'Dave Rudden writes brilliantly: his sentences are full of surprises, his ideas are shiny and fluid or sharp and shocking. He jabs at you with his language choices and makes you sit up and think, *Crikey!* He puts you deep inside the characters. This book reads beautifully: it keeps moving quickly between places, people, events, strangeness. You get thrown around and left a bit dizzy – in a good way'
Times Educational Supplement

'An immersive fantasy shot through with dark humour'
Bookseller **magazine**

'Etheric, beautifully grotesque, immensely satisfying descriptions'
The LA Review of Books

'Rudden is an author to watch. *Knights of the Borrowed Dark* is a pacy, entertaining read, but it has heart too'
Guardian

'This book will have you running from your shadow and fleeing from the darkness of your imagination'
Mr Ripley's Enchanted Books **blog**

Dave Rudden has performed in over four hundred schools, libraries and universities since the launch of *Knights of the Borrowed Dark* in 2016. He enjoys extinction-level events, putting things in his beard and being cruel to fictional children.

Knights of the Borrowed Dark series:

KNIGHTS OF THE BORROWED DARK

THE FOREVER COURT

THE ENDLESS KING

Follow or book Dave Rudden at
Twitter, Facebook, Tumblr, Instagram
@d_ruddenwrites
@theruddlesstravelled
#KOTBD

PUFFIN BOOKS

KNIGHTS OF THE BORROWED DARK

THE ENDLESS KING

Praise for *Knights of the Borrowed Dark*:

'Scary and funny – my two favourites. Dave Rudden is more than a rising star, he is a shooting star'
Eoin Colfer

'Clear some time in your schedule before you read this, because once you start it is very difficult to stop'
Joseph Fink, *Welcome to Nightvale*

'The stuff of nightmares in the best possible way'
***Heat* magazine**

'Wonderful style. Reminded me of Douglas Adams'
R. L. Stine

'This debut . . . is action-packed, atmospheric and powerfully imagined. But it is most notable for writerly wit and unexpected turns of phrase . . . this is engaging storytelling for any age'
Sunday Times

'Marvellous dialogue and prose, in much the same style as Derek Landy and Darren Shan'
SFX

KNIGHTS OF THE BORROWED DARK

THE ENDLESS KING

DAVE RUDDEN

PUFFIN

PUFFIN BOOKS

UK | USA | Canada | Ireland | Australia
India | New Zealand | South Africa

Puffin Books is part of the Penguin Random House group of companies
whose addresses can be found at global.penguinrandomhouse.com.

www.penguin.co.uk
www.puffin.co.uk
www.ladybird.co.uk

First published 2018
001

The author acknowledges that the excerpt from H.G. Wells' *War of the Worlds* has been abridged slightly for the purpose of the epigraph.
The author and publisher are grateful to Penguin Random House LLC for permission to quote from Kurt Vonnegut's *Mother Night* (1962, published in Great Britain by Vintage Classics).

Set in 10.5/15.5 pt Sabon LT Std
Typeset by Jouve (UK), Milton Keynes
Printed in Great Britain by Clays Ltd, St Ives plc

A CIP catalogue record for this book is available from the British Library

ISBN: 978-0-141-35662-4

All correspondence to:
Puffin Books
Penguin Random House Children's
80 Strand, London WC2R 0RL

Penguin Random House is committed to a sustainable future for our business, our readers and our planet. This book is made from Forest Stewardship Council® certified paper.

For my parents

'No one would have believed in the last years of the nineteenth century that this world was being watched keenly and closely by intelligences greater than and yet as mortal as us. No one gave a thought to the older worlds of space as sources of human danger and yet across the gulf of space intellects vast and cool and unsympathetic, regarded this earth with envious eyes, and slowly and surely drew their plans against us.'

H. G. Wells, *War of the Worlds*

'We are what we pretend to be, so we must be careful . . .'

Kurt Vonnegut, *Mother Night*

'Long live the King.'

Anonymous

CONTENTS

PROLOGUE
HINGE

'And they all lived happily ever after.'

Theo closed the book with a snap, flashing his audience a bright, wide smile. They did not smile back.

The silence stretched painfully. Theo's smile began to tremble at the edges. There was something horribly hungry about the eyes of children, which was why he had spent most of his life enjoying how his presence made them look at the floor.

Up until . . .

Stop it, he thought, squashing the memory before it could unfold. *Squashed* was an apt description for his audience as well: not one of them older than four, legs kicking off the edge of their chairs with the irritating squeak of baby fat on plastic.

The chairs were silly. Everything in this room was either too small or comically oversized. Personally, Theo saw neither the educational nor entertainment value of a thirty-centimetre-long pencil, and there was absolutely no reason to have this many different colours of crayon. Could the teachers not just ask the children to draw solely blue things? Or grey things? Then everyone could just have a pencil. *There.* He'd just saved the orphanage at least –

The children were still staring.

'What?' he said, and waggled the book in the air. 'They *did.*'

One spoke up. 'Until their deaths.'

On the shelves, the stuffed animals' grins stretched sinisterly against their zips. Theo's mouth went dry. '*What?*'

'Mr Colford said that it used to be different,' another piped up. 'He said it used to be: *They lived happily ever after, until their deaths.*'

'He thays accurathy's imporfant,' another mumbled.

I am surrounded by idiots, Theo thought, and these half-cooked bread rolls in front of him weren't even the worst of it.

'And right he is,' Theo responded, sagging smile floating on his grim features like an oil slick on a duck pond. It didn't matter. The point was, he was trying. He'd been trying ever since –

'Accuracy. Right. Very good.'

'Pigs don't live very long,' another of the creatures – no, *children* – murmured, and suddenly a spirited discussion broke out as to whether *talking* animals meant *magical* animals, and whether the magic would make them live longer or not.

'Yes,' Theo said, face now so rigid it was starting to hurt. 'Fascinating! Maybe draw a picture of it!'

He unfolded from the ludicrously small chair and stalked past Miss O'Keefe, who had been watching with the smallest of smiles on her wrinkled face.

'Would you like the pictures sent up to your office when they're done, Theo?' she said as he passed.

Director Theodore Ackerby's smile twitched. 'Of course.'

He tried very hard not to slam the door on the way out.

This was your idea, he reminded himself as he made his way through the corridors of Crosscaper Orphanage. And it had been. Gone were his hallways of soothing green and beige; now they were a riotous patchwork of brightly coloured murals painted by the students – *regardless of talent*. Each door was a different colour, windows festooned with stickers – *which are* never *going to come off* – and the only consolation was that with the children doing all the work he hadn't had to pay them a cent.

The air was full of the dry buzz of fluorescent lights. *Expensive* fluorescent lights. None of the teachers had questioned why someone so typically . . . frugal had suddenly decided to outfit every centimetre of the once-dim orphanage with lamps, not to mention the giant spotlights that covered the entire courtyard. When all were turned on – and they *were* turned on, every one of them, every night – there wasn't a scrap of darkness within the orphanage walls.

It was the only way they could get the children to sleep.

'Theo!'

He had almost made it to his office. The voice belonged to Mr Gilligan, the science teacher, who had the sort of wide, gormless grin that camouflaged a razor-sharp sense of humour. Ackerby sighed, and prepared himself.

'Theo, I was just wondering . . . Yes, sorry, Theo, I was just wondering: this new marking scheme I was thinking of implementing, Theo, I thought it would be good if . . .'

Mr Gilligan's voice faded to white noise, punctuated far too often by the sound of Ackerby's first name. He'd revealed it at the same time as he'd traded his suits for bright, itchy jumpers, and the calming austerity of his corridors for a thousand circus shades.

Familiarity. Safety. That's what was needed. Ackerby had read books on the subject. The Incident had driven away half the staff. The children had been terrified. So much destruction, so many repairs, the *courtyard* – he had needed to adapt. They all had.

So he was Theo now, and he wore a smile, no matter how much it tortured the muscles of his face.

'Yes,' he said, when the assault ceased. 'Whatever you think is best. Now, if you don't mind –'

A light flickered overhead.

There were moments, near-invisible moments, that your life swung on like a hinge. A bike tyre skidding on ice, a missed flight, a foot slipping off a step before regaining its balance. Or not. Every life had them, waiting like the secret flaw in a diamond, where something previously safe could suddenly fracture and *shear*.

It had happened to Ackerby before, but he'd not then had the wit to recognize it, and he would never let it happen again, to him or those in his charge.

Mr Gilligan's voice washed over him, unheard, unheeded, because the fluorescent tube above their heads was shivering. Not as if the power had been interrupted, or the bulb was about to fail, but as if . . . invaded, infected by a tiny scrap of night.

'It's happening again,' Ackerby whispered.

'What?' Mr Gilligan said. 'What are you –'

The science teacher's teeth clacked shut as Ackerby pulled himself to his full height. His spine protested – the . . . the *Incident* had bent him, shaken him, forced his shoulders into the kind of weak slump any idiot could climb.

Well. Not again.

'Mr Gilligan!' His voice struck the colour from the younger teacher's cheeks. A tiny, satisfied part of Ackerby imagined the disappearance of every child's smile within earshot. 'Assemble the other teachers. Empty the classrooms. Take the children down to the bunker –'

A grand name for the basement, but it had concrete walls and a thick door and it was underground, and *that* was what mattered.

'– and defend them with your life. With all of your lives. Do you understand?'

Mr Gilligan's jaw had dropped. 'But Theo –'

Ackerby's growl could have silenced the sea. '*Director.*'

Mr Gilligan bolted.

It didn't take long for the orphanage to snap into action. The director had spent enough time drilling it into them, after all, and, despite their utter mediocrity, they had learned their lessons well.

That hadn't been surprising. Some bad dreams you never forgot.

Doors slammed open, trickles of wide-eyed children becoming a flood, all heading downstairs. The director strode against the tide, glaring into the eyes of each teacher he passed as if to tattoo his orders on the inside of their heads. As much as they annoyed him he knew he could trust them, simply because they were the ones who had stayed. The others . . .

Disgusting.

Theo had spent his whole life in places like this. You didn't just abandon them when things took a turn for the horrible. A turn for the horrible was why places like this existed.

Bulbs abruptly shook in their fittings, the corridor pulsing through a rainbow of sickly shades. The children began to run, and the director waited until the last of them had disappeared round the corner before he did the same.

The snarl of slamming wood followed him, though not a single door moved as he passed. Carpet hairs stood as stiff as needles under his feet. If the director had allowed even a single clock within Crosscaper's walls, he was *sure* it would be ticking out of time.

The spotlights. The director had been a coward when horror had come to these corridors, and he was fairly sure he was one now, which was why he'd reduced the requirements of bravery down to the single flick of a switch.

These things moved in darkness. *Now let them choke on the light.*

His office doors were open. They were *never* open. He tried to stop, but the momentum of adrenalin and terror forced him over the threshold before his old bones ground to a halt. Outside the windows, the sky was weeping, raindrops pummelling the glass as if desperate to escape.

There was a figure standing behind his desk.

'No,' Ackerby whispered. 'It can't be. Not . . . not *you*.'

Denizen Hardwick gave him a bleak little wave.

'Director. I need your help.'

1

FAMILIAR GROUND

Some time earlier

They approached from the air.

Cloud broke before the plane like waves round a prow, and Denizen Hardwick pressed his long nose against the window because it seemed that in his absence someone had stolen the ground away. In its place was another night sky, rising to meet their descent.

Lights. Millions and millions of tiny lights, and all Denizen could think was that constellations had always been a bit of a romantic notion to him – just people looking for pictures in stars a billion miles apart. This pattern had order, though, a sprawling, organic order, like the pinprick skeleton of a beast he couldn't see.

A city.

Walls and towers and narrow streets draped in seaweed tangles across a huge mountain peak, outlined by glittering coral colonies of gold. The plane shuddered as it dived, and Denizen realized that he knew that glow. He'd been living by it for nearly a year now.

Candles. How many must there be that we can see them from the sky?

It was like something from a fairy tale. Not a modern myth, scraped clean of darkness, with animal companions and villainous musical numbers. This was a fairy tale with battlements, arrow-slits and murder holes, a story where the bottom of the portcullis was stained with blood.

In the old tales, villains killed you. In the old tales, fairies took your kids.

And at the mountain's summit . . . a shape. A citadel, dark amid the light.

Denizen's mother leaned over from her seat beside him.

'Welcome to the home of the Order of the Borrowed Dark, Denizen. Our first fortress. Our last fortress. The House We Will Hold.'

There was a rare reverence in Vivian's voice.

'Welcome to Daybreak.'

'I am *never* flying again.'

White as an envelope, Simon Hayes staggered out on to the tarmac, his long limbs heron-hunched inwards as if afraid the slowing propellers might take one of them off.

'You're hardly going to walk home,' Denizen said wryly, though he couldn't deny his own wave of relief when his feet also hit solid ground.

'I can't believe you're handling this better than me,' the taller boy said, his grin robbing the words of any malice. 'You *never* handle things better.'

Denizen mock-scowled. 'That is . . .' He thought for a moment. Between the orphanage of their childhood and the grim mansion of Seraphim Row in which they now resided, the boys had spent less than five weeks not in each other's pockets. Simon knew more about Denizen than Denizen did. 'Fine. Well then, I'm owed.'

He shouldered his bag and glanced around the deserted airfield – little more than a strip of flat tarmac and a couple of sheds, tiny in the gargantuan shadow of Monte Inclavare, Adumbral's sole peak. Even when Denizen had his back to the mountain, he could feel it bearing down on him, a tidal wave just before the plunge.

The fractures of his iron eye itched.

The Order had claimed this country back before it *was* a country – just a mountain valley in the Apennines, a place the world had long forgotten. Or been encouraged to forget. The Knights had little time for human wars, and Denizen could easily imagine kings coveting this land, only to be met with iron lips and iron words: *Leave us alone*.

Abigail swung neatly from the cabin doorway, landing lightly on the tarmac.

'That was fun,' she said, and laughed at Simon's less-than-enthusiastic look.

Monte Inclavare was crowned by the city of Adumbral, and there was a fortress called Daybreak at its heart. This fact was not widely known. Nor was the existence of the Knights who called it home. It had taken Denizen and Simon thirteen years, a near-apocalypse and the violent blossoming of their own magical talents to learn of the Order of the Borrowed Dark, but Abigail Falx had always known her destiny was here.

'So who do you think it'll be?' she asked, tying up her dark hair. 'The Master of Neophytes, I mean. It's a different Knight every year, you see. There was word *Gedeon* was retiring, but surely he'd stay in Russia, train an apprentice. Oh my *God,* what if it's Gedeon –'

She bounced lightly on her heels as she spoke, ponytail slashing the air, fists jabbing with what Denizen assumed was perfect technique. It usually was. Abigail wasn't in the habit of wastefulness, and that included her thirteen-year head start.

Simon was still glaring at the plane.

'Even if it had been a big one. The kind of plane where you don't know you're on a plane. That's all I'm asking. It's one thing to be travelling in a metal tube that only stays up because it's going too fast to fall down –'

'That's not precisely how it works –'

'Thank you, Darcie –' Simon said, as a second girl stepped from the plane, wearing the polite grimace she always adopted when someone was being inaccurate – 'but it's another to have it bounce around and then steady up again like it suddenly remembered it was a plane.'

Abigail shrugged. She had greeted the turbulence with a fierce grin, which was generally the way she approached everything. Denizen had *thought* he caught the briefest look of relief on her face when they landed, but he assumed that was because the four-hour flight was the longest she'd ever sat still.

'There's not much demand for flights here. Only Knights come to Adumbral.'

Denizen could count on one hand the amount of times he'd ever seen Darcie Wright take off her glasses in public, but now they dangled forgotten from her hand, revealing eyes of bright, silver-haunted iron.

A Knight's first and foremost weapon was the wellspring of voracious fire beating like blood through their veins, shaped by the eldritch language they called Cants. The fire *wanted* to be used, even though every time it stole just a little bit of its wielder away – turning them to metal, black and hard and cold.

The Cost. Power always had a price, and if Denizen had learned one thing in the last year it was that some were more visible than most.

'I remember my first year here,' Darcie murmured, drawing a dark hand through her riot of ebony curls. 'But then you leave, and time passes, and your memory convinces you it couldn't have been that big. That spectacular. You shrink it, to fit it in with what you know of the world.' She smiled. 'But then you return and it all comes back. Like a sunrise. You remember that here, of all places, the rules of the world don't apply.'

She slipped her glasses into her pocket. 'I love it here.'

With a shared conspiratorial grin, Denizen, Abigail and Simon followed suit, removing their black gloves to reveal dull iron hands.

'Well, there should still be a bus,' Simon continued, mock-grumpily. 'And hang on . . . Adumbral's all –' he waved a hand at the mountain – 'this bit?'

Darcie nodded. 'The city-state.'

'And Daybreak's the fortress at the top?'

She nodded again.

'Well then, why didn't we just skip to the top with the Art of Apertura? It's not like there would have been much difference. Cold sweat, eyes screwed shut, imminent chance of death –'

'The difference, Simon Hayes, is that we do not punch a hole through the universe just so we can avoid *motion sickness*.'

Malleus Vivian Hardwick stepped from the plane, her movements as controlled and lethal as the propellers' slowing spin.

'It's a long war. We only have so much skin to give.'

It took only one look at any Knight Superior to confirm the viciousness of their war, and Vivian more than most. Her credentials were written in scar tissue and Cost, her career a knot of battles and sacrifice notorious the world over.

Well, within the secret garrisons of the Order, at least. Denizen had been thinking about that a lot on the flight, in particular where that left him.

A long-handled hammer swung at Vivian's waist – both her symbol of office and the weapon that had carried her through as many hells as Denizen had frowns.

'Yes, Malleus,' Simon said instantly.

They had all given skin one way or another. Once, Denizen's Cost had been just an ink blot in his palm. Now, it rose up past his wrists in black manacles, and splinters had found their way into his left eye. Not like Darcie's – hers were the mark of a sacred duty – but a reminder that the power in his heart cared more about being free than its host.

If he covered his right eye, the world became a stained-glass window, all shades of grey, indigo and blue. Knights had a natural ability to see in the dark, but since the summer Denizen had found it a little easier to see the dark in things instead.

Even the light.

You mind your house, I'll mind mine.

He locked that thought away. He'd been doing a lot of work on that. Vivian had even said he was coming on nicely, which for Denizen's mother was the equivalent of a celebratory parade. Their eyes met, and Vivian's expression, which normally held the grim promise of an oncoming train, softened into a slight smile.

'It is good to be home,' she said.

Denizen had been seeing that smile more and more recently. He was becoming quite fond of it.

'There's our lift,' Simon said, pointing.

Knights fought in the shadows, and birth and blood had gifted them with the *Intueor Lucidum*: sight in darkness. Denizen's vision was a tracery of silver – brighter in his left eye than his right – and he could easily make out the black jeep making its way down the slope towards them. He was almost surprised by its arrival. The leader of the Order didn't exactly care for the Hardwicks, and Denizen wouldn't have been surprised if they had been left to walk.

A warm wind drew sweat from Denizen's cheeks as the jeep approached. *That'll take some getting used to*. Ireland stuck out into the Atlantic like a foot from under a duvet, but they were further south now, and Denizen felt the unfamiliar electricity of being *somewhere else*.

He hadn't travelled much. There had been an unplanned, unwilling and unpleasant trip during the summer, but being kidnapped by the Family Croit and served on a platter to their mad, grieving goddess hardly counted as a holiday, even by Knightly standards.

Then again, Denizen thought, staring up at the immensity of Monte Inclavare, *does this?*

'I. Can't. Wait.' Abigail kept leaving them behind only to double back, her eyes bright with excitement. 'We're *finally* here, and –' Her own words pulled her up short, eyes widening. 'Not that we didn't appreciate your training, Malleus. We –'

Vivian waved a hand. 'I understand.' Her smile deepened a fraction. 'Now your *real* training begins.'

'She keeps saying that,' Simon muttered to Denizen. 'Why does she keep saying that?'

Considering the paces Vivian had already put them through, it *was* an unnerving statement, but Denizen's worries ran far deeper.

Back in Crosscaper, the most you had to worry about was homework and sports. Joining the Order had traded those worries for a vicious war against extradimensional shapeshifters called Tenebrous, and, while Denizen obviously hadn't *enjoyed* facing off against clockwork women, murderous crows and, on one occasion, an animated dustbin, at least all you had to worry about in those situations was dying.

However, Daybreak was the most secure fortress on the face of the planet. He was completely and totally safe, which meant he was completely and totally safe to worry about other things. Such as:

1. *The leader of the Order and I have . . . trust issues.* Hopefully, there would be some important business that called Palatine Edifice Greaves away, and they would never have to be in the same room again. For the rest of their natural lives.
2. *What have the other Neophytes heard about me?* Denizen had found it difficult enough to make friends as Denizen Hardwick: bookish, ginger, freckled, sceptical of all things but most of all himself. Now he was Denizen *Hardwick*, the son of a respected Malleus, with his own list of messy encounters both with enemies *and* the people he was supposed to get along with.

Which led him on rather neatly to the last point. Denizen was very purposefully not thinking about that one. He loved words, and he'd picked up a suitably military one from Vivian for exactly this situation.

3. *Redacted – editing or withholding information for security purposes.* Generals did it all the time, apparently, to protect those under their command.

Denizen was no general, but he and Vivian both agreed that certain . . . things were best locked away.

No matter how much it hurt.

The jeep pulled to a stop, the driver sliding out to open the doors for them.

Relax, Denizen told himself. *It's a year. You have your friends. You're in the safest place you can be. This is a new start! Yes. That's it. You're going to bury any untoward . . . thoughts, and keep your head down. The last thing you need is stuff from your past coming back to bite you in the –*

'Oh my God.'

Darcie's exclamation made Denizen look up, just in time to meet a crooked, familiar smile.

'That bad?'

It was Grey.

2
ANOTHER COUNTRY

For a long time, they drove in silence.

Denizen fought the urge to stare at Grey, just as he had the day they'd met. Halfway between scepticism and desperate curiosity, world-weary with no real knowledge of the world, Denizen had gone into that first meeting with thirteen years' worth of mistrust, but Graham McCarron was Grey to his friends, and it said a lot that it had only taken Denizen half an hour to find that out.

Neither one of them were those people any more.

The jeep climbed the winding road. Abigail's eyes were flicking between Denizen and Grey. Darcie's hand was tight on Denizen's arm, and if Vivian – never the most . . . relaxed of people – sat any straighter she'd snap like a rubber band.

'So how have you been?' Simon asked Grey politely, and he had never been more of a hero to Denizen than in that moment. 'We only met . . . briefly.'

Even he faltered there – there really was no good way to say *after you got mind-controlled to betray us all.*

'You mean after I got mind-controlled to betray you all?'

Darcie flinched. Simon looked ill, as if whatever he'd been about to say had abruptly reversed back down his throat. And Vivian almost seemed to relax, as if the edge in Grey's words was something she understood.

'The doctors say I should talk about it.' There was a strange, strained distance in his voice, as if he were trying to speak a language he hadn't used in years. 'There have been a lot of doctors. They all agree with each other, which I guess is a good sign.'

He smirked at that, and for a moment Denizen saw his mentor again, the wry and smiling Knight who'd been so kind to him in those first weeks of a new and terrifying life. And then the smile vanished, and a different person sat in front of them, like the most depressing magic-eye picture ever drawn.

Grey had always been slender, but now he was thin to the point of worry, his cheekbones knife blades poorly sheathed under skin. His once-long hair had been shaved painfully short on either side, a fringe half-hiding one eye. He'd abandoned his customary tailored suits for a faded vest, bare arms taut with muscle and the Cost's advance and, in the only country in the world where a Knight had nothing to hide, his hands were gloved in black.

'What . . .' Darcie's voice was careful. 'What else have the doctors said?'

The road climbed Monte Inclavare's spine, the bare earth on either side studded with candles like a new crop of wheat. Grey swallowed deeply before responding.

'The Order can't find any trace of the Clockwork Three in my head, but, considering that we didn't even know Tenebrous could get inside people's minds, they don't really know what to look for.'

The Man in the Waistcoat. The Woman in White. The poor, wretched Opening Boy. Three of the worst Tenebrous the multiverse could vomit up, with a vendetta against Denizen's mother that they would have done just about anything to satisfy.

Denizen didn't hate the Tenebrous he fought, but death by Vivian had been far too good for the Three. They'd killed Denizen's father, Soren. They'd killed Corinne D'Aubigny and left her husband Fuller Jack to mourn her.

And they'd puppeted Grey, turned him against his comrades, and left him empty as a discarded glove.

'They're dead now, anyway,' Grey continued, mock cheer in his voice. 'So that door is closed. And the doctors make me listen to wellness tapes. So I'm sure everything will be fine.'

He chuckled. The others did not.

'But enough about me – how's home? How's . . .'

He trailed off. Seraphim Row had been home for Grey far longer than it had been for Denizen, and, looking back, Denizen could see echoes of himself, Simon and Abigail in Grey's friendship with Fuller Jack and Corinne D'Aubigny.

Just one of many casualties the Three had left in their wake.

The window. Look out of the window. The walls of the city loomed ahead, sheer and brutal with battlements, and

Denizen was about to ask something inane about their height or *anything*, just to break the silence, when Darcie sat bolt upright in her seat, trembling.

It wasn't exactly seeing the future: Darcie had been clear on that a number of times. But watching puddles showed you the first drop of rain, and watching the skin of the universe with a pencil in her hand told Darcie where a Breach would occur.

Now, though, it was her eyes that sketched, slamming left and right in their sockets with typewriter clicks of iron. Abigail caught one of the *Lux*'s flailing fists. Denizen hissed as Darcie's nails dug into his skin, scratching as if trying to draw –

Her voice was a toneless drawl.

'*Hereherehereherehere–*'

And then Denizen felt it too.

You could say it was a little like slowly realizing that the food in your mouth was rotten. You could compare it, perhaps, to the shocked betrayal of tearing your skin on a nail and the queasy fascination of watching your own blood well.

But it wasn't like any of that. Not really. It was what it was.

A Breach.

The field of candles ended a few hundred metres down the slope and, as the jeep growled to a halt, a swathe of flames flickered as if teased by an invisible hand. Dust plumed upwards beyond the field's edge. The air bent inwards. Darcie slumped like her strings were cut.

Vivian was already halfway out of the door before Grey grabbed her arm.

'*Wait.*'

The Tenebrous unfolded like frost condensing on a car window, if frost were black and dull and maggoty with movement, if nervous systems were made of dirty char. Dust rose to bulk out the waving tendrils with grainy muscle, skin and spines and a skull that even as they watched split into a snarl –

And then a bang of torn air, an explosion of grit from the back of the newborn monster's skull, and a long spear of black steel was suddenly vibrating in the ground behind it.

One mightn't have been enough. Humans were systems – complex, interconnected, fragile – but Tenebrous were black oil and scrap scavenged from the worlds they invaded, and Denizen knew from experience just how much it took to put them down.

It died on the fifth bolt, coming apart with a fading, mournful scream. The entire encounter had only taken a couple of seconds and Denizen realized that the shoulders of Monte Inclavare were bare for a reason.

There were no trees between here and the walls. No plants. *No cover.*

A killing field.

'You missed out,' Grey said calmly, turning the car key once more. 'Sometimes they use the rocket launchers.' The jeep began to move, and the Knight started, his eyes suddenly hunted. 'I'm sorry – Darcie, are you OK?'

The *Lux* nodded, a tear cutting a path of darker black down her cheek.

'I'm fine. The veil between worlds is thin here. It makes things more –'

Denizen's heart still pounded with adrenalin, drowning out her words, and with every beat trickles of gold spread through the cracks and crevices of him, searching for freedom. Cants shifted in his head, yearning to be filled with flame, to break the world and *burn* –

– and, with an ease born of practice, Denizen trapped them, raising in his mind a fortress of imaginary iron and dense, unthawable ice. The inferno wailed like a trapped cat, but Denizen and Vivian had worked for months on this technique, poring over maps of castles and engineering manuals, every trick of the siege trade.

Funny the things you could bond over.

'You should have stayed at home,' Vivian was saying, voice tight with concern. 'This is the one place in the world that doesn't need a *Lux*. You should have –'

'I'm seeing my friends off,' Darcie responded mildly, and, though Cants still pleaded in his head, Denizen grinned to see Vivian abruptly sit straighter. 'The world will manage for a day or two. And so will I.'

'Yes, well,' Vivian said, clearing her throat and turning to Grey. 'You'd think they'd learn not to come here.'

'Learn?' There was an uncharacteristic cruelty in Grey's voice. 'Tenebrous don't *learn*. They either Breach outside and have to face the walls or run off the city's candlewards like water off a windscreen. *Then* they have to face the walls.'

Ahead, gates the same bruise-black as Denizen's palms lurched open with a groan of something prehistoric sinking into tar. Their sheer size would have been reassuring if Denizen didn't already know that walls could be bypassed, even ramparts as impressive as these.

Like rats forcing their bodies through pipes, or damp worming into a wooden floor, Tenebrous could Breach the very walls separating our universe from theirs. Walls hadn't stopped the Clockwork Three from killing Denizen's father twelve years ago, or returning last year to provoke open war between humanity and the Tenebrae's Endless King.

Walls hadn't saved Grey.

They passed beneath the shadow of the battlements and Denizen could feel eyes on him. Slits in the stone glittered with drawn arrows. Barricades cupped the other side of the gates, so, even if an enemy did manage to break through, they'd simply be running into a pen, at the mercy of the archers above.

'Bit much,' Simon whispered, as if afraid someone would hear.

If Grey responded, it was lost in the clang of the closing gates.

The cobbled road became even steeper within Adumbral's walls. Buildings clung together like birds on a wire, the streets all sharp corners and narrow, cramped inclines. Dublin was an old city, but this place was *ancient*. Everything seemed to bulge in odd places, or sag like soldiers at the end of a long, exhausting march. And everywhere candlewards – glowing from window sills, strung across alley mouths like prehistoric Christmas lights, keeping the rot from getting in.

'It's only the walls that are manned, right?' Abigail said in a hushed voice. 'Nobody actually lives in Adumbral?'

'Not any more,' Vivian said. She didn't elaborate.

'Oh, you haven't heard?' Grey said lightly. She looked at him sharply, but he ignored her. 'The Order didn't always hide in the shadows, avoiding those they gave their lives for. No . . . once we tried to have lives as well.'

Gloved fingers drummed a one-two rhythm on the steering wheel. Denizen stared at them as if they were snakes.

'Grey,' Vivian began, 'there will be time enough for . . .'

'This is their home now,' Grey not-quite-snapped, as the jeep coughed its way up a particularly steep hill. There was something ahead, looming over the crowded skyline, but to see it properly Denizen would have had to lean into whatever battle of wills was going on between Vivian and Grey. And he wanted to hear the story.

'Adumbral, the first city of the Order,' continued Grey. 'A place where we wouldn't have to hide the Cost, a place where we could speak freely, a place where we could be ourselves.'

Darcie was turning her glasses over and over in her hands. The silence of the city was palpable. It reminded Denizen of Eloquence – that remote and crumbling castle where the Family Croit had festered for centuries.

Cornices like puckered mouths, pillars rounded as exposed bone – it was nothing as obvious as architecture and nothing so subtle as time, but there was a wrongness here, a chill.

'So many families,' said Grey. 'So many Knights. And you know what happens when too many of our kind gather . . .'

It was one of the first lessons Denizen learned. Tenebrous broke the barriers between worlds, but the presence of Knights and their Cants *eroded* it. That was why they had developed the candlewards. Because if you didn't, and the walls between worlds frayed too far . . .

Denizen paled. 'The Tenebrae got in.'

Grey looked at him sharply in the rear-view mirror, and Denizen realized it was the first thing he had said since they'd been reunited.

'As it always does,' the Knight finished bluntly. 'The longer we lived here, the more porous the barrier got. People began to disappear. A few at first. And then dozens. Just falling out of the world.' His voice was grim. 'Or being taken. And then one day . . . one day they came. From every shadow. From every crevice. Twisting the city to make their bones.'

That was what was wrong with the buildings. How had Denizen not seen it? The crooked angles, the leering gaps . . . Tenebrous had tried to claim them, the way the doomed creature from earlier had claimed dust as flesh. And yet still Adumbral stood, frozen in half-unmaking. A stillborn city that stubbornly stood.

'How . . .'

'We developed the candlewards,' Vivian said, in a tone that was halfway between her *things aren't that bad* and her *this conversation is over* voice. She was a lot better at one than the other. 'They stopped Adumbral from succumbing and it taught us that a level of . . . separation is required. To keep safe those we love.'

'And isn't that working out well for all of us?'

Grey's words were ice water, bitter and brackish. Abigail recoiled from them in a way Denizen had never seen her duck from a blow. Simon's eyes went owl-wide.

Darcie's voice was soft. 'Grey . . . it wasn't your fault.'

'*I know it wasn't*,' Grey said shortly. 'Everyone knows it wasn't. And everyone makes a really good effort at looking me in the eye and pretending it doesn't matter. But people are dead.'

The rest of the journey passed in silence. Grey pulled up outside what might have been a warehouse, had there been anyone left in Adumbral to have wares. Now it was where the Order kept their vehicles, row after row of jeeps identical to the one they were leaving behind.

Denizen racked his brain for something to say, *anything*, but everything that came to mind was impossibly tangled with meanings he didn't intend. So instead they wordlessly collected their bags, and were about to walk away when Grey let out a long and rattling sigh.

'Sorry. *Sorry*. You don't need this. Who would?'

Ahead, a fortress rose.

'There'll be tests enough.'

3
THE POINT OF LIGHTHOUSES

Knights never did anything without a reason. They couldn't afford to. The Cost made misers of them all, and that had spread to their training, their traditions, even the emotions they let themselves feel. But, despite that iron control, the Order were still human, and a simple, sombre poetry had found its way in all the same.

Denizen made it eight steps up the slope before his calves started to burn. No wonder no human army had ever attempted to besiege Daybreak. What would have been the point? Even the thought of battling your way through the killing fields, the walls, steep streets where five warriors could hold a hundred . . . only to find yourself *here*.

The buildings of Adumbral thinned out before the barren summit of Monte Inclavare like the ragged tonsure of a hermit. On three sides was the city, dead and gold and as empty as a burial mask, and the fourth was a sheer cliff all the way back down to the mountain's roots, who-knew-how-far down below.

And in between . . .

Daybreak was a lighthouse. Of course it was. It's not that Denizen was an expert – he'd never been anywhere near one before in his life. That was sort of the point of lighthouses. If you were near one, you were going in the wrong direction. It wasn't even that he figured it out from the surroundings – there were no ships to be warned, no rocks on which they could run aground, no sea in which to drown.

Except there was, wasn't there?

Out in the fresh air, away from the candlewards and distractingly traumatic reunions, Denizen could feel it: a *frisson* at the edge of his awareness – the constant reminder that this world was an island floating in a deep black sea, and the Order a single point of light.

Daybreak jutted accusingly into the sky, massive as a tower block, topped with a defiant fist of stone and glass. Denizen half expected a beam of white to lash from those panels to sweep the surrounding shadows away, but the huge lantern remained shuttered, as secret as the Order itself.

'Uriel would love this,' Simon said beside him, and Denizen agreed.

There was every chance that Denizen would still be in a Croit dungeon, had their youngest son not stood against the doctrine his Family had literally beaten into him his entire life. Uriel had paid for that, and it was a debt that still kept Denizen awake at night.

'I wish we'd been able to convince him to join us,' Denizen responded sadly. 'But –' He frowned. 'Hang on – how do you know he'd love this?'

Simon stiffened. 'Oh, I just . . . um . . .'

There was something at once very uncharacteristic and very familiar about that stutter. 'We've been . . . emailing.'

'Oh,' Denizen said.

Then: '*Oh*,' Denizen responded.

'*Right*,' Denizen continued, abruptly glad that everyone was staring up at the lighthouse, because he'd gone so red he could probably have warned off ships by himself. 'Hey,' he said. 'That's great! I mean . . . cool. *Cool*. Do I . . . need to do anything?'

'You can close your mouth for a start,' Simon said with an awkward smile. 'But no – we can talk later. It's not a *thing*, you know?'

'Right! No – obviously!' Suddenly aware that he was so flailingly desperate to convey his okayness that he might possibly be making things less OK, and also possibly be presenting a danger to low-flying aircraft, Denizen stopped speaking.

'Come on,' Simon said. 'Let's go and check out our new home.'

The girls were looking back but not at them, instead watching the car park where Grey had driven. A frown twisted Abigail's features. Darcie just looked sad.

'Should we . . . should we wait?'

'No.' A thread of softness entered Vivian's voice. 'Give him time.'

The doors of Daybreak – thick and tall and marked with the hand-and-hammers – were shadowed beneath another host of arrow-slits and chutes for boiling oil. Denizen wouldn't have been surprised if there were more high-tech or arcane defences that he couldn't see. The Knights had no problem mixing mechanical, magical and medieval arts when it came to protecting what was theirs. This was a war where the enemy could come from anywhere.

I guess it's important there's some ground you hold.

Simon turned to Abigail, who was now vibrating so hard with excitement that she could have phased through the door.

'You're finally here.'

Abigail grabbed him by the lapel. '*I. KNOW.*'

'Ack.'

'Sorry.'

Vivian withdrew a long iron key from her pocket, slipping it into the huge lock on the door. Uneasily eyeing the sharpened spikes of the portcullis above, Denizen shuffled a little closer to her.

'We just let ourselves in?'

'We just let ourselves in.'

'That's a bit . . . anticlimactic.'

Vivian shot him a look as the door opened with an industrial *clonk*.

'You were expecting a butler?'

Maybe.

You couldn't have called the two men sitting inside butlers, except in the Artemis Fowl sense of the word. Draped across wooden chairs, they watched Vivian and the others enter with what could have been mistaken for disinterest, if you ignored their eyes.

The foyer – *did castles have foyers?* Denizen resolved to look that up later – was a long, bare room, devoid of even the cluttered detritus and ornaments that turned Seraphim Row from a creepy mansion to a creepy mansion that people lived in. There was no art on the walls – rather, the art *was* the walls, and now he could see that set into every wall was a mosaic of war.

It reminded Denizen of Retreat, the Order's asylum, but, whereas those carvings were all Knights marching, these were warriors in the thick of battle. *Actual* battle – Denizen could see plaques underneath depicting names and dates in flowing script.

It made sense in a way. You could have carved every single Knight to ever live and they wouldn't have covered one wall of Retreat. Perhaps the lost souls imprisoned there needed to imagine the Order as an army rather than a few determined souls.

Here in Daybreak, the enemy was acknowledged. Tenebrous by their very nature were hard to depict, but the artists had done their best – chips of bright stone at odd angles to distort reflections, water rushing behind translucent glass so that the figures danced and twitched. No two were alike, writhing in anger, or delight, or pain.

Try as he might, he couldn't help scanning the twisted shapes in case one had been crafted from moonstone and sapphire and silver.

Stop that.

Vivian led them up a flight of stairs. Denizen found himself thinking that, even though they passed the occasional Knight in the corridors, Daybreak felt like Seraphim Row, but in a way that had nothing to do with the Tenebrae.

'How many Knights live here?' he asked.

'There's a standing garrison of one hundred,' Darcie said, 'rotated in and out on a yearly basis. There isn't a lot to do here bar training, archiving and maintaining the defences. Knights stay for a while and then move on.'

That was it. Despite its age, despite the grim nobility of its design and the careful detail evident in every mosaic tile, Daybreak felt . . . temporary, full of the evidence of the passage of people, but with none of their personality or soul.

Like an airport or a train station – a place you went to, to leave.

'I'd go mad,' Abigail said, reading each and every plaque. 'That's why they keep it to a year. Everyone wants to be out *doing* something, and here is just –'

'A way to serve the Order,' Darcie said, and, though there was no sternness in her voice, Abigail bowed her head a little. Darcie's talents were too valuable for the front line, but they'd just seen the toll her duties took. 'We all do it in our own way.'

They paused beneath a massive archway, just as Denizen noticed the mosaics had come to an end, the already-quiet halls now totally deserted. 'Speaking of which,' Darcie said, a tad awkwardly, 'this is where I leave you.'

They turned in surprise.

'*Luxes* have different quarters,' Darcie explained. 'They're . . .'

'Fancier?' Simon offered innocently.

'*In a different part of the castle*,' Darcie finished. 'They need us out in the field, not here, so they like to make a fuss when one of us comes home.'

'The way things are done here,' Vivian interrupted, 'you might find it an . . . adjustment.' The words crackled with warning. 'We're not in Seraphim Row any more.'

They really weren't. Vivian didn't stand on ceremony. Or, rather, she stood on it all the time, grinding it into the dirt. At home, the ranks went as follows:

– Vivian.

– Everyone else.

It was very simple. And now it wasn't.

Darcie looked so apologetic that Denizen felt bad.

'Hey, no, we understand. When are you guys heading home?'

'Tomorrow night,' Vivian said. 'I have some meetings and then we'll catch the evening flight out.'

'I'll try and see you tomorrow if I can,' said Darcie. 'But if not . . .'

She grabbed them all in a fierce hug. Denizen found himself surprised at just how fierce, but then again he'd never seen her with a book less than five hundred pages long. That gave you serious upper-body strength.

'Keep in touch,' she murmured into the crush. 'Let me know how you're all getting on. Simon, you keep dropping your fists before you go for a high kick. That's telegraphing. And Abigail . . . go easy on yourself. All right?'

'What do you mean? I'm –'

Darcie pulled back, her hands still resting on their shoulders.

'And, Denizen . . .'

A blush pinked Denizen's cheeks. 'What?'

Darcie's stare would have been intense even had her eyes been human.

'Take care.'

He nodded, and she held his gaze for just one second longer.

'Good luck.'

They watched her go solemnly. Darcie had been the first person Denizen had spoken to in Seraphim Row. She'd been unfailingly kind and considerate, guiding and teaching them while also shouldering a burden the rest of them barely understood.

It's just a year.

It had been a year since they'd met. A lot could happen in a year.

He was really going to miss her.

'This is the Neophytes' Solar,' Vivian said, leading them into a great heptagonal room, the walls set with wooden doors. 'Female cells, male cells, meditation cells, Neophytes' Library . . . Training chambers are two floors down. You'll congregate here for your allocated nightly social time –'

'Allocated fun,' Simon murmured to Denizen. 'My favourite.'

Vivian glanced at the slip of paper in her hand. 'Abigail, you're cell F12.' She sniffed. 'Hmph. I was F11. My name should be scratched beneath the bed, if you get a chance to look.'

Denizen's brain tried to supply an image of thirteen-year-old Vivian, but just wasn't up to the task. Her scars, her Cost, her aura of contained determination and rage – had she ever worried about making friends? About being up to the job her heritage had handed down?

'Where is everyone?' Simon asked, looking around the deserted room.

'Getting some sleep, I imagine,' Vivian said, and Denizen suddenly realized how late it was. 'Which is what you should be doing. Your first session tomorrow will be at seven in the primary training chamber. Rest. Memorize the rules. The Order doesn't go in for hand-holding – you are Neophytes of the Second Rank now, and expected to comport yourselves as such.'

'There are rules?' Simon asked in panic.

'There are ranks?' Denizen echoed with alarm. 'I didn't know there were ranks. Why didn't I know there were ranks?'

'Neophytes of the First Rank aren't expected to concern themselves with hierarchy,' Abigail said airily. 'And of course there are rules. Show up on time, no boys in the girls' cells, all that kind of thing.'

Simon frowned. 'Wait. Why not?'

Glacially, Vivian raised an eyebrow.

Denizen felt a very odd sensation of his blood simultaneously rushing to his face while also trying to hide from embarrassment. They'd all been living in such close proximity that Denizen had sort of forgotten that Abigail was . . . you know. *A girl and stuff.*

'Oh right,' Simon said in a small voice.

'Some of the rules here are a little old-fashioned,' said Denizen's mother, which was an impressive statement from someone wearing a warhammer. 'But others are there for very good reasons.'

They all nodded, Abigail seeming caught between trying to look respectful while also being highly amused.

'Goodnight, boys,' she said. Vivian gave her a grave nod. 'Abigail. It has been . . .'

Abigail's eyes went wide.

'An honour,' Vivian finished. 'And a pleasure. Your parents will be very proud when they read my report.'

'There are *reports*?' Simon and Denizen said together, while Abigail beamed like a solar flare.

'Oh. Thank you. Wow. Um. Goodnight!'

She practically floated to her dorm.

'Well,' Vivian said, and a note of uncertainty had entered her voice. The room was suddenly deathly quiet.

'Yeah,' Denizen responded. 'Um . . .'

'Cell M17,' Simon said, head angled to read the note hanging carelessly from Vivian's hand. 'I'll just . . . give you some spa–'

Vivian lunged.

Denizen was no natural warrior, but a year made a lot of difference, especially under the tutelage of Vivian Hardwick. It took him barely a second to quell the sudden but not unexpected inferno, dropping into a fighting stance –

– just in time to see Malleus Vivian Hardwick give his best friend the most awkward hug Denizen had ever seen. She let go just as quickly, leaving Simon rocking slightly on his heels.

There was the faintest drop of red in Vivian's cheeks.

'You're a good boy,' she said in a strained voice. 'Look out for each other.'

'Huh,' Simon managed. 'Um. OK –'

'*Goodnight, Simon*,' Vivian said. He vanished.

'I'll walk you,' she said when they were alone, and a strange flutter moved through Denizen's stomach as he realized that, bar about three weeks last year, this would be the first time in twelve years he and his best friend would be sleeping in separate rooms.

Vivian pushed open the door, and Denizen forced a smile.

'Are you allowed in the boys' cells?'

She shot him a look. 'I'm your *mother*.'

Fair enough. The long corridor on the other side was lined with doors, each one trisected by columns of carvings. Denizen peered closer. *Names*, marching back through time. Generations of boys who had trained for war right here.

There he was. End of the hall.

DENIZEN HARDWICK

Well, I suppose it's official then.

The door opened at his touch, revealing a simple bed, a wardrobe and a small desk, above which was pinned a sheet of paper. *The rules*, Denizen supposed. Some of them were in bold. And underlined.

'So,' Vivian said.

'Yep,' Denizen replied.

The silence stretched, and Denizen wondered how obvious it was from his face that he didn't know what to say and whether Vivian knew how obvious it was on hers. Eventually, she just cleared her throat.

'Greaves won't move against you openly, not after the summer.' Her voice was low. 'He might think he can still bring you round, convert you. But you're wise to his charm now. Avoid him. Keep your head down.'

Six months ago, her changing the subject from emotion to enemies might have annoyed Denizen, but now he understood – that was just who she was. Besides, the Palatine wanting to exploit your unparalleled fluency with the Cants was one thing when you were in Dublin, and another when you were right on his doorstep.

And that wasn't the only thing about last year that Greaves wanted to exploit.

'Denizen? Are you all right?'

Denizen nodded. 'I am. I really am. The fortress exercises are working really well. I'm in control. I am.'

Her lip twisted. 'And . . . the other thing?'

'Redacted,' Denizen said with a firm nod.

'*Good*,' Vivian said. 'Keep it that way.' She sighed, and ironed some of the roughness from her voice. 'Sorry. I know I don't need to explain how important it is that we distance ourselves from . . . past events. For your own safety.'

'I understand,' Denizen said.

She looked around approvingly at the thick, stone walls. 'And you'll be safe here. There's no way *she* can contact you.'

'I know,' Denizen said. And he did. *Though it's not like she tried. Ever since the summer. Not a message. Not a word.*

Fire curled its fists in his stomach, and Denizen dragged his thoughts away.

Redacted. *A most useful word.*

'Good,' Vivian said. 'If you need *anything*, contact me and I'll be here.'

Denizen gave her a wan smile. 'Greaves will love you just showing up.'

She smiled back. 'He can try to stop me.'

The Hardwicks had lived for nothing but duty for a thousand years. Vivian had shed blood – she'd shed *him* – she'd given her life a hundred times only to find no Tenebrous able to take it. For a long time, she'd shed her emotions as well. Duty was everything.

To hear her so easily put him before all that made something in Denizen's heart give way.

'I'll stay out of trouble,' he said. 'Greaves'll forget I even exist.'

'I hope so,' she said, and gathered him up in a hug. It wasn't something with which she'd had a lot of practice, and she'd evidently mixed up hugs up in her head with choke-hold techniques because it was ten whole seconds before he got his breath back.

Releasing him, Vivian lingered for a moment at the door, picking at a splinter on the door frame. They'd talked over every single eventuality that might arise after this moment, but the one thing they hadn't prepared for was the moment itself.

'Be safe,' she said, and was gone.

So that was it then, Denizen thought, lying down on the bed fully clothed. He was here. A Neophyte of the Second Rank – whatever that meant – surrounded by strangers in the heart of the Order's power, the safest place on the planet.

But wasn't that the point of lighthouses? If you were near one, you were going in the wrong direction.

It took Denizen a long time to fall asleep.

4

THE TERRIBLE SECRET OF ABIGAIL FALX

Abigail Falx had only spent three weeks in formal education. It had been her mother's idea – she thought it would be *educational* for Abigail to interact with other children. Up until that point, Abigail hadn't really interacted with other children. Mostly, she interacted with punching bags. Or painted targets. Or knives.

It had been educational. She could say that much. She had definitely discovered things she hadn't known before.

She'd learned, for example, that some teachers didn't appreciate children being forward and hard-working and *right* as often as they possibly could, which to ten-year-old Abigail made no sense whatsoever. She'd also learned that other ten-year-olds were terrible at threat assessment, ignoring crucial details to focus instead on her shaky grasp of their language and her skin being half a hemisphere darker than theirs.

That had proven to be a severe tactical error.

That had been the end of the experiment. Now she stood in a place where her drive would be appreciated – a place that would take her as seriously as she took herself. Then, as now, sneaking down early to be the first one at training, Abigail resolved to be worthy of it.

'Oh!' she said. 'Hello . . .'

Eyes flicked to her, and then flicked back. The walls of the chamber were mirrored so students could examine their form, which gave Abigail a selection of angles to see the three students who'd beaten her there and herself standing awkwardly in the doorway.

Obviously, it's good that they had all had the same idea, she thought, avoiding her own gaze as she took her place in the line. *It shows commitment. Cohesion. And*, a part of her couldn't help thinking, *the teacher isn't even here yet, so it's not like they can tell* which *of us arrived first.*

Time passed. She wasn't going to gawk. They hadn't gawked. Besides, it was a useful mental exercise to analyse each of the Neophytes instead.

First on the left: a pale and sinuous girl with an idle, vicious cast to her features that had instantly reminded Abigail of a weasel or a mink. *A Croit?* She'd heard some of them were being integrated.

Second: a Neophyte even shorter than Denizen, who had somehow managed to perfect the pinched, fretful look of a bank manager. A bank manager whose bank was failing.

Third: a dark-skinned young man – 'boy' didn't seem appropriate, partly due to his beard, his towering bulk, and partly because he had as many scars as a Malleus. He hadn't reacted to her entry at all.

More Neophytes filed in. Tall, short, thin, broad – there was Katerina, a girl she'd played with on a kitchen floor in Munich as Abigail's mother had been stitched back together upstairs. There was a girl with the traditional sunburst tattoo of the Eguzki family (bit over-the-top, Abigail privately thought), a pair of twins with dreadlocks – boys and girls from every corner of the globe.

She missed Simon or Denizen entering and, though part of her wanted to greet them, she knew they'd understand. This first meeting with the Master of Neophytes was crucial. She had to make a good impression.

Gedeon.

Nathaniel Gayle.

What if it's Vivian*?!*

Stop it.

She let out a deep breath. It didn't matter who it was. What mattered was that she was here now. She was ready to learn, to be challenged, to be –

'I sincerely hope none of you did the showing-up-early thing,' Grey said, striding into the chamber, 'because it impresses absolutely nobody.'

The Knight stalked into the centre of the room, gaze drifting from Neophyte to Neophyte as if only mildly interested in what he saw. Abigail felt his eyes rest on her for a second, before flicking away.

'Right,' he said, clapping his hands. 'I will be this year's Master of Neophytes, forgoing active duty to specialize in the art of training *you*. I've read every report each of your Mallei has filed. I know your experience, your temperaments, your Cants and your Cost.'

He started to pace back and forth, and Abigail felt something in her curdle as she remembered all those mornings in the back garden of Seraphim Row, duelling back and forth, Grey frustrating her with his mercurial grace.

Real swords?

Real swords. You need to get used to the weight. And you're not going to hit me.

Grey flashed them a hard, lupine grin. 'The question is . . .'

The fire of her heritage trickled up Abigail's spine before she shut it down. She had a lot of practice at that. Not controlling the fire – though she did, of course she did – but containing her anger.

It had been necessary, in those first weeks after the Clockwork Three's attack. Abigail wasn't used to loneliness. Where her family went, they went together. And moving to Seraphim Row had taken away one family but provided another – weird and mismatched with an absolutely inspiring leader – and she'd made do.

And then –

Grey's smile vanished. '*Why me?*'

Like mercury.

The Knight darted sideways, from standing still to sprinting, and he planted a foot in the fretful boy's chest to lift him from the ground. The line didn't break. It hadn't time. Abigail's second heartbeat had barely tripped over the first before twenty-four became twenty-one in a chorus of yelps. Grey spun like a dancer, skittered like a nightmare, and when the third beat came –

That was the other thing all the Neophytes had in common: children might have broken; children might have run. But none of them had been children for a very long time.

Mink Girl lashed out with a roundhouse kick, but Grey was no longer there to receive it, and two blunt *thwocks* of flesh put her down. He rolled over the back of a lunging boy to hammer his feet into another, and somehow it was only the kids who hit the floor. Bodies moved past her, or fell, or were struck, and Abigail just stood there, remembering flowerpots, and questions called out amid flashing blades –

'And breathe.'

Eight of the twenty-four Neophytes were down. Some had frozen where they stood. Others were halfway to the weapons racks on the walls, and standing in a circle of groaning, prone bodies was Grey, skin slick with sweat.

His gaze fell on Abigail. 'I said *breathe*.'

No – not Abigail. There was a rising glow in the mirrors, the colour of sunrises and ripe peaches, summer-warm and dazzling bright. They all turned.

The boy was nearly as tall as Grey, shoulders straining against his training top, hair a shock of gold two shades darker than the amber billowing underneath his skin. His hands were outstretched, and there the light was brightest, sizzling like a fuse.

'Release,' Grey said, his voice just a little out of breath. '*Release* it, Matt. Think cold. Think calm. Whatever you need to do.'

It took an age for the light to die out, or maybe that was just how long it felt. They all knew that struggle, and Abigail averted her gaze respectfully. She wouldn't have wanted anyone staring at her either.

Grey waited patiently as the line re-formed.

'It happens,' he said. 'No warrior escapes being taken by surprise. *That's* when the fire will try and get out. When you're distracted. Angry. Off guard. Our lives are a balancing act, and there will always be moments where you teeter on the edge. What matters is pulling yourself back.'

Abigail pressed a fingernail into the cold, comforting hardness of the Cost in her palm. They all had their methods of calming the fire – Abigail's parents had their faith, and she had them. They believed in her, and she worked to be worthy of it.

This was Grey's preferred method of teaching – throw as much as possible at you, just as this war would. It was why she hadn't moved. He was doing it to make a point. She had wanted to make a point as well.

'So why me? Of all possible choices, why was I chosen to teach you?' He spun on a heel and twenty-four Neophytes tensed, but no attack came. '*Anything*, people? Did you come here to learn or be right?'

'Because you're a Knight?' the Eguzki girl called from behind Abigail. It was a good answer. Fighting alone, turning impossible odds possible – that was what the Order did. It might even have been Abigail's answer . . . had she not been determined to keep her mouth shut. She'd had a lot of practice since Grey had been taken away.

'I might not be,' Grey said. 'Didn't use my power, did I? I might have been Secret Service, Spetsnaz, SAS . . .'

'We're not going to be fighting SAS,' the Eguzki girl responded confusedly. Grey's face hardened.

'*We don't know who we're going to be fighting.*' He slammed a fist into his palm. 'Two gendarmes find you breaking into an apartment a minute ahead of a Breach, and you're going to what – stop and explain yourself? A Tenebrous replaces the head of a Montenegrin crime cartel and you have to put down six innocent men without –'

He snapped gloved fingers, and a band of light rippled through him from head to toe like the snap of a flag, before disappearing as if it had never been.

Abigail heard intakes of breath. *Such control.*

'Innocent men?' came a voice. 'You said they were criminals.'

'But not Tenebrous,' said Grey. 'And innocence comes in varying degrees.' Another finger snap. 'Groups of two.'

OK. *OK.* A welcome distraction. The room crowded with the controlled chaos of teenagers seeking partners they knew, or wanted to know, or wanted to fight. Abigail just ran through stretches, concentrating on her form. She was sure that Denizen and Simon would be bolting for each other like sailors for shore.

'Hello.'

The Eguzki girl. Taller than her – *longer reach* – with a loose, short stance – *agile but unstable*. Abigail had sparred against Denizen, Simon and Darcie enough to know them, on a level that she sometimes thought transcended even their friendship.

But this person was new. *Fun*, she thought, with a nervous, appraising thrill.

Abigail had always excelled at observation, ever since her sixth birthday when she had solemnly sat her parents down and told them she'd figured out they weren't bear wrestlers. Every day of training since then had underlined for her that seeing threats before they became threats was the difference between getting hurt and not getting hurt, the difference between her parents debriefing her on their missions and . . . not coming home at all.

She knew that people sometimes thought she was uncomplicated, just because she said what she thought and didn't waste time overanalysing the things that didn't need to be overanalysed. They were wrong.

Abigail wasn't uncomplicated. She was busy.

'Begin.'

And Daybreak and Grey went away in the stinging song of impact.

Left hook.

Right hook.

Block.

Everything else fell away, the universe reduced to limb and locomotion, the constantly changing space between them both.

Jab.

She's right-handed.

Circle.

Jab.

Arms and hands and elbows, coming at her hard – sun-baked and fractal with muscle.

Trap.

Lock.

The girl's eyes widened, but by then Abigail was already moving, taking her arm with her. *My arm*, she thought triumphantly, and flung her out of their universe and on to the ground.

Or would have, had the Eguzki girl not suddenly gone limp, dead weight buckling Abigail at the knee. They both went down, but Abigail was on the bottom, a knee in her ribs. She gasped –

'And breathe.'

The weight went away, and, though a part of Abigail wanted to ignore the hand her opponent held out, she made herself take it.

'Sorry,' the girl said. 'Dirty trick.'

It had been. It had also been the first time a Neophyte had put Abigail on her back in a year.

'It was a good one,' she said, and she surprised herself by grinning back. 'I'll remember it.'

'Change partners,' Grey called, and the shuffle began again. 'And I'm still waiting on an answer. You're here to learn. Why am *I* here?'

'To teach?'

A shake of the head, and then Abigail's opponent punched her so hard in the face she could feel the bruise she left on his hand.

'To learn?'

She scissor-kicked a blonde girl to the floor. An iron wrist pinned her throat. She didn't see Denizen. She didn't see Simon. Her gaze became muddy with exhaustion, and her skin swam with sweat.

And all of it entirely failing to distract her from those familiar eyes watching her; that voice so bright with laughter and cracked with strain. She'd never spoken about what it felt like losing Grey, because it had hit the others so hard – and wasn't it her duty to look after them first?

Or maybe she'd kept quiet because then she'd have had to tell them that she didn't feel loss. She felt like she'd been failed.

'I know why you're here.' The boy who'd nearly lost control of his power. *Matt*. Standing or in tangles of limbs, the others slowly stopped their sparring.

'Oh?' Grey said, his shoulders set in a familiar fighting stance. The boy flicked the sweat from his face, eyes as blue as Abigail's above an aquiline nose and a jaw like the butt of a spear.

'You're the traitor.'

The word breathed around the room, as rank as an imminent Breach. *Traitor.* The word didn't get much use in the Order. Their war was as black and white as a war could possibly be. Tenebrous didn't see humans as collaborators. They saw them as food.

Grey's arms had folded. No trace of fire moved through the pewter paleness of his arms, but it must have been there all the same.

Food, or a toy to be played with.

'I heard about you,' Matt continued, and something ugly broke the surface of his voice. 'You turned on your cadre. Got one of them killed. That's why you're here. As . . .' He frowned. 'Punishment. Or –'

He looked around, as if for suggestions or support, but Neophytes were turning away or looking annoyed. Maybe they didn't believe him, or maybe they were keeping their mouths shut out of respect.

Hadn't Abigail kept quiet too?

'He's right,' Grey said quietly. 'I am a traitor. Was. Am. It's not the kind of thing that ever washes off. A year ago, three Tenebrous enthralled me. Made me act against my will.'

Gasps echoed round the chamber, but Abigail's teeth were clenched. Oh, she had been told about the Three forcing themselves into his head. She knew he hadn't been in control of himself, that nobody blamed him, that he blamed himself.

'I thought I was invincible,' he said. 'On good days. And then on bad days I looked at the Cost, and I looked at my scars, and I thought, *When I die, it will mean something.* That it'll be . . . poetry.'

He lifted his hands. 'I'm the only Knight who wears gloves in Daybreak. I can imagine you were wondering why.'

Grey tore off his left glove to reveal a hand of iron caught somewhere between clockwork and a claw – a snarl of gears and pins and shafts knotted to form a palm, fingers curled in on themselves like a dying spider.

The chamber was suddenly very quiet. Matt looked sick.

'A Tenebrous reached into me and did something no Tenebrous had ever done before. Maybe they'll never do it again – I don't know. And neither do you. They take their forms and their powers from what they see, and they have a whole damned multiverse to draw on.

'That's what we're at war with.'

He forced the glove over the broken machinery of his hand.

'I can teach you, but not prepare you. I can train you, but training only takes you to the edge of the darkness, and not a single step more. That's what I am. I'm a lesson that we are not invincible. That there are things that cannot be prepared for, and may not be survived.'

NO. Abigail's heritage coursed through her in whips of molten gold. She'd based her life on the opposite. She'd turned herself into a weapon precisely so that, when the moment came, all that time and energy and training would keep her and those she cared for safe. And he stood there, saying that it was all for nothing?

It was why she hadn't fought him earlier, played into their old games of question-and-attack. It was why she had listened to Denizen and Darcie mourn the comrade they had lost, but never spoken of it herself.

Knights were supposed to do their best. All the Order asked of you was everything, and all it gave you in return was the knowledge that you'd done all you could. And through some secret flaw, or weakness, or inattention, Grey had let in the dark, and Abigail's new family had paid for it.

'Spar,' Grey said tiredly, and the tableau began to move. Abigail suddenly found herself face to face with Simon, looking more like a crow than ever, sweat-soaked hair already feathering in the heat.

She brought up her hands half-heartedly.

'Do you believe that?' she said. 'What Grey said?'

'I've a better question,' Simon hissed. '*Where's Denizen?*'

5

A BETTER QUESTION

There's a special kind of waking when you know you're late.

Denizen was out of bed and three steps across the room before his brain realized he was conscious. *I'm late. I'm late. I'm late.* He didn't have to check his phone. He knew exactly what time it was. It was *late*. It was late o'clock. Knowing him, it was twenty-five past late, and now adrenalin was spiking harder in him than it ever had during combat.

It's my first day and I'm late. I'm trying not to stand out and I'm late. I'm late I'm late I'mlateI'mlateI'mlate –

The thoughts scudded into a panicked rhythm as he lost four seconds, blindly staring into an empty wardrobe, another two spinning in a circle with his brain sparking nothing-thoughts, until he remembered he hadn't unpacked –

– *IthoughtI'dhavetimeinthemorningI'mlate* –

– and blizzarded himself into his clothes as quickly as possible. Vivian had bought them just for the occasion: white cotton, light, perfect for training and running and being late, late, *latelatelatelate* –

He left his room at a run.

As if being a disgrace to his friends, his lineage and the entire Order of the Borrowed Dark wasn't enough, Denizen soon found that the shoes were a size too big. He discovered this after one came off mid-gallop and he had to rush back for it, lest he disgrace all of the above and be doing it in his socks as well.

It was then that he realized that he had no idea where he was going. *Why do I never pay attention to what people are saying?* One stone corridor looked much the same as the other, and Denizen fell into a sort of panicked back-and-forth dance. *Am I even running in the right direction?* He might have been making the situation worse rather than better *like he always did*, but would it have been too much trouble for them to *maybe* put up a sign?

OK. Calm.

'Lost?'

And it wasn't the accent, deep and smooth as a Tube tunnel, and it wasn't the rich tone of confidence and camaraderie. Denizen knew who was speaking simply because it was the absolute last voice Denizen wanted to hear, and that was a category with a *lot* of competition.

Turn round.

No.

You have to eventually.

Slowly, still thrumming with adrenalin, Denizen turned, inclining his head in what could have been mistaken for a nod of respect, but was actually an attempt to hide an involuntary grimace.

'Palatine.'

Edifice Greaves smiled. 'Denizen Hardwick. Welcome to Daybreak.'

Denizen had spent his childhood inside fantasy books, and they'd imprinted certain expectations in him as to what heroic secret societies were like. What he hadn't realized was that, just as you needed heroes, you also needed someone like Edifice Greaves.

'Disorientating, isn't it?' Greaves said, swaying aside to let a group of Knights pass.

Oh now *there are Knights*, Denizen thought, and briefly wondered if Greaves had ordered these corridors cleared so he wouldn't have anyone to ask for directions, which told you just about everything you needed to know about the Palatine.

'It's actually part of the design,' he said, tapping the folder he held against the wall. 'Dead ends, false staircases – anything to confuse possible invaders.'

'Oh,' Denizen said warily, trying to surreptitiously back away. 'Cool. I actually have to . . .'

'Get to training?'

This time the grimace was unavoidable. He'd been hoping to slink away and do his best to find the others, or maybe just lose himself in these corridors forever. But now Denizen was trapped in more ways than one: continue to be *latelatelatelate* or accept help from Edifice Greaves.

It wasn't that Greaves was evil. He wasn't. He ran the Order. He made things work. If front-line Knights like Vivian were the teeth of the gear, then Greaves was the bar that made the great gear spin. He was tall and he was handsome, and charm hung about him like an invisible cloud. That was a stupid reason for Denizen not to like someone, but experience had taught him that Greaves's effortless charisma was as mechanical a strategy as Daybreak's confusing layout.

The Palatine grinned. 'Follow me.'

Greaves swept past Denizen – *I was going the right way!* – to tap a recessed button beside a pair of doors. They hissed open – *A lift! I was* so *far away from the right way* – and, with a sweep of his hand, Greaves indicated the tiny, lamplit rectangle within.

They rose in silence, maybe because Greaves was simply helping a wayward Neophyte, maybe because he sensed Denizen's mistrust, or maybe because he was biding his time until Denizen lowered his guard.

Who knew? Denizen had never learned to play chess. He couldn't remember how half the pieces moved and he was too busy thinking about making the right move *now* than trying to make it half a game away.

He couldn't imagine how good you'd have to be to play chess with people.

'Sorry, Palatine, are you sure this is the way?'

Greaves's smile did nothing to comfort him.

'Don't you trust me? And stop worrying. The Master of Neophytes is hardly going to punish you if you're with me.'

I'm not with you, Denizen thought acidly, and then stiffened. *Oh God – who's our tutor? I'm already behind.*

Finally, the doors slid open to reveal a simple wooden staircase. Greaves bounded up the steps, placing one hand on the door above.

'Right through here.'

And grudgingly Denizen followed him into the dazzling Adumbral sun.

Stars burst against his eyes, and Denizen swayed against a wind eagerly trying to sweep him up into the sky, which was suddenly a *lot* closer than it had been previously. His stomach made a spirited attempt to get back down the stairs, but only made it as far as his toes.

'We're . . . we're . . .'

'A long way up,' Greaves said with relish, rapping his knuckles against a huge pane of glass so hard that Denizen flinched, as if that impact might send the whole tower tumbling down. Though his vision was still silvered and teary, he could now see that they were at the summit of Daybreak just beneath the swell of stone that formed the . . . top bit. *They should have told us it was a lighthouse. I would have read up if I'd known it was a lighthouse.*

Greaves looked right at home, because he always looked at home and also, Denizen realized, because he actually *was*. This was the seat of the Palatine – maybe you couldn't help but be confident with a whole country laid out before you. Greaves leaned out into the sun and drew a massive breath, sun shining on the delicate frosting of grey in his black beard. *Had those grey hairs been there before?*

'Beautiful, isn't it?'

No idea. I'm not looking down. The sun had turned Greaves's skin the rich brown of new-tilled earth. By comparison, Denizen could already feel his beginning to crinkle. He fixed the Palatine with Frown No. 9 – You Are Making Fun Of Me.

'I can't help but notice,' he said through gritted teeth, 'that this isn't the Neophytes' first training session.'

'There it is,' Greaves said. 'You're an odd reversal of your mother, you know that? Vivian Hardwick has never had a thought she didn't instantly state, and with you it's all going on beneath the surface.'

Maybe this wouldn't be so different from regular school, after all. Everything he'd been through since Crosscaper, and Denizen was still at the mercy of an adult amusing themselves. 'Why am I here? What do you want?'

'I want to know what you're capable of. Really. If you cut loose.'

They were the wrong words to say. Denizen was tired. He was stressed. He'd been led on a wild-goose chase by a person he thoroughly disliked and it hadn't even had the good grace to be downhill. The candlewards were very far away; there was a taste of Tenebrae in the air and, even without all that, the power within needed no excuse at all to raise its head.

'Denizen . . . I saw you.'

Coils of flame snaked through Denizen's stomach, climbing every beat of his heart, reaching out cautious tendrils to probe the fortifications he and Vivian had built.

'You threw Cants against that creature the Croits worshipped with a confidence and variety far beyond your years.'

Confidence? It wasn't how he'd felt at the time. The Redemptress of the Croits hadn't deserved her death, and he'd done his best to stop it, despite seventy-eight separate desires to burn her to ash.

'You have great power, Denizen . . .'

Vivian's tutelage had helped, showing him how to shape a fortress of ice and resolve, compressed blue-black like coal forced to diamond. And yet . . . Fire – gleaming at every keyhole and knocking at every door, and Denizen was both the walls' only guard and the enemy's man inside. He *wanted* to give in. He wanted to cut loose. He wanted . . .

'And I have absolutely no need of it.'

'What?' said Denizen, jerked out of his reverie. 'You don't?'

Greaves raised an eyebrow.

'You used your power with a dexterity I've never seen . . . and it doesn't interest me a jot. Do you know why?'

Denizen really didn't. The Hardwicks had sought to keep his fluency in the Cants a secret because Greaves had never seen an opportunity he didn't take with both hands – and because of who exactly had given them to him.

'The average Knight – if there is such a thing – learns maybe ten Cants,' Greaves continued, 'enough to get the job done. There are no prizes for showing off. Not in battle. Not with the Cost.'

Another of Vivian's controlling techniques – the walls of his inner fortress may have been ice, but their core was iron and consequence. Denizen's fluency eased the Cost a little, but he suffered it all the same.

'So I'm wondering, in your *expert* opinion, if the twenty-four Neophytes currently training in Daybreak had your . . . insight, how much of the city do you think they could take out? All at once. Cost be damned.'

Denizen didn't have to think. He knew. Sometimes it was all he could do not to see the world as overlapping patterns of devastation, as if it had already happened and all he had to do was say the word.

'There are a few variables,' he muttered, 'but you're talking a third of the city. Maybe more.'

Greaves whistled. 'That's a lot.'

Denizen didn't say anything.

'And the entire Order? Say, a thousand Knights?'

Denizen looked out on the stunning vista – the gnarls of forest, the mountain peaks – and imagined a second sun building below the first, tearing apart street after street, tumbling buildings aside in smoke and cinder.

'Why are you asking me this?'

'*Because it isn't enough*,' Greaves growled. His shoulders slumped in a sigh, as if the admission had drained him. 'It never has been. We train and we fight and we die and it doesn't change anything.'

For a second, Denizen really wanted to believe the look of honest frustration in his eyes.

'Do you think being a Palatine is all budgets? Do you know how many letters of condolence I have to write? Knights *die*, and I have to console with one hand and order coffins with the other. And that's just us. When the war spills over into the real world, it's me that has to clean it up. Anonymous donations, diverted funds . . . orphanages. They're a vested interest.'

He folded his arms.

'And all of it a holding action. All of it wading through the shallows, waiting for the tsunami to strike.'

His fingers tightened on the balcony rail.

'And then the Clockwork Three introduced Mercy to the world,' he said, 'and you two had a *conversation*.'

And there it was. The information Denizen had been trying to keep redacted. The one piece of contraband he'd desperately tried to leave behind.

'It didn't take much to figure out,' Greaves said. 'Half the Order would well believe it was Vivian Hardwick who pulled our fat from the fire that night, but it was the daughter of the Endless King, wasn't it? She taught you the Cants so you could free her from the Three.'

'That's . . .' Denizen's mind was working furiously. 'One way of putting it?'

And it was. It didn't incorporate Simon trapped in an orphanage diseased by misery, or Grey being twisted into a weapon against those he held dear. It didn't allow for the heartbreaking story of what Vivian Hardwick had suffered, or the sight of Corinne D'Aubigny dead in Fuller Jack's arms.

And it certainly didn't account for Mercy.

Denizen could have exhausted his considerable vocabulary describing the Endless King's daughter and never come close to describing a single second of her ever-shifting form. And his words gave out entirely when they came to describing their late-night walks through Dublin, or the first time she had giggled through a human throat.

And, against all the advice of his best friend and common sense and to the utter horror of his mother, Denizen had managed to develop a crush on her.

'You saved her, and she came back to thank you, and for the first time in history a Tenebrous talked of peace. *Of peace.*'

There was nothing in the rules about having feelings for a Tenebrous. Presumably nobody had been that stupid before. Second, Vivian Hardwick's feelings about *his* feelings had been made perfectly clear. Hammers had been involved. Third . . .

Third, it had been six months. Six months since Mercy had made the whole world about *her* and *him*, and then not spoken to him since.

'And it didn't happen.' Greaves pushed back against the rail in frustration. 'The Croits took that chance from us . . . but I *saw* it. Just for a second, I saw an end to this cold war that has slowly eaten our people for a thousand years. And, if another chance comes, *we will be ready.*'

Denizen had had enough. '*What* are you talking about?'

'You,' Greaves said. 'I don't care if you could cut your way through a dozen Redemptresses. I don't care if you were immune from the Cost and we could just drop you into a Breach like a holy hand-grenade. There is a *connection* between you two, and our best chance for peace is not bleeding out pointlessly on a Dublin street.' His voice was stern. 'You're going to serve the Order in a different way.'

'But . . .'

'But what?' Greaves said acerbically. 'You're not your mother, Denizen, not some lifer Knight raised to the blade. How far do you think you would have got in any of this if that brush with Mercy hadn't gifted you with such fluency?'

'It wasn't –'

'No more lies, Denizen. No more games. You used thirty-seven Cants in your battle with the Redemptress. I counted. Vivian could have trained you round the clock for six months and you wouldn't be that good.'

Utterly paralysed and absolutely flailing at exactly the same moment, Denizen struggled for words.

'You . . . you counted?'

Greaves flashed him a shark's grin. 'I multitask. And I'm right. Without Mercy, you wouldn't be here.'

Greaves was right. He'd barely survived as it was. Denizen didn't enjoy fighting. He'd come to Seraphim Row to find out what happened to his parents, then to control his power – which was not going well – and then he'd wanted to help . . . but did that mean fighting?

You do enjoy it. Letting that rage out, letting it flow through you to wreak your will upon the world, flinging power left and right like a child's dream of a wizard . . .

Denizen shivered, and refroze his melting fortress walls. That wasn't him. That was the fire.

Wasn't it?

'You'd live here,' Greaves said, 'training in the arts of a Knight, plus diplomacy, history, negotiation. And when Mercy returns *you'll* be the one talking to her. I wish there was another way, but we don't have anything close to an expert. We have you.'

'What about . . .' He swallowed. 'What about Simon? Abigail?'

'They'd visit. Knights pass through Daybreak all the time. They'd be transferred out of Seraphim Row at the end of this year anyway.'

Something twisted in Denizen's stomach. 'R-really?'

'We go where we're needed,' Greaves said. 'It's a big world with a lot of holes in it.'

There was only one more card Denizen could play. 'Does Vivian know you're offering this?'

She'd been the Order's first choice for Palatine, or so the rumours went. Not because of manoeuvring – then as now, Vivian had the political grace of a meteor strike – but, if there was one thing Knights didn't argue with, it was results. (Privately, of course, both Hardwicks knew that Vivian would have been a disaster. Forms, schedules, logistics . . . However, there was absolutely no point in letting Greaves know that.)

'You think she'd disagree?' One look at the Palatine and Denizen knew he'd been outplayed. 'Her son contributing more to the war effort than a hundred

Mallei? You'd be doing your name proud. And you'd be a lot safer.'

'You don't just mean by staying here, do you?'

'No,' Greaves said simply. 'The more Cants you know, the more they want to be said. And you know thirty-seven. At least. How's that working out for you?'

As if responding to his words, Denizen felt the yawn and stretch of seventy-eight Cants, alien shapes with lives of their own, and little regard for the teenager struggling to hold them in place. Fighting made that carefully constructed fortress far harder to hold.

And here was one far more secure.

Denizen reeled. He had been systematically beaten, as surely as if he'd sparred with Abigail. There was nothing he could say, and even if there were . . .

Mercy doesn't want to talk to me. She hasn't contacted me since she saved my life.

'We go where we're needed,' he whispered.

Greaves's eyes found his. 'And you're needed *here*.'

6
DEMANDS

It was a long time until lunch.

Greaves hadn't shown Denizen the way to the training chamber. Maybe the Palatine wanted him alone to think about his offer, or maybe there hadn't been enough time left, or maybe he'd even – rightly – noted that Denizen was in no mood to try and catch up.

Instead, Denizen had been left in what he supposed you'd have to call the Daybreak canteen. It probably wasn't what *they* called it. Canteens generally didn't have swooping ceilings hung with snow-white pennants, or well-worn flagstone floors, but Denizen had eaten in a canteen for eleven of his fourteen years and there was a certain *canteenishness* about the place all the same.

Denizen sat in an alcove where he could observe the whole room – the long benches, incongruously modern coffee machines and the counter, behind which lurked a Knight whose apron and disposable gloves did absolutely nothing to dilute his air of contained murder.

Denizen wasn't at all fazed to see Knights manning the mashed potatoes. The Order weren't the types to outsource their dirty work. *Besides*, he thought sourly, *if anyone could talk a hard-bitten warrior into a hairnet, it would be Greaves.*

It was *so* like Greaves. The last time they'd met, he'd leaked false information to Denizen to see if his loyalty lay with Mercy or the Order, and now he'd even found a way to turn that to his advantage. And yes, in fairness, he was doing it to keep the world safe, but that was the problem with Greaves – you had to use the phrase *in fairness* a lot.

And it made sense. That was the worst part. Daybreak was where Denizen could do the most good. Here, with Greaves, and away from . . .

Denizen thought about his birthday, just a few weeks gone – clustered around a single table in Seraphim Row's huge kitchen, gifts and stories and a little paper hat that Vivian had resolutely refused to wear but folded primly and put in her pocket. Jack had sung, his voice rich and warm as a forge fire, and . . .

I could write. Email. Surely Greaves wouldn't mind –

And there it was – this was Greaves's territory. All communication would have to go through him. Giant as this place was, Denizen suddenly felt very trapped.

You're being selfish. He picked at the ancient wood of the table. Nearly a year ago, Denizen had put himself in between a Tenebrous and a child. He could have run. Nobody would have known. But he'd made a choice.

He'd stayed then. He should stay now. And time would pass, and year after year of Neophytes would come and go, and his friends would write, and maybe they wouldn't start to resent him for being safe in his tower, but sooner or later, one way or another, the letters would stop.

And he'd be here. *Waiting for someone who might never actually show up.*

Denizen shrank back as teenagers began slipping through the door with the careful gait of bodies who'd been sparring all morning. There was a coltish not-quite-thereness to their movements that was disquietingly familiar, like seeing a stranger in your clothes. There were so *many* of them.

Denizen scanned the crowd and –

'Guys!' Denizen winced at the eager squeak that came out of his mouth. 'Guys!'

Fortunately, Abigail clocked his frantic waving before it went on too long, and they wound their way to him through growing crowds.

'I hate to break it to you,' Simon said, when they had got close enough, 'but you're late for training.'

With a jolt of horrified embarrassment, Denizen realized there was a lump in his throat. *Stop being ridiculous.* He swallowed, and forced a grin to fill the silence.

'Yes,' Denizen managed. 'I'll explain, but – how did it go?'

Abigail threw herself into the back of the alcove, her face like thunder. Simon and Denizen exchanged glances. Denizen had had personal experience of just how patient Abigail could be, but generally that expression meant something was going to get broken.

'Is . . . something wrong?'

Abigail's shoulders rolled in a fluid shrug. 'No.'

One eye on Abigail in case breaking stuff was still on the menu, Simon sat down as well.

'Grey is our Master of Neophytes.'

'Oh!' Denizen said, and suddenly Greaves's offer gained new and tangled dimensions. He could vouch first-hand for Grey's teaching skills, but he couldn't deny that his former mentor might not be in the best . . . headspace for teaching.

But if I stay I'll see more of him. Yesterday the thought would have cheered him immensely, but that was . . . *Before?* Was that what he was about to think? Was Denizen going to avoid his friend just because the war had changed him? Wasn't that what war did?

And isn't it kind of your fault?

He was jolted out of his reverie by Abigail abruptly jumping from her seat and stalking towards the queue for food.

Denizen frowned. 'Is she all right?'

'I don't know,' Simon said. 'She's been super-quiet since training. And I know you guys were trained by Grey, but I have to say, if the rest of the year is like his opening speech . . .'

'What do you mean?'

Simon pressed both his hands down on to the tabletop between them, but not before Denizen saw them shake.

'Denizen . . . I spent a month hiding from the Clockwork Three in Crosscaper and I don't think I ever even really *saw* them, not properly, but, when you're being . . . being hunted like that, I felt like I knew them. You know?'

Light streamed in through the high windows, but the taller boy's eyes blinked furiously, as if trying to see in the dark.

'The Boy used to cry. Constantly. I could feel the sound in my hair, on my tongue. The Woman in White had this skittering, loping walk, like she would occasionally move to all fours . . .'

'I remember,' Denizen said softly.

'And the Man in the Waistcoat . . . he thought he was so funny. He'd make little jokes to himself as they went around destroying the classrooms, read out those stupid posters that Mr Colford used to put up about staying positive –'

Mr Colford had been their favourite teacher in Crosscaper. Denizen had never heard Simon refer to anything he did as stupid before.

'He had this way of mocking all the good things he found, all the good things in the world. He read the birthday card you sent me and he made it sound *horrible*. And, on top of all that, they twisted Crosscaper around them. Our home. Our childhood.

'They made it theirs. And now, *now* I know that's what Tenebrous do, but at the time I thought I was going mad. I thought they were in my head.'

'Look . . .' Simon spoke so rarely of those weeks that, when he did, Denizen felt like he had been handed something incredibly fragile to hold, and a single wrong word would break it forever. 'Simon, they didn't even know you were there. They weren't in your head.'

'I know,' Simon said. 'They were in Grey's.'

They sat in silence until Abigail returned, carrying a tray loaded with enough food for all three of them.

'You need to eat,' she explained, 'even if *someone* didn't come to training.'

'Hey,' Denizen said. 'What's wrong?'

'Nothing,' Abigail said, flashing them both a grin. 'So where were you?' Her eyes widened. 'Was it a . . . walrus situation?'

'We never agreed to that code name,' Denizen said. 'But . . . yes.' Both Simon and Abigail's faces darkened as Denizen explained Greaves's offer, warily eyeing the closest tables so they weren't overheard.

'He wants his eye on me,' Denizen trailed off dismally. 'It must be that. He wants me close because he thinks I'm . . .'

'Like Grey,' Abigail said, her voice stony. 'But you're not.' She sighed. 'Compromised, I mean. You had to save Mercy. We do what we have to – whatever victory demands.'

'Exactly,' Denizen said. Which was true. It was only in the subsequent months that thoughts of a decidedly squishy variety had bloomed. At the time, all he'd thought was that Mercy was very loud and he was probably going to die.

'I don't think Greaves judges Grey for what happened either,' Simon said. 'He's tried to help him, from what I can see. And yes, I know, *Greaves*, but that's something about him I'd actually believe.'

'You're right,' Denizen said. 'I just . . .'

'You just don't want to be left behind,' Simon said, and smiled. 'Because we have *very* short memories, and as soon as I'm not sleeping at the foot of your bed I'm definitely going to forget you ever existed. Won't we, Abigail?'

'Forget about who?'

'Exactly.'

'*Guys*,' Denizen said. 'You're not *funny*.'

'Yes,' Simon said, and Denizen told himself that it was the lingering thought of the Three that put the hollow edge in his smile. 'We are.'

Denizen looked at the plate in front of him, loaded with the same sort of primeval mush that Vivian served in Seraphim Row – so healthy you could have used it to terraform Mars.

'Now eat,' Abigail said, iron in her tone. 'We have a long day ahead.'

She was right. Lunch gave way to languages, a towering mantis of a woman named Madame Adler marching the gathered Neophytes through French verbs with military precision.

There was a lot to take in. It wasn't that their training had been haphazard; it was just that it had been dictated by Vivian's sensibilities, some subjects pursued with her typical vehemence, and others . . . not. Darcie had made a fair stab at picking up the slack, but listening to a friend was one thing, a stranger surrounded by strangers another.

'That wasn't so bad,' Abigail, who spoke French already, said as they walked to their next class.

'French I'm fine with,' Simon said, 'but first thing tomorrow we have Latin. *Latin.* That is not a tomorrow language. That's a yesterday language. Three or four thousand yesterdays, in fact.'

'Well, technically, we should have been studying Latin all year,' Abigail, who also knew Latin, said. 'It was just far easier to ask Darcie.'

The thought sent a pang through Denizen. Even their conversations felt a bit uneven, like a familiar song played with an instrument missing. *Get used to it*, a voice hissed cruelly in his head, as they navigated their way through the corridors. *In a year, you'll be playing solo.*

'So,' Simon said. 'Have you . . . have you decided what you're going to do?'

'No,' Denizen said. 'I haven't. But –'

Abigail cut him off. 'What do you mean, *what he's going to do*? He's going to stay.'

Denizen flushed with shock, marbled with the first stirrings of anger. 'Well, I haven't had a chance to think about –'

Abigail sighed. 'That's not what I mean, Denizen. Think back. Did Greaves actually *ask* you?'

'Em . . .'

No. No he hadn't. He had neatly skewered each of Denizen's protestations, but, now that Denizen thought about it, it hadn't felt like an argument, with both sides having an equal chance of convincing the other.

It had felt like an order.

'I'm sorry, Denizen,' Abigail said, 'but things are different now. I'm not saying Vivian ever went easy on us, especially not on you. But she did things her own way, and so does Greaves. We mightn't like him –'

'We *don't* like him,' Simon interrupted but his attempt at humour fell flat.

'– but he's in charge. He gets to give us orders and, unless they're morally wrong, we have to follow them. That's what being a soldier means. And from the sound of it he's right. If *she* shows up again, and you can help, then you should. This is what you signed up for. It's your duty.'

Denizen's shoulders slumped. She was right. She really was.

Yield not to evil, but attack all the more boldly. It had been the Hardwick motto for more than a thousand years. Vivian might have done her own thing, but only after a lifetime of sacrifice and battle. She'd earned the right to bend the rules a little.

Denizen, in fairness, had not.

7

BATTLEFIELD

They went to be social.

The Neophytes' Solar had settees, tapestries, rugs on the floor to take some of the chill from the flagstones – even a dusty TV and DVD player with a single box set of world history documentaries underneath.

It softened the chamber a little, but there was only so much you could do with a stone box. Abigail appreciated them trying to provide somewhere homey, but the first thing Neophytes learned was that everywhere was a battlefield, if you knew where to look.

Abigail scanned the room. A few little cliques had already formed, but many teenagers just sat alone, awkwardly trying to look around without being seen to do so. Simon immediately made a dash for the closest chair, curling up as if he were hoping to disappear between the cushions.

'We'll have to talk to them sometime,' Abigail said quietly, perching on the armrest. She was trying to be patient with the boys' reluctance, but her whole childhood had been spent finding strange adults trying to hide bandages under their sleeves at breakfast.

In Abigail's family, elders were referred to as *aunt* and *uncle* by tradition, but for those Knights that passed through the house it was more than that – they *were* family, by blood spilled rather than shared.

'I know,' Simon said grumpily. 'I just wish Denizen had stuck around. I wanted to talk to him about . . . stuff.'

'I think he's talked out,' Abigail said, though in truth she'd also been a little disappointed when Denizen had begged off social time and gone to his cell. 'Come on.'

'Gah. All right. I'm just . . . picking one. Hang on.'

'Nope,' she said, and yanked Simon out of his chair before he had a chance to protest. Ignoring his white-hot glare, she approached the tiny Neophyte with the bank-manager frown, who was sitting ramrod-straight on a plush footstool, gaze fixed on the window as if thinking of diving out of it.

Abigail could feel eyes on her. Nobody else had made such a bold move across the floor. But there was her mother's voice: *Sometimes you have to go first. That way you make it easier for everyone else.*

'Hi,' she said. 'How's it going?'

The kid looked at her with an expression of pure panic, hair cropped short around features almost too delicate to hold eyes that big. When the small Neophyte spoke, their voice was surprisingly deep. 'I'm sorry?'

'How are you?' Simon repeated, trying to nonchalantly lean against the wall before realizing it was a little too far and straightening himself out. 'We're Simon and Abigail. I'm Simon.' He frowned. 'That was probably obvious.'

That got a tiny smile. 'Not always. I'm Edwina de Montfort. Ed to everyone but my parents. It's an . . . ongoing conversation.'

Abigail smiled gently. 'For them or you?'

Ed shrugged. 'Them. I know I'm a he.'

'Ed it is,' Abigail said, grinning, and shook his hand.

Simon blinked, and then stuck out his hand as well. 'Cool. What's your garrison?'

'London. My family have been in Islington for . . . well, forever. You know.'

'No,' Simon said. 'I'm . . .'

Abigail pointedly didn't look at him. Simon's parents had died in a car crash, but his Knightly gifts spoke of some connection with the Order that no amount of research had been able to uncover. It had been a long time since he'd had to tell anyone.

'I'm a stray,' he said finally. 'Don't really know where I came from.'

Ed nodded sympathetically. 'I'm sorry to hear that. But you're here now. We're all family in a way, I think.'

When Abigail was a kid, she'd wanted to be a princess. Her mother was Iranian, and Abigail's childhood had been full of stories of women who'd fought and ruled, and what *ruling* meant. It was a duty. You served your people and your kingdom, and it was the quiet, automatic kindness in Ed's words that made him part of the private kingdom that Abigail kept in her head.

It wasn't a proper kingdom. Proper kingdoms had maps, and flags, and weren't able to fit in a bobble hat. But, proper or not, Abigail felt responsible for the people in it. She'd known Ed for all of eight sentences, and now she would risk her life for him. It was as simple as that.

That there are things that cannot be prepared for, and may not be survived.

She shivered.

'My family go back a long time,' Ed was saying. He had a small bud of a nose, and eyes that were wide and morose. Now that Abigail and Simon had revealed themselves not to be terrifying, Ed was directing a prey-animal stare to the rest of the room. 'Don't ask me to name all my ancestors. My dad makes me do it at Christmas.'

'Both Knights?' Simon asked.

'My dad. Mum spent the whole of my thirteenth birthday glaring at me and giving me ice water. I think she was going to tell the Palatine that I wasn't allowed to go, until Dad told her if I didn't get training I could explode in my sleep. He thinks he's really funny. But I actually really like training, and . . . me and Dad have lots to talk about now.'

Ed tensed once again as three more Neophytes entered the chamber. One was the Eguzki girl Abigail had sparred with earlier, neck tattoo bared. Another was the squat, blocky boy, every inch of his exposed skin a tangled forest of scars. His eyes burned with an intensity that had nothing to do with fire, and everything to do with rage.

'Who is –'

'Matt Temberley,' Ed said wearily, and it was only then that Abigail noticed the third boy, the one who had called

Grey a traitor – blond and broad, those long curls arranged in a meticulous cascade.

He stalked to an empty seat, spinning it round before flopping into it artistically. Even his hair flopped artistically, before settling back exactly in its pre-flop position.

Something about his expression annoyed Abigail. It was . . . disrespectful. They were in a magic castle. He didn't have to look *bored*.

'Oh yeah,' Simon said. 'That guy. Do you know him?'

Ed nodded. 'We've met a few times. He's garrisoned in Edinburgh. I think he practises to make his hair do that.'

Abigail looked away before Temberley noticed her staring, but not before she caught the weariness on the Eguzki girl's face as he made a comment and jogged her elbow to see her response.

Maybe it was the trio's arrival, or Abigail's bold move, but the atmosphere of the room turned concave, once-separate groups coming together like an invisible zip.

There were introductions in a dozen different languages. Simon and Ed got caught up talking to Stefan – Madrid garrison, very arm-wavy – so Abigail detached herself and ended up in a spirited conversation with Dmitry about crossbows. Abigail didn't speak Ukrainian, and Dmitry's English wasn't perfect, but there was a surprising amount you could get across with hand gestures – if you were talking about crossbows.

Groups split and re-formed. As different as they all were, there were enough similarities for it not to matter.

Not just being Neophytes, though that helped – shared training, favourite weapons, a pride in their purpose, a lore – but mostly because they were kids, and they were new, and in a very strange place indeed.

'So go on then. Who's fought one?'

And the moment was over, and the war returned.

Slowly, everyone turned to look at Matthew Temberley, who had steepled his fingers under the jut of his chin.

'Who's fought a Tenebrous?'

It was the one word that transcended the language barrier, the one word no one had said so far.

'Edinburgh's full of them,' he continued. 'Our *Lux Precognitae* – our cadre has a *Lux*, by the way – says that the Tenebrae runs like water through the city's stones. It's no wonder *normal* people think the whole city's haunted.'

Silence but for Etienne – Mink Girl from earlier, surprisingly friendly, excellent braid – quietly translating for the girl at her side.

'Matt Temberley,' he said. 'My kill count's eight. That's *kill count*, not just seeing them. I don't even know how many I've seen. It's a pity –' he cracked his knuckles – 'that you can't mount them. You know, for trophies? Once, right, in the Queen Anne Room . . .'

His hands carved shapes out of the air as he talked, as if slicing invisible Tenebrous to pieces. At one point, golden light fluttered beneath the skin of his hands and everyone tensed, but then he let out a deep breath and the glow dissipated as he went on to say how his cadre – but mostly he – had run the dread beast Anarabix down.

'That's . . .' Stefan's voice was as burnished as his skin, a drawl both sun-warm and utterly neutral. '. . . great.'

It didn't seem to be the response Matt was looking for. His expression darkened, as if he'd suddenly realized that conversations had more than one side.

'What about the rest of you? Any war stories? Any *scars*?' He said the last word with a strange kind of relish, and Abigail had been trying to be nice up until now, but it had been a very long day.

'Scars don't make a Knight,' she said. 'And we'll all have them soon enough.'

He definitely heard her. His eyes almost – but not quite – snapped to her before he re-crossed his arms and regarded Simon instead.

'What about you? I saw you spar earlier.' A grin slid across his face. 'You must have a scar or two.'

'Clocks,' Simon said, without missing a beat.

'What?'

'Can't. Be. Around. Clocks.' Simon's voice was as sharp as a new razor. 'Spent a month hiding in an orphanage from Tenebrous. They had a thing about clocks. Now I have a thing about clocks.'

'Oh,' Matt said, and then rallied. 'Well –'

'My Malleus fought a Tenebrous in Salut.'

Emilia Garcia – also from Madrid, missing two fingers on her left hand so she punched like a chisel. 'She let me come. My first time. I had never seen her cry before. It put her down and went for me, and when our eyes met . . . I saw Grandfather.

'That was what let her kill it. It made itself look like the people you loved, but it could only do one at a time.'

Matt opened his mouth, but Ed spoke up, each word an effort.

'I haven't seen one at all yet. I've trained and trained, but . . . they say they won't risk me until it's the right time.' Hands scrubbed up and down arms. 'I don't have any scars at all.'

'Well . . .' Matt rallied. 'Not to worry, sweetheart, it's like what's-her-face said –'

Ed winced. Abigail scowled at Matt.

Sweetheart?

And then a second later –

What's-her-face?!

'– you'll get your stripes.'

The scarred boy had been resolutely staring at the wall since they'd come in. A jolt of horror thrilled its way through Abigail's gut as Matt turned –

Oh no –

'What about you, big man? What's your story?'

This close, Abigail could see that the estuaries of scar tissue were too messy for blades, and nearly too messy for claws. He looked . . . chewed.

Abigail wouldn't have thought it possible for those eyes to chill any further. Though there couldn't have been more than a few months between them, his voice was crushingly deep, as if winched out of the centre of the earth.

'My cadre was Berlin. I had just Dawned when the Pursuivants hit.'

Abigail's heart missed a beat. As vicious as they were loyal, the Pursuivants of the Endless King had left no stone unturned in their search for their master's daughter. At first, it had just been scouting missions – warning shots across the Order's bows – but with each failure the clashes had become bloodier until finally Vivian, Abigail and Denizen had found her. They had almost been in time.

'Hagen . . .'

The Eguzki girl leaned forward, but he waved her away.

'I do not remember much,' he said. 'They came through the walls. I fought. *We* fought. I remember stabbing and stabbing and then . . .'

Scarred fingers tightened against each other, as if trying to wring out the words.

'It shouted *mercy*. Over and over again, in the most terrible voice. Why would it say that? Why would they speak of mercy, when they showed us none? It left then. I think it thought me dead. The Knights who found me . . . they thought I would die too.'

His eyes darkened.

'But we are at war.'

8
A DIFFERENT PRISON

The look on Simon and Abigail's faces when he abandoned them followed Denizen all the way up the stairs and into bed. It wasn't that he didn't want to get to know the others – he'd be spending a whole year with them, so presumably they'd have to talk sometime. He just couldn't do it tonight.

It wasn't life or death. That was the worst thing. Denizen had risked his life to face the Woman in White because, if he hadn't, a toddler would have died. Life or death. Simple.

This, however, was just *life*, and Denizen wasn't sure he could deal with it.

'Hello,' Grey said.

Denizen sat up with a start. He must have been closer to sleep than he realized – the Knight had somehow slipped into Denizen's room like a ghost, an impression not helped by the *Lucidum*'s pearlescent shades.

'Grey . . .' Denizen said. 'Why are you in my room late at night in the dark?'

'Is it dark?' Grey asked, taking a seat at the end of Denizen's bed. 'I didn't –' He stopped abruptly and shook his head. 'I forget to turn lights on sometimes. You know how it is.'

No, Denizen thought but kept his mouth shut. Once Grey had been the easiest person to talk to in Seraphim Row. But now Denizen felt as if he were struggling with a language he didn't understand – no, worse, a language he had once known but whose meanings had now been rearranged.

Grey even moved differently, no longer stalking like a leopard on the wrong side of hunger. Now there was a hesitancy – as if he was afraid of catching himself on sharp and hidden things.

'Is . . . everything OK?'

Denizen's voice was unsteady. It wasn't fear – though Cants stretched in his head as if recognizing a fellow predator. It wasn't pity either. Denizen had grown up in an orphanage. He *hated* pity.

It was guilt.

Red spilling down Grey's nose, the wild look in his eyes as he managed to drag the gun aside.

They'll kill you.

A mad, bloody smile.

One can only hope.

'What?'

Denizen started. He had been staring. 'Nothing. Sorry. What's up?'

Grey scrubbed a hand across his face. 'Don't worry about earlier. Greaves told me he needed a word. You'll have time to catch up. It's exciting, really. My favourite subject was history. Century after century, all those battles, all those choices people made to lead us here. Being a part of something bigger than yourself, you know?'

He looked at his hands. 'Meant a lot to a kid who didn't belong to anyone.'

'Grey . . .'

'Now science is less fun. I don't know if they should even be allowed to call it science. It's mostly just flammability scales and how to turn cleaning products into napalm. And then next term there'll be *law* or, more accurately, *loophole management for secret organizations*. It's amazing what you can convince parliaments to write into their constitutions if you get there in the right century. Ah, article three, subsection two: how many times have you saved my –'

'*Grey*.'

He sighed. 'Yes?'

'Why didn't you answer any of my letters?'

Grey snorted. 'What would I have said? *Hey, kid, good to hear from you. Sorry I put a bullet in your mam?* Not the best postcard.'

'You could have said *something*,' Denizen retorted. Long-suppressed anger was building, and he mentally hardened himself against the accompanying flame. 'I know you were trying to get better . . . but I had to hear about where you were from *Greaves*, and he dangled it in front of me like a carrot.'

'Yeah,' Grey said tiredly. 'He's like that. For what it's worth, I don't blame him. Or envy him. Logistics. Budgets.

Paperwork. Every time a battle's won, we lose another somewhere else. Sometimes the fighting's the easy part.'

His wan smile was testament to that.

'I suppose you know that he wants me to stay here,' Denizen said. '*Forever*. While my friends fight and . . .'

How would it happen? A pat on the shoulder and his mother's obituary? His arms pink and unmarked and Simon paler and colder with each visit until the day there was no visit at all?

Grey's lips tightened. 'You say *stay here* like it's a bad thing. Think of the people you'd help. The lives you'd save.'

'I should be out there,' Denizen said stubbornly. 'I'll meet Mercy, I'll do whatever he asks, but I should be out there with my friends. With my family.'

And that was part of it too. He'd only just got his mother back. He wasn't going to be separated from her again.

'I was wondering when *she'd* come up,' Grey snapped. Denizen flinched. The last time he'd heard Grey sound so angry was when the Three had been at the wheel. 'She's really done a number on you, hasn't she?'

'What do you mean?'

'That's Vivian's logic,' Grey said. 'Her selfishness, out of your mouth.' His fists opened and closed, and that was all the oxygen the fire needed. Denizen struggled for a moment, slamming door after door until its advance was stalled.

Grey hadn't noticed. He was looking at a different set of walls.

'Remember how she acted before *they* attacked? Remember her silence? Her damned air of mystery? *Do you know how different things could have been if she had just told us about the Three?*'

A bitter sunrise flushed Grey's drawn features, his eyes brimming with pallid light. With a shock, Denizen realized that all this time he'd been thinking about the Order forgiving Grey. He'd never once considered whether Grey would forgive them.

'I'm sorry,' the Knight said abruptly. 'I shouldn't have . . . I shouldn't have got angry. I just . . .'

His eyes found Denizen's. 'I used to get excited, can you believe that? Feeling a Breach in the air used to make me feel afraid, sick, the usual – but part of me liked it. Liked the fighting. Liked being *brave*. That was magic. Real magic.

'And then the Three came, and all they left me was the wrongness. Nestled inside me like a tumour, and all the fire in the world couldn't clean me out.'

'Grey . . . I –'

'I remember what you were like when you first came to Seraphim Row. Scared but *defiant*. You stood up to Vivian Hardwick five minutes after meeting her, which is more than I did. I knew then that you'd say yes. It might take you a while, but you would be a Knight.'

He stood abruptly. 'When we first met, I told you I'd do anything to make this war end.'

'You did,' Denizen said quietly.

Grey tossed him a fold of black cloth.

'Put this on. We have somewhere to be.'

*

You'd think, Denizen thought, hitching up his black robe for the twentieth time, *that I'd start knowing better than to follow Grey on night-time excursions.*

They hurried down a corridor, rough flagstones unwarmed by buttery candlelight. Grey had donned a black robe of his own and on him it looked dramatic and impressive. Denizen just looked like he was wearing a duvet cover.

'Where are we going?'

A smile, somewhere in that shadowed hood.

'Remember your thirteenth birthday? When I was supposed to wait out your Dawning away from Seraphim Row so if you did turn out to be normal you'd never know the Order existed?'

'And you brought me to Vivian anyway, so she'd have to talk to me.'

'Exactly.'

Grey's next words were under his breath, but Denizen caught them anyway.

'*Edifice is going to kill me.*'

Onwards and downwards, Denizen trying and failing to keep an internal map in his head. Each corridor looked the same. Only the murals changed, depicting battle after battle, creature after creature, blurring into a centuries-long serpent of war.

Grey seemed to know exactly where he was going, turning corners and opening increasingly iron-studded doors without hesitation. Around them the corridors were devolving – the stone rougher, the murals caked with dust.

'Are these the dungeons?' Denizen asked. He'd never seen proper dungeons before.

'Oh no,' Grey said. 'The dungeons are much nicer.'

He paused at the next door, and lifted an iron key from under his robe.

'I can't believe I'm doing this.'

'*Grey.* Doing *what*?' Denizen's legs were too sore for ambiguity.

Grey had pressed his ear to the door, frowning. He looked back at Denizen and sighed.

'OK. You weren't the only Neophyte to get a midnight visitor. About ten minutes before I woke you, all the others were herded up and brought down here in their finest cultish chic.'

'Then why –'

'Because *you*, Denizen, weren't supposed to get a midnight visitor at all. You were not to be included, for the exact same reason he wants you to stay in Daybreak.'

'To keep me safe,' Denizen whispered.

'Exactly,' Grey said. 'He is *going to kill me*. Pull your hood forward. Hide your face.'

Denizen did so, and Grey turned the key.

'On three.'

For a moment, Denizen couldn't help but grin at him.

Grey grinned back and swung open the door.

The chamber beyond was searingly bright, the air arid and desert-hot. Looking at the floor provided no escape from the light, and Denizen realized through watering eyes and the sudden hollow clang of his steps that the floor was polished metal.

Spoken steel – forged by a Knight's fire to burn Tenebrous like a cobweb touched by a flame. Grey propelled him forward, the heat palpable even through the exposed iron of his hands, before Denizen was unceremoniously shoved into a knot of other robed teenagers.

He wanted to turn, but the hand on his back had disappeared and so instead Denizen ducked his head down, shuffling through the group, listening for –

'I'm just saying – it's nice to finally get black robes. Magical organizations should have black robes.'

'You look like a tent with half its poles missing.'

'Hi, guys,' Denizen whispered.

They both jumped.

'You found us!' Abigail whispered. 'I tried to go back for you, but they wouldn't let me.'

'You missed all the fun,' Simon said. 'Abigail has a boyfriend.'

'Simon, I will punch your neck out the back of your head.'

'That isn't possible. Right, Denizen?'

'I don't know,' Denizen said, half because he didn't and half because the relief at seeing them was a physical pain. 'But I'd bet on her every time.'

'Neophytes of the Second Rank.'

Greaves's voice was still deep and rich, but all the warmth in it had gone. Denizen had always thought

him . . . not soft exactly, but able to hide his sharp corners when needed.

Now he was the Palatine.

'There are many tests you will endure before you become a Knight,' he intoned.

'Your bravery. Your will to fight, and your will to walk away. You will be tested by pain. By loss. By loneliness. Children will recoil from you in the street. Those you love will choose easier lives than loving you. You will live in candlelight, in shadow, in fire.

'And there will never be victory. I say this as it was said to me, and I didn't believe it either. There will be a prophecy. Some secret trinket. Some act of resistance snatching triumph from the dark. But no such thing exists. You must understand the work that we do.'

Denizen's stomach turned. Not from nervousness. No – he *knew* that feeling. It shook the strings of his heart and, one hand on the hem of his hood to keep it steady, he slowly raised his head.

The chamber was a hexagon, and six great lamps glared from the walls. There were Knights, two in each corner, all armed, all robed in black.

And, above, something squirmed.

The light from the lamps was so bright it was almost solid, but where the beams met it took on a different hue – sickly, colourless . . . tainted. That, even before his iron eye began to ache, told Denizen what it was.

He'd never seen a Breach like the one outside Adumbral's walls yesterday. He'd likely never see a similar one again.

They were as unique as paper cuts, as unique as the creature they birthed. Sometimes you saw the hole in the air; sometimes you merely felt its effects; sometimes the Tenebrous was just *there*, like the sudden appearance of a spider.

But this one just hung there, a rippling, bubbling gap.

'You may know of Os Reges Point,' Greaves began. 'Five wind-scoured peaks in a vast and stormy sea. A sacred place where we may consult the Emissary of the Endless King, where human and Tenebrous can speak in peace.'

He raised his hand, splaying dark fingers against the harshness of the light, and Denizen remembered those massive spires, reaching as if to pull down the sky.

'Five *fingers*. The fingers of the Endless King.'

Shock breathed silently through the chamber, the Palatine's words holding them to muteness with the soft power of his voice.

'That dreadful, mighty creature built a body unequalled by any Tenebrous before or since, and walked this world, breeding legend and terror in its wake, before leaving that body behind. *Ossa Regis* – the Bones of the King. That walk ended in dark water . . . but it started here.'

The rupture waxed and waned, twisting like a worm on a hook.

'A wound that will never heal. A path no other Tenebrous would ever use. A path *protected* by the reverence of his subjects. And for us, this Breach is a Glimpse of our purpose, a vantage on to our eternal crusade.'

It ached to look at. It ached to be around. It was an affront to everything the Order stood for, and it languished there like a prisoner of war.

'This too is sacred ground.'

The Palatine's eyes were stony. He raised a hand, and with a spike of fear Denizen thought Greaves was pointing at him before the hand swung left.

'Miriam Bell, please step forward.'

A Neophyte approached hesitantly, pushing her hood back to reveal blonde curls and sharp features. The Knight behind Greaves stepped forward as well, a harness and cord in his hand.

Denizen stared at it a moment without comprehending. It looked like . . . *a bungee cord*? Bungee jumping had always seemed like madness to Denizen – surely it was bad enough falling off something without still being around to remember it – and it was doubly confusing to see it here.

The cord was dark with etchings. *More spoken steel.* Knights didn't go for show – like its wielder, the favoured metal of the Knights looked no different until battle began.

With swift, sure motions, Greaves and the other Knight attached the harness to Miriam's slim shoulders. Each buckle was tugged on, each strap checked, Greaves even lifting her by it for a moment before clicking the cord into place, just as another Knight wheeled forward a set of steps. The whole process had taken just long enough for the Neophytes to realize its purpose.

Miriam's eyes were fixed on the Breach. She had gone very, very pale.

'Miriam Bell,' Greaves said. 'Do you want to be a Knight?'

'Yes,' she said, and her voice did not waver.

Greaves nodded. 'You will take fourteen steps. No more. No less. Then tilt your head upwards . . . and open your eyes.'

Murmurs rippled around the Neophytes before a look from Greaves quelled them. *Open your eyes*. The one rule of being in the Tenebrae, on the rare occasions the Order braved its depths, was that you never, ever opened your eyes. Knights could see in the dark, but that didn't always mean that they should.

The floor trembled as another figure entered the chamber – a monster of black armour fully twice as tall as Denizen, its seams drawn in burning gold. Huge shoulders vaned with smoke-stacks loomed over a blunt helm with a cyclopean, glaring eye.

Hephaestus Warplate. One of the Order's most potent weapons, only unveiled in greatest need. There was a Knight somewhere beneath all that steel, strength and speed augmented by those ancient, Cant-forged plates.

Spoken steel clanged against spoken steel as it lumbered forward to clutch the cord in two gigantic fists, and, as Denizen watched, it braced itself to pull.

'You will never speak of what you see there, do you understand?'

She nodded.

'Then go, Miriam Bell,' said Greaves. 'And then I will ask you the question a second time.'

She nodded again and began to climb the steps. Denizen's heart hammered with every footfall, the Glimpse quivering like a beating heart . . . and then she was gone, but for a cord hanging motionless in the seething air.

Denizen had traversed the Tenebrae before, fallen through an inky sea so cold it stole thought from your head, but never once had he taken *steps*. Was there solid ground somewhere in the Tenebrae? Where did this Breach lead?

With a growl of plate and flame, the Hephaestus Knight pulled and, just as suddenly as she had disappeared, Miriam Bell was there again, chest heaving as she frantically sucked in air. Greaves was immediately by her side, helping her down the steps.

Denizen had never seen eyes so wide. She was shaking so hard you could hear it, and a Knight came to her with a blanket and draped it around her shoulders.

Greaves's voice rang out again. 'Miriam Bell, do you want to be a Knight?'

Her voice was a shadow. 'Yes. God help me, yes.'

And then quietly she started to cry.

As Miriam was led away, Greaves turned back to the Neophytes. In fairness, he didn't look like he was enjoying this either. One by one, the Neophytes ascended the steps and, seeing as Denizen had not been given – or taken, if he were being honest – the chance to get to know them yet, it felt voyeuristic and uncomfortable to see them in this moment.

A short, squat teenager with more scars than Denizen's mother stepped out with a look of grim confirmation, as if he'd expected the worst and got it. A girl with half her head shaved staggered out and nearly fell, but said yes all the same. A lanky boy whispered something to Greaves that Denizen didn't hear, before being led through a different door.

And then it was Abigail's turn. She'd been eagerly watching the process like a crossbow bolt straining against its trigger. She stepped forward when it was her turn, before her name was even called, and Greaves opened his mouth –

And then Grey reached up and pulled down Denizen's hood.

'*Denizen?*'

Only experience with Greaves let Denizen catch the high-speed carousel of emotions racing across the Palatine's face. Greaves had forbidden Denizen to attend the ceremony, and it mightn't have provoked too many questions, but now that he was here, and now that Greaves had said his *name* . . .

It was a neat little trap.

'Hardwick,' Greaves finished, with barely a pause. You mightn't even have noticed it, if you weren't expecting it. Or if you were Abigail, who now wore a look of shock and anger that turned Denizen's heart to lead.

He tried to get his mouth to work, but already the Neophytes were parting, and Greaves spoke again, confident enough to nearly convince you that it was the alphabet and not him that was wrong.

'Denizen Hardwick. Do you want to be a Knight?'

And abruptly Denizen forgot about Abigail. It was a big question. It was *the* question. The Knights were deadly serious about not forcing people to join. Forcing people with literally volcanic emotions was a terrible idea. Denizen had seen that with the Croits. Lies always came out, and there were no worse lies than those used to control.

The Order was honest, at least.

'I do,' Denizen said, thinking of a little girl in a little garden.

The harness went around Denizen's shoulders. It had to be tightened a depressing amount before it was snug. He could feel the Palatine's frustration in every tug of the straps, but then Grey was at his shoulder, clicking the cord into place.

'I knew you'd pull something like this, Graham,' Greaves hissed.

'I'm trying to help. He walks in, he sees what he needs to see and you'll get the answer you want,' Grey replied lightly, squeezing Denizen's shoulder. 'Good luck.'

The Hephaestus Knight tugged on the tether once, nearly pulling Denizen over, and then it was just him and a set of simple wooden steps. He could feel the Breach like needles raking his skin, snagging on every pore.

You've been in the Tenebrae before. He'd even opened his eyes there, just long enough to see the briefest glimpse of terrible shapes, long enough to know he never wanted to do it again.

But the tears in Miriam Bell's eyes. The tremor in her voice. What was he going to see?

One step remaining, and Denizen's gaze glitched over a wound in the world, a scar on reality. A tear was clotting at the corner of his iron eye, and he fought the urge to scrub it away. There were a lot of people watching.

Fourteen steps. Do it.

He took a deep breath – and a comet took him off his feet.

Denizen tumbled and in that single weightless moment he heard a voice of silk and storm, a voice he hadn't heard in six long months.

Mercy's voice.

Denizen Hardwick, I need your help.

9

COMPROMISED

They hit the ground together. It probably saved her life.

A single lance of flame seared the length of Denizen's spine, before Greaves and Grey's voices came as one.

'Hold your fire!'

That's considerate, Denizen thought, but even his sarcasm dimmed in the face of the light. *Her* light – a halo of lightning that felt cool on his cheeks even as it danced scorch marks on the floor on either side of him.

The moment of peace didn't last long. Footsteps vibrated Denizen's head against the floor as the Hephaestus Knight thundered forward to yank on the cord. It snicker-slid to where he lay –

– and then came back empty, severed neatly by one of Mercy's errant, sizzling strands.

To the hulking warrior's credit, he barely mis-stepped. Faced with a long length of broken cable, he did what any Knight would do and improvised – cracking it like a bullwhip to take off Mercy's head.

It bounced off Denizen's Anathema Bend instead.

'*Ow*,' Denizen said, climbing awkwardly to his feet. The fused shield of air dissipated, but he kept it to hand – and *only* it, despite how many other Cants eagerly offered themselves. There were a lot of weapons pointed at him right now.

At both of them.

Greaves had drawn his Malleus hammer – the most powerful weapon in the Order's arsenal, able to kill even the most deadly Tenebrous outright. Light dripped from Knights' hands, danced in eyes, glared from the titanic threat of the Hephaestus, like a volcano about to erupt.

Most of the Neophytes were in fighting stances. So, he noted with pain, was Abigail.

'Can everyone . . .' Each word was the careful cutting of a wire. 'Please. Calm. Down?'

Nobody said anything. Finally, the Hephaestus Knight reached up to remove its helm, and Denizen's heart sank beneath sea-level.

Vivian Hardwick stared at the daughter of the Endless King with undisguised hate. She had looked less belligerent with the helm on.

'Oh,' Denizen said forlornly. 'Hi, Vivian.'

'*Stop using my son as a shield*,' she hissed. Denizen felt Mercy stiffen behind him, but before she could do anything words spilled out on autopilot. *Life or death*. He was almost grateful.

'Lookobviouslythisisasituationbutldon'tthinklosingour-temperswillsolveanything!'

Silence.

'Didn't catch a word of that,' Grey said, but Greaves had already regained control. He turned to a Knight.

'Assemble a cadre and take the Neophytes on night exercises.'

Robed teenagers stiffened with shock, but not half as much as Grey.

'You're sending us away?' he countered. 'Why –'

'I'm sending *them* away,' Greaves interrupted. 'You, I need here.' He turned to Mercy and Denizen. 'My office. *Now*.'

'I'm Master of Neophytes,' Grey said, but Denizen could see he was torn. 'Shouldn't I go with –'

'*Do as you're asked*,' Greaves snarled. For once, he could have given Vivian a run for her money. His gaze fell on Mercy like an executioner's axe.

'You need help? Then talk to me.'

The last time Mercy had been received by the Order of the Borrowed Dark, there had been a certain amount of ceremony and pomp. And yes, weapons, but this was the Order – there were always weapons. But there had also been invitations, and a truce, and a sort of plan.

It wasn't the usual reception, but, then again, there was nothing usual about the daughter of the Endless King, a Tenebrous never before seen in the Order's extensive histories who spoke with the Endless King's authority, but, more *importantly*, who used that authority to speak of peace.

Funny how one word can change everything.

'What do you mean, *fugitive*?'

Greaves's office occupied the entire circumference of the lighthouse's highest floor, just a level below Daybreak's great unlit beacon. Outside the vaulted windows Denizen could see nothing but night.

Hundreds of candles hung in steel lace lanterns from the roof, gently tinkling in the wind so that lattices of shadow chased each other across the marble floor. A constant reminder, as if the Palatine needed it, about what lay beneath.

I believe I am using the word correctly, Mercy said, eyes downcast. She was a girl of fog and witchlight, too faint to see one moment and eye-achingly real the next. Her hair was limned white at the edges by billowing frost, and her features changed with every beat of Denizen's heart, drawn and redrawn over and over again.

It, Denizen. Not a she, not a girl. A thing. A monster.

But can't she be both?

Tenebrous built their form from stolen things. Mercy had chosen light – *a particle and a wave* – so she would never have to be just one thing at a time.

The air was thick with the taste of the Tenebrae.

Knights surrounded her, and Denizen could feel the Cants nocked like crossbow bolts under their tongues. Greaves sat behind a monster of a desk, and Denizen hovered by Vivian, who even out of Warplate loomed like a cavalry charge.

'I thought you'd left?' Denizen whispered. 'Not that I'm not glad to see you,' he added hastily, 'but –'

'Knife.'

Denizen dragged down the neck of his robe to reveal the strap of the sheath. Vivian had beaten the Three to death with a shard of a stone Malleus hammer, which she'd then ground down and polished into a knapped stone blade for him. It was a very Vivian gift to give. It was also very like his mother to make sure that they were armed before they had a conversation.

'Good,' she said. There was the tiniest flush of pink in her cheeks. 'I . . . didn't want to miss your Glimpse.'

'Oh! Em . . .'

'Not that I thought you weren't going to make the right choice,' she said quickly.

'No, of course!' Denizen said just as quickly, and then they both looked at the floor until, inevitably, his eyes were drawn back to Mercy.

She looked so *tired*. Gone was the artillery-strike anger of their first meeting, or the diamond calm she'd displayed when wielding that same stone knife to free him from the Redemptress. Now that hand was clutched, flickering and charred, to her chest, and there were phantasmagorical shifts of colour around her eyes, the way a human's skin might flush after crying.

'Denizen.'

He dragged his gaze away from Mercy. 'What?'

Denizen's mother had very few expressions. This one's meaning was very clear.

'I'm over it,' he said quietly. The walls in his head were high and skin-stealingly cold. 'Really.'

She nodded. 'OK.'

Greaves repeated his question. 'What do you mean, *fugitive*?'

I am a refugee. I am a fugitive. I am unsafe in my realm.

'I don't understand,' Greaves said. 'You're the King's daughter. When you were in danger before, he nearly tore this world apart looking for you. *People died*.'

The map of Daybreak set into the wall of Greaves's office was the first mosaic Denizen had seen here that didn't depict war and death. Denizen liked maps. He found them calming. And tracing the delicately labelled tiles meant he didn't have to look at Mercy right now.

I know they did.

'Then why would he abandon you now?'

Mercy barely seemed to notice the armoury surrounding her, as if all her fear was reserved for something else.

'*Answer me*,' Greaves snapped, and Denizen jumped.

He'd never seen the Palatine like this. Self-control was as crucial to a Knight as practising with a blade and, normally, the Palatine shuffled emotions like cards in a deck, playing both his hand and everyone else's to his own best advantage.

But there was an openness now, a *clumsiness*. Denizen could see glimpses of the truth beneath, and it chilled him to his core.

Greaves was frightened.

Finally, Mercy raised her head.

My father was challenged for rule of the Tenebrae and he . . . he lost. The reign of the Endless King is over.

For once, it was her words rather than her Tenebrous voice that froze Denizen's heart.

The reign of the Endless King is over.

'But it's the . . .' Greaves's voice was incredulous. 'It's the *Endless* King.'

I know.

The Palatine shook his head. 'We don't have time for games –'

I KNOW THAT!

They all went down beneath a barrage of sound. Greaves disappeared behind his desk, Vivian dropped to one knee, and only her hand on his arm stopped Denizen's feet leaving the ground. Blades alternately froze and softened as Mercy flared, her voice bursting across them like winter and summer in a single breath.

And then that terrifying avatar was gone, and a translucent girl stood there again, one hand clasped across her heart.

I know that.

'Then let us help you.'

Denizen's voice was soft, almost a plea. And then, after an eternity, she nodded, and Denizen could almost see patterns shifting inside her, the way you could be tricked into seeing meaning in fire or cloud.

We are not meant for love. We are creatures of will, and that will must be selfish. When you grow up in the shadow of the omniverse, it is all you can do to cling on to yourself.

That is why we are changeable. That is why so many of us are mad.

That is why my father was so intoxicating. Traveller, warlord, thief – the Tenebrous who'd Breached a thousand worlds, the Tenebrous who'd stolen a sun. He never spoke of its source, but, when he fixed that jewel of flame in the sky, he *changed* our world, instead of being changed.

She sounded very proud.

He ruled for millennia by sheer force of will, by undeniable skill and fury. He *made* himself King, and we could do naught but accept.

'It's not a name,' Vivian said suddenly. 'It's a boast.'

Mercy smiled wanly.

It was a promise. *I am Endless.*

Her smile vanished.

And then I was taken, and for the first time the King knew fear. Fear for me. Fear for my loss. And by the time Denizen saved me . . . it was too late.

Denizen thought of the fragile fortress in his head, the battle to keep his worries under control, and imagined a mind so ancient and powerful that it could hold an entire world in sway . . .

. . . and then imagined fear creeping in like rust, darkening doorways and chewing through foundations. The horror it must have felt. The doubt.

It consumed him. Withered him. Faded him. The command he needed to keep your world safe –

'*Safe?*' Grey snapped. 'Is that what you call it?'

'Grey –' Greaves began, but Grey cut him off.

'The battles we've fought. The people we've lost. And you talk of *safety*?'

Mercy's eyes blazed.

You have no idea how bad things would be without him. You think you've seen the worst of our realm? Mere renegades, beasts – a *fraction* of what the Tenebrae holds. You have no idea what real war is.

But I fear you're about to find out.

As a rule, Tenebrous did not have rules. Not in their shape, their powers, or the way they hurt people. But the Endless King *did* have rules, or at least a sense of honour. He was *known*. Denizen had no head for tactics, but Abigail did and, as a rising wind shook the windows in their frames, he remembered something she had once said.

Unknown quantities, Denizen. That's what kills you.

I've spent months speaking with my father's voice, playing factions against each other, trying to maintain . . .

The Concilium. A display of command so daring that of course the Forever Court would have believed it to come from the King. It had even outed a traitor, and revealed the King's hand in the creation of the Order itself.

You mind your house, I'll mind mine.

Mercy's sigh sounded like feathers falling.

But they came anyway. Usurpers. Wretches. *Sharks*, smelling blood in the water. A nightmare, a betrayer and a . . .

Her voice trembled.

They cast my father down and I do not . . . I do not know where he is. The throne at the heart of the Tenebrae

lies empty, and now the Usurpers must prove themselves before my people so a new King can rise.

Denizen leaned forward, ignoring Vivian's sharp look.

'But you're his daughter! Can't you –'

Mercy shook her head. **Not for us the messiness of your world, with its bloodlines and child kings. A ruler of the Tenebrous must be unassailable in will, or be eaten alive.**

Sheets of rain were drumming against the windows. There was just enough space in Denizen's head to briefly feel sympathy for the Neophytes out there – *what even* are *night exercises?* – but that led to thinking of earlier, and that led to –

Sacred ground.

Greaves got there before him.

'Triple the guard around the Glimpse,' the Palatine snapped at the Knight by his side. 'As many Mallei as we can spare. And –'

'Wait.'

They all turned to Vivian. In the flickering candlelight, she looked less human than Mercy, a grave and graven goddess of war.

Her voice was a hiss. '*Prove themselves how?*'

Tenebrous were harder to read than Knights, but Denizen had practice, and, even though hers was a face of ever-changing light, he could read Mercy's shame. She held out her one good hand, not to Greaves, not to Vivian, but to Denizen.

I didn't have anywhere else to go.

'Sir?'

The Knight who Greaves had spoken to held up her phone. What spilled forth was a dead growl of defeated technology, echoing far louder than the speaker should allow. Hands went to pockets, flicked light from screens, and one by one the drones rose like a hive of dying bees –

And a raindrop hit the window hard enough to leave a spiralling crack. Slowly, very slowly, Denizen and Vivian turned to watch it inch sluggishly down the glass.

The raindrop was black.

Vivian bolted for the window, the rest of them a second's breath behind. Beyond was Adumbral, laid out in shadow and candlelight, the view so spectacular that Denizen could not even bring himself to feel nauseous. The sky was the colour of a new bruise, the moon huge and scarred by falling rain.

I'm sorry, Mercy whispered. **I –**

Whatever she had been about to say was lost as Daybreak shivered like a struck bell. Swords fell from the walls to clatter against flagstones. Hangings detached themselves, the victories of long-dead Knights folding themselves into anonymous cloth. Windows came apart in waterfalls of glass.

Denizen had been lost in Daybreak. He'd stood at its highest point. He knew exactly how big it was. He shouldn't have been able to feel it sway.

Thunder cracked pain across his eardrums, and with it came *despair*, a nausea of the soul, bypassing Denizen's senses to assault his mind. If the Breach from yesterday had been a probing needle then this was an avalanche, squeezing Denizen's eyes in his sockets, curdling the blood in his veins.

Knights staggered. One vomited against the back of her hand. One of Grey's hands was spasming open and closed and he didn't seem to be able to make it stop.

'But the candlewards –' Greaves's eyes were as wide as a child's. 'They –'

Stop a Tenebrous Breaching inside the city. Not from *above*. Mercy's voice was forlorn. **You know, it's actually quite clever.**

And maybe someone, somewhere would have cut Denizen some slack. The reek of the Tenebrae, revelations, an uprising – there was a lot going on. He was fourteen years old. The room was comprised entirely of people who had more experience of situations like this.

But, in that moment, he *knew* he'd never forgive himself for how long it took to turn to Greaves and snarl, 'Palatine!'

It took the man an eternity to focus. 'What?'

Horror carried Denizen's voice over the wind and the rain and the wrongness.

'*Night exercises*.'

10

ARMY OF ONE

Neophytes were trained to be self-reliant. When the ranking Malleus couldn't be contacted, when you were separated from your cadre and the enemy adapted . . . you should too.

Abigail wondered if the Knights were regretting that carefully cultivated independence now.

'Tell us what's happening!'

'What is the point of –'

'We can be trusted! We need to know –'

The truck wound through candlelit streets, and, as they left Daybreak, the teenagers did exactly as they had been trained – using their initiative, trying different routes of attack –

'Isn't telling us an opportunity for us to learn?'

'Was that Tenebrous made of light? I've never read of –'

The Knights did not reply. Two sat up front, another two riding with the Neophytes in the truck's canvas bed: a tall Sikh man with olive skin and a dark blue turban, and their French tutor, Madame Adler, the freckled planes of her face stark beneath a veil of black-and-silver hair.

Both of them had the exact same expression.

Abigail was fairly sure her expression was similar. *Mercy.*

Abigail had met the Endless King's daughter precisely once, on a hillside at dawn, after one of the most terrifying and exhausting nights of her life. They'd little more than exchanged a glance, but that had been enough to set Mercy apart from every other Tenebrous she had ever faced.

They hadn't been trying to kill each other, for a start. And Mercy spoke of peace, and had risked her life to save Denizen, something Abigail would never have believed of a Tenebrous before.

But the one lesson drilled into Abigail from the day she'd learned the word *Tenebrous* was that when it came to Those Who Walked Under Unlit Skies you couldn't trust your senses. That was fundamental. That was how you tracked them. That was the trail they left behind.

And in Mercy's trail . . .

Weeks desperately searching through old books while blood-spattered reports crowded Vivian's desk. Ravaging Pursuivants searching for a word that had never before sat in a Tenebrous's mouth. Abigail's father, and the pained smile as he assured her he'd walk again.

Across from her, on a rough metal bench, Hagen was running a finger along the scars on his hands. Left to right, tip to tip, eyes closed as if deciphering Braille. Abigail thought back to his story in the Neophytes' common room.

Why would they speak of mercy, when they showed us none?

Maybe it was for the best that they'd been sent away.

'He'll be fine,' Simon whispered beside her. 'Won't he?'

She turned back to stare at the lighthouse, looming like a canine in Adumbral's ravaged gum. Abigail tried to draw strength from its battlements. Daybreak was impregnable. The whole city was.

At least until Mercy walked in.

'Of course he will,' Abigail said. 'Forget the Knights, *Vivian's* there. She won't let him get hurt.'

'I know.'

Simon hesitated, mouth working as if probing a loose tooth.

'It's just that when Mercy shows up, Denizen tends to . . .'

Abigail shot him a sympathetic look. 'Get dragged into things?'

Simon swallowed. 'Yep. I *think* Mercy doesn't mean any harm – she hasn't hurt any of us. Not . . .'

Not directly. If it had been some great treasure that had been stolen by the Three, Abigail wouldn't have blamed *it* for what had been done in its name. She wouldn't have blamed a person. But a *Tenebrous* . . .

Hagen was still tracing his scars. Her father still walked with a limp. And you could mean well, you could try your best to do your best, and still . . .

Mercy might mean no harm, but that didn't mean she didn't bring it with her. She'd crossed over twice to the human world, and both times had been a nightmare. Maybe they hadn't been nightmares of her making, but she heralded them, as sure as the ticking of a bomb.

Adler rapped the back of the driver's seat and the truck pulled to a stop. They were in a plaza amid a distressingly organic tangle of lanes and pathways. Buildings had twisted against themselves here, as if trying to escape.

The Knights who had been sitting up front – a wrinkled, Cost-swathed man with a goatish sprig of beard, and a Malleus named Coiled who had once worked with her father – opened the back of the truck for the Neophytes to disembark.

Empty windows gaped down as the teenagers formed up. The air was cool but not cold. Clouds scudded across the sky, almost too fast to be real. There was a hard-edged pressure to the air, and the familiar sting of adrenalin calmed her.

Mercy had looked . . . desperate. And scared. Abigail didn't like the thought of Mercy being frightened. *Humans* were frightened. Humans were frightened of Tenebrous and, though Denizen had shared everything he knew about her, Abigail still couldn't *quite* bring herself to think of Mercy as even *close* to human. That wasn't wise. It wasn't tactical.

A drop of rain stung her nose. Abigail flinched, and then became immediately annoyed for doing so. She stopped herself rubbing the soreness away, but around her the others were also shrugging away drops, pulling up hoods and straightening sleeves.

You'd think after a year in Ireland I'd be used to rain. Not that it had been the first rainy place she'd lived – before the penetrating slyness of Irish rain there had been the shocking skin-patter of Indian monsoons and the everywhere-wet of Burmese humidity. Why should this be any –

Abigail's stomach heaved as a drop came down, exploding on her outstretched hand. She stared at the oily black sheen, bright with the water with which it would not mix. They separated even as she watched, the darkness launching itself into the air as a spiral of smoke.

Adler's voice was a roar. 'BREACH!'

Suddenly they were all back to back, Simon's knobbed shoulder blades pressing into the back of her head. Knights circled them, turning shoulders and closing gaps; the goatish man grabbed Ed by the scruff of the neck and pressed him into the throng.

The rain was coming harder now, biting and stinging like wasps.

'Find cover!' the Sikh Knight called.

They ran, jerking and hissing as the wind flung rain into faces and under hoods. Simon ran with his hands clasped over his head. A boy she hadn't spoken to yet fell with a yelp, and two others stopped to pick him up by the shoulders.

And through it all, through the sudden panic and the pain, came the gut-squeezing, eye-watering pressure of the universe bending out of shape. Questions came down with the rain – *a Breach? Here?* – but speculation was dead weight and she left it behind.

They fell into an open doorway just as a cloudburst tore the air to shreds, cracking cobbles with shattering pops.

Even on the ground floor, Abigail could hear the roof strain under the assault. What would happen if it collapsed?

How do we fight this? How did you fight the sky?

The Tenebrae furred her nerves, prickled her skin. Bodies banged off her, wide eyes in soaked hoods, and, despite their experience, their training, their iron and the light streaking intermittently through their skin, the Neophytes didn't look like Knights-in-training at all.

They looked like children hiding from something far bigger than themselves.

I can teach you, but not prepare you.

Shut up, Abigail thought ferociously.

I can train you, but training only takes you to the edge of the darkness, and not a single step more.

He hadn't even come with them. Vivian wouldn't have left them, even if she'd been ordered to stay behind.

That's what I am. I'm a lesson that we are not invincible.

Things had got bad and, once again, Grey was nowhere to be found.

And then Malleus Coiled – just a little woman no taller than Abigail, as stocky as an artillery shell with shockingly bright green eyes – cleared her throat, and every eye turned towards her and the lump of iron she carried on a long, thick chain.

A Malleus hammer, of a design Abigail had never seen.

'Eyes on every exit,' she said crisply. 'And the stairs. This floor is our fortress. Our Daybreak. Now *go*.'

The purpose in her voice steeled them all and, for a moment, instead of standing in a building emptied by a long-ago failure, they stood a chance to do something right. Lightning cracked outside, the tendrils wrapping Abigail's heart in stuttering beats.

And then, like a tap turning off, the maelstrom became nothing more than a half-hearted shower *plipping* into the seething mass of ink now filling the street. It just *sat* there, not draining away or dispersing, rippling like something alive.

Coiled approached the doorway, light spreading through her in peals of gold. Some of the Neophytes held their power close too, glowing fitfully, Cants already visible as shapes beneath their skin.

The Sikh Knight opened his mouth, but whatever he had been going to say went unsaid as the mat of slick, sickening black suddenly retreated in one pulsing movement. It rippled and rose in defiance of gravity, caving in a door across the street to disappear with a wet slurp.

Abigail couldn't help herself. Her heritage rose within, insistent, hungry, and instead of tamping it down she embraced it, letting it burn the doubt away. *This* was the war they had been trained for, and it was impossible for her not to want to act when sweat was trickling down her spine and the air was hateful in her mouth.

Normal people ran from that feeling. Knights ran towards it, to do what must be done.

Simon was beside her, his hands already raised. Ed was trembling hard but stood with her as well. They took their places, an arrowhead in the plaza, and pride briefly beat back the night.

This is where I belong, Abigail thought. *This is what matters. This is our kingdom.*

The building shifted with a groan of masonry. Dust billowed out from the door the nightstuff had struck down, but before it could reach them it retreated as if pulled by a vacuum.

Or . . . lungs.

One hundred mouths. The motto of the Order, in her father's voice. *One hundred tongues*.

One iron voice.

The building imploded. The tenement crumpled as if crushed by a giant hand. Holes opened as bricks tore free, windows opening in screaming mouths. Neophytes ducked as a sudden sucking tore debris from the street in a gritty hail. Abigail's robe flapped treacherously, tangling her legs; through eyes buffeted by hair and cloth she caught a glimpse of Malleus Coiled, her hammer unmoving at the end of its chain.

And from the vortex burst *limbs*, as black and crooked as spider legs, as long as Simon was tall. With insectile industry, they snapped flying rubble from the air, passed it from needle claw to needle claw.

Turning.

Sifting.

Sorting.

The weakest Tenebrous could only inhabit tottering frameworks, whatever their dim minds could devise . . . but the oldest were limited only by materials and their own twisted imagination. Abigail had never seen a truly ancient Tenebrous clothe itself before. It was the most spectacularly ugly thing she had ever seen.

'Back!' the Malleus shouted as a massive stone arm erupted from the murk to blindly sweep the air. More followed, clicked and clattered into place by the black – a barrel torso, an ogreish head – and still those nightstuff claws scraped and scrabbled, hewing out a monstrous shape.

Detail followed detail, wrenched into reality. Abigail could hear *breath*, low and grinding, and with it a smell of the sea – the oceans of history polluted and dead. It was that, more than anything, that told her: *I know this thing.*

The last time they had met it had been massive, four metres from fettered ankle to brutish helm, rust-caked and stinking of salt like a sunken battleship from a forgotten war. Now it was the height of a double-decker bus, and there was a bright, rustless band around its boot to show where a shackle had been.

That there are things that cannot be prepared for, and may not be survived.

The Emissary of the Endless King carried a colossal shard of metal in one bestial fist. Its roar was the death of an empire.

I FOUND MY SWORD.

11

GLIMPSE

They ran. What else could they do?

Denizen ran after the Palatine, he ran after his mother and he ran after the Tenebrous who had been bundled along with them. He ran through a thousand shouted orders: armouries opened, rescuers dispatched, Darcie bundled to the Palatine's office, her hands pressed to her head.

He ran as if the hole at the base of Daybreak had been uncorked, and gravity was dragging him down.

The official entrance to the Chamber of the Glimpse was a slab of spoken steel as belligerently immovable as Monte Inclavare itself. It would have been immensely reassuring if a Tenebrous had not already Breached behind them.

Well, that was fine. Some walls were still going to stay up, Denizen thought, eyes firmly on the gates and *not* on the wraith-girl prisming between silver and blue. The fire wasn't the only thing Vivian had been teaching him to keep out of his head these last six months. Normal teenagers probably didn't welcome romantic advice from their mothers, but the Hardwicks had their own normal, and, if there was one enemy Vivian could be said to have vanquished over her long career, it was unnecessary feelings.

Whatever crush he'd had, he'd crushed it. He'd been doing *so well* too, though a part of him pointed out that it was very easy not to think about people who didn't seem to be thinking about you.

She hasn't even looked over –

'Denizen!' Vivian snapped. The chains were being unlocked. Weapons were being distributed. With phones down, Greaves was now in the centre of a maelstrom of Knights running to his side, receiving orders and then pelting away. 'You need to go back to the Neophytes' cells and wait –'

'I'm not going anywhere,' Denizen retorted, and took a deep breath. 'You are.'

'*What?*'

'They're sending out cadres to get the others. To get my *friends*. I need you to go with them.'

You could have handed out Vivian's glare as a weapon. 'I'm not leaving you –'

'Yes,' Denizen said. 'You are. If anyone can bring them back – you can. We don't even know if the Glimpse is compromised. But Simon's out *there* with God knows what. I'll be fine. If anything comes through . . . I'll run, or something.'

He was lying and he knew it, and she knew it too. Six months ago, she would have unceremoniously marched him to his room. A year ago, there wouldn't have been a conversation at all. But that was then, and this was now.

'*Stay at the back*,' Vivian said. 'Remember what I taught you. *Everything* I taught you. And don't hesitate to do what you need to do.' He nodded, and her grip relaxed on the hammer just for a moment, as if her hands wanted to do something else.

And then she turned and ran. Denizen didn't spare a thought for whoever had previously been in charge of the rescue mission. He knew who he trusted. Of course, now that she had gone, that was precisely nobody.

Greaves was staring at the opening gates so intensely that Denizen wasn't even sure the Palatine realized that he was there. A host of Knights were crowding a corridor never built for so many, and more were arriving all the time – hard-eyed, scar-knurled, corded with muscle and iron. Denizen counted eight hammers – *eight* – and for an instant the unreality lapping against them receded.

Grey refused one, his hands on the twin swords by his sides, and Denizen remembered the last time he had seen his former mentor wield a hammer, and the question of trust assaulted him one more time.

I'm *staying here because I serve the Order.* I'm *staying here because it's where I can do some good. That's why.*

Not because he could *feel* the canker growing behind these doors.

Not because staying here gave him an excuse to let the fire out.

Not because of –

'Oh, *now* he wants to stay.'

Edifice Greaves had drawn a black steel hammer from its black silk sheath – the weapon all one piece, polished, faceted and *heavy*. Muscles strained against his expensive shirt.

'And where did Vivian –' He shook his head. '*Hardwicks*. Just –'

Grey slipped between them. 'Kid, we have this.' Behind him, the doors were opening.

The Tenebrae was swelling, and Denizen's synapses misfired in response. His hands felt cold, then too hot. He tasted gun oil, had to touch his nose to check for blood.

'Why don't you go and get Darcie –' began Grey.

'*Don't*,' Denizen said, the syllables sharp in his mouth. 'Don't use her to get rid of me. That's what *he'd* do.'

Greaves didn't even have the decency to look ashamed. But Grey did, and Denizen suddenly felt a pang of guilt. And then the doors opened, and all he felt was afraid.

The Glimpse was bleeding.

The edges of the Breach were hot with infection within its cradle of light, the criss-crossed beams heavy and orange with pus. Its every pulse darkened the air around it, as if necrotizing, as if eating healthy flesh. Tears sprang from Denizen's iron eye at the sight of it. He felt the sudden need to vomit, to scream, to drink deep of the fire and perform urgent surgery before nothing could be saved.

'See?' Grey said, backlit by the diseased glow. 'Totally under control.'

Denizen didn't dignify that with a response. Instead, he drew the stone blade his mother had made him. He'd called it Falter because if he was going to have a magic weapon he was going to name it. Like Simon and the robes, some things were just tradition.

'You know I can fight. Besides, you were keeping me from combat so I'd help with diplomacy.' He gestured at the suppurating wound in the air. 'Well, I think we've gone beyond diplomacy –'

Ohhhhhhhhh . . .

It came from everywhere and nowhere. It unspooled through the Glimpse. It scraped itself from the shadows. It slunk through the gaps in the atoms in the air and stalked slowly up Denizen's spine, caressing each vertebra slightly out of true.

You have no idea . . .

The Man in the Waistcoat had purred like a detaching fingernail. The Redemptress had wailed like a broken-hearted hurricane. But this voice suddenly, horribly, reminded him of Mercy – the way she played her strangeness like an instrument, muted one moment and deafening the next.

The Knights' response, in comparison, was voiceless – a lifting of weapons, a blazing of light. Behind pupils, beneath tongues, between the whorls of fingerprints – and, cautiously, always cautiously, Denizen let his light out to join them.

Careful.

Sluicing through him, channelled by will but seeking, always seeking for an emotion, a weakness, through which it could escape: the Knights between him and the Breach, and the simple, automatic hatred he felt for them being in his way –

That's not you.

Mercy cowering at the sound of the voice, and Denizen's red-hot rage that she was allowed to be weak when it was because of her he had to be strong –

That's not . . . that's not . . .

The thing's voice was a purr.

I knew you'd run to them.

She shrank then, like a candle flame battered by breath.

You think aping their form will make them trust you? Make them forgive you? Make them . . . love you?

It tutted. ***Freak.***

Mercy spat sparks. **My father will –**

Your *father*, the beast growled, **is the prize in all this, dear girl. The worlds are watching. Three challengers to the throne, three who have** ***suffered*** **the most at his hands. Only the worthiest will have the honour of taking his place and taking his head. We each have our challenge, Mercy . . . and killing you is** ***mine.***

'Spooky,' Palatine Edifice Greaves murmured, the simple human sarcasm a balm against the sick smugness of the voice. 'Is there a body to go with this vaudeville act or should we do you some shadow puppets?'

'I can do a duck,' Grey offered.

Denizen took a shuddering breath that was the closest he could come to a laugh, and it was then that he realized why the air was so dry, why the whole chamber was spoken steel. *A clean room* – kept sterile so a Tenebrous wouldn't have a mote of dust with which to build a body.

Very Edifice Greaves.

Ah. The little king, hiding behind promises that should never have been made. Would you like to keep your castle, dear Edifice? You only have to do one thing, and I will preserve all edicts my . . . predecessor left behind.

'I –'

Just give me the child.

A hundred voices. A thousand, squirting through the room like sewage down a hose, thick and wet and *needy*, desperate with hunger and hate.

And Greaves did not immediately respond.

One ruler to another. A trade. That is diplomacy, is it not?

He wouldn't.

The frustration in the Palatine's eyes. The terrible burden of fighting an unwinnable war. The words he had said before the Concilium, when peace had been a distant dream:

'*We have lived this war for so long. If what happens here today has even the* chance *of ending it . . . For that, I'll make any promise. For that, I'll do anything.*'

He couldn't. Could he?

'We don't build peace on the deaths of children,' Greaves responded, and relief was nearly painful in Denizen's chest.

I've studied humanity *extensively*, Edifice Greaves. We both know that's not true. The voice sighed in mock disappointment. **So be it. Mercy?**

Between the searing gold of the torches and the blighted uncolour of the Glimpse, she could barely be seen at all.

Remember that you came here. Remember that their deaths are on your –

Greaves slapped the haft of his hammer into his palm. 'Right, we get it. You're going to grind our bones to make your bread. Can we get on with it, please?'

The Tenebrous laughed, low and breathy.

That's not what I'm going to use your bones for.

The Glimpse began to *stretch*, distending like a boil. Denizen shifted his grip on Falter. Grey drew his swords with a rasp of steel.

Come on. The fire rose in Denizen, hot and vindictive. Every Tenebrous spent their first few moments frantically hiding soft oil in stolen debris, but there was nothing here for them to take, to twist. Nothing but fire. *Come on.*

It was a day of things not happening the way they were supposed to.

What leapt from the Breach was not a black flood blindly seeking form; it was *already* formed – a ratcheting hulk of pistons and eyes that deflected the first barrage of flame from its massive shoulder before a second volley smashed it down.

The remains never had a chance to hit the floor – sucked back into the Glimpse on stringy pseudopods of black, like a parody of the test of Miriam Bell. The next Tenebrous managed three whole seconds of life before a Hephaestus Knight Denizen hadn't even noticed pounded past him to squash it almost comically flat.

That corpse too was retrieved. The chamber rang with a vast sigh, as if something huge had tasted the air and found it pleasing.

And then the Glimpse exploded.

Denizen was suddenly face to face with a Tenebrous. He had no idea how. It swung a fist made of a crumpled shopping trolley and he deflected it with the reflex twitch of an Anathema Bend before another Knight cut off its head.

Another, then, with a mouth of flexing syringes, that he killed himself. A limb – human, Tenebrous, he didn't know – cracked him in the face, and he careened straight into the path of something that could have been a spider had you made it out of rubber and stretched it to two metres tall.

Falter opened its belly in slops and smoke.

There was no line. No direction. Denizen lost track of everything but moving Falter and trying not to fall. Even the fire was silent – he hadn't the breath for it to escape. He cut. He stabbed. He slashed. A frond of grit and cephalopod muscle picked him up and *threw* him, and he only stopped because a wall was in the way.

And, in that surreal, floating moment, a light across the chamber, bright and blue amid warring black and gold.

Mercy.

The thing that had flung him didn't seem interested in following up, but there was another in front of Denizen now, and another, and half the time he had no idea if he was even killing them because the battle kept whirling them away and he had been stabbing for *at least* a hundred years and why were they still fighting?

Usually, Tenebrous Breached by themselves or in tiny bands thrown together by shared madness or opportunity. They found the Knights, or the Knights found them, and one way or another things were quick.

But this wasn't.

Frown No. 1 – I Don't Understand, even as Falter snagged in skin that had modelled itself on either shark's teeth or an escalator, and it was scant consolation that the beast didn't seem happy about it either. It spun, giving Denizen barely enough time to throw the palisades of his mind wide and let a single Cant free.

The Qayyim Myriad – orbs of hungry fire that pounded into the creature's sternum, throwing out soot and crisping flesh. Denizen punched impacts up its chest, tearing away its jaw and blowing a hole through the back of its head.

It staggered, squirming against physics and physiology to replace the appendage it had lost, and Denizen struggled as well, shutting down channels in his head and reopening others, searching for a way to let the fire out without letting the fire *out*.

It raised a hand that became a claw that became a scythe, and, caught between agony and arson, Denizen could do nothing but watch as a perfect line of polar blue slit it in half. The Tenebrous bellowed – hateful, heartbroken – and dissolved, revealing a nuclear winter in the shape of a girl.

One hand was still clasped to Mercy's chest. The other ended in a hard-light blade of incandescent white. Spots of black sizzled on her cheeks before dissolving away.

'Mercy,' Denizen whispered.

She stared at him blankly, and then lunged.

KILL HER. It was his training. It was the fire. It was his mother, and the fact that when a monster came at you your duty was to *put it down first*.

Flame punched from his hands, and it took every bit of strength to turn them aside, even as Mercy's blade just grazed his shoulder to halve a Tenebrous's skull.

He hadn't . . . he hadn't even *seen* it.

I nearly . . .

Move, Mercy growled, and spun him so they were back to back. The floor was already choked with debris that squirmed as monsters drank it in, and, of all things, Denizen's shins ached with bruises and bangs.

A writhing nest of hair and veins grabbed his throat and he would have died then and there if not for the accidental backswing of a Malleus hammer. He fell, rolled, slashed inhuman ankles with Falter's stone edge, before driving it into a thigh and dragging himself upright.

'PULL BACK!'

There was such anger in that voice. Retreat was a curse to a Knight, proof of failure, a sign that nothing was as it should be. But suddenly hands were on Denizen's shoulders, hands he almost slashed out at before he recognized them as iron.

Oh, he thought stupidly, *that's where we were*. Three metres from the door, just about where he'd found Simon and Abigail earlier. He'd completely lost track.

The pristine chamber had become a junkyard wet with rising black, and no sooner did a twisted shape fall than it became reborn somewhere else. Knights still battled in diminishing bands, but now they fought to free each other, sacrificing themselves so that others could get to the doors.

In the centre of it all was the Glimpse, and the Glimpse had expanded. It had widened, and forcing it still wider was a forest of hands and arms and black, grabbing fingers, a tangle of human limbs.

Like a crowd. Like an army.

But that wasn't what gave Denizen pause, even as the head and torso of a young man pushed its way out of the mass like the stem of a strawberry, stretching and smiling like a teenager after a long lie-in.

The shape looked human. Properly human. They had never been very good at it. The eel-of-tweed had made the most effort Denizen had ever seen, and even it hadn't fooled people for very long. There were so many details to get right, all those evolutionary and behavioural quirks that marked people from . . . not.

But the boy's body looked perfect, and even the web of straining limbs had a polish and art that Denizen had never seen before. They bent like limbs should bend and, as Denizen watched, more heads began to push through, each one accurate, each one human.

Except that they were all made of iron, as flawless as if carved by the Cost itself.

The Usurper looked at Denizen and grinned from a dozen mouths.

Daybreak, it whispered.

12

WHEN THE RUST GETS IN

Abigail Falx could run a mile in under eight minutes. She was deadly with a rapier, had won awards with a crossbow, and was merely excellent with the staff, hand-axe and scythe. She was a black belt in kick-boxing, could put a 200-gram knife through a wedding ring at fifteen paces, and had once left a bruise on Vivian Hardwick's cheek.

Someone somewhere was shouting, but then the Emissary growled, low and deep as muscle pain, and all Abigail could do was stare at the largest Tenebrous she had ever seen.

There was no body inside that armour, just a sloshing, slopping sea of black, now tall enough to stare a bull elephant in the eye. Plates bulged oddly. Elbows jutted. Its chest-plate seemed half a mile across, cracked concentrically around a hole Abigail could have fallen into without touching the sides.

There had been a hammer there. She had been there when it had been removed.

I FOUND MY SWORD.

The Emissary twisted at the hip, a ponderous grind of gorget and greave, and cut the nearest building in half.

Masonry groaned as a night-black blade longer than Vivian's car carved through it with the ease of a butcher jointing a calf. Dust billowed. The roof collapsed inwards. And every shard of stone that touched that sword puffed into a haze of grit, as if not just sliced but disassembled on a molecular scale.

With an almost delicate snuffling, the Emissary leaned forward and breathed it in.

I FOUND IT. I *FOUND* IT.

Was that her imagination? Did the Emissary seem to *grow*? Flanks heaving, details sharpening . . . did it swell with everything it ate?

I FOUND . . . I FOUND *YOU* AND . . .

It stared down its sword, still buried in the building's corpse, and its gauntlet unfurled with the clanking grind of an assembly line to lovingly stroke the blade.

And then it looked at her. **WE ARE HUNGRY.**

All her life, Abigail had been trained to fight. She'd chosen Cants the way other kids collected trading cards, she'd honed her body and she'd *studied*, because Tenebrous didn't have muscle groups or pressure points. Each Tenebrous was a new language that overwrote itself with every passing second. Her father had taught her to observe. Her mother had taught her to appraise. And when she turned that expert eye on the Tenebrous before her . . .

Nothing. She had nothing. The Emissary was too big. Too . . . too impossible. You couldn't dent that armour with a Malleus hammer, not unless you welded it to the front of a tank. She could have given every ounce of herself to the Cost and not so much as singed it.

The sheer *scale* of it slammed down like a guillotine, surgically disconnecting not just Abigail's muscles from her brain but her muscles from her memory – every moment she'd ever spent replacing the human urge to flinch with the Knightly urge to fight.

The Emissary was, in every way that counted, bigger than her.

ABIGAIL FALX.

It took her in top to toe without even moving its head.

LITTLE ABIGAIL FALX.

And it *knew* her.

LEFT TO ROT. LEFT TO RUST. LEFT FOR *CENTURIES* WITH NOTHING BUT WIND AND RAIN AND EVERY HUMAN DESPERATE ENOUGH TO COME TO ME FOR HELP.

On the last word, its voice *jumped*, like a dying radio, and a voice trickled from under that helm, stretched by volume but unmistakably, horribly human.

WHEN THE TIME COMES . . .

Her voice.

I WANT TO BE GOOD ENOUGH.

She'd said that to Denizen on Os Reges Point. She'd told him that Knighthood was what she wanted because it was where she'd always known she was headed. She'd told him that she trained because there would be a time when life and death depended on her.

DO YOU *FEEL* YOU'RE GOOD ENOUGH, ABIGAIL FALX?

'Stop!'

The voice rang out, as loud as human lungs could deliver, but still pathetically small compared to *it*. The Emissary was deafening even at rest, a low-level grumble of joints and chains clanging with every gurgling breath it took. Like standing next to the ocean. Like the noise in your ears when you were about to drown.

MALLEUS COILED.

The Tenebrous was so large it had to take a step back to turn in the narrow street, palm pivoting lovingly on the hilt of its sword. Coiled, in comparison, barely reached the Emissary's knee, standing with her arms folded as if the now eight-metre-tall behemoth was a student stepping out of line.

This was Abigail's moment. This was when she should act. The weight of the beast's gaze was gone, and air and thought were rushing in to fill the gap. It had turned its back on her, the most simple and elementary mistake, and this was her moment, so *why was she hesitating*?

A tactical error. A fatal mistake.

And then –

'Now!' Coiled yelled, and the other Knights leapt from the roofs above.

Adler hung in the air as if physics didn't quite know what to do with her, before bringing an axe down to hack a chunk from the Emissary's helm. The Sikh Knight landed on one pauldron and ran, actually *ran*, across the beast's shoulders before whipping a blade into the darkness between helm and neck.

It howled.

Coiled was already darting between the creature's tree-trunk legs, whipping the iron sphere into the gaps where hamstrings should be. The Emissary lurched in a circle of dust, leaving itself open to the wrinkled Knight's jab of flame.

No movement wasted. No gap in the dance. A single swing of that massive blade would have broken any of them in two, so instead the Knights baited and dodged like hunting-dogs trying to take down a stag.

Abigail's heritage boiled up inside her and she tensed, wanting to lend her fire to theirs, but then Coiled saw her and froze.

'Abigail! Get –'

The dance faltered. Just for a second. Just for a beat. Abigail saw it. The Emissary saw it too.

The Tenebrous turned, suddenly lightning-fast – that poisonous Tenebraic inconsistency – and caught the Malleus with the bulldozer tip of its boot.

Coiled *flew*.

It felt like a play, a backdrop. It felt like the stories Abigail's mother used to tell her when heroes and monsters battled back and forth and every step and blow was world-shaking.

Coiled landed beside her, a broken bundle of limbs, and Abigail could no more take her eyes from the Malleus than she could have arm-wrestled the monster behind her.

The little woman had hit the wall three metres off the ground. She'd taken a lump of the corner with her and it lay in pieces around her like a halo, slowly being soaked with blood. She stared up at Abigail with one eye already closing, the other a bright and shocking green.

'Abigail . . .'

How could Abigail hear her? There was a howl behind her, a roar of flame – the dance was broken now and Knights were falling. The Emissary was bellowing like an air turbine. She shouldn't have been able to hear someone whispering so quietly through a half-collapsed chest.

'Abigail, you should have . . .'

Should have done *something*. This was her duty, her heritage. What she had been made for, what her parents wanted for her, the crux of who she was. Life or death.

DO YOU FEEL YOU'RE GOOD ENOUGH, ABIGAIL FALX?

The Emissary answered questions. Abigail had hers.

She fled.

13

GHOST STORIES

Denizen hadn't taken three steps out of the chamber before his muscles simply let go, dumping his frame in an awkward heap on the floor. He didn't even register the impact.

What he did register was a hand closing on his arm like a bear trap. Terror pushed aside tiredness, and he swiped raggedly at whatever held him.

It was Grey, dragging him along the flagstones so that the chamber could be sealed. He caught a blurred glimpse of Knights with their backs pressed against one door, roaring as if they meant to push it back by sound alone, and then a lone Hephaestus leaning into the other, taking step after deliberate step.

The doors slammed shut, but not before a hand trapped itself between, snap-scrabbling at the air with knuckles that didn't move the way knuckles should move. With a deliberate backhand, Greaves smashed it to shards.

'Seal it,' he snarled. 'And light it up. I want them to *burn*.'

Denizen stared numbly at the door as the remaining Knights – *this corridor had been . . . it had been full* – pressed bare hands to the exposed metal. Light purled beneath their skin, faint at first, then brighter, streaky with effort. After a moment, the lines and carvings on the doors began to glow as well, the spoken steel channelling their fire.

Soon the whole wall glowed geometric with precise lines of illumination. And with the light came sound – rising low from under Denizen's senses, an earth-deep rumble that pitched louder and higher until he had to press hands against ears to drown it out.

Tenebrous. More than Denizen had ever heard before. It sounded like . . .

It sounded like hundreds.

Light flickered across Graham McCarron's stony expression as he listened to Tenebrous burn inside the chamber walls. There was no smell. Sealed. Airtight.

How long will it hold them?

'Upstairs,' Greaves said. There was a ragged wound down one side of his face. '*Now.*'

Rain was still beading on the balcony when they returned to Greaves's office – the drops clear with no trace of black. Denizen had no idea if that was a good sign or not.

Greaves wasn't giving orders any more. There didn't seem to be any to be given. Cadres had been stationed round the Glimpse, some to power the spoken-steel wards, and others if those wards . . .

A woman with a dragon tattoo on her cheek and a man with a sweep of dyed blue hair across his scalp entered the office, Mercy between them. Even that small detail was unnerving: her honour guard had halved. They had better things to be doing right now.

I am sorry, she said. It seemed to be her go-to phrase. **I –**

'What is it?' Greaves said. He had one hand on the head of his hammer. It was as dented as Vivian's now. 'That *thing*. The thing that spoke to us.'

I don't –

'You *do* know,' the Palatine snapped, and scraped the weapon across the desk with a whine of iron and wood. 'It knew you. It called you its *challenge*.'

We follow the strong, Mercy murmured. The fury she'd shown in battle had drained away. Now she seemed . . . resigned. **Usurpers are rising. Those who think they could be King.**

And, like a dog sensing an earthquake, Denizen turned just in time to see Vivian come through the door so hard it slammed open and closed in the same breath. Everyone jumped. Hands went to hilts.

Denizen, however, did not jump. He was used to it. Vivian could slam a bead curtain.

'Do you want to explain,' Vivian hissed, 'why we nearly just lost the next generation of the Order to the *Emissary of the Endless King*?'

That was two hammers being waved in Mercy's face now, and still she didn't flinch. Perversely, it made Denizen think of Crosscaper. What did Simon always say? Oh yes. *Don't panic.* If you were here, the worst had already happened.

He is my father's Emissary no longer.

The reflection of Vivian's hammer was a spot of darkness on the brightness of Mercy's eyes.

Obviously.

A muscle twitched in Vivian's cheek. Knights did not *get on* with Tenebrous. That was an understatement. But it also wasn't a patch on how Vivian felt specifically about Mercy.

They did not *get on* at all.

'You. Led. Them. Here.'

I chose a side. I don't want anyone else to die.

'*Tell that to* –'

'Enough!' Grey snapped, and Vivian was so surprised that she actually shut up. 'The Neophytes? The cadre? Where –'

His friends! He hadn't even –

'Coiled, Adler, the others . . . They covered the Neophytes' retreat . . . and paid for it with their lives.'

Knights hissed, or slammed hands into fists, or swore, and Grey just seemed to . . . deflate, clutching his right hand with the mangled machinery of his left.

'And the Emissary?'

Vivian shook her head. 'We don't know. When we've finished our search, we'll formulate a response. The Neophytes –'

'Are mistaken,' Greaves said, and the hope in his voice was worse than fear. 'You didn't speak to the cadre? It's something else. They're *wrong* –'

'They're Neophytes,' Vivian retorted, 'not children. Not idiots. I interrogated them myself. And it's *grown*, Greaves.

Nine metres tall, and wielding that damned sword it always talked about –'

'It's shock,' Greaves snapped, and somewhere Denizen found the headspace to be insulted. 'They're –'

'They're right.'

Darcie stood in the doorway, so frail Denizen had to stop himself from running to her side. She'd shrunk since he'd seen her last, disappearing into the folds of her coat. Even her hair had drooped, flat and tangled, against her scalp.

'So much movement on the other side of the veil. Like pressing my cheek to the side of a beehive. Feeling that vibration. That awful, awful hum.'

She licked her lips, the motion convulsive and sad.

'Like they're crawling on the inside of my brain.'

'That's *enough*,' Greaves snapped, turning to a slim lynx of a woman behind him, her skin dappled brown and black with the Cost. 'Phones are out. Islington, Berlin: we need reinforcements.'

The Art of Apertura. The Cant that allowed Knights to step from one shadow to the next. The woman nodded and three things happened in quick succession:

Darcie lurched forward. Mercy went out but for her eyes – just two points of light like fireflies frozen in flight. And the voice of the light and the *Lux* overlapped in fear.

'*No!*'

No!

And that unnamed Knight opened a hole in the universe and died before the sound of her Cant left the air.

It was quick. That was the only mercy. Tendrils of black lashed out from that half-opened hole like a century of spiderwebs from a growing spinneret, and the Knight's expression didn't even have time to change before her feet left the ground.

And then the rent in the air closed. It had to, when the life supporting the Cant went out.

It seemed that they stared at that patch of air for an unforgivably long time.

It is as I said. There is no escape. Not by the Art. You are surrounded. You are besieged.

Detail returned to Mercy with every word, like a radio tuning back in, like an artist pulling lines from ink and paper.

It is difficult to plan when you are liquid. *You* are rigid things. Stacking one thing upon another comes easily to you. For us, it is far harder. We are flowing. We are impermanent. We are . . .

'*Mercy*,' Denizen hissed, 'start making *sense*.'

And, finally, the lines fell into place.

You have been anticipated. That is what I am trying to tell you. A cloudburst infiltration. Hundreds of Tenebrous using the concentrated distortion of their presence to disrupt communication with the outside world. We are creatures of will, the weak follow the strong and what proves strength more . . .

'Than destroying everything the last King built,' Denizen whispered. 'Destroying the greatest enemy of your race. Destroying us.'

Mercy nodded.

You are the Emissary's challenge. I didn't come here for my salvation. I came here for yours. This is not a raid, a ravening . . . This is not a Breach.

It's an invasion.

'Then . . .' Vivian actually seemed at a loss for words, 'what do we do?'

Edifice Greaves just looked at her blankly, as if he had vanished into himself, an empty hotel with the lights left on. Denizen had seen many of his masks, but he'd never seen him simply *off*, the gears all seized up.

'Palatine,' Vivian repeated. 'What do we *do*?'

And Greaves's lips moved without speaking and, through some quirk or luck, Denizen read them perfectly.

I don't want to die like this.

Vivian's voice was horrified. 'What did you –'

She didn't finish her sentence. Actual shapeshifters couldn't have changed as quickly and competently as the Palatine did in that moment. One by one, he pinned them all with a leonine grin, the same nuclear confidence he'd possessed at the Concilium, when there had seemed there was nothing he couldn't do or say.

'I *said* – we do what we always do. We fight. And we win.'

And suddenly Denizen understood Edifice Greaves perfectly. He'd never known which mask was real – the affable rogue, the earnest leader, or the pragmatist who'd lie through his teeth to test the loyalty of a thirteen-year-old.

Or the briefest glimpse of a coward that the Palatine hadn't been able to hide.

They were all real, and they were all irrelevant. Greaves wore masks so he could be whatever the moment needed, and now he would do the same. That was all there was to it.

'Two goals,' Greaves commanded. 'One solution.' He pointed at one of the Knights. 'I want everything priceless and movable evacuated beyond the walls. Break out the shortwave radios – they're old, they're basic, they might hold up. Pull the wall cadres back and issue every set of Hephaestus Warplate we have. If they're coming here, then at least they're not going anywhere else.'

He turned on Mercy. 'Right?'

Mercy's voice was hesitant. **Yes.**

'Fine. They want the world? Then they'll have to come through us. Same as it's always been.' He turned to Vivian. 'Until you come back with the cavalry.'

'What?' Denizen couldn't blame Vivian for looking confused.

'You're leaving,' Greaves said, his voice burning not with Knightly fire but with *command*, and Denizen felt the gears begin to turn again. 'The Emissary circumvented the Glimpse. How many other Tenebrous are going to be clever enough to do that?'

It is not a matter of cleverness, Mercy said. **The Emissary's hate made him strong enough to attempt such a thing, but most Tenebrous will flock to the point of least resistance instead.**

'Why parachute in when there's a hole in the wall already?'

Exactly. But the Emissary will have to come here eventually, if he is to prove himself. Each Usurper declared their challenge –

Something sparked in Denizen's head at that, but he was too exhausted for it to flicker to life.

And the weakest of us will flock to them. Others will wait to see what happens to those Tenebrous daring enough to attack the Order of the Borrowed Dark.

'And act accordingly.' Greaves looked to Vivian. 'We have to turn this around before that happens. Get the Neophytes out of the city and clear of this Tenebraic interference. Then you're going to contact the outside world. The rest of the Order. PenumbraCorp. The damn Croits. *Everyone*. The counter-charge, Vivian Hardwick. You're leading it.'

'Palatine . . .'

'What?'

Vivian opened her mouth, then closed it again. 'I have misjudged you.'

'Yes,' Greaves said. '*Constantly*. Now go out there and do what you do best.'

A fierce smile darted across Vivian's face. 'Yes, Palatine.'

'Good!' He spun on a heel. 'Madame *Lux*. Accept my deepest apologies. We're having a bad day. Are you fit to serve?'

Just for that moment, Darcie's eyes fixed on him. 'Always, my Palatine.'

'*Good*. I need the Emissary's movements. I need to know whether other *Luxes* have detected this anomaly, and I need to know if we're *losing people* because they're trying to use the Art of Apertura to get here. Your knowledge or your best guess. And as for you –' He rounded on Mercy. 'I'm sure my predecessors would be rolling in their graves at this, but, if you're here to help, you're here to help. Are you?'

Mercy flickered. **In any way I can.**

'Then welcome to the Order of the Borrowed Dark.' In fairness, he managed to say the words without flinching. 'You'll stay here. I need everything you know about what's coming against us.'

Yes, but –

'But *what*?'

You cannot beat this. I respect you, I commend you, but you can't.

The warmth that had entered the room at Greaves's proactiveness began to drain away.

I came here to offer you a different path.

Ever since she'd touched Denizen's Malleus dagger, her hand had been clasped across her chest. It looked like she was promising them something, hand on heart.

If you get me out of the city, we can start looking for my father. We give him back his throne and *he* will bring the other Tenebrous into line.

They all stared at her.

'Do you . . .' The Palatine raised an eyebrow. 'Do you know where he is?'

I . . . No. But if you could spare some forces to help me search –

'Not a hope,' Greaves interrupted. 'Not a *hope*. He can have his crown back when we've taken these Usurpers' heads.'

Then I'll do it myself, she retorted. **You don't understand –**

'The time for your giving orders is over, Mercy.'

Denizen knew that tone. This was no longer the Palatine speaking to a foreign dignitary; it was a general commanding his troops.

'I can't spare forces for a wild goose chase. You don't even know where the King is. Besides, you can't leave. One of the Usurpers needs to kill you to take the throne. We are not handing them that. Not today.'

He turned to her honour guard.

'Take her somewhere secure, while we formulate a defence.'

You're *locking me up*?

'Comfortable quarters,' Greaves said. 'Our very best. You did say you came here to help.'

I . . . Mercy lowered her head. **Yes.**

'Good,' Greaves said. 'Because I will not be the last Palatine this Order has.' He glared at the Knights around him. 'Right?'

Light darted beneath skin. It was the closest to applause that the Order got.

Vivian flexed her hands on her hammer. 'I'm taking my son with me.'

'Of course,' Greaves said, already marshalling the Knights. 'It's like Denizen said: diplomacy's over. This is war.'

It was inevitable, of course, that Denizen's scepticism would catch up. Impressive speeches and dynamic action were exactly what they needed after so many losses in so little time, which was precisely why Greaves had delivered them. But even as Vivian began to steer Denizen towards the doors, even as the Order began to rally and rattle their blades, Denizen couldn't help but look back one more time . . .

His eyes met Mercy's, and they glittered with fear.

Greaves would do whatever was required.

This is war.

Just give me the child.

14

THE BACKSWING BEFORE THE BLOW

Daybreak had never made much of an effort at being anything other than a fortress, but now even that flimsy pretence was being stripped away.

Extra candlewards were placed in alcoves and arrow-slits. Tables were flipped for barricades and nailed over doorways, cutting off exits, turning corridors into killing fields. Blades were carried unsheathed in hands, until it seemed Denizen walked through a hall of mirrors, his worried reflection glittering from a thousand sharp angles.

Vivian was walking so fast that Denizen almost had to run to keep up, but a year of training had increased his lung capacity so he could at least both talk and jog. The only reason he hadn't said anything yet was because he didn't know what to say.

This was definitely a situation. There was no denying it. It was the most *situation* situation Denizen had ever seen, and it had been a busy twelve months. But Greaves had rallied a defence, there was a plan to both save the

Neophytes and call reinforcements, *and* they had their very own inside man. Girl. Tenebrous. *Whatever.*

Denizen didn't know how long it would take for the counter-charge to come together, but when it did hit, it would strike with the force of a meteor. So danger, and peril, and death on either side, but a clear and inarguable path. It was all they could do. It was what was required.

He couldn't get the memory out of his head: Mercy, hovering small and alone in a room of bared swords, and the gears turning once more in Edifice Greaves's head.

'Vivian, I –'

'Denizen, there's something I need to tell you.'

She pulled him into a doorway just as a cadre marched past, laden down with more sharp objects than they had hands to wield them with.

'What's wrong?'

She didn't answer, dragging a handkerchief from her pocket and spitting into it with a jerk of her head. Denizen went bright red as she turned his head with a twist of her fingers, and began matter-of-factly – and painfully – wiping blood from his temple.

'Can't this wa-*ow*!'

'Infection kills more soldiers than swords,' Vivian said absently, and then her eyes locked into his. For once, anger wasn't in the ascendancy.

'Abigail is missing,' she said. 'Or she was. It's entirely possible they've found her by now. We recovered most of them – including Simon – without much difficulty, but . . .'

And Vivian looked away. Vivian – who had never backed away from a fight in her life.

'I would have stayed to look, but I had to report to Greaves. He would have argued with anyone else.' Her fingers flexed into fists on her hammer. 'Our best people are out there, going house to house –'

'Our best people?' Denizen whispered, incredulous. Something awful and unknown was building within him. He'd never worried about Abigail before. He'd never had to. Darcie – yes, most recently just a few moments ago. Simon – obviously, he was the only person worse at fighting than Denizen. But of all of them Abigail was the most competent, the most focused, the most . . . *Knightly.*

And since when was that a guarantee of safety?

'*You're* our best people,' Denizen hissed. 'How could you leave her? She's . . . she's out there somewhere, afraid . . .'

'Denizen –'

'Oh God, the *Emissary* . . . What if it –'

'*Denizen.*' She jerked her hand back, handkerchief hanging down like an admission of surrender. 'I know. All right? I know. But . . . I had to make sure that you were safe.'

There was the tiniest quiver in Vivian's hand. With both of his, Denizen clasped it still.

'I understand. I do. But I'm safe now. You have to go out there and –'

She shook her head. 'I trained Abigail. I know what she'll do. Avoid the Emissary, regroup at Daybreak; she's probably downstairs already. We'll need an hour or so to put together supplies. And we have our orders.'

'No, Vivian –'

'*We have our orders.*'

Her gaze flicked past Denizen's shoulder. He turned –

– and Simon nearly took him off his feet.

Someone had apparently slipped a bunch of muscle into Simon's frame when Denizen hadn't been looking because those lanky arms closed round him like an adolescent vice. Denizen made a strangled noise into Simon's shoulder.

'Are you all righ–'

'What happened to your –'

'The *Emissary* –'

'I heard –'

'Abigail.'

Their mutual, stuttering catch-up halted around a gap that should never have been there. Normally, Denizen didn't talk a whole lot. It was a great deal more fun to watch Abigail and Simon spar – figuratively: nobody enjoyed sparring with Abigail except Abigail – but now . . .

'More cadres have gone out searching,' Simon said. Even with the bruises and the scrapes, it was these words that seemed to pain him most. 'She's . . . she's not the only one missing. They say they'll find her. The Emissary's gone to ground.'

'He doesn't want to fight yet,' Vivian said grimly. 'Not all of us. He's biding his time.'

And the longer he waits . . .

How many Tenebrous would see the Emissary's daring and draw strength from it?

'Then we *can't* leave,' Denizen said. 'Not until we find out what's happening. We can't just abandon her!'

'What do you mean, *leave?*' Simon said, but Vivian cut him off.

'We give it until another patrol reports back,' she said. 'I'm sorry. Delaying the counter-attack puts the entire world in danger. We need to crush whatever this is before more Tenebrous flock to the Usurpers' banners.'

'And what about what Mercy said?' Denizen had to force the words out past Vivian's suddenly flat stare. 'About finding her father? Letting him end this?'

'Even if I believed her about what's happening . . .' Denizen's eyes went wide, but his mother wasn't finished: 'And even if we had forces to spare, this is clearly an attempt to make us reinstate her father as Endless King.'

'Well – *yes*,' Denizen said. 'It is. So?'

'*So we are not the lackeys of some monster warlord, to be used and discarded at his will*,' Vivian growled. 'We fight this war our way, with our weapons. Not with . . . politics. The time for that is long gone.'

'But –'

But Vivian had already resumed her stalking, striding into the Neophyte's Solar and silencing it without needing to speak a word. She swept her gaze across the room, and every back straightened.

'Beneath Daybreak lies the Asphodel Path, the crypts in which the Knights of Daybreak are laid to rest. These tunnels have another entrance, where the inhabitants of Adumbral could visit their . . .'

She paused.

'Anyway. We will use these to traverse the city, staying out of sight of the Emissary, and resurface close to the Aurelian Gate. From there, it's a straight hike down through no man's land. This Tenebraic . . . interference has a limit. We will find it, and contact the outside world.'

'What about the Neophytes left in the city?'

Denizen couldn't see where the question came from, but felt a momentary pang that it hadn't come from him.

I would have asked. It's just . . . there's a lot going on.

'The city is being combed, both for the Emissary and our two missing Neophytes.'

Wait – two?

Frustration crackled off Vivian's voice. She was leaving one of her own behind, and Denizen knew she would have torn this entire city apart brick by brick if not for the fact that her son was here, and Vivian had decided to put him first.

'They will be found,' Vivian said simply, and Denizen told himself she was speaking to him. 'We have our own mission. Prepare yourselves. Food, supplies and weapons will be provided.'

She paused, and when next she spoke her voice was soft, as soft as Vivian's ever got.

'Your Order needs you,' she said. 'It needs you to be calm. It needs you to be brave. These are the things it has always needed from you and this situation is no different.'

Daybreak trembled, and the trainees trembled with it. Eyes widened. Faces paled. Not a muscle flickered in Vivian's frame. For a moment, she seemed sturdier than the fortress around her.

'*This is no different*. We are Knights. We fight. We move forward. We do not retreat. We do not run.'

'Aren't we running now?'

It was the Neophyte who'd asked the previous question. Denizen caught a brief glimpse of wide worried eyes, half-hiding behind the crowd. As someone who had interrupted Vivian's rants quite a few times, Denizen braced himself for the inevitable explosion.

It didn't come. Instead, Vivian simply raised her hammer until every pair of eyes was fixed upon it.

Malleus hammers weren't just weapons – they were symbols. The Order paid no attention to race, religion or gender – fire and iron had none, after all – but only the most tenacious Knights were trusted with the weapon Vivian now held. The Order simply couldn't afford to lose them, and so they were bestowed upon the people who were guaranteed, hands down, to bring them back.

'We are not running,' Vivian said, and everyone in the room jumped as she spun the hammer in a tight, brutal arc, rolling it around her wrists like the hidden axis of a planet.

Denizen had tried lifting one of those hammers once. He knew just how heavy they were. To wield one, you had to understand gravity, the mechanics of a swing, that centrifugal drag, every movement a key rotating in a lock.

Vivian hadn't named her hammer. She wasn't the naming type. There was no inscription or motto or crest. But both it and Vivian may as well have had *inevitable* carved into their very core.

'This isn't running, Neophyte,' she said, and there wasn't a hint of strain in her voice. 'This is the backswing before the blow.'

She stared at them for a moment longer. 'Prepare yourselves.'

Knights entered the room with backpacks and bundles. Vivian had already vanished through the door. Simon's hands were opening and closing into fists, as if ready for the fight that was undoubtedly coming. *Or one that's already over*, Denizen thought, with a pang of guilt.

'We can't leave Abigail behind,' Simon said, echoing his thoughts. 'We just can't.'

'Maybe they'll find her.'

'You didn't see it, Denizen,' Simon said. 'Like . . . I've seen Tenebrous. I've *fought* Tenebrous. And they're horrible. All horrible – all different flavours, new one every time. But –'

Denizen remembered fists held over D'Aubigny's head, clenched fingers, a rain of rust. The sheer, caged *hatred* that had been in the Emissary's voice, the kind of hatred that could only accrete over hundreds of years in the wind and the rain . . .

'It's just one Tenebrous.'

Simon opened his mouth to protest, but Denizen shook his head.

'One *big* Tenebrous. I heard. But it's a city. Abigail's smart. Smarter than both of us when it comes to these things. They'll either find her, or she'll make her way back, or she'll show up with half the Order to save us. You know what she's like.'

'Yeah. You're . . . you're right.' Simon rubbed his face, and then pulled his hand away, as if only now realizing how dirty it was. 'We should get ready.'

'Yeah,' Denizen said, and suddenly the thought of leaving had become horribly real once again. Was that it? Was he just going to leave?

Walls shivered, inside his head and without. Yes. It was. For once in Denizen's life, what duty demanded and the right thing to do had aligned. It hurt, physically hurt, to leave Darcie behind, but that was her choice. *We're needed.*

Abigail was another matter entirely, but, as much as he hated it, Vivian was right. None of them seemed to have any illusions about how long Daybreak's garrison could withstand the forces arrayed against them, even without the odds set to worsen with every passing moment.

That left . . .

Nobody. Absolutely nobody. You're not thinking about anybody. There is nobody to think about. And that nobody came here because she wanted to help, and you wouldn't be doing her any favours by getting in the way . . .

'Denizen?'

Simon was saying something, but all Denizen could think was that for all the many masks he had seen Mercy wearing – trapped princess, regal queen-in-waiting, remorseful fugitive or blazing warrior – he had never seen her frightened until he left her behind.

That was all it took. That flicker. That fear. Denizen could have erected every battlement known to the human race in his head, forged them out of the hardest iron, reinforced them with the coldest ice, and still Mercy would slip between them. Like a knife. Like the ghost she so often resembled.

Like she had never left him at all.

'I'm fine,' he told Simon, as around them the castle shook. 'Definitely fine.' His voice was heavy. 'I just . . . I need to go and get something.'

15

TEETH OF THE GEAR

You're an idiot.

Denizen scuttled through Daybreak's innards, wincing at every step he took. It wasn't that he was worried about being overheard – since that first battle at the Glimpse, the tremors shaking Daybreak had been more and more pronounced.

It felt like footsteps, like the approach of something huge.

He wasn't even worried about being seen: with only a hundred Knights to go around, and a castle's worth of preparation to make, the halls he now traversed were deserted. Any warrior he did pass probably assumed he was on some important errand on behalf of his mother or the Palatine himself.

They *definitely* wouldn't guess what he was actually doing, because they were intelligent, and he was not.

No, what Denizen was really wincing at was that every step he took was another nail in his coffin. What that coffin contained changed from moment to moment, as fluid as the mosaics on the walls.

There was his career in the Order, though that had already pretty much been on life-support since birth.

He didn't care so much about what the other Neophytes thought, but he could just *imagine* Simon's reaction to what he was doing. *Don't think about it. He'll understand eventually. He always does.*

And then there was his relationship with Vivian. That thought nearly froze him mid-step before he forced his limbs to move once again. He'd disobeyed her before, but this made every previous infraction look like . . . well, the trouble normal teenagers got into.

She'll understand too.

I hope.

Hope was what Denizen was running on right now. Hope was his destination, and hope was his path, more than the half-remembered map from Greaves's office. Denizen liked maps. He would have been absolutely fine this morning had someone just thought to put a map in the Neophytes' Solar. But that seemed like centuries ago, and it wasn't the primary training chamber he was trying to find now.

'Comfortable quarters. Our very best.'

Greaves hadn't been wrong. The *Luxes'* quarters were a whole lot nicer than the Neophytes' cells – a series of plush apartments that wouldn't have looked out of place back in Dublin. The castle shook again, harder than before, and all the paintings jumped off the walls in a clatter of wood and glass. Denizen fought the sudden, stupid urge to go and fix them. Which was Darcie's room? *What would she say?*

She'd understand. Darcie knew that Greaves would do anything to ensure victory. The Usurper had told them that Mercy was its challenge – what could Greaves negotiate for with a bargaining chip like that? He wouldn't hesitate to sacrifice Mercy if it bought the Order time to respond.

What loyal Knight wouldn't?

Besides, Darcie has to be here. He didn't have time to search anywhere else.

Knights chose the Cants that suited them, and, though Denizen knew all seventy-eight, there were some he had gravitated to more than others. The ones most linked to property damage, as it happened.

What does that say about me?

It says I have a habit of ending up in stupid situations.

Like this one?

This isn't stupid. It's necessary.

Can't it be both?

Sluggish from his regime of denial, the Cants stirred muzzily in his head, and Denizen took advantage of their lethargy to seize the one he wanted. He'd only ever cast it once before – a dirty trick in a fight that had been far too dirty already – and, though the phrase *bending light* had always seemed softly at odds with the belligerence of the other Cants, nevertheless there was a violence to this one as well.

Denizen spoke the Starlight Caul, the syllables so sharp that the torchlight hit them and split, flowing round Denizen like a stream round a rock. An arm's length beyond, the world was as normal as a passageway in a besieged magical fortress was ever going to get. Behind him, the flow of light closed up again, drawing even a Knight's eye away from the fourteen-year-old boy who'd carved himself a little teardrop of invisible night.

He began inching forward, senses stretched in the hopes of detecting Mercy's umbra. It was very nearly enough of a distraction from the fact that Mercy had already made her case to Greaves and got precisely nowhere. The thought of peace had been one thing six months ago, but neglecting the defence of Daybreak at this crucial hour to *save* a Tenebrous was a step too far.

Denizen wasn't even sure he could argue with the logic, and with Vivian Hardwick in the room he hadn't dared try.

There was no reason to think he would have any more luck with the honour guard, and every reason to think they would simply march him back to his mother. He hadn't a hope in a fair fight against a Knight nor the guts for an unfair one.

All he knew was that she had come to help them, and he couldn't leave her behind.

You have to listen to me.

Only Mercy's voice saved Denizen from being caught. He reflexively ducked into a doorway just as Grey came round the corner. Denizen hurriedly narrowed that teardrop of darkness around him in case the Knight advanced, but he just stood there, staring at nothing, a hand pressed to the stone wall. Denizen had seen Grey switch off before. He had his own mask, the same as Greaves, and sometimes Denizen felt honoured that he had seen past it and sometimes guilty that Grey had to wear it at all.

This wasn't either. This was Grey unobserved, and the raw exhaustion on his face should have made him look older, but it didn't – it gave him the expression little kids wore in Crosscaper's courtyard when the gates closed with them on the inside.

He looked trapped. Afraid.

Mr McCarron, ***please.***

And then it was gone. Grey rebuilt himself like a Malleus donning plate, and that scared little boy disappeared. The Knight turned back to the voice and, like a ghost, Denizen followed.

Luxes obviously didn't visit very often. Everything in the apartment at the end of the hall was covered in dust sheets. Mercy sat on the end of the bed, and Denizen could see through her to the mattress cover beneath, undulating as if it couldn't quite decide whether someone was sitting on it or not.

She was staring plaintively at Grey, who was draped across a chair like a discarded coat, but it was a woman who answered first, her Mohawk frost-bright against her dark scalp.

'Be quiet.'

It wasn't her tone that stopped Denizen in his tracks, though it was at once surprising and not surprising at all how quickly the Knights had stopped treating Mercy with any kind of courtesy. No, it was the hammer at her waist, drawing Denizen's gaze like a magnet.

A Malleus. *Of course.* Only the best for a trusted ally, valued prisoner or crucial bargaining chip.

Some long-ago fight had turned her left eye into a blind gem set in silver scars, and she swallowed wetly before wiping her mouth with the back of her hand. Her pointed glare at Mercy spoke volumes as to the source of her distaste.

Denizen, by comparison, felt barely anything from Mercy at all. He had never liked thinking about her umbra the way he thought about other Tenebrous, but he couldn't deny that she did carry an air of distortion around her. Now, however, she was so muted she was barely there at all.

Except she was. That was the problem. And if he left her behind, there was every chance Greaves would betray her, or Daybreak would simply fall and she'd die at the hands of the Usurper. And every second that went by felt not like the ticking of a clock but the building of one thing on another, the whole tottering edifice about to come down –

And something in the woman's posture changed. It wasn't that she had looked comfortable before – she had possessed the same air of pre-lightning-strike tension all Mallei did. But now she looked *pained*, swallowing so thickly that Denizen could hear it across the room.

'Grey, I'll be right back.'

Grey nodded, and Denizen leapt out of the way before she strode right through him. Denizen couldn't blame her for needing a moment. Mallei didn't usually spend much time in the company of Tenebrous: they usually killed them on sight.

And then there was one.

His mentor. His friend. The person standing between Denizen and the Order's only real chance of victory.

Do you really believe that?

He had to. Denizen realized it with a crystalline clarity that went beyond crushes and gardens and almost-kisses and mistrust. He had to do this. He had to believe he could both help the Order and free Mercy, that freeing Mercy *was* helping the Order . . . because if it wasn't then he was wrong, and everyone else had been right.

And all I have to do is strike down the man who's suffered far too much for me already.

A single careful line of fire fed the Cant in Denizen's head, but others were clawing desperately for the flame that could give them life. It wouldn't even have to be him that did it. He'd just have to not hold himself back any more. *Not* doing something wasn't the same as *doing* something, was it?

That's why you came here.

You don't have much time.

Didn't he betray you?

That was what clinched it. *No*, Denizen thought. *He didn't.*

He'd talked to Grey when Grey had a gun to his head. He wouldn't put one to Grey's now.

And then the decision was made for him.

You can come out now.

Denizen lost his grip on the Caul, the glow from the torches finding him once more, and it was no consolation at all to learn that Grey only moved at a fraction of light speed.

'Ulp,' Denizen said around the sword point under his chin.

'*What the hell are* you *doing here?*'

Daybreak trembled, and Denizen felt the blade shiver with it.

'Can you put the sword down, please? It's a little hard to think –'

'*Denizen*,' Grey snapped, whipping the sword away so quickly it took a drop of blood with it. Denizen watched it hit the wall, and dreamily considered that the seventy-eight Cants in his head hadn't even had a chance to stir.

He tried to raise a hand to his throat, but, blades still in hand, Grey half pushed, half tossed him into the room beside Mercy.

'You can't be here. You *can't*. What are you thinking –'

All right, Denizen thought, staring into Grey's livid face. *I've got this far. Here goes.*

'Emm . . .'

Oh, good grief.

Denizen's here to tell you the same thing I've been telling you. The Order can't hold back an entire universe of shapeshifters, and the more that come, the more that *will* come.

Your only hope is reinstating the King. If we find him, I can help him regain himself. We can combine forces. Destroy the Usurpers. Both our peoples will live.

'Exactly!' Denizen blurted into the silence that followed. 'What she said.'

Why didn't she make that much sense earlier?

Grey's expression shifted from homicidal shock to homicidal incredulity. 'Denizen, I can't go against Greaves's orders. He told me to –'

'Greaves will trade her back to whatever's on the other side of the Glimpse!' He flinched. 'Sorry, Mercy.'

It's fine.

Grey sighed. 'I know what you think of Greaves, but he's not an idiot. Even if he'd *contemplate* such a thing, he knows not to make deals with Tenebrous. And buying off one Usurper doesn't stop the Emissary –'

But if it buys him a day . . . if it buys him an *hour* . . . what then? When he believes that a cavalry charge will save you? What wouldn't he do to give Vivian Hardwick that extra time?

There. The tiniest flicker of doubt.

'I can't stand here listening to this,' Grey said. 'I just can't. You're supposed to be leaving the castle. If Munroe catches you here, she'll –'

'Yes,' Denizen said. 'We're leaving in . . . ten minutes. Probably. And when we do, Mercy has to be with us. I don't know about . . . about finding the King or whatever, but she just can't stay here.'

Grey's eyes were wide. 'You're insane. That's insane. What? *What?* You want to sneak her out under Vivian's nose? You think that's better than staying here? Vivian would let her die without batting an eyelid!'

He flinched. 'No offence.'

None taken. I focused my umbra on Munroe to drive her out of the room, but she's vomited up most of what she's capable of vomiting, so I imagine she will be returning soon.

Grey's head was in his hands. 'This is treason, Denizen.'

'Come *on*,' Denizen pleaded, painfully aware of the seconds ticking away. 'We're trying to save the Order, you know we are. There's nobody else. You know she's not a villain. You know she's not a monster. You . . . you gave her *books*, back in Crosscaper. She's just a *girl*. She's trying to help us.'

'I know she is. But I have my orders.'

'Is that why you're down here?'

Grey raised his head.

'The Master of Neophytes – except when they need you. His trusted adviser, except when you're not. A guard for a prize prisoner, except she has a guard already. Why are you down here?' Denizen pressed. 'If you're trusted?'

Is this what it feels like to be Greaves? Denizen despised how the Palatine made levers out of loyalty, machinery out of need – reducing the sum total of your life experience to a set of buttons he could press. People weren't lab rats. People weren't toys.

'Grey . . .'

Say it.

'You put her in a cage before. Don't make that same mistake again.'

Very Edifice Greaves.

Grey stared at him for the longest moment, and though every fibre of Denizen wanted to apologize, to take it back, to scrub himself raw of every word he'd just said . . . he met his mentor's gaze, and every drop of pain that was in it.

As penance for what he had just said. As penance for betraying his friend. And because that's what the Palatine would have done, to drive his point home.

'No.' And on that word Daybreak *rocked*, actually rocked, like a punch-drunk boxer on his last legs. 'I see what you're saying, I do . . . but I can't betray my Order again. I just can't.'

He sheathed his blades with a muted click, and Denizen suddenly wished that the Starlight Caul could be reversed, simply so he wouldn't have to see the look on Grey's face.

None of them were wearing masks any more.

The Solar was still a hive of activity by the time Denizen returned. Weapons were being handed out under Vivian's expert supervision. Neophytes were testing mobility in harnesses and sheathes.

Simon looked up as he approached, screwing the cap on to a canteen of water.

'Here, I grabbed you one.'

'Thanks,' Denizen said woodenly.

Simon frowned. 'Did you get what you were looking for?'

Denizen shook his head.

'All right,' Vivian said from the middle of the chamber, clapping her hands. 'We're leaving. No – *one* sword. Are you trained to fight with two? No. Then *one* is enough. For God's –'

Any other time, watching his mother try and deal with teenagers might have amused Denizen. But he couldn't find it in himself. What was he going to do? How could he have been so stupid? How could he have lived in books for so long and still not been able to find the words to convince Grey he was making a mistake?

How could I have said that to him?

How . . . how could it not have worked?

'*Right*,' Vivian said, in exasperation that had nothing to do with the apocalypse and everything to do with having to talk to young people. 'Are we *finally* –'

'Ready.'

They all turned to see Grey standing in the doorway, hair casting a scythe of shadow across his face, a coat folded over his bare arm. 'Palatine's orders,' he said airily. 'Can't be letting you rush off into battle by yourself.'

Vivian frowned. 'Fair enough. And who's this?'

A girl stepped forward. She had Darcie's skin and Abigail's grace, wrapped round a body that somehow took Simon's gawkiness and gave it the sort of studied elegance that made Denizen think of a flexing bow. Her eyes had the malachite sting of poor lost Ambrel Croit, but her smile was crooked and hesitant, unsure if it should be there at all.

It was disconcertingly familiar.

'One of the Neophytes. Caught her a bit lost in the corridors so thought I'd bring her along.'

His eyes met Denizen's.

'It's not safe here.'

16

RETREAT

This is not a dream.

Jasper Falx had left Alaska when he was barely out of boyhood, but it had never truly left him – tucked in the stretch of his syllables, unfolded in his anger or his laugh. It faded like freckles when they were on the road, but here at the lodge where he had been born it was as thick as crusted snow.

Wrapped in two coats, a scarf, mittens and an old *roosari* of her mother's, Abigail could only feel sunlight on the very tip of her nose, but that was enough for her to know exactly where she was. This far north, daylight was different from Sumatra or Borneo or Madagascar – all brightness and no heat, polishing the frozen lake below into a dazzling mirror, snow-covered hills shining like the spotless tops of clouds. She'd hiked those hills. She and her dad had climbed the huge black peaks beyond them.

This is not a dream.

This is a memory.

'Sholea Sassani-Falx, I am trying to –'

'I know you're trying. I've been listening to you practise this speech every morning for a year. I found it trying too.'

'It wasn't *every* morning –'

Realizing it was a memory gave Abigail a languorous sort of power, sliding from detail to detail like a ride at a theme park. *This was more than a year ago*, she thought, looking at her ironless hands.

This was before.

She mouthed along with her parents' bickering, watching her mother, dark as teak, hiss at every touch of the wind. Eyes the shade of bubbling copper were all that could be seen between collar and shawl, and the wind came off the lake as cold and sharp as if they had wronged it.

This was where it happened.

Her father's voice washing over her. Her mother the model of innocent attention, then winking whenever Jasper couldn't see. Rafi had to stay inside out of the cold, but Abigail knew he would be watching . . . was watching . . . had been watching from the window above.

Abigail fought the urge to wave. She hadn't the first time, and now she was reliving it she didn't know if she could. Besides, it was easy just to let things happen, to watch the movie of her own life play out.

I would have liked him to join us. That's all. I wouldn't have changed anything else. Not today.

Not the day she Dawned.

It would be dark very soon. Abigail had lived in cities rich with street lights, but out here there was nothing to slow the night from falling but miles of crisp cobalt sky.

Abigail trembled with excitement even though she knew exactly what would happen next.

I was so worried. Worried that it would never come, wondering what her parents would do if she turned out to be . . .

Ordinary.

Normal.

Falxes had an incredibly high rate of Dawning. Her mother's family did too. There had been a grand-uncle who'd chosen to be an imam instead, but he'd possessed the power; he'd just chosen to help people in another way. She didn't know of any relative who'd simply been . . .

Lacking.

Abigail knew this moment. She knew how it would end. It would unfurl from every cell, from her stomach and her heart and the two people before her, the two people whom she loved more than anything, and all the thousands upon thousands of ancestors before them.

The power came, and my skin turned to gold, and slowly I undid my scarf and slipped from my shoes and the snow melted beneath my feet.

I felt newborn. I felt perfect.

It will happen now.

She waited, tilting her head upwards for that first blush of inner sun . . . and shivered, as the wind hardened against her cheeks. She frowned. *That's not how it happened. The cold lessened. The wind fell away.*

Her mother and father smiled in unison, just as they had when this had happened for real, but the movie was skipping, the memory faltering. Abigail felt unstable, unmoored, like a wrong note in a favourite song, like a rotten bite of a favourite food.

'We're proud of you, Abigail. Our daughter, the Knight.'

The frozen lake still glittered. Her parents still grinned, blank and sinister. The lodge before her was as familiar to her as her own face in the mirror, but the shadows had deepened, and ice gleamed wherever she looked.

'So proud.'

The words echoed, as if bouncing off walls she couldn't see, and Abigail turned to stare at the horizon, an unwilling extra in her own best day.

This isn't how it happened.

'So proud.'

Their lips moved in unison, drowned beneath the teeth-chattering rumble of the ground underfoot. Snow slid from the roof of the lodge in sheets. She heard windows break, and panic thudded in her at the thought of Rafi and shards of glass, but when she tried to run to the door the wind congealed around her to hold her in place.

And the bright cold of the sunlight began to slip away.

This isn't –

And the trees swayed against their roots like the swell of a tide.

How it –

The mountains were moving.

The range separated, each massive peak of stone chafing free in world-drowning waterfalls of dust. It happened with such slowness, and all Abigail could do was stare, the voices of her parents like needles in her ears.

This isn't how it happened.

Not peaks. Fingers.

The colossal fingers of a horrific hand.

'Proud. Proud. Proud.'

Sucked up by the wind, pebbles rattled like snakes along the ground. One clipped Abigail's head and spun her round, but there was no blood, and no pain, just horror as trees tore themselves free to arrow towards the hand, as hills were skinned of snow, dirt lifted in miles-wide scabs –

Her mother smiled as she came apart in sighing threads of dust.

Her father in shreds, pulled apart to feed the beast.

And the dull roar of the Emissary's paw as it gathered the whole world in its palm, and, as everything upended, Abigail felt herself being disassembled, atom by atom, tumbling towards a Tenebrous the size of a planet, and the black hole in its core.

Its laugh was Armageddon.

'Abigail?'

From one nightmare to another, and Abigail was moving before her eyes opened – the crossbow of her body loosing with a snap. She unfolded from a sitting position – *I was sitting?* – and felt the meaty tremor as she drove two fingers into soft flesh and twisted, balancing her opponent on the hook of her hand.

'*Hnnngh!*'

Something about the sheer pathetic humanness of the noise brought Abigail back to herself, thinned the howl of adrenalin in her blood. That noise didn't come from a throat you designed yourself: it came when your own biology was working against you.

Slowly, the world returned.

Time and dust and Tenebraic twisting had hidden whatever this building might have been. Rafters bulged like ribs. Windows narrowed to squints. The *Intueor Lucidum* didn't help – seeing every detail only mattered when the details made sense, and the Tenebrae had wrung sense out of this architecture a long time ago.

'Let me *go* –'

Oh yeah. That.

Abigail withdrew her hand, and Matt Temberley staggered back with a look of relief that soured to resentment in the space of two steps. He rubbed his chin where her fingers had dug in.

'What was *that* for?'

Abigail tried to blink some sense into her brain. She could still feel the heatless burn of winter sunlight on her skin, her mother's old clothes protecting her from the cold, the sickening lurch in her stomach as gravity shifted, as up became down, as the universe tilted into the gullet of a beast . . .

She started in panic. *My Dawning. It didn't . . . oh no, oh no* –

But there it was, coaxed out of hiding by sudden terror, a faithful hound protecting its mistress. Light filled her, and she had to fight back tears of sheer gratitude.

'Whoa –' Matt was backing away, his face no longer silver in the *Lucidum* but illuminated, pale and afraid, by the light flaring from hers. 'What are you –'

Breathe. It was just a dream.

'Sorry,' Abigail said, forcing the fire away. 'I just . . .' Everything was muddled, her blood still a heady cocktail of adrenalin and fragments of the past. *How . . . how did I get here?* There was a memory, as light as a spiderweb, of a scrabbling, panicked run. Her trousers were ripped, dark with blood at the knee. And then –

DO YOU FEEL YOU'RE GOOD ENOUGH, ABIGAIL FALX?

Five a.m. starts so she could run at her own pace instead of waiting for everyone else. Hours of sword practice until her hands bled and healed and bled again. That was how muscle fibre worked – you tore it and it came back stronger.

And when the moment came, when her comrades needed her fire, her bravery . . . *I gave them cowardice.*

She'd worked so *hard*. She thought she had understood how the world worked and how she fitted into it. There was such power in understanding your body, knowing how hard you could punch, how fast you could run.

Capable. That was the word. She had always known what she was capable of, and had added to it every day. Until today, when she realized that she wasn't capable of anything at all.

Something hot leaked down Abigail's cheek. She could feel it try and fail to move the grime on her skin.

Matt was staring at her as if she might grow wings, his hair lank and stringy with sweat. The studied coolness and nonchalance, that sense of strange ownership of everything around him that he seemed to display had . . . diminished, as if just a little air had been let out.

He looked like she felt. Uncertain, as if the world had moved in a direction it shouldn't.

A hand, rising to blot out the sun, growing larger and larger with each piece of the world it stole . . .

Abigail shivered, and Matt twitched in response, but, when she didn't hook his jawbone or light up like a fuse again, he straightened and moved towards her. She flinched away from his outstretched hand.

'Hey! Hey, don't . . . don't freak out. I just . . . found you here. I was . . .' He looked decidedly shifty for a second. 'I was looking for stragglers. Other Neophytes. I thought I'd searched the whole place, but you had crammed yourself back in there –'

An alcove – just a nook of stone, but carved with the kind of delicacy that made Abigail think that at one point it had been important. Maybe some long-dead Adumbralian had knelt here before a little shrine of household gods, or just left flowers to take the bleakness from the stone.

Anger then, chewing some of the cobwebs away.

'So you just went to grab me?'

'You were staring at the wall and rocking back and forth,' Matt said, evidently with no idea how close it came to getting him killed. 'So I thought I'd . . .'

'Call out my name?' Abigail said, and though it *probably* wasn't exactly him she was angry at, this wasn't the time to be clueless. 'Grabbing a Knight who doesn't know you're there is a good way to get yourself hurt.'

Matt's eyes narrowed. 'You're not a Knight, *sweetheart*. Maybe you should be saying thanks that I knocked you out of whatever state you were in.'

Palm-strike. Base of the nose. He'd be dead before he felt it.

Abigail stopped her fingers before they could curl into fists. Not because he didn't deserve cartilage shards slicing into his brain like soft cheese, but because the thought was unworthy of her. They were both tired. They were both scared.

Be the bigger person. Her mother had always said that. *Lead by example.*

'I wasn't in a *state*,' Abigail said, as pleasantly as she could through gritted teeth. 'I . . . I got separated from everyone. I was just . . . I was trying to figure out what to do next.' Her heart skipped a beat. 'Oh no, did they have to send a search party? Is everyone else all right?'

Her spine stiffened with shame. She hadn't even thought about them. She'd been languishing in her own misery when the people she was supposed to be protecting could have been hurt. What was wrong with her?

She turned away, and Matt followed, though at least this time he kept his hands by his sides. 'Hey, wait, it's OK.'

She pinched the bridge of her nose, trying to take deep breaths, and then turned so quickly that Matt backpedalled. 'Let's get out of here. Where are the others?'

'Ah,' Matt said. 'Well, that's the thing . . .'

They stepped outside, and Abigail could almost have felt nostalgic for the remnants of her nightmare because at least that had been in her imagination. Now the rising murk of the Tenebrae was all too real – a gelid clamminess that left her sweating despite the coolness of the dark. Leaves rustled down the empty street though there was no breeze to move them, and Abigail wanted to tell herself that they were the source of the whispers she heard, but she knew that would be a lie.

'We got separated,' Matt said. 'Adler told us to run back to the truck and I was *trying* to get everyone to head back, but everyone was just panicking and running and . . . and screaming –'

His voice was sure, almost cocky, but there was an edge to it, as if he wasn't entirely convinced by his own story. Abigail was barely listening. *Where was everyone?* She had to get back and make sure her comrades were OK. She'd abandoned them once. She wouldn't do that again. She'd make everything right –

There had been blood on Malleus Coiled's lips. There had been things broken inside her.

Abigail pounded her fist into her leg to make the tremors stop. Matt didn't notice, caught in his own reverie.

'So I went back. Didn't want anyone to get left behind, like? And, hey, lucky for you I did, right?'

The glare she gave him should have wiped the smile from his face, but no such luck. It was almost fascinating. She'd grown up hawkishly observing people around her, and Matt was more like those cartoon characters that ran off cliffs but somehow kept going because they refused to look down.

It took a moment for what he was saying to sink in.

'Wait – so you're alone? The others aren't with you?'

'Yep. I mean – no. They're not. They're probably back at Daybreak, assembling a rescue cadre. Not that we need rescuing? But yeah.'

Abigail stared at him for a long moment.

'What?'

'Nothing. Just . . . nothing.' She looked around. 'Do we . . . do we know where the Emissary went?'

'No,' Matt said. 'And I don't want to know. We're better off going back to the Order, telling them we're OK and then just . . . letting someone else deal with it. They can figure it out. It's not our job.'

'*Yes*,' Abigail hissed. 'It *is*. We need to . . .'

She trailed off. What did they need to do? Matt might be incredibly annoying, but he had a point. They were two unarmed teenagers against a creature that could crush them in a single fist. She had as much chance against the Emissary as . . . *as the Knights I abandoned*. Proper trained Knights, Knights who didn't hesitate when they were needed. She was in even less of a position of strength compared to the last time she'd faced the Emissary.

DO YOU FEEL YOU'RE GOOD ENOUGH, ABIGAIL FALX . . . ?

'It's our duty,' she said. 'We need to at least try.'

'So we can *what*?' Matt snapped. 'Die? Like the Knights? I don't know what you think you have that they didn't, but they're dead. I . . . saw it. Do you want to go up against that? Do you *want* to die?'

Would they still have loved her had she turned out not to be a Knight? At her *real* Dawning – not the horrible nightmare version – she'd searched every angle of their faces for doubt, for a sign that they were preparing to love her any less.

It was the only time they'd ever disappointed her.

You can't disappoint them now.

'We don't have to fight it,' she said. 'We just have to find out what it's doing. That's all. We can . . . tail it. At a safe distance. Listen to it . . . or something. And then –'

Matt's eyes were wide. 'Then we go back to Greaves. With useful information. Valuable information.'

'Exactly,' Abigail said. 'That's what a Knight would do.'

'That's what a *hero* would do,' Matt said, and for once she matched his breathless grin, though a canker of her nightmare remained, cold and sharp against her heart.

That's what they would do.

Her mother's face breaking apart. Her father reduced to dust.

'Let's get to work.'

17

IN CURRENT COMPANY

'Hey.'

One canvas backpack – standard issue. One pair of hiking boots – size 6. One lightweight shirt and matching combat trousers with extra knee padding and MOLLE webbing, to which would be clipped one combat knife, one sheath and one canteen of water – all to go underneath what Denizen absolutely refused to call a *tactical poncho*.

The column of Neophytes trotted after Vivian along the shuddering veins of Daybreak, and Denizen went through the list again because lists were even more comforting than maps. *Where did the Order get this stuff?* It was one thing seeing armour and weapons that had been lovingly maintained from generation to generation, and Denizen knew there were online marketplaces for anybody's apocalypse of choice, but surely *combat kits for teenagers (bulk order)* would raise some eyebrows?

'Hey, *you*.'

It was probably where they'd got the black robes too. Did that not worry people? Battle ponchos were one thing, but . . .

Denizen weighed his knife in his hands, fully aware that holding a weapon and staring off into space was bad manners in any company, but also knowing that if his brain stopped freewheeling he wouldn't be able to help craning his neck to further up the line, where jogging along with everyone else *was the daughter of the Endless King.*

Any minute now. Daybreak's shaking had worsened, and Vivian now held the radio to her ear constantly, jaw set as if she felt every update from the Glimpse as a personal blow. There were plenty of distractions, but all the warriors around them, teenager or not, had been trained to detect creatures that toxically, painfully did not belong in this world. Would they cry out? Would they sound the alarm? Or would they just –

'Hey!'

It was the accusatory tone that finally snapped Denizen out of his reverie. There was a tall boy beside him, staring at him through hair as long and straight as falling ink.

'You're *him*.'

There wasn't much you could say to that. Now that Denizen thought about it, since he and Mercy's first meeting, there was only one *him* anyone ever meant. *And to think I was worried about just being Vivian's son . . .*

Well, at least he had some practice. Frown No. 4 – Give Nothing Away – locked into place.

'I'm who now?'

Maybe the non-committal tone would have worked with a normal teenager, but the Neophyte's gaze was like a sniper scope. 'You were about to step into the Glimpse when that thing came out. You *defended* it.'

Heads were turning. Denizen squirmed, briefly considering hiding in his conflict poncho, but before he could answer a girl joined them, vastly muscled, a sun tattoo on her thick neck.

'Leave him alone, Stefan,' she said. 'The thing was using him as a shield.' She gave him an appraising look. 'Nice Bend, by the way. What was the Cost?'

To his horror, Denizen found himself blushing. *Say something!* The line was slowing, more and more Neophytes crowding round. Simon had gone up to the top of the line to speak to Vivian, and Denizen suddenly felt very exposed, assailed on all sides by questions with a disheartening attention to detail.

'You weren't at the first training session, were you?'

'Did they take you to Greaves's office after that creature attacked? What did he say?'

'Forget that, what did *it* say?'

Denizen always felt outnumbered. That was a fundamental part of who he was. There was only one of him in the world, after all. He should have been paying attention to the Inquisition in front of him, this wall of faces and narrowed eyes, but instead all he could do was ask himself a question of his own:

Was this how Mercy felt?

'Is there a problem here?'

Vivian talked the way she fought – clipped, brutal and with the goal of putting her opponent down as quickly as possible. Suddenly looming over all their heads, it was very clear from her expression that she wasn't *enquiring* if there were a problem so much as offering to become one.

Stop using my son as a shield.

There was something very satisfying about how quickly the Neophytes dispersed. Stefan still gave them a lingering look that stopped only when Vivian met it with a scowl.

'Sorry,' Vivian murmured under her breath. 'I know mothers aren't supposed to sweep in and save their kids from –'

'Vivian,' Denizen whispered back, eyes still on the retreating teenagers, 'you can save me whenever you want.'

Only Denizen could hear her tiny pleased *hmph*. They began moving again, and Denizen attempted a quick not-at-all-suspicious examination of the girl at Grey's side – shapeless under her poncho, her hair tucked messily under a cap, stray strands standing out against the black material like forks of summer lightning.

Mr Observant hasn't noticed her, Denizen thought pettily, and then immediately kicked himself for tempting fate. People often went their entire lives without sensing Tenebrous. In present company, there was nothing strange about her arm being bound to her chest, and the strain on her face mirrored every Neophyte's in the line.

We're all under strain, Denizen thought. *Why would she be any different?*

Because the second she loses concentration for even a heartbeat, the second her facade cracks and a drop, a flicker of her umbra shows . . .

Then what? His focus had been on freeing Mercy. He had no idea what Greaves would do when he found out she was gone. He nearly stumbled as he suddenly realized he had no idea what Grey had been required to do to free her. He had no idea what Vivian would do if and when she found out, and what it would mean for him when she did.

'I'm sorry you got piled on.' Simon fell in beside him, shooting Stefan's back a dirty look. 'Stefan's all right, really. Everyone's just . . .'

'I know,' Denizen said distractedly, though, if he were being honest, Stefan's personality was far less relevant than the fact he was currently blocking Denizen's view of Mercy. Why couldn't she have morphed into someone tall?

Wait – there she was, walking alongside that massive German kid. Were they *talking*? What were they talking about? How was she able to have a conversation?

How is she better at blending in than me?

Denizen looked away before Simon could notice his blush.

'I see they gave you a sword.'

Simon, who even after a year had so far only successfully sparred against his own elbows, shrugged. 'I'm not even sure what good it'll be. And not just because I'm using it.'

A dark shadow passed across his face.

'You didn't see the Emissary.' The taller boy wrapped his arms around himself. 'And Abigail's still –'

'I did,' Denizen said, trying surreptitiously to look over Simon's shoulder and only achieving an excellent view of the taller boy's armpit. 'It was chained in Os Reges Point. We went there last year.'

'*No*,' Simon said, and there was something in his voice, but Vivian was walking by Mercy, close enough to touch, and Denizen's heart was pounding so hard he was afraid it was going to give him away –

'*Denizen*.'

Simon was glaring at him. Denizen blinked. 'What?'

'What do you mean, *what*? What are you looking at –'

Denizen shook his head frantically, but, before he could dissuade his friend, Simon had craned his neck, achieving very easily what the shorter boy couldn't. He frowned.

'Who's that? I didn't see her at training.'

'Absolutely no idea,' Denizen responded, not at all suspiciously. 'I was just . . . just looking, I guess.'

Simon raised an eyebrow.

'Right,' Simon said. 'Well . . . OK. It's not the best time to start getting a crush.' His sudden smile made Denizen feel like a monster. 'What is it with you and dangerous crushes? It could be worse, I guess. At least it's not –'

Like water icing over, the colour drained from Simon's face, his smile glassy and frozen and trapped.

'Oh no,' Denizen said, again entirely unsuspiciously. 'Simon, I –'

There seemed to be something in Simon's throat.

'Simon, it's not what you think –'

'*ISN'T IT?*' Simon hissed, and then immediately clamped his hands over his mouth as Neophytes turned in surprise. Denizen flushed guiltily.

'Is it maybe exactly what I think?'

In unspoken unison, they slowed down to open a gap between them and the others, a gap Simon's voice swiftly rose to fill.

'What were you thinking? What is actually going through your head?'

'Nothing!' Denizen retorted, and then winced. 'I mean, nothing bad. The thing beyond the Glimpse said it wanted Mercy. You know what Greaves is like – he would have *traded* her.'

'You don't know that.'

'I didn't want to take the chance. Mercy said if we find her father, he can fix all this – crush the Usurpers and take back his throne. Everything goes back to normal.'

Simon was just staring at him now, and Denizen could see the tiny flecks of gold spiral up through his eyes. It struck him that he'd never seen Simon lose his temper enough to have his power manifest under his skin before.

'Wait – was that where you went before we left?'

Denizen swallowed. 'I . . . yes. I went back and I used the Starlight Caul – you don't have a monopoly on it, you know –' He tried to smile, but it died in the air between them. 'And I . . . *convinced* Grey to help me.'

Simon buried his face in his hands. 'Of course you did. *Of course you did*. And now – what? What's your plan, O fearless rebel? Or did you bother to think that far?'

'Yes I did, actually,' Denizen said. He could feel his own fire chewing on the barricades in his head, fighting to be heard. It had its own opinions on people who disagreed with Denizen.

'We get her out. Vivian will lead the counter-charge like Greaves said, and I guess . . . I'll help Mercy find the King.'

The fire in Simon's eyes vanished. 'Oh. You will.'

Simon had always been better at keeping a lid on his power. He'd first manifested it to hide, after all, but he was also just a much calmer person. Denizen, however . . . The big book in the nurse's office in Crosscaper had called it *catastrophizing* – the dubious talent of overthinking your way to disaster. When Denizen got tangled in the negative consequences of things that hadn't happened yet, Simon had always been there with the shears.

Anxiety was real to the anxious. It never worked when Denizen told himself that what he worried about wasn't real, but the fact was he trusted Simon a lot more than he trusted himself. He'd never thought about it going both ways.

He'd never thought it could break.

'You'll run after her,' Simon growled. 'While the rest of us are fighting and dying for our world, you'll head off with her. Because that's what you do.'

It was a moment before Denizen realized what Simon meant. What he himself had said.

Vivian will lead the counter-charge and I'll . . .

Leave.

His friends. His family – the little of it that he had. His Order. His species. Mercy had been back in his life for five full minutes and already he had betrayed all of them, and was planning to do it again.

That's not what I'm doing. I'm trying to help everyone. In the long run. Isn't that what Greaves does? Isn't that what Vivian did, when she left me behind? Why am I not allowed to do what the situation needs? Why is it only me who has to –

It was so hard to focus on keeping that rigid structure in his head when fire was the only simple thing left in his life. So hard to be strong, and see disappointment in his best friend's eyes.

'Simon, I'm not abandoning you. I'm not abandoning anyone. This is just something we have to do. To save people. You can't . . .'

Can't be mad at me. Please don't be mad at me.

'You went back for her,' Simon said, his voice flat. 'You went back for her and broke the rules to make sure she was safe.'

'Yes,' Denizen said, daring to feel a spark of relief. 'That's all I was doing.'

'And what about Abigail?'

Denizen stiffened.

'What about our *friend*, Denizen? The girl who goes to the chipper for us when neither of us can move after running? The girl who risks her life for us day in and day out, when our stupidity nearly gets us killed? The girl who's now alone in a city with the scariest thing I've ever seen?'

For a moment, Denizen was convinced Simon was going to hit him.

'Would she have left you behind?'

'It's not that . . .'

Simple. Except . . . what if it was?

'She would have gone back for you,' Simon snarled. 'Abigail Falx would actually have broken the rules for you. And you don't even *spare a thought* for her.

'You don't even . . . I *told* you something really important on the way here, or tried to tell you, or was trying to tell myself, I don't know, and you haven't even bothered to try and talk to me about it either, because you're too busy to –'

It took Denizen a second to remember what Simon was talking about, and that second gave anger all the head start it needed on shame.

'*We're all busy, Simon,*' he snapped, and then shame caught up, and he tried to mollify his tone. 'You know I don't care if you're . . . that you're . . . You *know* I wouldn't care –'

'Yeah, well – funny the things you'll make time for,' Simon snapped back. 'And I know you don't care, but I want you to *care*. I want you to maybe have a talk with me about something *I'm* feeling instead of what you're feeling, or *maybe* worry about our missing friend, but you're too busy chasing the girl who's brought nothing but pain and misery and death to our door.'

'*I* am *thinking of Abigail. I'm trying to think of everyone. I'm trying to –*'

'No, Denizen, you're not. Do you know what I was doing when you were breaking Mercy out? I was trying to get your mother to stay and find our friend.'

'Simon . . .' Denizen felt a prickle in the corner of his eyes, and for once it wasn't fire rising, but a lump that took the place of words he knew weren't enough. 'I didn't think –'

'No,' Simon said quietly. 'You didn't. You don't, when she's around. And that's not good enough, Den. It just isn't.'

He shook his head. 'I'm going to check how the others are doing.'

'Wait,' Denizen whispered. 'Please don't –'

Simon glanced at Mercy one more time. She was staring back, and it might have been distance or imagination or simply Denizen's guilt, but in the half-light of the hallway her eyes looked sapphire blue. *Abigail's eyes.*

'It's fine,' Simon said. 'You have everyone you need right here.'

18

ONE OF THESE THINGS IS NOT LIKE THE OTHER

'If we do find the Emissary,' Matt said, 'I'm going to go out in a blaze of glory.'

Abigail fought the urge to introduce a blaze of glory to his face. People talked more when they were nervous. She'd heard that, but it wasn't something she'd had much experience of.

'Like it probably wasn't even that big, when you think about it. Combat can mess with your head. Or it was the . . . angle. Tenebrous can play tricks on the eye, you know. It's like a power they have –'

Navigating the calcified warrens of Adumbral, hands held out the way D'Aubigny taught her, trying to separate one flavour of wrong from a city soaked in it for centuries –

'We've definitely had ones that big in Edinburgh. The whole city's half in the Tenebrae – did I mention that?'

Deserted streets. Plazas like the flat plane of a stomach before ribcage swells of structures and alleys so narrow they could have been the lines in a cupped palm. Abigail could have understood nervousness, might have accepted it, if every second sentence weren't –

'They should have given us weapons. They should have given *me* a weapon. My sword is just sitting in my cell in Daybreak. What good is that?'

For someone who spent most of her time hitting her friends as hard as she could, Abigail considered herself a reasonable person. When you could set people on fire with one hand and stab them with the other, it was sort of a requirement. But she'd been up for more than twenty-four hours at this point, and the hairs on her neck had been up for ten. She hadn't shed a drop of sweat, despite the rising temperature, but it bubbled and pricked the inside of her skin as if desperate to get out.

And Matt was . . . Matt was *commentating.*

'. . . I'm not saying I couldn't take Hagen, because I do have a longer reach, but also, *look at him.* He's like a tank –'

It didn't help Abigail's mood that, for something that had dented the world so harshly, the Emissary had now vanished as if it had never been. No footprints. No trail to follow. It shouldn't have been difficult to track something that huge, even through a city so twisted by Tenebrous, but with all her training, all her experience, Abigail was reduced to straining her senses and hoping against hope that the path she took was the right one.

Your training didn't help you against the Emissary.

'I can't believe he ran. I mean, they all did. I was going to stay and fight, but then the little girl, your mate, she was just standing there –'

Your training didn't stop you abandoning your comrades.

'A good claymore, and things would have gone differently. I'd have shown that thing just what happens to creatures stupid enough to attack Adumbral –'

'*Can you please keep quiet?*' The hiss escaped Abigail like a kettle full of arsenic, boiling and venomous and wincingly loud. You couldn't trust sound not to travel with the Tenebrae griming the air. Every time she moved her head, it smeared strange tastes across her lips, prickling her skin and turning her stomach, and she had to lean into that sickness, and pray that the thing they hunted wasn't hunting them.

'I'm just *saying*.' Matt had folded his arms, and Abigail abruptly felt the tiniest prick of guilt. *You're not really angry at him*. Well, no, she absolutely was, but it was partly because he was being an idiot, and partly because anger kept her focused, and if she didn't stay angry she'd still be curled up staring at the dust.

'Sorry,' she said. 'It's just . . .'

The bowed heads of the buildings. The bulbous growths on their sides where things had once tried to birth.

'I know,' Matt said. 'But, um . . .' He kicked at a cobblestone. 'You're right. Finding the Emissary is what's important.' He brightened. 'Do you think Greaves will knight us on the spot? I hear they do that sometimes, for Neophytes who do something crazy brave. Hey – is that . . .'

Abigail's eyes narrowed. 'Is that what?'

'Is that why you stayed behind? To go up against the Emissary?'

Bright and blue and guileless, Matt's eyes threw her own reflection back at her, and it wasn't someone she recognized at all.

'*Yeeesss*,' Abigail said. 'That's what I did.'

And just like that, she was a liar as well. Abigail never lied. Had it been Denizen or Simon in front of her, she would have just told them the truth automatically. *So why can't I tell him? You ran. You abandoned your comrades. You abandoned the Order and the crusade you're supposed to serve.* Tell *him. Why does it matter?*

Because it matters to me.

Not what Matt thought. He didn't seem to have any thoughts he didn't say out loud, and most of them seemed to be about himself. But she had been alone in that room with her panic and her dream, and she wasn't alone now. Now she had someone to let down, which meant she *couldn't* let him down.

Just like that, a kingdom.

'*Awesome*,' Matt said and, to Abigail's immense discomfort, punched her on the arm. 'That's totally what I was doing too. Let's find this thing and report back.'

'Right,' Abigail said. 'And Greaves will definitely knight you when you bring back strategic information about the Emissary.'

Matt grinned. 'Right?'

She turned away. 'In fact, he'll probably put you in charge of the strike team that'll take it down.'

Matt went pale. 'Don't be ridiculous.'

She got half an hour of silence out of that.

They crept through a city on the edge of unreality, the sky above it turning from opal to anthracite to the murk of a half-formed pearl. Nothing grew between the cobblestones but dust, as if even the weeds were afraid. She had to keep dragging her eyes from them to re-immerse herself in the dead stench of the Tenebrae – categorizing, dissecting, evaluating every nuance of its reek.

It was a matter of sensitivity. Not physical sensitivity – even before the Cost, Abigail's palms had been calloused from countless hours of training – but Tenebrous leaked through the very fabric that separated realities. Muscle and flesh were no barrier at all.

Abigail lost herself in that wrongness, navigating by it like a sailor would a storm. They split crossroads between them, checked doorways, followed the unease until it drowned out the pain in Abigail's feet, the hunger pangs in her stomach, dragging her forward until it was all she could feel.

A single inhalation from those massive stone lungs, and the wind ripped from the earth like a sheet from a bed, like skin curling from a wound.

Her feet torn from the ground, her parents' ashes in her mouth –

Abigail jerked back to herself so hard she nearly fell. For a moment, she'd been . . . she'd been . . . but no. Just another street, blurry in her exhausted eyes. How had they even got here?

She looked around to try and place herself. Matt was leaning against a wall, scrubbing his face with his hands as if trying to rub life back into it. Abigail couldn't blame him. She'd never fallen asleep on her feet before. The air was so bloated and *full* with the Tenebrae that Abigail, still swaying like a sail, almost thought that if she were to collapse it would buoy her up.

And it was then she felt it, like a current of algae-choked water moving marginally quicker than the congealed scum around it. Not better, not by any stretch, but newer . . .

The Emissary.

Her fingers were abruptly fists, curled so tight they hurt. Matt felt it a second after she did, or maybe he just felt her stiffening spine disturb the thick and choking air.

'Abigail?'

'*Quiet*,' she hissed, the fire of her heritage chasing adrenalin round her chest. *Where is it? Where is it?* Nothing that big should have been able to sneak up on them. They should have been able to hear it – the cannon crack of its footsteps, the bovine blast of its breath – but all around there was silence, mutant buildings and a growing wrongness in the air –

Abigail had to force herself to take another step forward. Then another.

This was a mistake. Why have you done this? What made you think you could?

Do you feel you're good enough –

She turned the corner, and froze.

The piazza was twenty metres across, and every centimetre of that space was covered in Tenebrous. Black liquid arced up from the stones like nervous systems, like ink drawings of trees, a whole forest of reaching tendrils and stiff, hooked fronds. A Cant leapt unbidden to Abigail's lips, but stopped as she realized not a single Tenebrous was moving – all as motionless as her.

White was threaded through the black like sickness, like a horrid reversal of the Cost. Arctic air tightened the skin on her face, and, though she'd never heard Tenebrous make a noise without a mouth to produce it, a soft moaning filled the air – like ice cubes popping in water.

Like children having bad dreams.

'Where do you think it came from?'

Abigail didn't even jump when Matt's voice sounded right beside her. The scene in front of her was too strange. The edges of the fronds were softly straining, curling like buds in frost, as if plaintively reaching for help. She edged closer, and saw that it was indeed frost that held them, but beneath the dusting of silver there was another whiteness – a rind of . . . of . . .

'Hey, where do you think it came from?'

And before she knew it she was running, footsteps ringing like church bells until it seemed she hung in the air for an eternity between each step. Matt yelped but, just before she could run into the thicket of paralysed Tenebrous, she cut right, circling them to see –

There – a splatter of white on a cobblestone. *There* – a drop crystallized on a fallen pillar. *There* and *there* and *there* . . .

Unlike Denizen and Simon, Abigail had grown up in Order garrisons. For her, there wasn't anything strange about swords on the walls, or bars on the windows, or first-aid kits everywhere. Above all, she had lived her life in the soft light of candlewards.

There was an order within the Order – the Gardeners – who spent years simply keeping the candlewards in Adumbral maintained, changing old for new, opening the cunningly wrought lanterns that shielded them from rain.

All that work was for nothing now. Candles had been stomped flat into flowers, great clusters kicked in sprays of white, plucked brutally from their perches to leave broken stumps behind.

Abigail took a shaky step forward, picking her way across plates of flattened wax. This street's candlewards hadn't just been doused – they'd been annihilated. There was such an awful *thoroughness* to it, she thought, staring into a ten-centimetre-deep hole in the stone at her feet, like a massive-calibre bullet scar.

She looked round, and – *yes*. On either side of her, there were cobblestones that were particularly cracked and crushed. *It had knelt*. Abigail did the same, shuffling back as if to try and ape its monstrous dimensions. *It had knelt here*. The effort it must have taken, to heave that bulk down by degrees, all to extend a finger and push that candle into the ground.

The effort of it. The hate.

It took her a long time to realize that Matt had approached her, his face a mixture of horror and awe.

'I don't understand. What happened here? How is there another Tenebrous inside the city?'

When you hunted something, you hunted all of it. You hunted its feet and its hands and its hair and its spoor to know what it might leave behind. You hunted its hungers and its fears and its desires to know where it might go. You hunted its strengths and its weaknesses to know where one ended and the other began.

Abigail didn't understand the frost and the cold, or what had trapped these Tenebrous here before they could pull together a body. But it had been able to Breach because the Emissary had destroyed the candlewards . . . and it wouldn't be the last.

'I know what the Emissary is doing.'

'You . . . what? How?'

'Look around you,' she whispered. 'Adumbral was invaded before. There were so many Knights here that it tore the fabric of reality. And Tenebrous bled through.'

'Until the . . . *oh*.'

Abigail's voice wasn't hushed because she was worried about being overheard but by the sheer enormity of what she was about to say. 'It's destroying the candlewards so that other Tenebrous can Breach. So Adumbral falls into the Tenebrae at last.'

'We need to get back to Daybreak,' Matt whispered. For the first time, Abigail completely agreed with him. 'Now.'

19

WE BURY OURSELVES

Denizen made lists of things because cataloguing provided perspective, and trying to decide exactly which frown he was using was a distraction from what had caused him pain in the first place. If it fitted an existing category, that meant he had survived it. If it didn't, well, Denizen could distract himself by creating a new one. The problem was, that only went so far.

Simon is angry with me.

The taller boy was walking ahead, and even that degree of separation was a turn of the blade. Denizen and Simon never separated. Not willingly, anyway – there had been Denizen's induction into the Order, but that had lasted three whole weeks before the universe copped on to itself and gave magical powers to Simon as well.

Simon dipped his head to say something to another Neophyte, and in Denizen's chest the knife turned to jagged ice. He'd tried losing himself in categorization of the pain, but all it did was lower his mood and crowd his head.

Their surroundings just accentuated his gloom. *The Asphodel Path* – the crypts of the Order: low-ceilinged tunnels lined with alcoves as tall as Vivian, spaced a few metres apart. On the floor in front of each alcove was a candle, white and thick. Some alcoves were empty, their candles unlit, and others were closed with simple doors of polished wood etched with a date and a name. In front of those, the candles were lit.

And, as everywhere else in Daybreak, there were mosaics of Knights – not at war as above, not marching triumphant as in poor cursed Retreat, but standing, hands clasped or at their sides. Their faces were unlined, the Cost discreet shadows at wrist or lapel. There was something strange about them. It took Denizen a while to figure it out.

They looked at peace.

'Place gives me the creeps,' came Grey's voice by his ear. Denizen jumped. The tunnels were wide enough for two Neophytes to walk abreast, but most walked alone, deep in thought, stepping nimbly to avoid the candles on the floor. It was one of the more esoteric skills you picked up in service to the Order.

Though they were deep beneath Daybreak, Denizen could feel the vibrations of the battle above every time he clenched his teeth. It wasn't that the vibrations had become worse, but they had moved from intermittent to a constant rattling roar. That was all the Tenebrous had to do really – keep coming, keep the pressure on until the Knights could do nothing but break.

And Simon was ahead, talking to someone else, and Stefan – *Stefan* – was tapping his iron knuckles against the wall as they passed with an irritating *clink clink*, and Denizen was so desperately grateful that *someone* wanted to talk to him he almost forgot just how guilty he felt about manipulating Grey.

Denizen had never seen anyone smile and look so angry at the same time.

Almost.

'Grey, I –'

'This is where they come, you know? In case you ever wondered. We do our best to recover bodies from the field. For the families. And to keep the big secret. Don't want any pathologists blunting their knives and writing an illuminating medical report. And some garrisons have their own graveyards –'

Fuller Jack took his breakfast in the garden. It would have brought a smile to Denizen's face, watching the huge blacksmith carefully position himself on the back step, if not for the tinny tremble of the saucer and the headstone he'd carved himself.

Show me something you can build from revenge that you can't from moving on.

Some things were easier said than done. Some things were only ever a work in progress.

'– some Knights want to come home.' The smile was a proper grimace now. 'We leave our homelands behind so often that this place becomes home instead. It's funny.

Live long enough with the Cost and soon there's just a kernel of life inside you. Like being behind the walls of a fortress.'

Denizen looked at him sharply, but Grey's gaze had slipped to the graves they passed and the names that marked them. It was like a dark mirror of the Croits' necropolis – that mad, proud city of the dead. The Croits shouted their history in a forgotten corner of the world. Here, the fallen of the Order were almost . . . shy.

'And still we manage sentimentality.'

'So they come here?'

'We bury ourselves,' Grey said. 'With the work we do. But the Order's kind enough to keep off the rain.' He raised a hand to not quite brush a door as they passed. Denizen had noticed that but for Stefan – *clink clink* – everyone else seemed determined to stay as far away from the walls as possible.

'And, with the last of our strength, we light a candle.' For just a moment, the grin twisting his features was genuine. 'Bringing light – our last act. *That* I like.'

'Grey,' Denizen said. 'Grey, I'm sorr–'

'Do you know what I tell Edifice?' Grey said. 'When he feels guilt for the things he has to do?'

'No,' Denizen said. He'd never imagined Greaves in that position.

'I tell him to make it count. If what you did was the right thing to do, then *make* it the right thing. It's easier to ask for forgiveness than permission, and it's a hell of a lot easier to ask for it after you've saved the world. We can . . . we can talk later.'

'OK,' Denizen said, and, though what Grey had said was nothing close to forgiveness, there was enough hope in the phrase *we can talk later* that some of the ice in his stomach melted.

'Also, I'm going to make you apologize to Munroe *personally* for making me knock her out and hide her in a cupboard,' Grey said. 'So I figure if you survive that we'll be square.'

'*Oh*,' Denizen said. '*Right*.' He swallowed. 'We're going to be in so much trouble, aren't we?'

'I was considering retirement anyway,' Grey said. 'And I'll radio Greaves when we're far enough away that it makes no difference. I just hope we're –'

'This is the right thing to do,' Denizen said. He had to say it out loud. He wanted to hear it. 'It's the *Endless King*. We find him and everything will be OK. How is . . . how is *she* holding up?'

It wasn't the question he wanted to ask, but Denizen had been doing his very best to convince people that his actions were for the greater good, and that noble sentiment would be extremely undermined if his next question was, *Why hasn't she come over to talk to me yet?*

Because we're being discreet. Because we're undercover. It made complete sense – Mercy staying away from Denizen had always been the safest thing to do. She just seemed to be a lot better at it than he was.

'The candlewards aren't helping, but she's surviving,' Grey said. 'But aren't we all? I'll keep an eye on her. You just concentrate on figuring out the next step.'

'What?' Denizen said, in a voice that *definitely* didn't crack with panic.

'This plan is yours and Mercy's, genius,' Grey said, with no little amusement. 'Getting out of Daybreak is only the beginning, isn't it?'

He grinned even wider at Denizen's stricken expression.

'You'd think you'd have learned from the last time you saved the world.'

'I know,' Denizen said gloomily. 'It just seems to upset people.'

'Stop.'

Vivian's voice rang out down the corridor, and the Neophytes halted. The Malleus was standing very still, face tilted to the ceiling, the radio forgotten in her hand. Grey left Denizen's side, slipping past and through Neophytes, and they fell into a whispered discussion.

Denizen understood her logic – she didn't want to panic anyone, or share information before surety – but he had also been dealing with her for more than a year now, and had become very good at reading lips.

Grey: *What's wrong?*

Vivian: *When did the vibrations stop?*

'Malleus?'

Stefan's tapping fingers had stilled on the mosaic beside him, all that earlier belligerence faded from his face. He looked very young.

There was a spot of black on his cheek.

It wasn't the Cost. Stefan had been very much in Denizen's face just a few minutes ago, and Denizen remembered his skin being clear. Vivian opened her mouth, but Stefan jerked his head minutely to stop her.

And abruptly the stain was larger, the corridor so quiet that Denizen could hear the drop hit Stefan, just a gentle tap of oil on skin.

And then the mosaics ate him alive.

Bright tiles flashed like a magician's cape, and Stefan was just *gone*, devoured by an iridescent flex of stone. There was a muffled detonation, like a door slamming on the other side of a house, and then a ripple ran through the walls from where Stefan had stood, like a great beast prowling just the other side of the tiles, or as if hidden machinery had just shivered into life.

Or the peristaltic spasm of a throat.

The radio squawked in Vivian's hand.

'*MULTIPLE BREACHES. TENEBROUS ON EVERY LEVEL. FALL BACK TO THE COURTYARD. THE GLIMPSE IS LOST. THE GLIMPSE IS LOST.*'

There was a Tenebrous in the wall. No, the Tenebrous *was* the wall. *Both walls.* Ceiling and floor, the entire chamber. Stefan was dead . . . and so were they.

All it had to do was squeeze, and it would crush them alive. Or flood the Path with whatever Tenebrous possessed instead of digestive juices. Or chew them up, or drown them in soil, or *maybe*, just maybe they'd manage to take it with them and simply die in a cave-in instead.

And, horribly, Denizen realized a part of him was delighted. Walls fell. Walls were meant to fall. And if these could, if Daybreak's could, then so could his.

That treacherous thrill.

At least you could go down in flames.

That tyrannical temptation –

'*Look.*'

Still cloaked in human guise, Mercy pointed at the floor. On either side, the mosaics groaned, tiles popping free as unseen oil seeped and shifted and re-formed, but the flagstones of the floor remained untouched.

The candlewards. They were protecting the floor, or discouraging the Tenebrous, or blinding its senses, or maybe Stefan had just been unlucky because he'd been under that drop. Denizen had no idea how Tenebrous wormed their way into materials, how they hunted or how they sensed the world around them.

But Mercy did.

Careful not to touch the walls, Mercy edged her way round stock-still bodies until she was at the front of the line, where Vivian had stood. The Malleus herself had her hammer raised, but was staring at Mercy instead of taking a swing that might have doomed them all.

Follow, Mercy mouthed with her borrowed lips, and they did.

Hesitantly, Mercy led them through the tunnel. A low moan that might have been confusion or shifting earth seeped from the walls, but Mercy's progress was steady and, one by one, they followed her. Denizen focused on stepping exactly where the Neophyte in front of him had, not for the first time wondering at the mind crackling electric in Mercy's skull.

If the candles beneath them were candlewards then they had to hurt or diminish her as much as they did the tunnel worm. But, more than that, she had to be scared, as scared as they were, because for so long her lineage should have been a passport, a guarantee, and now it wasn't.

Maybe it never had been. It hadn't protected her from the Three, after all. Tenebrous fought each other as much as they did the Order, and being of a shared species was no guarantee of safety in any world. Either way, her steps were deliberate, and considered, and unafraid.

Or maybe she just pretended they were, because that was what a leader did in this, a time of war.

The walk lasted an eternity, each pulse-pounding second written in sweat on Denizen's brow. Tiles popped from the walls, and Denizen put it down to coincidence that each falling shard left a painted Knight frowning, or snarling, or screaming through missing jaws.

He flinched as a particularly violent tremor made a whole mosaic face slide free, the stone behind suddenly splitting to reveal an eye, bright and white and glistening blind.

Denizen froze as a shard of glass pushed its way through the jelly of the eye, fumbled by the soft white into a pupil, vertical and green.

It blinked, and narrowed.

'RUN!' Denizen screamed, and sent a seething pulse of fire into the eye with his very next breath. The crater grew teeth and howled.

And then they were running, and flames were flashing, and ahead the walls tried to close and swallow, but flinched back when an arrow whickered past Denizen's ear and punched into the tiled body of a long-dead Knight.

Black was beading between the tiles, popping them free in volleys as hard as bullets, sharp as knives. Fins and growths of earth lurched blindly outwards, only to be lopped off or scorched away. The inside of the beast was suddenly oven-hot, but whether that was from so many Neophytes or the beast itself Denizen couldn't tell.

Something *spanged* off Falter in its sheath. Heat was running down Denizen's cheek, but a far greater blaze was climbing his skull from the inside, trying to force his body to turn back and *FIGHT*. The tunnel worm yawled around them, and Denizen felt a horrible and absurd symmetry between them, two creatures being torn apart from the inside by flame.

And then his hands clanged against something else – something cold, something unmoving and real. *A ladder.* He clung to it, gasping, but the chill through his skin just wasn't enough to douse the inferno beneath it.

Walls shattered in Denizen's head, melting in a heartbeat, ice turning to mist, to steam. The fire was suddenly inside his fortifications, or had crept in a long time ago, or had never left. He didn't register the Neophytes running by him, ignored the jostles and bangs as they scrambled up the ladder. Let them run. *Let them flee.*

JUST LET ME –

And Vivian's hand caught him in the throat, just the right side of pain. The two Hardwicks stared at each other, and maybe the fire recognized the woman who had taught Denizen to control it . . . or maybe it just did what everyone always did when Vivian Hardwick glared – it guttered and shrank.

'Nothing fancy,' Vivian hissed, and, grabbing his shoulders, aimed him back down the tunnel like a flame-thrower.

Got it, Denizen wanted to say, but didn't dare open his mouth until the last possible moment. It felt so automatic now. Molten light lunged from the pit of his stomach, and the Cants dived down to give it shape.

With long practice, with cold iron hands gripping his throat and shoulder, with a Croit's focus and a Hardwick's rage, but more than anything with *permission*, the castle in Denizen's head shifted and remade itself.

A channel. A cannon.

A tide of eyes and tiles and stone teeth roared towards them, and Denizen Hardwick roared volcanic in return.

After that, everything was a little bit blurry. His feet left the ground, first from recoil, and then from Vivian throwing him over her shoulder. He didn't even have the energy to be embarrassed. That all went towards rebuilding the melted fortress in his head.

And then there was sunlight on his face instead of trying to explode out of it, and it was very, very welcome. Denizen would have liked the ground to be at least fifteen degrees colder, but beggars couldn't be choosers, and at least now it wasn't trying to grow teeth and digest him.

Each blink sent plasma arcing through the back of his skull. Every time he unleashed his power, it became harder to hold back. How difficult would it be the next time?

'Denizen?'

He looked up. It had somehow become nearly morning; dawn flaring over the jagged skyscape. They were in the city. They'd made it out of Daybreak. One tower in particular loomed over him, until it somehow grew a hand and reached down.

Denizen's words, scared into hiding by the unearthly language that had just pounded through his skull, were only just coming back, and this was far too important to mess up. So instead he just took Simon's hand when it was held out to him, and squeezed it as if he could convey everything through that.

'Are you all right?'

'Yes,' Denizen said, and yelped as Simon pulled him upright. 'Sorry. Are you –'

'I'm fine,' Simon said. 'We all are. Except . . . Stefan.'

Denizen's entire body was an ache at the moment, but there was still room to feel another pang. He hadn't known

Stefan. Their confrontation earlier had told Denizen precisely nothing about the boy, and now he'd never know anything at all.

The others had clustered in the shade of a huge arch. Grey was moving between them, checking for wounds, whispering soft words, and only left when he got a smile or a nod in return. Denizen couldn't help but notice that, even after he had left, some of them still watched him, rubbing their arms where he had briefly laid his hand.

The entrance to the catacombs was hidden under a manhole cover, and Vivian lingered by it as if debating fusing it shut. Denizen approached, a trifle shakily, and she gave him the closest she ever got to a smile, just a small quirk of the lips.

Denizen returned it. They did actually make a pretty good team, even if . . .

Vivian's smile vanished.

Oh no.

Slowly, achingly, Denizen turned round.

Mercy was chatting to one of the Neophytes, her expression the perfect mix of bone-tired and elated at her own survival. She wound a bandage round her bad arm, and Denizen knew that she'd be proud of how tiny spots of red soaked through it when she was done.

That level of realism had probably taken a lot of concentration, which explained why Mercy hadn't noticed the Neophyte's horrified expression, or the fact that at some point a tile must have punched through the top of Mercy's skull like a spoon removing the top of an egg.

Lazy curls of white light escaped into the breeze like the pennant of a knight.

Gaze after gaze fell upon her, until finally Mercy looked up.

'What?'

20

AS ABOVE, SO BELOW

Dawn melted over Adumbral like spoiling butter, the day oozing across the sky.

They'd taken refuge in what had been a guardhouse, once-thick walls eroded eggshell-thin by the elements and time. They didn't plan on staying long. Vivian had made that clear as she placed sentries, with weapons drawn, at the windows and on Mercy. Denizen, she had bid stay put with a glare before disappearing upstairs with Grey.

The dismissal should have stung. Six months ago, Denizen would have indulged in a long and complicated inner monologue about how cold a mother had to be to prioritize someone else over her son.

Now it just made sense. She had to be sure of the Knights under her command, and Grey had a . . . history of his actions not being reliable. There was a big difference between Grey freeing Mercy because he thought it was the right thing to do, and Grey freeing Mercy because she had made him.

Deciding whether Denizen could be trusted could wait, because he'd made it fairly clear that he couldn't.

He sighed. Humans could feel when they were being watched – a prehistoric by-product from when noticing the weight of a gaze might be all that saved your life – but Denizen was learning that there was an equal and opposite chill when nobody would look at you at all.

They're just being careful, Denizen told himself. And it might have been true. When Vivian Hardwick told you to watch the approaches, you watched the approaches. *I mean, what kind of soldier would intentionally put their comrades in danger?* But theirs was a careful awareness. You needed to know where something was so you could not look at it.

Even Simon had it, and that hurt most of all.

The only person who was looking at him was Mercy. Denizen was doing his best not to look at her in case it made it seem as if they were secretly plotting, which felt a bit like closing the stable door after the horse had turned into a Tenebrous and eaten everyone's family. But she was back in her true form now, and he could tell by the swirling dance of her shadow on the wall that she was facing him.

He wondered what she thought of all this. He wondered whether she was afraid.

How could you not be? Denizen had spent a lifetime trying to understand people, but he would have needed a dozen more to understand Tenebrous. At least humans were all working with the same facial expressions, the same body language – every Tenebrous was unique.

Even Mercy, the nearest to human he'd ever met, displayed inconsistencies and gaps that couldn't help but remind Denizen of just how alien she was. It was why he'd been absurdly glad she'd shed his friends' features. People weren't . . . props. You couldn't simply take their skin and smiles to play the part you wanted.

But, with the little experience he had, Denizen was realizing that Tenebrous were far more frightening when they had emotions and actions he could *almost* understand. He'd seen it in the Redemptress. God help him, he'd seen it in the Three's unreasoning hatred, because he'd come close to it himself.

And he'd seen it in the thing beyond the Glimpse. It hadn't come for him. It hadn't come for the Order. Leading an army against the most secure location in the material universe was just a *by-product*.

It had come for *her* –

'Denizen?'

Grey was coming down the stairs. He didn't say anything more. He didn't look at him as he passed either but that was OK. Denizen was sort of getting used to it.

The room at the top of the stairs must have been an armoury, its walls set with tall metal racks, the weapons long since gone. Sunlight slipped through the arrow-slits in sharp quarrels of gold.

Denizen's mother had pulled up her shirtsleeves to reveal the muscled iron of her forearms, the black scratched white in dozens of places. She was fingering one of those dents now, her face turned away, and Denizen absently wondered if she even felt the cuts any more, or had the distancing Cost rendered pain an abstract, just something to ignore?

'Let me guess,' he said, with an awkward smile, 'you're not angry, you're just disappointed.'

His smile disappeared as she looked at him. There weren't tears. Vivian had cried exactly once in front of him. She didn't even look angry, or as close to not angry as Vivian ever got. Instead, her shoulders were slumped, fingers curled against the haft of her hammer like a walking stick or cane.

What arose in Denizen then was cousin to the dread that had assaulted him when Tenebrous had set foot in Daybreak, or when it had rained black from a cloudless sky. A sense that the world was not the way it should be.

Vivian looked defeated.

'Yes,' she said simply. 'I am. I thought we'd come further than this.'

'I had to save her,' Denizen said. 'You *know* that Greaves would have handed her back when things got desperate, and the Usurper would have just taken her and laughed and killed us all anyway. It was the right thing to do. It wasn't because of . . . *feelings*.'

On the last word, his voice splintered, not due to fear of Vivian, but fear that he had done this to her, that he had broken something he couldn't fix, and from now on she would always look at him with that empty, pained exhaustion.

'We don't know what Greaves would have done,' Vivian said quietly. 'You don't, and I don't. We don't know what help Mercy could have been to Daybreak, and removing her will have consequences that neither of us right now can fully see. And you bullied Grey into helping you. That will have consequences too. You will have to be ready for them.'

'*Bullied?*' Denizen said in a strangled tone. That wasn't what he had done. That wasn't a word he wanted anywhere near him. He'd just . . .

'He's not even angry, Denizen. He just doesn't want to let anyone down any more.' She shook her head. 'As if it's a choice.' When she met his gaze again, there was that old Vivian anger . . . but muted, as if she didn't think it would do any good. It terrified him, that look. Other people gave up. Not her. Not his mum.

'But that's not what I'm talking about either.' She sighed. 'Why didn't you come to me?'

Denizen's eyes widened.

'I *understand*, Denizen.' Her lip twitched. 'Not your loyalty to that *thing*, but . . . I have been reading a lot. About emotions. It has not . . . previously been a field of study for me. And I understand that you're used to relying on yourself. You had to, when I left you behind.'

Her voice did not crack when she said the words, and Denizen knew she was right. For a long time, mistrust hadn't been a habit, it had been a survival mechanism.

'We learn patterns of behaviour to serve us in wartime, and then, when peacetime comes, they are nigh-impossible to unlearn. We rely on ourselves at the cost of those who rely on us.'

'But this is wartime,' Denizen said in a helpless, hollow voice.

'Yes,' she said. 'And we need all the help we can get.'

They stood there for a long moment.

'I'm sorry,' Denizen said. 'I'll try harder. I will.'

'Thank you. Now we need to –'

'Would you have helped me?' Denizen asked suddenly. 'If I had come to you, instead of sneaking around behind your back?'

'I don't know,' Vivian said. 'But that was my choice to make. And you made it for me. Now we have to make the best of it.'

'What do you mean?'

'The mission hasn't changed,' Vivian said grimly. 'We have to get beyond Adumbral before Daybreak falls. The Order need to be rallied.'

'What about the Endless King?' Denizen said. 'Mercy said –'

'Yes,' Vivian said. 'It's been saying a lot of things. None of it specific. None of it useful. I don't trust it, Denizen.' She sighed. 'But I trust you. And if you think there's something to what it's saying . . . I will hear it out.'

And there it was, treacherous and tiny. A spark of hope.

'You mean . . .'

'There are other Knights who can lead the counter-attack.' She bared her teeth. 'I was never much of a team player anyway.'

The fierce pride Denizen felt then was all too brief, as Grey shouted from downstairs. Vivian sprinted, Denizen not far behind, and they found the others clustered round the north-facing windows, straining against each other to see out.

Mercy stood at a window on her own and – now that the damage was done – Denizen went and stood beside her, Neophyte and princess, to stare out at where a lighthouse stood ablaze.

Smoke cracked the robin's-egg blue of the sky, light booming and flashing through the rents in Daybreak's sides. Vivian flicked through the channels on her radio, but all that came forth were growls of static and something that could have been the crackling of flame.

'We need to . . . We need to . . .'

Grey was stammering, but the end of his sentence wouldn't come. How could it? A hundred Knights was more firepower than Denizen could even imagine. What could a few children add to that?

And then, just as it had with the Emissary, the Tenebrae gathered and deepened and *pushed*. The side of Daybreak bulged like a blister after a burn. Stone shrieked as *something* burst free, wreathed in smoke and the crashing fall of masonry, and Denizen realized that it wasn't an explosion at all.

It was a hatching.

Denizen lived and breathed fantasy books. Their tropes had been the furniture of his childhood, and it had been a source of great frustration that joining the Knights had proved so many of them false. Magic wasn't magical, swords had no names, heroes were just people, and monsters could be kind-hearted girls with the blood of their own people sizzling on their cheek.

And what wormed its way out of Daybreak's puckered wound was not a dragon. It couldn't be. Dragons were supposed to be graceful, and majestic, and beautiful, in a strange way, so clever and bewitching that you were warned about their voice rather than their flame.

The king lizards of fantasy, dominating every book from here to Crosscaper.

But Tenebrous got bodies wrong, and this creature was no different. Its tail whipped in cramped, hinged angles, like a cheap toy, every bit of its sixteen-metre form laced with strange, stunted barbs. Its wings were pitted panels of stained glass – literally stained – cracked and shoddy, wet with mildew that Denizen could smell from here and . . .

It was the Tenebrous from the Glimpse, the one that had tried to push its way through, the beautiful iron boy rising from a matted knot of bodies. But that had only been a fraction of the beast, sent through to . . . to mock them.

Now they were seeing it in full.

The dragon was made of bodies. Iron bodies. *Knightly* bodies, all braided together, melted like taffy into a sinuous, feline shape. The spurs protruding from it were arms, or legs, or heads, bristling out as if trying to escape.

No wonder one of its minions had gone straight for the Asphodel Path.

They were . . . they were collecting.

That's not what I'm going to use your bones for.

The thing began to chuckle, low and deep and black, and Denizen, who had once obsessed over how fantasy authors designed their dragons – four-legged, bat-like, snouts smooth or crocodilian – found himself baring his own teeth in disgust because its head opened outwards like a flower, like a lamprey, like a hand.

It couldn't even get the *voice* right.

'Edifice,' Grey whispered in the terrible silence, and he was halfway to the door before Vivian's voice rang out.

'What. Are. You. Going. To. Do?'

He didn't turn. She had to physically grab him to stop him. For a second, Denizen thought Grey was going to strike her. His chest was heaving, his blades half out of their sheaths . . . but Vivian made no move to guard herself. She just stared him down instead.

'He gave you an order, Graham,' she whispered. 'And he can't do his job if we don't do ours. Now, are you going to disobey him or not?'

Grey shrugged her off, slamming both his blades back into their sheaths. Tension hummed between them, the temperature rising as two caged suns fought for dominance. Eventually, he shook his head.

'It's easy for you, isn't it? To put duty down and then pick it up again? Like it's a goddamn sword.'

Vivian didn't reply. Instead, she turned to the gathered Neophytes.

'Nothing has changed.'

Behind them, the Usurper still circled, riding the thermals of Daybreak's death. Its chuckle was wet and obscene.

Meeeeerrccccyyyy.

21

TRAJECTORY

'So . . . how are you?'

Candlewards winked from the basilica's ceiling like the eyes of a thousand roosting bats. Once, Abigail had imagined them as an army at her back. Now all they did was remind her of fallen soldiers.

And the more soldiers that fall, the more that are likely to.

Her mother had taught her that you fought when you had to. You didn't waste skin or blood, not just because Knightly blood was precious but because an army survived on morale and the more you lost, the more you were likely to lose.

How many candlewards would it take? Was there a tipping point? It wasn't like the Order had ever experimented. You generally didn't take chances when it came to bits of the world falling *out* of the world. Abigail didn't even know what that would look like. Would the shadows spread like an oil slick, polluting everything they touched? Would the whole country begin to sink like storied Atlantis? Or would the sun simply go down one day and never rise again?

It was a moment before she realized Matt had spoken. 'What?'

He shrugged. 'How . . . how are you? Finding everything, I mean. You know. Before all this happened. Being a Neophyte and . . . stuff.'

She frowned. The wan candlelight had got tangled in his long blond hair, pouring shadows into the hollows of his cheeks. For a second, his face didn't look capable of the arrogant sneer it had worn since the moment they'd met.

Wrong-footed, Abigail didn't respond immediately. It wasn't something she had often considered. She was in the place she was supposed to be. Not this sepulchre of marble and dust, but *here*, first in Seraphim Row and then in Daybreak. Losing focus was what stopped you running that last two hundred metres, doing that last stomach crunch or sit-up.

'It's where I'm meant to be.'

Matt nodded. 'Yeah. Must be pretty par for the course. You are a Falx, after all.'

'Oh, now you remember my name,' Abigail said, with a half-hearted grin.

'Well . . . I read up on people before I got here.' Matt looked down at his hands. 'Falxes. Been Knights pretty much since . . . what, the tenth century?'

'How did you . . .'

'And then Ed's family . . . even longer? If that's possible. Same with Stefan, Patricio, Ulver . . . Your family trees must look like nervous systems. I don't . . . I don't know how you all keep track.'

He still hadn't looked at her.

'Man, you should see our garrison. The Fourth Vault of Edinburgh – all oak and polished stone. You hear 'underground' and you think it'll be cold and damp, but every bit of the place is covered in rugs and cushions and tapestries. And on one wall we have this board. Every Knight's lineage from the first moment their first ancestor Dawned. It's . . . it's really something.'

'Yes,' said Abigail.

She should have said more – this was one of those moments. It wasn't that Abigail was bad with people, it was just that they were complicated and she . . . wasn't. It was energy conservation – *don't sweat the small stuff*. It was a nice contrast to Denizen, who was extremely sweaty about small stuff, and Simon, who had arrived at her philosophy from the opposite direction.

She didn't panic about little things because of what might happen, and Simon didn't panic because of what already had.

Say something. Pick something safe.

'What about your fa–'

'We should get going,' Matt said, suddenly slipping on his shoe and standing. 'Daybreak isn't far, right?'

'No,' Abigail said, mystified by his sudden change of topic. So far, the one thing she knew about Matt for certain was that his favourite subject was himself.

Daybreak stood out against the skyline, no matter where you were in Adumbral. Finding it had been easy – it was reaching it that had proved exhausting. They'd stopped here to get their breath back, nominally because good soldiers paced themselves, but also because they'd soon have to appear before Greaves, and he'd probably take them a lot more seriously if they weren't gasping for breath.

Of course he'll take you seriously. You're delivering valuable tactical information. He knows you.

And another voice, weary with spite.

But does he know you abandoned your comrades? How are you going to explain that?

And it wasn't even Greaves she was worried about. She'd been debriefed by her Malleus more times than she could count, and not once had there been a hint of disappointment in Vivian's eyes.

How do I tell her?

There Daybreak swelled, the triumphant spire briefly quelling her doubt, even though . . .

'Is that smoke?' said Matt. Thin trails of black and grey slunk from arrow-slits, creasing the sky.

'It looks like –'

The end of his sentence was swallowed by a groan so earth-shatteringly loud it rattled her organs, arriving nausea-deep in the pit of her stomach, and then the ground *heaved* and suddenly she was on her back.

When had that happened? She was on her back and there were rocks in the sky. Abigail stared at them, utterly confused. Dust-trailed, slow as clouds, they tumbled –

Some had windows in them. They began to fall.

The first boulder obliterated a shopfront six metres from Abigail's supine form, showering her in grit and dust. *No.*

Not obliterated – *replaced.* That was how big they were. The shard rocked a little as it settled, as unsteady as Abigail climbing to her feet, and she tore her gaze away from it to stare at Daybreak – cross-sectioned like a shattered skull, vaults exposed, staircases truncated like severed veins.

It was horrifying. It dragged awe from her like vomit. It was . . . it was an *insult.* Daybreak *was* the Order. In a world that didn't know they existed, it was the one place a sect of wanderers could call home.

A huge piece of the castle still spun upwards like a comet in reverse, as if it were desperately trying to escape what was happening beneath it.

Abigail thought in trajectories. That was how she'd been trained. A bowstring had been drawn back eleven hundred years ago by the first Falx to come here, and she was the point of the arrow they had loosed.

But everything that went up came down. Gravity was always waiting. *Sometimes there is nothing you can do.* And now gravity pulled meteors down on her, trailing tapestries like feathers from a murdered bird.

Larger, and larger, and –

Something hit her from the side, and Abigail was almost delighted as her brain registered something she could hurt. She got in a couple of good punches before the debris impacted in a spray of cobbles that would have torn her to pieces had she not been flattened first.

There was an arm across her waist. She stared at it uncomprehendingly for a long moment before its owner pulled away.

'You saved me,' she said.

'I did,' Matt responded, seemingly as surprised as her. 'I really did.'

Dust rained down, painting them Pompeii-grey. Matt took her hand, or maybe she took his, and they dragged each other into cover, as from the massive wound in Daybreak's flank came a noise, clear and cold and radioactive with glee.

MEEEERRCCCYY . . .

The Neophytes cowered as its shadow crossed them, and *now* Abigail sweated, clammy and cold, as a single violent wing-beat flung them on their backs. It didn't see them, even as its passage washed filthy air over them, even as they were both suddenly drenched in cascades of brittle threads, like blackened straw.

She shuddered as they dissolved on her skin. They looked like . . .

Eyelashes.

MEEEERRCCCYY . . .

'Please. Please. Please.'

Abigail didn't know which of them was whispering, or how long they lay there, almost praying for another rock to come down. Dead and buried in one fell swoop, hidden from the horror in the sky.

Abigail could see the Neophytes' Solar – a honeycomb of cells exposed to the air. The Breaching monstrosity had squirmed through the castle like a larva, chewing its way free, and, lying there, all Abigail could feel as its umbra receded was embarrassment, as if she'd accidentally walked in on someone in the shower. Castles were taken. They changed hands.

They weren't torn apart.

'We've got survivors! Survivors, here!'

The voice was so gloriously, mundanely *human* that Abigail could have wept. She clung to it like a lifeline before hands found hers and pulled her up. And then she saw the Knight's face, and that fleeting reassurance disappeared.

Bruises were storm-clouds round her eye socket, a laceration red and weeping on her cheek. There wasn't a piece of skin without soot or dust or blood in varying states of dryness, but none of her wounds shook her so deeply as the tears staining her cheek.

'What . . . what is *happening*?'

Her voice was small, scratchy with confusion and dust. The Knight spoke, but not to her.

'Get them to the Palatine. Now.'

It had been a chapel, though to which god or goddess Abigail couldn't say. The Palatine, surrounded by Knights, did not look up as she and Matt were marched in.

Greaves was a blur, giving orders in a ceaseless murmur, the Knights peeling off almost before the words left his mouth. Others were being bandaged, or sorting through weapons, or spreading maps out on the floor.

Something had cracked Edifice Greaves's left arm off at the elbow, leaving behind a splintered stump of black and scarred white. He paid it no mind at all.

'Sir?'

A Malleus with a shock of white hair cascading across her dark scalp turned to acknowledge their escort. Normally, a look of disapproval from a Malleus would have made Abigail jump to attention, but she was so very tired, and instead just stared through eyes grainy from exhaustion and dust.

'Not now, Middlehurst. We –'

'I found two survivors. Two Neophytes.'

Abigail hadn't thought Greaves knew they were there, but the circle suddenly flexed apart as he stepped through. Muscle memory dragged her to attention, even as Matt gave a weary, lopsided salute.

'Palatine, I have to report –'

'Vivian,' Greaves snapped. 'Did she get out? Why did you split up? Is Mercy still –'

'We weren't with Vivian,' Abigail interrupted. 'We . . .'

Coiled coming apart against the wall.

Do you feel you're good enough –

'We were separated,' she said. 'Is . . . is Vivian not here?'

Her Malleus. Her Malleus was gone, and Abigail was not with her.

Frustration twisted Greaves's face. 'No, Abigail Falx, she is not.' His gaze flicked to Middlehurst. 'Arm them.'

He bent to scribble something on a note held out to him and the circle closed as if the Neophytes didn't exist. Middlehurst placed hands on their shoulders, but Abigail twisted free.

'Greaves! You need to listen – the Emissary is destroying candlewards. He's trying to let the whole Tenebrae in. You have to listen –'

Greaves just shook his head.

'The Emissary hasn't been seen since it Breached. *Daybreak has fallen*. We're tested on a dozen different –' He caught himself, suddenly aware of all the eyes on them both, and nodded at Middlehurst.

'Get them out of here.'

'What's *more important* than the candlewards? If they – Palatine!'

But the circle had already closed.

22

PREY ANIMALS

Its name was Dragon.

Wing-beats like thunderclaps, each impact of iron on air deafeningly, ear-poppingly loud. Dust wheezed down streets, stinging eyes and scraping throats, before being rasped back up as if determined to hurt twice – breath from an infected, struggling lung.

Just Dragon. That was all.

It rattled its talons against rooftops as it flew, and Denizen, creeping from doorway to doorway, couldn't help but picture the damage that must be doing to the bodies it had stolen for its claws – just one more insult to throw in their faces.

Dragon. A monstrous name for a monstrous thing.

I can *smell* you, Mercy. Just a trace, beneath the stink of candlewax.

Its snarl burrowed right into Denizen's bones. Vivian led them in a trembling procession, flinching back into cover every time its shape darkened the sky. Addled with terror and the Tenebrae, to Denizen it began to feel like *they* were following *it* – waiting for that serpent's shadow to pass over their heads so they could scuttle behind . . . until it banked round again, and they hid like mice in the shadow of a tiger.

You're here, aren't you? You couldn't bear to leave them. You've bound your banner to theirs. *Pathetic.* You and your hope, the Emissary and his vengeance . . .

Yes, there was another Tenebrous somewhere in the city, wasn't there? Denizen had forgotten. There was the Emissary, and Greaves, and Abigail and Darcie – *they got out, they had to get out, they've been two steps ahead of everyone since the day we met* – but right now Denizen's entire consciousness was reduced to the clenched fist Vivian held high.

How *un-regal.*

Any minute, Dragon would blast across them like a whip between the shoulder-blades, and that fist would jerk forward – giving the order to desperately sprint to the next scrap of cover.

Why bother, little girl? Is humanity that hard a habit to break?

It had broken free of Daybreak an hour ago, circling, *mocking*; sometimes just calling Mercy's name as if it expected her to rush out and face it. Denizen had never thought there were so many ways to say the same word. An insult, a promise, a vindictive, desperate plea –

***Meeeeerrrcccccyyy.* Do you . . . do you even have a choice?**

There was no way to get used to a Tenebrous's voice. Whenever you thought you had a handle on it, it squirmed out and away, evolving like a virus to attack you twice as strongly. Denizen had thought he was *almost* immune to its viciousness, and now it suddenly sounded . . . sad.

Did either of us?

Twenty-odd teenagers flattened against the wall of a collapsed granary, trying to make themselves as small as they possibly could. Grey and Vivian were ahead, Simon behind, and the rest were just sensory data to Denizen, obstacles he had to traverse or avoid. Scurrying like rats towards the Aurelian Gate, and it said something as to how frightened Denizen was that he couldn't even feel relieved that Mercy was no longer everyone's concern.

Oh, she was still there – flitting along beside them like a dream unknit by sunlight – but it would take either bravery or insanity to breathe a question now. Denizen had ended up huddled beside two of Stefan's friends earlier, and though tears still streamed freely from their eyes their faces were blank and resolute.

The monster skirled overhead, and Vivian's fist flung them forward, panting and heaving into the shadow of a shopfront. Denizen was really gaining an education as to how many teenagers you could comfortably fit in a small space, and he dug his feet in to avoid being popped out by the elbows mutinously climbing his spine.

JUST *FACE* ME!

The words became a shriek, then a dive, and then a detonation that banged Denizen's heart against the roof of his mouth. The knot of Neophytes became a single organism – wretched, fighting itself – and then they spilled into the darkness of an abandoned shop.

Landing on people who had gone through Order training was only marginally less painful than landing on stone, which, coincidentally, was also what Denizen had landed on. *A building*, he thought with dreamy horror, *it dived down on a building*. Not the one they were in, but, like a cockroach paralysed by the kitchen light, Denizen realized that the illusion of safety that had been keeping him sane was exactly that.

'*Get up*,' Vivian hissed. She was lifting great stringy clumps of dust from the floor and roughly smearing it over the Neophytes' faces. *Camouflage*. Or an excuse to gently slap sense into them – and it was working, teenagers dully lining up to follow her once more.

With slow, deliberate strokes, Hagen brushed grey dust over his dark skin, his eyes burning from a nest of scars. Denizen met them once, and then looked away fast.

Worry about the other Neophytes later. Try and keep the friends you have.

As if on cue, Grey appeared in the doorway, engaging Vivian in hurried whispers. Denizen moved towards them, but he'd barely taken a step before she raised her fist and they all went rigid and then –

I GROW BORED, MERCY.

Its voice was devolving, rendered into a roar by the stress of passing through that composite throat. Denizen's shoulders prickled as Dragon droned overhead, and then Vivian lifted her fist and flung the Neophytes out into danger again.

All except Denizen.

There was still the constant pressure of the Cants in his head, offering all sorts of pyrotechnic solutions to the problems he was facing, plus all the myriad worries about his friends and his future and his family, any one of which would have been a perfect reason for a bit of anxious paralysis . . . but that wasn't it either.

It was because he heard sobbing.

It was a quiet hitching sound – the tears of someone who didn't want to be heard. They were also hauntingly familiar.

Crosscaper. That kind of crying had been the soundtrack to Denizen's childhood, and he was climbing the staircase at the back of the shop before he knew what he was doing. In Crosscaper, that kind of crying came with a choice: respect the person's privacy or reach out.

Denizen had never been a reaching-out kind of person. Or a person who needed to be reached – he had Simon and books, and that had always been enough. In Crosscaper, he would have just let the sound die away or someone else would deal with it, and he *knew* that Dragon was circling round again, but . . . he'd cried like that before too.

The third floor of the building was a hollow square latticed by sunlight and swirling dust. Candlewards winked in clusters from the corners. One wall had fallen away, gaping wide enough for Denizen to freeze at the thought of being seen from the air.

And Simon stood in the middle of the floor, the breeze pushing his hair back from his face.

Denizen made a start towards him. '*What are you* –'

Simon slashed a hand through the air, and Denizen froze. Not because there was so much of Abigail in his curt gesture, but because he was now close enough to see that it hadn't been Simon sobbing at all.

A Neophyte sat on the lip of the third floor, legs dangling over the side, eyes fixed on Daybreak and the smoke-gauzed tear in its side. Their tactical poncho did nothing to bulk out his form, short-cut hair rippling in the breeze.

He didn't look at Denizen as he approached, but his eyes were so wide they probably didn't have to. Those huge staring orbs could have drunk in the whole city.

'Ed,' Simon said, fourteen years of calm pressed into a single syllable. 'We need to go.'

'I just want to see it one last time.' Ed's voice was nearly swallowed by the wind and the drop, and every molecule of Denizen trembled, waiting for the wing-beat that would drown them out. How long had it been? Was Dragon even now gliding above them, owl-silent with hearing sharp?

'I've been waiting my whole life to come here. My parents never brought me; they said . . . they said it was . . .'

The boy hacked out a laugh. 'They said they didn't want me exposed to the Tenebrae too soon.'

'*Ed*,' Denizen hissed, and flinched as pink fingers turned to white on the ledge's stone lip. Denizen had forgotten hands did that. *Does he have any Cost at all?*

'You *can* see it. It's right there.'

'It's *not*,' Ed snapped raggedly. 'Not the way it's supposed to be.' Tears streamed freely down his face. 'It was supposed to stand forever. That was . . . that was our *job*. And now it's falling and, and that *thing* is laughing at us.'

Just one. That was all it would take. The drag as those huge wings lifted would likely pluck Denizen, Simon and Ed out like dandelion seeds, spinning in the Tenebrous's wake. It mightn't even notice.

'This is how we lose,' the Neophyte said. 'After so long, this is how we lose.'

'*Ed, please get away from the edge*,' Denizen and Simon said together, and finally Ed turned to look at them with a glare that would not have shamed Vivian, or Greaves, or Uriel Croit, last son of a family with fifteen centuries of spoiling for a fight.

'I'm not going to *jump*. I'm a de Montfort. I'll do what I have to do. I'll fight. I'll fight Dragon itself if I have to. I just . . . I just wish it meant something.'

Simon's face was grey. 'What do you mean?'

Ed just shook his head. 'Neither of you went through, did you? Neither of you saw what's on the other side.'

The Glimpse. Ed had gone through. What had he seen? And how did it frighten him more than the nightmare circling above?

I'd be interested to see how you describe it.

Dust motes spun lazily, and with a sigh Mercy folded herself out of the air between Ed and the long drop. Ed's eyes widened, but, before he could pull back or react, the Tenebrous simply held out a hand and some bone-deep autopilot made Ed clasp it in his. A shiver ran through him at the contact, and Mercy gave his hand a single, deliberate shake.

I've never done that before, she said, her voice like frost crunching underfoot, her glittering form blurring Daybreak until it could have passed for whole. **Nice to meet you.**

'We need to *leave*,' Simon snapped, and Denizen had been so concerned with his friend being angry at him that he hadn't given any thought as to how angry Simon might be with Mercy. 'We don't have time for –'

Ed's mouth still hung open as if he wanted to speak but had forgotten how, and for a ridiculous second Denizen was both jealous and massively embarrassed.

Is that what I look like when she's talking to me?

I only wanted to tell you this. You do not see the best of our realm, Mercy said, displaying among her many talents an incredible grasp of understatement. **Before our sun was stolen, the Tenebrae was less a dark ocean than a . . . mosaic, many-coloured . . . bodies and minds in constant motion, free to be whatever the moment and the multiverse told us to be.**

There was a quaver in Ed's voice that had nothing to do with fear.

'R-really?'

Mercy giggled, a sound as incongruous as birdsong in a war zone.

Oh yes. Infinite worlds, infinite possibilities. An *omniverse*, repeating away forever. My father used to tell me

stories about them – some crowded, rowdy things, others intricate, delicate machines, and some just empty . . . just waiting.

Think of that potential. Think of all those gardens waiting to grow.

'Your father told you stories?'

I think all fathers do.

'My father used to tell me that every monster had a bit of good inside them.' Ed's voice was a whisper. 'And when we sent them back to the Tenebrae it was to think about that little spark and to come back in a different shape.'

Only someone who had spent so long thinking of Mercy's face would have noted the difference between a flicker of light and a faltering smile.

He was more right than he knew. There is far more light than darkness out there. Even the darkness is not so bad. Light creates darkness. It needs it. There needs to be . . .

'Balance?' Ed said, a second before Denizen could.

Both, Mercy responded. **That's all. No simple equations. No binaries. Just both. If we could just get beyond –**

'*Is this how you talk all the time?*' Simon Hayes grabbed Ed by the scruff of the neck to *heave* him upright, putting himself in between the pale Neophyte and the phosphorescent girl, and, as distressing as all this was, it was the abrupt loudness of his voice that raised the hairs on Denizen's neck.

How long had it been this quiet?

Simon, Mercy said, and reached out a shimmering hand. **I know you have seen much, but –**

It was *very* quiet. When had they last heard wing-beats? When had –

'Oh, would you *quit*,' Simon said, his Achill Island accent abruptly thickening in his annoyance. 'No wonder he –'

'Em . . .' Denizen said. 'Guys?'

Dragon tore the roof off the building.

One moment Denizen was staring at his friend, the next he was airborne, and only the lip of a newly severed wall saved him from a three-storey drop. Seconds smeared together as sound fought to catch up – the ear-splitting, too-close bang of Dragon's wings, the sabretooth roar of splitting masonry, the sudden scorch of sunlight –

Denizen saw the roof, miraculously still intact, shear into a tower some half the city away. That was how fast Dragon was moving. After so long hiding, cowering, running with his head held low, Denizen had an unwillingly perfect moment to watch the beast lazily bank round, to take in the turbine bulges of its shoulders, the roadkill kink of its neck.

And then Vivian's face was in his, as startling as a magic trick.

'*The Aurelian Gate. RUN!*'

23
INEVITABLE

This is your chance, Mercy!

Dragon didn't kill them immediately. That was the worst thing. The Neophytes pelted through vine-ribbed ruins and the beds of dried-up canals, and the cackling atrocity that chased them could have killed them in any number of ways, but it didn't. It played with them instead.

Your chance to strike me down!

Swooping as low as the huddled roofs would allow to shriek right in their ears before lashing itself upwards with a mighty beat of its wings. Landing on roofs so that bricks came down like rain, daintily plucking statues free and flinging them at the Neophytes like toys. *Following* them – joyously prowling, leaping from rooftop to rooftop with the spine-bending flexibility of a cat.

A cat the length of a city block. A cat made of braided human bodies, some crisp and perfect, others stretched to nightmare. The bodies rasped against each other with its every movement like a thousand snakes, like the wing-cases of a cockroach.

What kind of a monster *runs*?

Denizen couldn't look at it. He stared at the ground as he fled, not because its wings had churned the air to grit, but because if he looked directly at the monstrosity he would die. He would let it kill him, the way prey animals did, because it was better than being this scared and still alive.

He could hear the sobbing again, somehow, over everything, the plaintive wail of a wounded thing.

The Tenebrae beat off the creature like radiation from a nuclear warhead, slower to kill you but just as deadly. This was the monster that had broken Daybreak. This was the architect of the most daring attack this realm had ever seen, and it wasn't here for them at all.

FACE ME, MERCY!

It kicked itself into the air, Neophytes staggering away from an avalanche of rubble. The world was shaking apart. Shapes ran through the murk around Denizen, anonymous with dust. As soon as it looked like he was running in vaguely the right direction, Vivian let go of his hand to circle the fleeing Neophytes, snapping at the stragglers like a sheep-dog.

Another pass, Dragon howling like a hurricane, and the backwash dragged enough dust from Denizen's vision that he saw the city walls curving up into the innocent blue sky. *Have we come this far?* He staggered. A huge part of him suddenly just wanted to lie down and seep into the cracked pavement under his feet.

Far away, a tiny black dot was coming around again.

'Denizen!'

It was Vivian, standing in a doorway, hammer in one hand, the other beckoning fiercely. Denizen pelted towards her. Those twenty steps were somehow more terrifying than any he had taken before, but nothing could have stopped Denizen from running to the one person he would bet on against this thing.

He ran to his mother, his Malleus, in the hope that she could somehow make this right.

She dragged him into cover as soon as he was within arm's length and for a moment they just stood there, clutching each other. Someone was speaking –

'– missing Etienne, and Ruben, and Dmitry. We need to –'

'– my ankle, I've twisted my –'

They were in some sort of warehouse, long and low with huge windows, sunlight painting piano keys on the floor. Grey was cupping a girl's face in his hands, speaking low and quiet, but the girl was just staring at him as if she'd never seen him before. Neophytes were pacing, or huddling, or had just slumped like discarded kitbags.

'Simon!'

Denizen didn't see him. That was impossible, surely. His friend was half-ostrich – why couldn't he see him? Why couldn't he –

And underneath the panic came a *whistling*, growing louder and deeper and more urgent, like the last breath of air escaping a punctured lung. Vivian stiffened.

And then Dragon came down like a meteor. Like a bomb. Its ungainly slide levelled every building for a hundred metres, and its tail barely touched the wall separating them from the street, but suddenly it listed as if concussed, and all those piano keys had turned to fangs.

This is what is going to happen.

Denizen felt like a mouse before a cat. No – not a cat: cats and mice were both animals at different ends of the same scale. Denizen felt like a mouse before a *human* – hunted by something not just bigger but far more complex, something that could out-think and outsmart and take from him the most important person in the world.

Simon was missing.

Grey pulled him upright. Denizen didn't even remember falling.

'*We'll get him back*,' the Knight whispered. '*We just need to regroup. That's all.*'

A stealer of treasure. A true dragon, after all.

I am going to find you, if I have to level this entire city.

Denizen heard it scalp another building, rummaging into its innards like a rat with a corpse, and in that sudden dance of particles Denizen saw Mercy, stock-still and barely visible, like an old photograph of an ancient war.

And then . . . I'm going to take you to your father.

Her head came up.

I'm going to chain you up right beside him on that monument to his colossal arrogance, and *then*, dear girl, I'm going to chain the little Hardwick boy up with you.

Every syllable stole definition from Mercy until she was little but a smudge.

Out there, in the middle of the ocean. How long do you think you'll last? The Emissary was so *diminished* when he broke free. No wonder he has such an appetite now. If I chain you beside your father, if I chain a sweet little morsel of humanity at your feet . . . how long before it becomes too much?

How long before you eat each other?

Denizen was so frozen at hearing his name in Dragon's mouth that he didn't even notice Vivian at his side.

'It's right there,' she whispered.

'I know,' Denizen whispered back. The proximity to it was deafening. The shearing creak of its movements, the madhouse scrape of its barbs – he had been in actual battles quieter than Dragon.

'Not that,' she whispered, and, to Denizen's horror, she dragged him *towards* the half-collapsed wall. He tried to fight her, but her grip was irresistible, and she pressed him against a head-height crack in the wall.

'That.'

And past clouds of grit and warping air and buildings ground to nubs, through a black collage of purloined corpses twisted into lizard limbs, Denizen saw it, tucked away into the wall like an afterthought.

The Aurelian Gate. It may as well have been on the moon.

Grey was beside them, his blades drawn. 'We could . . . we could . . .'

'We could what?' Vivian hissed back. 'If we get them out of the gate, it's half a kilometre of open ground between here and any sort of cover. Dragon will have us before we get ten metres.'

We're done for.

The words came from nowhere, which meant they came from Denizen. And fire followed them – eating through every shred of ice and resolve Denizen could put in its way.

Simon was gone. They were trapped. Dragon had them. They were lost.

Cants were bullying aside his thoughts and fire was scorching the bottom of his heart and Denizen wanted nothing more than to let them meet because they were done for, and that meant he didn't have to try any more. Vivian's eyes were tracking wildly across the floor, the walls, as if reading script Denizen couldn't see.

And then they stilled.

'Yield not to evil, but attack all the more boldly,' Vivian said to herself. The family motto. *Vivian's* motto, and not just because he'd never met another Hardwick to compare her to. The words of their family were written into her as immutably as the shared greyness of their eyes, deep as DNA.

It was what had driven her to leave Denizen behind all those years ago, and what had driven him to forgive her for it. Staying with him would have meant giving up fighting, and that was one of the few things Vivian was incapable of.

'Mercy.'

Yes?

The Tenebrous condensed round the word, and the sudden cold only fed the fire in Denizen's stomach. What was –

'You heard what Dragon said. You know where the King is.'

Yes.

'And if Dragon is . . . can you get out of here? Can you bring the King back and end this?'

Her voice was solemn.

I promise you.

'I don't care about your promises.' Vivian's voice was almost a snarl. 'I care about . . . just do it. Prove that you haven't been a lie all this time.'

She turned away before Mercy could answer, and pulled Grey close, whispering urgently in his ear. Denizen strained to hear her, but Dragon took off again, the downwash crazing the air with grime, and her words were lost in the echoing boom.

All he caught was Grey's response. 'You'd trust me with that?'

There was no expression at all on Vivian's face.

'I never stopped trusting you.'

I'm going to find you, Mercy, if I have to tear this whole city down!

And then she and Denizen were face to face.

'Vivian, what are we going to –'

'Shh,' Vivian said, and caught his cheek with her cold iron hand. 'Do you know why we called you Denizen?'

'What?' Denizen said, so surprised he forgot to be quiet. 'I don't think this is the –'

There were iron flecks in her grey eyes. She wasn't being quiet any more either. 'I wanted you to be normal. I shouldn't have, but I did. But your father knew better. Always . . . he knew better. He knew you'd walk in dark places.'

'Vivian, what are you –'

Iron fingers tightened, and Vivian pressed her forehead to his, so hard it hurt.

'I am so proud of you.'

And then he was released, falling backwards into Grey's arms, and Vivian was running, hammer in hand, towards the street.

'NO!'

It should have been a roar. It should have been enough to make her come back. But before his lungs could find the strength there was a forearm round his throat, expertly flexing his breath away. Denizen scrabbled at it, drawing Falter with his other hand, but something slapped it away and he was getting weaker and weaker –

No. No! What are you –

His mother had left him. His mother had –

And then he was gone as well.

24

WAR'S END

The dust was settling.

It swirled around Vivian as she stepped out into the sunlight, the white of her cloak turned to ash. The ground had been chewed by the passage of massive claws, and she had to carefully pick her away across it.

There was a growing black speck in the sky.

With a smooth roll of the wrists, Vivian let her hammer whicker round her in a figure of eight. She had wielded it so long now –

– the speck the size of an acorn –

– that compensating for the drag of the hammer head was automatic, and the grooves and notches on the handle fitted perfectly into the scars on her hands.

– the acorn the size of a fist –

It was all about momentum, a hammer. You let the weight of it spin you, lead you. You let it show you where it wanted you to go.

Dragon screamed over her head like a fighter jet, the backwash driving Vivian to one knee. Her cloak was ripped from its clasps with a snap of fabric, and, when the wind and noise of Dragon's passing had died away, she turned and rose to find the Tenebrous gecko-planted on the great outer wall, directly above the Aurelian Gate.

There was a lot of it. Its wings spread hugely, turning the sunlight a reeking, patchy green, and it shook rubble first from one claw, then the other, the movements delicate and almost human. Its head unfurled like a mayflower dance, and, when it roared, all its mouths opened at once.

Dramatics. It was neither the most intricate or cleverest perversion Vivian had ever seen. When its bellow didn't move her, it cocked its head in confusion.

Not who I expected.

Vivian shrugged.

But no matter. There's a spot. On my back. You'll be perfect.

'The Clockwork Three.'

The beast went still.

'Before that, the Tearsipper Girls,' Vivian continued calmly. 'And Redpenny, the Hounds of Vox, Verdigris, Charnabal Cross . . .'

She remembered the names the way she remembered old injuries – forgotten aches and long-healed cuts. There were names that everyone knew, written deep and red in the histories, and names that even Darcie might not have recognized. There were names there she'd never told anyone at all.

I don't frighten you?

'You don't frighten me,' Vivian responded. 'None of you. You have never been what I'm afraid of.' A corner of her lip twisted upwards. 'I have carried this hammer for a very long time.'

Dragon's sigh blew stinking air down the street. Vivian didn't honestly believe these animals capable of emotions, but she allowed herself the brief satisfaction of imagining it sounded . . . disappointed.

Why are you smiling?

'Because now I get to put it down.'

And she swung the weapon into her waiting palm.

Dragon's head spasmed, blaring discordantly from a thousand throats, and with a hinging snap it charged, bounding like a lion, like a locomotive of darkness and iron and hate.

And Malleus Vivian Hardwick did what she had been born to do, what she had been raised and trained to do, what she'd always done.

She attacked.

25
THE TURN

'I got them out,' Darcie said, but there was no pride in her voice, just soft and hollow truth. 'We were fighting them corridor by corridor, and then I *felt* Dragon push through the Glimpse and . . . and we evacuated. We abandoned Daybreak.'

This tower was the third position they'd taken in as many hours. Abigail had managed to somehow snatch an hour of rest between the three, but all the brief moments of rest in between simply let exhaustion catch up.

Darcie hadn't slept at all.

'A rearguard stayed,' the *Lux* continued, 'to cover our escape, or maybe Greaves didn't quite believe me when I told him, but . . . sixty-eight Knights. That's how many I managed to get out before it . . .'

A floor below, a scream rose and then was abruptly cut off. You weren't supposed to move the wounded. You weren't supposed to use healing Cants like the Bellows Subventum because both the Cost and the pressure on the body were too much . . . but those were rules from the old war, the old Adumbral, the one that belonged to the Order and the Order alone.

Now they whispered. Now they hid, the once-silent city clogged with hoots and snarls and baying laughter no human throat could produce.

'I know,' Abigail said. 'We saw. There was . . .' The words felt foreign in her mouth. 'There was nothing any of us could have done. Not against something like that. It was the right thing to do.'

'I felt them die,' Darcie said simply. 'The boundary between worlds is so thin now that I felt their lights go out. I can feel the candlewards crumbling, the Tenebrous spilling from the Glimpse now, feeding on Daybreak . . . *colonizing* it.' She scratched her arms through her coat. 'I can feel them.'

'I know,' Abigail repeated. It was a pathetically small thing to say. It was also the heart of Greaves's strategy for holding the Tenebrous back.

She hadn't heard it from Greaves, of course. The Palatine was too busy coordinating the warriors who had made it out of Daybreak alive. But in the midst of the controlled chaos Darcie had been able to fill them in.

With the Glimpse lost, and more and more reports of Tenebrous Breaching *inside* the city, the Order had fallen back on the strategy that had defined them since their inception – intercepting Breaches, plugging gaps, with a *Lux Precognitae* directing their blades.

The web of ever-shifting, ever-responding cadres across the city was holding – so far – and Dragon had seemed to lose interest in them as soon as it had pulled free of Daybreak, but Abigail was under no illusion as to how long that would last. The city couldn't hold forever – at some point the numbers of Tenebrous spilling from the Glimpse or bleeding into the city would become too great.

And the Emissary itself wouldn't even face them.

'Have you . . . have you detected it? The Emissary?'

Abigail knew that, in this situation, coming across two Neophytes was like finding loose change under the settee when the debt collectors were kicking down your door, but Greaves had shrugged off their intel about the Emissary as if it were nothing. It didn't matter if they somehow managed to defend every alleyway and street corner, when at any point the whole city might fall. The Emissary was the target. Killing it would slow down the invasion. It had to.

'No,' Darcie responded, and, though she allowed no anger in her tone, Abigail could feel the space where it should be. 'It's the one thing I can't feel. It's hiding from me. Why come this far . . . only to hide?'

'It's had years,' Matt whispered. 'Centuries. Centuries to figure out what we do and how we do it. Centuries to plan what it's doing now.'

'Which is why we need to take it out,' Abigail snapped. 'None of this will matter if the Emissary pitches us all into the Tenebrae. We need to get a cadre together and –'

'A cadre?' Matt's voice was bitterly incredulous. 'You saw what the Emissary's become. What's wrong with you – you want to just go out there and face it head-on? Why can't you –'

'Children.'

Their mouths snapped shut at Darcie's stern tone.

'We have to trust the Palatine. More than that – we have to trust Vivian. This strategy is just a holding action until the Malleus leads the rest of the Order back here. *Then* we reclaim Adumbral and Daybreak itself.'

'And what if we can't?' Abigail said, and she was no longer sure if she was speaking to Darcie or herself. 'What if every candle we lose is another chance lost, another piece of ground we'll never retake? This isn't the same war. Things have changed. We have to change as well.'

They both fell silent as something like a foghorn mixed with a cat's yowl split the air, and then Darcie shook her head. '*C'est la guerre*, Abigail. This is war. There is no victory. Don't you think I want there to be?'

Sunlight still streamed through the windows, but they sat in a corner away from the light.

'I grew up on the same books as Denizen,' the *Lux* murmured. 'Secret temples and magic gems that make everything right again. And, when you join an order of sorcerer Knights, and they tell you you're *doubly* special, you research, you know?

'You hope.

'You begin to think that maybe you'll be the person to solve everything. To save everyone. You look for prophecies. Solutions. The lock for which you're the key. And I'm not alone. Maybe we all think we're chosen.'

Abigail didn't say anything. Neither did Matt.

'But that's not how the world works,' Darcie said. 'Greaves knows that to contain what's happening we do what we've *always* done. We do what works. And yes, this is . . . on a greater scale, but that's why we need to pull together harder than ever.'

She slid a notebook and pencil from her pocket with the grim care of a warrior drawing their blade.

'I have to get back.'

The Cost in Darcie's eyes had spread through her skin like an oil slick, a domino mask of dead black on living brown. Abigail knew her eleven Cants like she knew her own reach, but the toll Darcie's talents took was a mystery to her. How much longer could the *Lux* hold out?

How much longer could any of them?

Knights were climbing the stairs. One flashed them five fingers, and Abigail nodded in response. They couldn't stay in one place too long. Outnumbered, outgunned and attacked on all sides, the second that their defence became static was the second the Tenebrous would converge.

Maybe then the Emissary would –

'What is wrong with you?'

Matt's hand found her arm, but before he could walk her to the other side of the room she twisted round in his grip and jabbed the point of her elbow into the hollow of his. He yelped, drawing a glare from a passing Knight.

'I could ask you the same question,' she hissed.

Matt's eyes narrowed. 'Excuse me?'

'I just think that it's a bit *pathetic*,' Abigail whispered venomously, 'that now that you have a few Knights to look after you, all that high-and-mighty talk of being a hero has gone out the window. What happened to going out in a blaze of glory?'

'Are you listening to yourself?' Corded muscle stood out on Matt's arms as he folded them. He looked as if he would like nothing more than to strike her, and Abigail automatically felt her left foot slide backwards and her fists come up. Matt saw it too, and there was something triumphant in his scowl.

'You're just going to charge blindly in and what? Punch the problem away?'

'In case you haven't noticed,' Abigail countered, 'that's what *we do*.'

'Is it?' Like a card-sharp pausing before that final flip, just to let you know they've won. 'Or is it your way to make up for your little freak-out earlier? Saving the day to prove you're not just a kid? You can lie to yourself if you want, but the Emissary would crush you like it crushed those candles.'

And then the triumph was gone from his voice, the way it had gone from the day.

'Daybreak has fallen, Abigail. What are you going to do next to that? What are . . . Where are you going? Hey!'

Abigail took the stairs two at a time, the upper floor of the tower crowded with Knights hefting weapons or shouldering packs. Radios burbled and spat patchwork updates of a city at war.

Darcie was picking notebooks from the floor. That was how the *Lux*'s gift worked – tracing the trembles of realms against each other through paper and pencil and lead. Some were being pored over on tables. Others had been forgotten as soon as the Breaches within them had been quelled.

She frowned as Abigail entered. 'What's –'

The Palatine had said it himself. *This too is sacred ground.*

'Is Daybreak a candleward?'

Darcie's mouth opened and then closed again abruptly. Abigail didn't bother elaborating. Mallei competed fiercely to be assigned a *Lux*, and, though there were many things that separated soft-spoken, sixteen-year-old Darcie and Malleus Vivian Hardwick, they both had one very simple thing in common: when they were doing their job, you got out of their way.

'I did read . . .' Darcie whispered finally, hand twitching as if to pick up a book from an invisible shelf. 'But how would that even work? We barely understand the relationship of dimensional stability and flame –

'But back then it was desperate times and desperate measures. A city on the brink of plunging into the Tenebrae. Palatines willing to experiment. Magic, not science. And then –

'Candlewards are safer, more efficient, easier to hide –'

It was after Darcie had interrupted herself for the third time that Abigail decided to step in.

'Darcie, I'm sorry. I don't need you to figure out how it works; I just need to know – is the lighthouse a candleward?'

'I don't know,' Darcie responded simply. 'If I had access to the libraries, even the one at home . . . but I don't, and communications beyond the city are still down. What I wouldn't give to just –'

'Ask Greaves?'

It was only then that Abigail realized Matt was hovering uncertainly at her shoulder.

'Surely he'd know?'

'That's . . .' *Actually not a terrible idea.* 'Yes. OK. Let's ask Greaves.'

Matt broke into a bright grin.

'And, if it is, we have to find a way to light it.'

The grin disappeared.

'Hang on, what? That's ludicrous – the whole city's at war. Daybreak's *crawling* with Tenebrous –'

'*Because of the Glimpse*,' Abigail said. 'And because the Emissary is out there somewhere, probably knocking out every candleward it can get its hands on. How many more do you think we can lose? Can't you feel it in the air? Can't you feel how close we are to –?'

She didn't finish her sentence. She didn't need to. The air was fermented, as thick as tar. She could feel it on her eyelashes when she blinked. It felt as if one wrong move, one bad step, would tip them over the edge entirely.

Something distant and huge was dying, out in the city. Abigail heard it, a lowing that trembled her bones and stung her eyes. She'd never heard anything like it before. Did cities make noises when they died?

'A candleward the size of a lighthouse. Think of it. If it were lit, it would . . .'

She trailed off. She actually had no idea what lighting a candleward that large would do to the surrounding Tenebrous, and she didn't care.

'It would buy Vivian time,' Darcie said, 'and maybe compensate for what the Emissary has done. For a while at least.'

'That's all we need,' Abigail said, hope swelling like a bellows in her chest. 'It's *Vivian*. She'll come back for us –'

And, when she does, she'll see that I figured this out, that I was the one who fixed things. That'll make up for running. For letting her down –

'Abigail. Darcie. The Palatine needs you.'

It was the Knight who'd found her and Matt outside Daybreak. She gestured at them to follow him, but held up her hand when Matt went to join.

'Wait here, please.'

Abigail was suddenly caught between her own unworthy sense of triumph – *that's what you get for constantly arguing* – and guilt at the look on his face. *You would have hated to be left behind too.*

Her regret was short-lived. They were meeting Greaves. She'd ask him about Daybreak, he'd *have* to listen to her and they'd work out a plan together. Maybe that was why he was summoning them. Maybe Vivian would be there, and they could cut out the middleman entirely.

Maybe this was the turning-point, the moment where they stopped reacting and began to *act*.

Greaves was waiting for them in a side chamber on the ground floor, surrounded by pages laid out on the floor. You could have charged a battery with the Palatine's intent stare. A radio popped and growled in his remaining hand.

'Palatine,' Abigail began, trying to add respect to the urgency in her tone. 'Is –'

Greaves jerked the radio at her and, as if the motion had annoyed it, the staticky snarl rose – the sound of two worlds rubbing against each other until a voice finally managed to squeeze through.

'. . . *still . . . there . . . ?*'

Interference had scraped the voice almost free of personality, but Abigail would have known it anywhere, and hearing it took beats from her heart.

'That's Simon!'

Darcie let out a hitching breath, clasping Abigail's hand so tight it hurt.

'Where are they?'

'Are they OK?'

'Where's –'

'We're still here, Simon,' Greaves said. 'A cadre has been dispatched to you. We need to know – Mercy, Vivian, what –'

The radio buzzed, and the next words that came through were miraculously free of distortion, as if even the Tenebrae were unwilling to touch them.

'. . . *Dead . . . They're . . . they're dead . . .*'

26

THE FULL SET

Denizen woke, and knew that his mother was dead.

He lay in that certainty for a long moment as cold retreated from his skin – a cold he recognized because it was quite literally like nothing else in the world. There was only one cold that reached into you and turned your blood to slush, only one cold that bred a freezing ache in hand and eye.

The Art of Apertura.

Denizen lay on his back, feeling his clothes crinkle to dryness around him, and considered the art of parental extrapolation. As a child, he'd had no evidence his parents existed except for the fact that he did, and he'd spent years wondering what they were like. The other children in Crosscaper had photos or souvenirs, but all Denizen's parents had given him was life, and a host of questions.

There were five stages to grief, but Denizen had never got angry, or bargained, and he'd especially avoided denial because, if he refused to believe his parents were dead, he'd have to believe that they might be out there, but unable to be with him . . . that they might be out there and not *want* to be with him.

Schrödinger's parents – a riddle he'd been afraid to solve. And now it was solved for him. Vivian had to be dead, because if she weren't she'd be here.

'He's awake.'

Denizen pushed himself to his elbows. They were no longer in Adumbral. Ochre stone had been replaced by heather-thatched slopes, sweeping down to an ocean the colour of slate, waves clawing at the sky as if desperate to be rain. The smell of salt was a familiar sting.

The past never left you. It shadowed you, hunted you, and for Denizen it was scuffed granite and windows like narrowed, hostile eyes. It was corrugated sheds that smelled of half-sealed bags of compost, doors that moaned and drains that clattered like veins in a seizing heart.

Someone had come in when Denizen had been gone and lit the place up like a prison – spotlights glaring like guards from every corner on the wall – but Denizen knew it all the same.

Crosscaper. He was back at Crosscaper. He was back at Crosscaper with Grey. He was back at Crosscaper with Grey and he was an orphan and each thought squeezed more air from his throat until the Knight was suddenly at his side.

'Hey. Hey. Look at me.'

His handsome face was streaked with dirt and blood, his eyes red-rimmed from exhaustion and tears. He looked like Denizen felt.

'Dragon,' Denizen whispered, and the word, with its harsh, cruel consonants, felt right to him. The word should hurt.

Grey's voice was raw. 'The whole street went up. She must have taken out half the . . .' He swallowed. 'She gave it her all.'

Of course she did. That's Vivian. Was. *Was* Vivian. The past could follow him, but he couldn't follow it, and now it had gathered her up like it had his father. She'd left him again, and this time she wasn't coming back.

Something must have passed over his face, because Grey gripped his shoulder with the iron fingers of his good hand.

'She did what she had to do. She told the Neophytes to get clear and she told me to . . . to help Mercy . . .'

Distantly, Denizen noted how shockingly clear the air was of Tenebraic interference compared to Adumbral. What had been a deafening cacophony was now a single wavering note, echoing from a shape that might have just been a curl of mist.

'When Dragon died, the whole Tenebrae went quiet,' Grey whispered. 'I've never felt anything like it. As if Vivian scoured the air clean, just for a moment. I told the Neophytes to make a run for it and then I used the Art of Apertura. Vivian . . . she –'

'Did the right thing,' Denizen said, and, though the words were flat and calm, he could feel the grief expanding in his chest, preparing to crack him apart. 'She did what she had to do.'

The words arrived on the crest of a sob, dry and clipped, as if his body had started mourning before his brain was able to. 'And I'm not . . . I'm not mad. Why am I not mad at her?'

Grey blurred in his vision, and then the first real sob came, so racking and violent that tears splattered his hands like rain. They climbed out of him in great body heaves and he felt Grey shaking as he wept too. They stayed that way for a very long time.

I'm sorry for your loss.

Maybe it was the stronger taste of the Tenebrae that she brought with her, or some echo of his mother's contempt, but Mercy had barely drifted over before Denizen lurched to his feet. 'We need to get moving.'

Grey jerked back as the Neophyte took two staggering steps towards the orphanage, hands darting to his thin chest as if stabbed.

'Falter. My knife. I don't have . . .'

Denizen cut himself off before he could become hysterical. The ground seemed to shift underneath him, emotions fluttering in him like the subject and settings of a dream. There was a gap in his world now, and he struggled to account for it.

'Denizen . . .'

'I'm fine, I'm fine, I'm fine,' he said, his fingers tangled in his hair, pulling hard enough to hurt. 'I'm a Hardwick.' The pain helped. Every time his brain drifted to *Vivian's dead*, he dragged it away. 'It'll kick in any minute. That's what we do, you know? Grief hits, and then it's all about duty. We're so *similar*, you know? That . . .'

'Denizen, we can wait –'

'No.' And finally, *finally*, his voice was firm. He'd heard every platitude about grief there was by the age of six and, as was so often the case with Vivian, the normal rules didn't seem to apply.

Crosscaper's cook, Mrs Mollins, handed out *they've gone to a better place* with every bread roll, but Denizen couldn't imagine Vivian sitting on a cloud somewhere with a harp. A sword of fire, *yes*. Steel wings and holy wrath, definitely. She'd not be in heaven five minutes before criticizing the Pearly Gates for being militarily indefensible.

They're at peace. A concept so alien to both Denizen and Vivian that it just didn't wash.

No, what came to Denizen then were the words of one of Crosscaper's ill-fated substitute teachers. He didn't remember her subject or appearance. All he remembered was that one morning, when Michael Flannigan hadn't done his homework, she'd said, *What would your parents think?*

Whether she'd been fired because of the staggering stupidity of using dead parents to shame an eight-year-old or because she'd had the kind of personality that would use dead parents to shame an eight-year-old was up for debate, but it was her words Denizen clung to now.

What would Vivian think?

'Yield not to evil,' Denizen said. It didn't sound as impressive without thirty years of war and bloodshed behind it, but it would do for now. 'I'll break down later. Right now we have to . . .' A thought surfaced from the murk. 'Why are we *here*?'

A shadow crossed Grey's face. He turned away abruptly, staring down at the slump of buildings below. *They replaced the gates*, Denizen thought absently. Well, they would have had to. Denizen and his mother had demolished them the year before.

'We got dragged off course,' Grey said. 'The Tenebrae's all stirred up; the currents dragged us here or we got . . . confused or something. That's all. I wasn't . . . I didn't mean to . . .'

He was scratching at the malformed claw that had replaced his left hand.

'We just ended up here.'

'Specifically *here*,' Denizen said. The Order's stock-in-trade was battlefield sorcery. Their history might have stretched back fifteen centuries, but there still hadn't been much time for study. That said, *we just ended up here* was uncharacteristically vague.

'Yes,' Grey snapped. 'And?'

'Nothing,' Denizen said. 'I just –'

'You think I want to be here any more than you do?' The older Knight's eyes were blazing, not with flame but with fury, an anger so sudden that Denizen took a step back. They weren't far from where Grey had been puppeted by the Three to point a gun in Denizen's face, and the same sort of rage had twisted his features then.

And suddenly it was gone, as quickly as it had appeared.

'Sorry,' he said. 'I'm . . . sorry. It's been a day.'

'I know,' Denizen said. 'I just . . . What do we do now?'

We find a boat.

Mercy stood out as pearl against the iron of the sky.

You heard what Dragon said. *The monument to my father's arrogance.*

'Where?' Denizen and Grey said together.

She raised a hand of rippling silver to point at the sea.

That dreadful, mighty creature built a body unequalled by any Tenebrous before or since . . .

Five fingers. The fingers of the Endless King.

Grudges were lifeblood to creatures fuelled by will.

They're keeping him at Os Reges Point.

It was strange thinking about adults as complicated people.

Denizen had always assumed you just got to a certain age and . . . solidified. Teenagers were supposed to change. They had to learn and change and figure out what kind of adult they were going to congeal into, and Denizen had been looking forward to it because he'd changed so much in the last year that he was frankly exhausted.

After twelve years, Denizen had thought he had the measure of Ackerby: his habits, his patterns. He'd thought he knew the director at least as well as he knew Crosscaper, which was why it was both disconcerting and oddly fitting to find out how the orphanage had changed.

There was *art* on the walls. There were brightly coloured signs on the doors. The smell of armpits and sadness had been replaced by a nostril-curling whiff of bleach. Denizen slipped through the foyer, squinting in the glare of unfamiliar lights, and stared down at the floorboards where he'd found Director Ackerby a year ago.

Had you asked Denizen before the Three descended on Crosscaper, he would have put Director Ackerby squarely in the *orphanage directors first, women and children second* category. But, in those last moments before the Tenebrous had drowned him in troubled sleep, he'd tried to ring the fire alarm.

He'd tried to warn them. He'd tried to help.

Adults did change. Even after being given every reason and excuse not to, even after enduring more misery than anyone should.

Denizen's eyes prickled, and he ducked into a classroom to clear them. It was the only reason he wasn't caught. Doors were slamming open, and he watched, hidden, as students began to file by in stops and starts, teachers pausing them at each corner as if they too were hiding.

Mr Colford passed by, so close that Denizen could have reached out and touched him, could have simply fallen into step behind him and faded into the background. He'd been very good at that here.

And I am an orphan.

The urge was short-lived. Denizen could no more rejoin them than he could pull the iron out of his palm. He belonged to a different world now, and kids came and went from Crosscaper all the time. Just another topic at dinner – *Denizen Hardwick? Oh, he left.*

Ackerby's office was much like the man himself – shabbily majestic with a patina of dust. It felt like sacrilege to go through the director's desk, but on the one hand it was hard to find any desk impressive after Greaves's, and on the other they weren't going anywhere without car keys and the gate remote.

Passage to Os Reges Point required a boat and, while there was a harbour just beyond the closest village, *close* in rural Ireland without a car meant a couple of hours' walk. None of them had particularly good memories of Crosscaper, but Denizen knew his way around, and had volunteered to . . .

Rob Ackerby?

Denizen yanked on another drawer. There wasn't time for subtlety. Ackerby would probably come running as soon as he heard the gates open, though Grey looked half on the edge of murder already, so Denizen didn't exactly rate the director's chances.

'It can't be. Not . . . not *you*.'

The voice reached his senses a second before the Tenebrae did, and Denizen went bolt upright as the hairs on his neck stood on end so hard it hurt. The feeling was nothing as strong as what they'd left behind in Adumbral, but it still clogged his throat with nausea, painting sweat across his brow.

The director, by comparison, was almost an afterthought, frozen in the doorway with a shocked look on his wrinkled face. *This is what you came for.* It was an effort to speak around the fire in his throat.

'Director,' Denizen said, awkwardly raising his hand in greeting. 'I need your help.'

He frowned.

'Also, what on earth are you wearing?'

'Shut up, Hardwick,' Ackerby snapped reflexively, crossing his hands protectively over his scratchy mauve jumper. 'And . . . why are you . . . *They're not coming back, are they?*'

The last time Denizen had seen Ackerby he had been in the company of a tiger-lean girl with a crossbow, a madman with a broken jaw and – tears caustic in his eyes once again – a towering woman dressed in armour and scars, and Denizen *still* knew he was talking about the Clockwork Three.

'I won't have them back here. I *won't* –'

'I'm sorry to bring this to you,' Denizen said, and he really was, but Cants were swarming through him like agitated bees, darting into the thin bones of his wrists and shaking his pulse from the inside. 'I truly am. Where are –'

'In the bunker,' the old man snapped. 'I mean the . . . the basement. They're safe. What's happening?'

This far into the countryside every sound travelled. This far into the countryside the smallest light was a star. The baleful cry of a Tenebrous shook the window frames just as honeyed light licked the frost from the glass, and Denizen was running before the echoes died away.

It wasn't Dragon, which was good for a number of reasons, not least that Denizen didn't know if he would have been able to survive losing his mother and finding out she hadn't taken her killer with her. But, just as every Tenebrous felt a unique kind of wrong, so too did horror, and the revulsion Denizen felt when he stumbled on to the courtyard was a familiar one indeed.

Denizen remembered a stubby thumb of a head, human features swimming on top like scum on cream. He remembered buttons like eyes, and hair evacuating a scalp to make room for rising clockwork teeth. Obsession remade Tenebrous, and the Woman in White had hated Vivian so much it had grown to resemble her, and the Man in the Waistcoat had hated Vivian so much it had almost made him sane.

They had died here, in this courtyard. You wouldn't have known. Every scar in the courtyard walls had been filled in, every scrap of that spavined arachnoid form removed . . . and yet one sign remained, dug into the gravel and the stone.

Mercy and Grey stood over it, as pale as each other, the Tenebrous shuddering between light and smoke and the Knight with his swords in his hands.

'We – we – we . . .'

Grey was stammering, actually stammering, sweat a drizzle on his skin. Unreality palpitated off Mercy like the beat of a failing heart, the air cold enough around her to cut.

We came to see if you were . . .

Neither one of them had taken their eyes from the ground, and there was absolutely no need to ask why.

'It won't go away.'

To his credit, Director Ackerby didn't seem fazed by Mercy at all. Like all of them, his gaze was fixed on the words carved into the ground, the scars outlined by a thick rime of ice.

'We tried, after the Incident. We tried covering it, and burying it, and chipping away the ice, but . . .' There was a quiet, bitter rage in his voice. 'It's like the words are visible no matter what. It just won't go away.'

'No,' Denizen said distantly, his iron eye aching. 'I imagine it wouldn't.'

What would it look like, to someone who didn't have Denizen's sight? Did even Grey see it? Mercy would, of course. The wrongness that bled from the carved words was kin to what came from her.

The words couldn't be scrubbed away because they weren't carved on the stone. They were carved on *reality*, ripped into the fabric of the universe itself with a viciousness and anger that might never heal. Denizen saw each letter as a pulsing wound, no less deep than the Glimpse itself.

He'd heard those words. The Man in the Waistcoat had spoken them.

The last Hardwick.

THE FULL SET.

27

THERE ARE LITTLE KINGDOMS

It had only been a day.

Twenty-four hours. That was all. Twenty-four hours since the only things Abigail had had to worry about were her fear of flying and whether she'd remembered her favourite hand wraps. (She had. Abigail Falx never forgot anything.)

Twenty-four hours since Daybreak had loomed over them like a protector, like a parent. Twenty-four hours since her whole future had stretched out in front of her; a million chances to make those who mattered proud. As Simon tonelessly began his story, Abigail couldn't help but think that the reason so much had happened in a single day was because it was the Order's last on this earth.

'Dragon separated us,' Simon said. '*Herded* us. I saw Neophytes go down under a building. One of the girls freaked out and we were trying to drag her clear and we lost sight of the others and Dragon came down and I bent light to hide us. Most I've ever done at once. It was . . . all I was good for.'

'You did the right thing,' Greaves said. It almost sounded like an order – *believe it* – but Simon didn't acknowledge it. The last twenty-four hours had stolen away the boy Abigail knew, replacing him with a bad photocopy – all gaps and greys and tear-streaked dust.

'I don't think it was at all bothered about us. But, every time Dragon moved, buildings came down, and the air was full of dust, and we could barely see. It was like a war zone. It was . . . even being close to it was death.'

Greaves had dispatched a cadre to retrieve Simon as soon as they'd figured out where he was, Darcie guiding them through the maelstrom of Breaching Tenebrous and running battles. The Neophytes had scattered, maybe into the city, Simon didn't know – but eight had been retrieved.

Eight. Out of twenty-three.

'Simon,' Greaves said, laying the second syllable on the first as if trying to rebuild something very fragile. 'Where's Grey? And . . . and Vivian. Where are they?'

'It was like the sun coming up,' Simon said morosely. He scrubbed a hand across his face, and Abigail saw that his skin was flecked with a thousand tiny burns. 'The dust caught fire, and Dragon was roaring, and Vivian . . .'

Greaves leaned forward, and Abigail's heart was a battle drum in her chest. The shame was searingly welcome – how *dare* she despair? How dare the thought of giving up even enter her mind when Vivian was out there fighting for her, for them all?

There was always hope and, if there wasn't, you carved it out. And, if there was one person on which this day, this war, would turn, it was –

'She's dead, Abigail.'

Someone, somewhere was screaming. It was hard to pick out from distant explosions and the thunderous cries of monsters, but the shriek was there all the same. It took Abigail a long time to realize it was coming from her, and a longer time to realize nobody else in the room could hear it, because her teeth were clamped together so tightly they ached from the root up.

Vivian couldn't be dead. She *couldn't be.* There had been Verdigris. The Tearsipper Girls. Abigail had . . . had *researched* her. The Malleus had dragged herself back from death a thousand times, killed more unkillable things than any other Malleus in the history of the Order. She *couldn't be dead –*

'She took Dragon with her,' Simon continued in that same drab tone, as though he hadn't just demolished all their hopes, and Abigail with them. 'We saw the fight, but we couldn't get close and then it was just . . . over.

'And then . . .' *Now* his voice wavered, his dark eyes brimming with tears. 'We searched. *I* searched. The whole street was in ruins, but there were a couple of buildings standing and I wanted to find him. I needed to find him.'

Simon pulled something from his belt and let it fall to the floor.

Falter. A terrible name for a sword.

Simon was suddenly eclipsed by Darcie, half embracing him, half holding him up, but Abigail just stared at how fitting it was that something so unique, so priceless had been dumped on the floor like so much rubbish.

Two people. Abigail had lost two people. Two people at once. How could the maths be right? How could two separate people – two completely different universes of thought and memory and experience – die in the same battle, at the hands of the same monster? How was that fair? It was . . . it was . . .

It was pointless. Wasteful.

'And Grey?' Greaves asked urgently. 'Mercy?'

It felt like an insult to break the silence so soon, but what amount of time would have been enough?

'I didn't see them,' Simon said hollowly. 'There were bodies. Neophytes. Dragon . . . *Her.*' A jerky sort of energy seemed to fill him then. 'Can I go back? I want to look for him. I wouldn't have found this except that it was just lying there on the ground. I want to find him, even if it's just his . . . I want to *look*.'

'I'm sorry,' the Palatine said, 'but I can't risk another cadre. Every moment brings new Breaches. We're stretched to capacity. Beyond capacity. There'll be a time to mourn when we –'

'When we *what*?'

Anger. The longer this day went on, the more thankful Abigail was for anger. It filled out the cracks in her voice. It swamped her helplessness beneath a tide of red. Anger was *useful*. That was what Vivian had always told her. Anger was fuel.

'When we have time, Abigail.' Greaves's one remaining hand had gone to the silver sword pin on his tie, still miraculously clean. That just made Abigail even angrier.

'She was twice the Knight you are.'

Darcie stiffened. Simon looked at Abigail, then away again, disinterestedly, like he had already forgotten what she had said. Greaves just shook his head.

'I'll ignore that, Ms Falx. Just once. For the day that's in it. And Vivian Hardwick fought a good fight, but her fight is over. Ours is not. There's every chance her sacrifice allowed some Neophytes the chance to flee, to get word out, but until then I have an Order to keep alive. We have to hold this ground and buy time for –'

'You don't win *wars* by holding ground,' Abigail snapped. She could only imagine the look on her parents' faces if they knew she was shouting down the Palatine, but at this moment she didn't care. It wouldn't have stopped Vivian.

'Every step they take into this world makes it *their* world. The Emissary is out there, dismantling the barrier between them and us, and you're just going to *wait* here until there's nobody left?'

Though not a gleam of light appeared underneath Greaves's skin, the air was suddenly ominously warm. Abigail registered it the way she would have read an opponent readying a blow, but her mouth had apparently staged a coup of its own.

Was this how Vivian had felt? This righteous, unstoppable rage?

'You need to light Daybreak.'

Darcie had her eyes closed very tightly. Abigail wavered, but she couldn't have stopped now even if she'd wanted to.

'It's a candleward, isn't it? If you lit it, it might suppress the Breaches and give us time to stop the –'

'*Spare* me,' the Palatine snarled, 'from the sermons of fourteen-year-old strategists who have spent the last day getting *lost* instead of serving their Order and their cause.'

Abigail didn't cower. She definitely didn't. She'd cowered when the Emissary had bulldozed through a cadre of Knights like a child parting grass. Cowering was watching eighteen metres of screaming iron claw through the sky.

But the sheer sizzling contempt in Greaves's voice rocked her on her heels all the same.

'Allow me the *courtesy*,' he growled, 'of assuming that I know my fortress and my work. I sent a cadre to light Daybreak –'

I was right!

'– as soon as it looked like we were going to lose it. And then Dragon happened. And Daybreak remains unlit. Now our ancestral seat of power is a teeming mass of Tenebrous that I do not have the numbers to retake and I have to make do with what I have for as long as I have it. *Do you understand?*'

The last was delivered with such savagery that Abigail nodded automatically.

'I respected Vivian,' Greaves said, the rage in his voice suddenly gone. 'But, more than that, I *envied* her. Do you know why?'

'No.'

'Because she had the luxury of being uncomplicated,' Greaves responded. 'Now, get out of my sight.'

Darcie and Simon had vanished before he'd finished his sentence, and Abigail herself stayed only long enough to pick up Denizen's blade from the floor. *She wasn't 'uncomplicated'*, Abigail thought, as the Palatine turned to look out of the window at the city he was failing, and Abigail pressed her finger to the blade's razor edge to remind herself of that red and bitter rage.

She was busy.

Another hour, another camp.

Two Knights lost in a battle under the Sabelline Arch. The many-headed Maenus Carvolin defeated by Nathaniel Gayle to the wails of its watching kin. Darcie sketched paths and probabilities, a sixteen-year-old general steering cadres through a cat's-cradle of Breaches and beasts, the night's darkness fighting its own battle with the burning city below.

And Abigail waited. She watched. They gave her a sword and she sharpened it. They put up sentries and she marked their positions; they gave her porridge and she marshalled her strength.

Four Neophytes were confirmed dead. That was what Simon had seen. Whether the others had escaped, whether they had got beyond the gates or were lost in the city or were underneath the rubble would have to wait until a cadre could be spared. On any other day, even that would have been a catastrophic loss. Now it was a side note.

Greaves had split the Neophytes up, assigning them to cadres. There was no point trying to keep them from battle any more, but he could at least try to stop them all being wiped out at once. Ed had stayed with Greaves, possibly because you couldn't prise him away from Simon with a crowbar, and Abigail had *wanted* to try and speak to the others, but she had nothing to say and they didn't look like they wanted to hear it.

Saying things isn't my strong point, she thought. *Doing things is.*

They navigated the city by Darcie's sketches – ranging from faint and incomplete when no Tenebrous was inbound to vividly, violently dark. Adumbral's geography didn't change, but the Tenebrae beneath did, and so the maps had to be constantly redrawn.

Abigail collected each discarded sheet, and thought of how ships had once sailed by coastlines with monsters mere decoration, and now the Order sailed by monsters with the streets mere detail beneath.

Was that the guardhouse? Backpack across her knees, she surreptitiously tried to connect one sketch to another the way Greaves had done. *And that the basilica from earlier?* She had personal experience of how hard it was to navigate through Adumbral, and that was *before* she got to her destination, which happened not to be on any of the maps because it was the one place the whole Order was trying to avoid.

Eventually, she just hissed in frustration and jammed the pages in her bag. They were probably obsolete now anyway. She'd just have to do what centuries of Knights had done – navigate by her senses and adrenalin's edge.

Sometimes, she caught Simon studying her, but she always looked away. He wouldn't understand. Better to let him and Darcie mourn the Hardwicks – they would be far better at it anyway.

It was up to Abigail to avenge them.

The first two floors of the building were crammed with Knights, so Abigail went up to the deserted third, noting both the trail of dusty footprints that the sentries had left on the way to the roof and the overhanging cupola that should hide her from them. Three storeys down to the street – it was more of a climb than she'd like, but iron fingers made excellent crampons and she knew how to take a fall.

The stone blade rattled in her bag as she slung it over her shoulder. This was it. She just had to –

'Told you.'

Jump. The thought came unbidden into her head, more from recognizing Matt's voice than thinking she'd survive. The tall boy had scaled the stairs after her, and stood with arms folded. She opened her mouth to say something, *anything*, that would make him go away . . . and then shut it when Simon, Ed and Darcie appeared behind him.

'I . . .' Abigail didn't know what was worse: their faces or the smug look on Matt's. 'I was just . . .'

'You were just going to somehow sneak through an entire army of Tenebrous, scale Daybreak and then light the candleward at its summit,' Darcie said flatly. 'That was what you were going to do.'

'I knew it,' Matt said, oblivious to Abigail's viperish look. 'She's been all . . . fidgety. I knew she was going to try some sort of stupid heroics. Now let's all go back downstairs and –'

'You'd want the other window on the north wall, by the way,' Darcie said. 'The rooftop sentry just noticed the cupola and moved eight steps down. Also Daybreak's in the opposite direction.'

The only comfort in that moment was that Abigail knew she looked a fraction less surprised than Matt.

'I told you I can feel them,' Darcie said. 'Every Tenebrous in the city. Every Knight too.' She stepped off the stairs. 'I just have one question.'

Abigail nodded wordlessly.

'Are you doing this because you think it'll work? Or are you doing it for revenge?'

After so long of doing it to herself, lying to Darcie was no chore at all.

'I'm doing it because it's the only way to save Daybreak. Because Greaves won't do it. And Vivian would. Because it's the right thing to do.'

'All right,' Darcie said. 'Then we're coming with you.'

'*What?*' Abigail and Matt said together.

It was Simon who answered, his voice as hard as she'd ever heard it.

'I'm not staying here and hoping Greaves gives me something to do, or running messages between cadres just because I'm better at hiding than most.' His voice threatened to crack, but he stilled it with a breath. 'They killed Vivian. Denizen is . . . he's gone. So, if you think this will work then we do it. Darcie can guide us. I can hide us. They'll never see us coming.'

A fragile bubble of hope was blooming in her chest, and Abigail was terrified to argue in case she killed it. 'You're the one coordinating the defence. With you gone . . .'

'I'm not going anywhere,' Darcie said, and threw something to Abigail. 'But I'll guide you all the same.'

A radio. Abigail ran her fingers over the chunky, stippled rubber, the sleek black plastic.

'I've been politely ordered to sleep for four hours because it's been . . .' She frowned. 'A very long time since I've slept. And you're right. My duty is sacred and I would not abandon it. But you're my duty too. I can guide you round Breaches to Daybreak. And you'll have to describe the candleward to me. It sounds fascinating.'

Abigail's words fell across each other in their eagerness to get out. 'And Ed?'

'We have to do something,' was Ed's reply. 'I'm not staying here while you go and fight for us.'

'OK,' Abigail said simply.

'You people are *idiots*.' Matt had retreated back a couple of steps, as if he thought their insanity were catching. His gaze searched face after face, but if he was looking for regret or weakness he didn't find it. 'You can't think you're going to – you're not going to – Abigail, *seriously* –'

'Sorry,' Abigail said. 'Cover for us?'

'*Cover for you?*' A sigh pulled the air from him, so he looked shrunken and small, and then he drew it back in. 'Fine. You win. I'm coming too. I have to, don't I?'

'Actually, no,' Darcie said.

'Not really,' said Simon.

Ed gave a tiny shrug.

'Yes,' Abigail said, and surprised herself by giving him a real and genuine smile. 'You do.' She frowned. 'Though I guess this means we can't go out of the window.'

'I have an idea regarding that,' Darcie said. 'Though I don't know how I feel about it. We should –'

'Um, guys?'

They had been told to avoid the windows, not draw attention, keep noise discipline. It made sense, in a city at war. But, as anything to do with Edifice Greaves, there were wheels within wheels, reasons beneath reasons, and, as they joined Ed to stare out of the north window at Daybreak, Abigail was forced to admit that the Palatine might have had a point.

Gone was the gleam of its white walls, the soaring, defiant cleanness of its lines – replaced by a teeming crust of rot. *Tenebrous*. Hundreds of Tenebrous, a bristling mass that clambered over each other and the lighthouse like wasps in a hive.

Ed's voice was faint. 'Where . . . where did you say we were going again?'

28

IT TAKES A VILLAGE

Pollagh Dock was little more than two arms of concrete sullenly folded in the face of the Atlantic, littered with nets and pots and a great steel hook of an anchor, which Denizen was mildly surprised to see looked exactly like they did in cartoons.

They exited the director's car, and Ackerby, squinting in the darkness, pointed at a squat beetle of a boat with a belligerent, jutting prow.

'That one. The owner uses it for deep-sea fishing.' He purposefully turned his back as Grey bent to the task of nautical larceny, though that put Denizen and Mercy squarely in his field of vision, which was definitely no improvement.

The Tenebrous had managed to rein back her umbra – she wouldn't have fitted in the back seat otherwise – but there was no hiding what she was, and watching her craft a human disguise probably wouldn't have done much for Ackerby's nerves either. He'd had far too much experience of things *looking* human before.

The full set. Seeing *anything* carved into the skin of the universe would have made anybody break out in a cold sweat, but it was the words themselves that were terrifying.

There were any number of reasons why that phrase could be there. Maybe it was a common Tenebraic saying. Maybe there was a horrible speakeasy somewhere – misery on tap, toddler popsicles – and they all traded catchphrases . . .

Do it.

However, the way the Boy had *helped* Denizen to free Mercy, though it meant its own death as well, made it hard to imagine the Man in the Waistcoat having friends.

Please.

Vivian Hardwick rarely gave second chances. She'd burned the Three so badly on their first encounter that it had taken them eleven years to recover and, when they had once again raised their ugly heads, she'd taken great pains to finish the job.

Hadn't she?

With a clarity born of exhaustion and grief, Denizen knew he was currently held together by spit and wire and the demands of the moment. He could only think *around* Vivian – her actions, her crusade – because if he thought *of* her he'd have to accept that she was gone.

Compared to that, the pressure of rescuing the Endless King from Os Reges Point was welcome because it kept bits of him from springing off and exploding. Pressure was good. Pressure made diamonds. Leaving him behind after the Three's first attack had made his mother who she was.

And the thought that Vivian had somehow failed made Denizen sick to his stomach.

She hadn't used a hammer. The thought arrived in the scabby drawl of the Man in the Waistcoat, making Denizen shiver in a way that had nothing to do with the cold coastal breeze. It had only been a shard; even Vivian doubted it held the same potency.

It must. Look at Mercy's arm.

He raised his hand to his scabbard before realizing that Falter was gone. *I'll get it back. I promise. If I have to tear Adumbral apart looking for it.*

'We're ready,' Grey called. 'Fully fuelled and everything. Director, please pass on our thanks to Mr . . .' He examined a page tucked below the boat's dashboard. 'Cattigan. We very much appreciate it.'

'I'll get him to invoice you,' Ackerby croaked. 'And for the gates.'

Grey knocked off a sharp salute and dipped back into the cabin. With a sudden thrill, Denizen realized that there might be a bed, or at the very least a shelf they could tuck him on for a few hours. He was contemplating making a run for it when Mercy wafted closer on fronds of lightning, offering Ackerby a shy smile.

Thank you for your hospitality, Director. It will not be –

'I dreamt of you,' the old man said abruptly. 'In Crosscaper. When . . . when they came. I dreamt of a girl in a cage.'

Oh. Well. I –

'Don't,' he said. 'They weren't good dreams.' He thrust out his jaw. 'Stay away from my orphanage. What . . . whatever you are. Stay away from my children.'

Mercy opened her mouth, and then closed it again.

Of course, was all that she said.

'I guess that goes for me too,' Denizen said, and the pang in his stomach felt stupid and strange.

He didn't like Crosscaper. There was nothing in it to like, bar Simon, and he'd taken him with him when he went. It hadn't been Tenebrous who'd wallpapered those halls with bad memories – it had been long nights of asking himself why *him*, why *here*, why any child at all.

There was a reason the Three had grown fat there. There was a reason why, to him, homesickness was just a word. But still . . .

'No,' Director Ackerby said, and met Denizen's eyes squarely. 'Come back whenever you . . . you're always welcome. Always.'

An unexpected lump in Denizen's throat. 'Thank you.'

'Yes,' the old man said. 'Well. Good luck with . . . whatever it is you're doing.'

They left him there, standing on the pier, a hunched old man holding himself in the midnight chill, and just by coincidence Grey happened to bring the boat around Keem Bay and the grey little buildings nestled there. It was ironic, but for the *Intueor Lucidum* he wouldn't have seen anything at all.

The boat rolled under them like a coin across a conjuror's fingers, and Denizen sat near the gunwale (he'd read up on boats), staring up at the stars – flaws in the onyx of the sky. Achill Island receded, and so too did sound, bar the engine and the shrill of the wind.

'Mercy!' Grey called after an hour or so. 'Can you come here?'

She turned from her perch at the prow of the boat, strikingly bright against the night, and joined Grey at the wheel. Denizen stood too, curious.

'You know which way Os Reges Point is, right?'

Yes.

'Then take the wheel. I have to do something.'

It was a very rare thing to catch Mercy off guard, but her eyes widened at the Knight's words. **What?**

'It's OK – you just have to keep us steady. It's just like riding a bike.'

Mercy stared at him blankly.

'Yes,' Grey said, and Denizen stifled an exhausted smile. 'I thought that might be your reaction. Five minutes – that's all. Turn her gently and . . .'

She nodded, brow crinkling in confusion as, one-handed, she braced herself against the wheel. Waves jinked and jerked them sideways, and a slow smile dawned across her face as, with minute adjustments, she corrected and steadied them. Her light changed, from capillary crazes of lightning to a slow, rolling pulse, mirroring the flow of the sea.

Grey watched her a moment longer and then made his way back to Denizen, sitting down heavily beside him. Denizen realized with a start that however little sleep he had got, Grey had had even less.

'That was a nice thing to do,' Denizen said quietly.

'Well,' the Knight said, 'she knows where we're going. And . . . we don't know what she's going to find, you know?'

Denizen nodded solemnly.

Grey! Grey! Mercy's delight came in glittering waves. **I'm doing it!**

'You are!' Grey called back, and he flashed her a grin before turning back to Denizen. 'We have something to do.'

'What's that?'

'We're knighting you,' Grey said.

Denizen's eyes widened.

'Normally, it has to be a Malleus,' Grey said, with forced lightness, 'and there's Latin bits and arm-waving bits and robes and whatever, but it's been a very long day and . . .'

He swallowed.

'And Vivian knighted me, a long time ago, and I feel it's the right thing to do. There's no magic to it or anything, but . . . it's . . .'

'The right thing,' Denizen said hollowly. The world was still loosed from its moorings, but he felt something solidify at Grey's words. *There's no magic to it.* And there wasn't. Vivian would say as much herself. 'I understand.'

'Then kneel,' Grey said.

Denizen did so. He should have felt silly, and the rolling of the deck made it more of a challenge than it should have been, and Denizen was usually too busy asking questions and poking holes in moments to ever believe them sacred . . . but the sea seemed to calm and the wind quiet all the same.

'My Latin is terrible,' Grey said, drawing his sword with a rasp of steel. 'But I've got the gist.' Power climbed the blade in loops and whorls, first the colour of embers, then flame, then the summer sun.

'Denizen Hardwick,' Grey said, and there was no wryness now, no self-deprecation, no weakness and no fear. It wasn't the voice of a mentor, or a victim, or a friend.

It was the voice of a Knight of the Borrowed Dark.

'It might be fine,' Grey said. 'That mightn't have been a scream. That might not be blood on the ground. You can keep walking. You can ignore those hairs rising on your neck, that shadow in the window. You can walk on. Someone else might fix it. Someone else might face that hell.

'Some do. Most do. You can live your whole life in the light, and not look for darkness. We wouldn't begrudge you that. We would never begrudge you that. And if you do stay, if you do choose to fight . . . your reward is that choice, again and again and again. There is no magical binding. There is no Oath but this.'

The blade *burned.*

'We ask you, as we asked you . . .' Grey frowned. 'Last night. Two nights ago? Sorry, there's normally more time between those . . .' He shook himself. 'Ahem. Do you want to be a Knight?'

She'd always looked so imperious. So determined. So *hard.* But now all Denizen could think of was how much

Vivian must have cared, to go to war for people she'd never met. The thought rocked him, so much that he felt the blade sear his skin. Denizen had known how resolute Vivian was from the moment they'd met, but he'd never considered her heart until it stopped.

'I will fight,' Denizen Hardwick said, the way his mother must have on the day she lost her husband, and on every other day until the day she died.

Gently, Grey's blade tapped his shoulder. 'Then arise, Knight.'

Denizen wasn't sure how long it took them to reach the Point. There was nothing out here for time to grab on to – nothing to erode, or grow or bloom or die, nothing but them, skating across the surface of the sea.

Mercy held the helm, the moonlight passing through her and turning glacier blue. Grey watched the horizon, the shadows under his eyes dark even through the *Lucidum*, and Denizen stared too, trying not to ask himself questions he couldn't answer – about his friends, about Daybreak, whether the Order still fought or if the last hope for humanity was three figures in a tiny boat.

And then . . . the first fingertip rising over the horizon, and another, and another, as if they were cradled in the Endless King's palm. Mercy aimed for the smallest of the spires – *smallest*, at three hundred metres tall – and the temperature fell like a stone.

Their breath plumed. Denizen had to carefully draw on his fire, letting down some – but not all – of his guards until the fire was close enough to his blood to stop it freezing entirely. The waves around them sharpened, white edges turning to glass, until Denizen could have run his hand along them and bled red warmth into the depths.

The boat's passage through the water became the crunching rasp of slicing snow, until finally it ground to a halt, a full ten metres from the tiny stone pier. Their path behind them had already frozen.

Denizen stared down at the crust of ice, but, before he could even test it with his feet, Mercy blurred past them so fast that she left a sickly streak across his iron retina. Grey didn't hesitate, leaping out after her. The ice groaned but held firm, and Denizen followed, moving as fast as he could while wincing at every shudder and crackle under his feet.

The pier led to a vertical shaft straight up through the first spire, as if the finger bone had been removed without disturbing the surrounding flesh. Mercy shot up into it, her light melting the accumulated ice so that Denizen and Grey had to duck away from falling rain.

'Climb!' Grey snapped, light flickering and snapping under his skin.

It wasn't easy. Denizen had had a full year of training since he'd been here the last time, but a day and a night of fighting and running and *more* fighting had taken its toll.

Within fifty rungs, he was hissing breath between clenched teeth. After a hundred, a stray scurf of ice tore his knee, and it wasn't the pain that slowed him but the wind suddenly feasting on his open skin. His dripping blood became a welcome source of heat.

The bridge between the first and second spire was a rigid line bearded by frost. They sprinted across it, and another, and another, and Denizen could trace Mercy's passage from where ice had melted and refrozen in a thousand colours, as if she left rainbows in her wake.

And, as they rose, so too did the pall of the Tenebrae – distorting colours, separating sounds. Every moment felt disjointed, a movie laid out shot by shot with nothing to connect them. It didn't feel as poisoned here: not the arch malice of Dragon nor the muddied rot of lower beasts. This was the only place in the world where the Tenebrae felt . . . not natural, exactly, not to Denizen, but maybe natural to something else.

Different instead of *wrong*.

Finally, they reached the summit, the stars hanging down like Christmas decorations, bright and sharp. The air was fine with mist and ice particles, billions of them. It hid the crashing sea below, dusted Grey and Denizen until their clothes and skin were stiff and crackling with frost and reflected moonlight.

It made Mercy look like a queen.

She floated over an outline of rust – the spot where the Emissary had once been imprisoned – her light snapping at each mote of cold as if defending her in a thousand tiny dogfights. She didn't acknowledge them. Instead, blades slid from her hands, or *became* her hands, sizzling ice droplets out of existence as she stared down at . . .

The King. The *Endless King*. The Master of Shadows. The Lord of the Obscura. The Knights talked about him in such hallowed, terrified terms that sometimes it was hard to remember that the King was a Tenebrous at all. When he'd threatened the world over Mercy's disappearance, the Order hadn't even *considered* taking him on. Ants didn't fight a descending boot. They just got out of its way.

And afterwards . . . afterwards, Denizen had only really thought of the King through the prism of Mercy. The power she wielded through him. The sad way she spoke of him. The fondness. The threat.

He had never expected the King to be beautiful.

Where Mercy was silver, the Endless King was gold – not the dull hue of cold metal but molten, moving – currents of auric lava billowing like ribbons around graceful, elongated limbs, shrouding wide, noble shoulders until the true form of the King was something more glimpsed than perceived.

Denizen saw eyes like augered pits, a thin slit of a mouth never meant for smiling, cheekbones as sharp and hard as the head of an axe. He was reminded of funeral masks, of child kings and emperors long dead.

The Opening Boy had its foot on the King's neck.

At last, it whispered. **The full set.**

29

NO MAN'S LAND

Abigail firmly believed that, with enough training, anybody could become good at anything. Denizen and Simon hadn't had her childhood. She'd watched them spar, as knobble-kneed as calves, seen them fail and fail again to follow Vivian's movements, or Darcie's, or hers.

Anyone could become good at anything, but nothing was automatic. Nothing was owed. They'd all inherited magic from their parents, and metabolism and senses and size were the gifts of DNA, but you still needed to learn how to use them, and the key to learning was a thousand tiny decisions to keep going. To not give up.

She'd been surprised to learn it was the same with betrayal.

Faking an awkward smile when told they were moving on. Distracting a sentry with questions while Simon filched a radio from its charging stand. Watching Darcie draw out the route to their next camp and hoping nobody noticed how uncharacteristically unskilled one section of the sketch became.

Abigail counted each little crime the way she'd count footfalls on a particularly hard run, or the way she'd grade muscle pain when training became almost too tough. A way to take stock. To look at how far she'd come.

They broke camp, Darcie's map leading them through a city turning on itself in the most awfully literal way. Material gnawed from the sides of buildings, earth scooped up in bomb-crater blotches, the air a dreary, thickened fog that seemed only a heartbeat away from coalescing into madness and teeth.

Greaves led from the front – *of course he did; he knows the path is safe* – with Ed, Simon, Abigail and Matt a half-ignored cluster towards the back. Darcie, by contrast, was so surrounded by Knights you could barely see her.

And ahead, the minaret. That had brought a thrill of guilt – though of course Darcie hadn't chosen it, there was little of this plan any of them had *chosen*, just the need to do what Greaves would not – but its slim length did make Abigail think of soft prayers and home . . . and what her parents would think of her actions now.

Sometimes you have to go first. That way you make it easier for everyone else.

The stones moved beneath her feet. Breaches used to stand out like drops of ink in pure water. Now the atmosphere barely changed before a rent opened at head height, black liquid whipping forth.

There was a stirring, prideful moment as Abigail watched the best-trained warriors on the face of the planet respond to the threat with parade-ground precision – falling into overlapping lines, the Neophytes dragged out of the way, Darcie lifted, *lifted* off her feet – and the

Tenebrous had barely plundered itself a skeletal form before a dozen Cants tore it apart.

There was a second shape coming from the rent. This one was already formed – hulking, horned – and Abigail briefly met its narrowed eyes before she turned and ran.

Was it still betrayal if you were doing it for the right reasons? Was it still fleeing if you were running towards a greater fear? There had been plenty of time for Abigail to ponder this as Darcie searched for a Breach to lead the Palatine to – a Breach big enough to serve as a distraction, but not big enough to be a threat. It had been as difficult as it sounded. There were few small Breaches now.

The shouts of battle rose behind, and Abigail prayed for everything she couldn't control to come down in her favour. She prayed that the Knights would focus on the battle at hand, and she prayed that Greaves would bid his force continue to a safe base and not waste time and soldiers looking for her, and she prayed to be able to look Darcie in the eye if any of them died.

Ed, Simon and Matt were running beside her. That was one prayer answered at least.

They ran for exactly three streets – Darcie had been very precise – pausing beneath where a marching set of aqueducts met the bulk of a massive cistern. They paused in its shadow, *Lucidum* painting detail silver out of the dark, and Simon bent light to take them out of sight.

'Right,' Abigail whispered, unfolding a sheet of paper from her pocket. 'Let's see.'

Darcie had been *very* precise. Simon's hard-won affinity for the Starlight Caul was an advantage, but, without Darcie mapping out Breach sites, existing Tenebrous *and* patrolling cadres, they would have been lost. The notes she had provided would be accurate until she was next able to contact them –

Unless the battle brings more Tenebrous.

Unless she gets hurt.

Unless they all die –

– and Abigail used the quiet faith her friend had shown in her to slow the hammering of her heart, and start the *Lux*'s count.

Three minutes to get to the marketplace – a few wooden stalls still standing, bone-dry and brittle after centuries of sun. Pausing for a minute to let a stretch of paving ahead tear itself free like a manta ray shuffling from a sandbank, before propelling itself into the night with a single flap of flagstone wings.

They passed knots of abused air where nightstuff drooled up and down like saliva from a jaw, where statues of Order heroes charged by, animated by burrowing black, screaming the names of descendants they hoped to slay.

And as hateful as it was to see Darcie's bestiaries come to life – bloody-mouthed Cruachan, Sweet James and its wallpaper wings – the fighting was something Abigail understood. But then she saw the Widows of Victory – three women twice her height fused at the scalp into a pyramid of flesh and hair and sweat – just *stroll* through the streets, wearing an expression very similar to the one Abigail had worn when she'd first arrived at Daybreak.

Wonder.

They took shelter in the gardens of an ancient villa to wait for Darcie to make contact, but the brief relief from the monstrous tableau was no respite at all. Matt twitched at every sound, his fingers cramping tight on his sword, and Abigail had kept catching Ed walking with his eyes closed, like a child hiding from the bogeyman. As for Simon . . .

He hadn't complained. He never really did, not about things that mattered. But, even though hiding in the villa had let him momentarily drop his mask, there was still a parched, drained cast to his skin, and he had that gritted-teeth, seconds-counting determination you only saw when approaching the edge of exhaustion.

You can do this. She didn't dare say the words aloud. Part of her wanted to squeeze his hand or touch his arm, but she was worried about distracting him or . . . or how much Cost she might find. They had a long way to go. There, and back, and whatever they had to face on the way.

How much of Simon would be left?

The wait dragged on, Abigail *willing* the lump of plastic in her hands to speak, while simultaneously obsessively checking the volume dial to make sure it didn't give them away. She didn't have to imagine the Tenebrous that could pounce on them at any moment: she could hear their idiot babbling just beyond the walls, like a parody of birdsong.

'Hello? Abigail?'

They all sat bolt upright. Matt went to grab the radio, but Abigail got there first, clicking the send/receive button back and forth in the simple affirmation they'd agreed on in case they had to be quiet.

'Ask her what to do,' Matt hissed, and then flinched as Abigail, Simon and Ed all glared at him.

'*All right. Quick report. We're safe. Made camp. Two wounded, no casualties.*'

Abigail sighed in relief. When you were a Knight, it was the unknown that killed you. That was why *Luxes* were so cherished. It was their job, their *calling*, to send the Order into battle with as much intel as they could. And Darcie had volunteered to betray that calling in a heartbeat, because she trusted Abigail.

Guilt threatened to overwhelm Abigail before she tamped it down. *Just one more reason why this has to work.*

'*Your absence has been noted. Greaves is incandescent.*'

Simon and Abigail shared a look. Only Darcie could give a quick report and still use words with more than three syllables.

'*But I've found you a way in. At least I think I have. The front gates are mobbed with Tenebrous, but inside is relatively empty.*'

They could hear her disgust through the static.

'*Picked clean.*'

'Then how do we –' This time Matt shut himself up.

'*There's one area they seem to be avoiding. I'm not sure why. There was Tenebraic activity there, but it's as if . . .*'

There was a pause that usually meant Darcie was trying to explain something you needed extra senses to understand. *'As if it's been cauterized. It's the Asphodel Path.'*

'We're not using the Path,' Simon and Ed said in unison, panic bright on both their faces.

'Shh!' Matt snapped indignantly, but, before Abigail could bang all their heads together, Darcie continued.

'It's that or fight your way through God knows how many Tenebrous. The entrance isn't even far from here, if you . . .'

She delivered a series of clipped, precise instructions, Abigail jotting them down before Simon hid the four of them once again, sweat painting pink trails down his face through the dust.

It took them another aching, panting half-hour to find it – a manhole cover partially obscured by rubble. Ed and Matt began clearing it away, Abigail keeping watch, Falter a slick chill in her hands. It had felt right to bring it with them. To carry it where Denizen could not.

When the cover was clear, Matt gripped it, muscles writhing like snakes, and began to heave it upwards, centimetre by gasping centimetre. Ed didn't hesitate, dropping to his stomach and shimmying on to the ladder inside. Simon went more carefully, the air above them rippling as he fought to steady the Cant. Abigail took a deep breath, glancing around one last time, the ever-present pall of dust clearing just for a moment –

– to reveal a Knight. A lone Knight – as stout and boxy as a forklift, a pair of morning stars flickering around her so fast they had created their own mini-cyclone of grit. Her assailants were mere ghosts – the most diffuse Tenebrous Abigail had ever seen – filthy cinder outlines with clutching hands and bobbing, vulpine heads. There must have been a hundred of them.

'Abigail, come on!'

Matt had moved on to the first rung of the ladder, hefting the cover on his back like a red-faced Atlas, but Abigail couldn't move, watching the woman lose one morning star to grasping claws before punching the spiked ball of her other weapon through the smudged swirl of its head.

And, above, something was growing, drinking in every speck and ember, a gravel disaster of spectral limbs the Knight hadn't even seen. How could she have? To take her eyes off the fight would have ended it for good.

'You can't help her! Help *us*!'

How did you know? How did you know which betrayals brought you nearer to the greater good? How did you know which were a step closer to yourself and which were a step further away? Why, when everything else in Abigail's life was a composite network of decisions and effort and cause and effect, had it taken one heartbeat for the Emissary to make her betray herself?

The Helios Lance burst from her fingers with a kestrel's wail, blowing out the dust devil's half-formed brainpan. The Knight turned at its sudden screech, but Abigail had already dropped into the dark.

Ash puffed from her landing, her vision jolting to silver lines in the tunnel's gloom. She couldn't tell what it had once been used for, the walls now scorched to anonymity.

'What happened here?' she asked.

'Hardwicks,' Simon said, with a touch of his old humour, but his smile was short-lived. The air stung with the memory of smoke, and every step they took came with its own mourning shroud. And Matt, for some reason, had removed his shirt.

'What are you *doing*?' she said as he began wadding up the garment and tearing strips free. Simon just stared as Matt handed him a long shred and then gave another to Ed.

'Don't want to choke on the ash, do we?'

Ed stared down at the sweaty rag in his hand. 'Can I get back to you?'

'Suit yourself,' Matt said with a shrug.

Abigail soon learned that what they found was not an easier route but a trade-off. Simon no longer had to hide them behind the Caul, and she could hear him breathing more easily, but now their footing was less certain, the ash fine and soft and treacherous. They had to drag their feet free after every step.

Eventually, the tunnel began to curve upwards, the scorch marks becoming fainter. Soon they travelled through a corridor that could have been any in Daybreak – though odd, shallow channels seemed to have been cut into the walls, as long as Abigail's torso but barely a few centimetres deep.

'The mosaics,' Abigail said with a start, reaching a hand out to almost – but not quite – touch the bare stone. 'They took all the mosaics.'

'And anything that's not nailed down,' Simon said, peering into what might have been an archive, scraps of paper littering it like crumbs.

'Maybe that's why the Tenebrous are all outside?' Ed was clutching his sword so tightly that all his trembling had transferred to its point, making it buzz back and forth like a bluebottle figuring out where to land. 'That's good, right?'

Abigail nodded. 'We can do this. We just need to be careful. And not just of Tenebrous. Dragon tore through the upper floors on its way out. We may have to . . . climb in places.'

'Oh,' Simon said shakily. 'Cool.'

Matt looked equally despondent, but Abigail grabbed them both by the shoulders. 'We can do this,' she said. 'We just need to take it slow, watch our corners –'

Ed began looking around wildly for corners. Simon gave him a tired smile.

'– and keep together.'

Now that they were out of the tunnel, Simon hid them again, and they went on, ghosts infiltrating a ghost. Even the battle sites they passed were muted, scavenged down to the bone.

She could see the outlines of where barricades had been, and wondered if they were now grim trophies adorning the monsters that had broken them. They passed discarded mosaic tiles, and she wondered whether Tenebrous had been too glutted to pick them up, like millionaires ignoring pennies in the street.

Only once did they see a Tenebrous – a gangling, marsupial shape that padded by them so quickly none of them even had a chance to react. Abigail kept her blade out after that.

Their ascent seemed to stretch into infinity. Whispered correspondence with Darcie, staircases blurring into staircases, Abigail becoming dizzy with backtracking and path-crossing. In some places, the floor had canted, sourceless breezes cooling the gluey sweat on their limbs, and Abigail knew that they were close to Dragon's exit wound.

At one point, Matt opened a door and *there* it was – a hole the width of a basketball court, with the multi-storey shattered intestines of Daybreak beyond it on the other side. Matt closed the door again.

'Are you all right? What's wrong?'

'Nothing,' Simon replied to Darcie faintly. 'Just . . . we have an obstacle.'

'I'm sorry, but there'll be another Breach near you soon. You need to go this way – it's the fastest route. What's the obstacle? Can I help?'

'I don't think so,' Simon said. 'Matt? Open the door.'

Matt took two steps back down the corridor, and opened the door with the tips of his fingers as if trying to stay as far away from the edge as possible.

'It's fine,' Simon said. 'It'll be grand. The edges are kind of . . . ragged, I guess? We can just . . . climb around it?' His voice had gained a sort of sing-song, falsely positive quality. 'OK. I'm just going to do it now. And you guys have to do it too because I'm not turning my head to look back when I get out there. OK?'

And, before they could answer, he was out of the door. A yelp escaped Ed before he clamped his hands over his mouth, but, between the howling wind and the knowledge that even *Tenebrous* probably weren't insane enough to do what Simon had just done, noise discipline had stopped being a priority.

'Oh God. Oh God. Oh God.'

The words escaped Ed with every step closer to the doorway, as if being dragged against his will. He pressed himself against the frame, foot balanced on the shorn lip of the drop, and then inched out after Simon with the methodical shimmy of a caterpillar.

'Ed, *wait* –'

And then it was just Matt and Abigail and the honeycomb of exposed rooms beyond. As she watched, the floor in one gave way, and a wardrobe slid down the newborn slope, vomiting out clothes before tipping over itself.

She dragged her gaze up. *Heights*. She hated them. Always had. The plane ride over had been torture – trapped in a tiny metal tube, her life at the whim of forces she couldn't control.

Do you feel good enough, Abigail Falx?

Those were the words that pushed her out. She moulded herself to the door frame as Ed had done, her shoulders as tense as climbing hooks, and insinuated herself out over the gap. It was as Simon had said: Dragon's violent emergence had left a collar of stone, the remnants of corridors and hallways and rooms and lives, just wide enough to traverse.

What he had neglected to mention was that in some places the collar was wider than in others. That some stretches were coming away entirely. That rubble and belongings would occasionally just tumble down and that, in every direction Abigail looked, was the hotchpotch horror of her Order's eviscerated home.

Keep going. Keep going. Every step was a bang of elbows, a scrape across calves. But she was a warrior, she was a *Knight* – nearly, someday, probably – and she wouldn't be defeated by mere gravity. Hadn't she crossed the bridge at Os Reges Point? That was at least as terrifying as this.

But you were trying to put a brave face on then.

I'm always *trying to put a –*

She looked down. Abigail had never been held at gunpoint. According to Denizen, it was really unpleasant. But that was what looking down felt like – staring into the barrel of a gun a city street wide and ten storeys deep, and at the bottom . . . blackness. Blackness as dense as a bullet, but *churning*, heaving and swelling with a sound like all the sinks in creation being unblocked at once.

It drove her soul to the roof of her skull, rolled her eyes back in her head. For a second, she was absolutely sure she blacked out, except that she seemed to be awake to endure it. She swayed, nearly pitching forward –

'There's a monument at home.' Matt was at her side, bare chest beaded with so much sweat he looked like he'd been caught in a monsoon.

Abigail couldn't even think of responding. Her words would just *fall*, and drag her out and down –

'My parents make me climb it every year.'

It was strange, the anchors that pulled you back. Abigail had no idea why this stood out to her now, of all places, but this was the first time she'd heard him mention his parents. The thought steadied her, just for a moment, and words spilled out.

'Is it . . . is it tall?'

'Giant,' Matt said, smiling grimly. 'And the stairs get smaller and smaller as you go up it, and when you get up there . . . You know when you're so high up you feel if you did fall you might fall up instead of down?'

'No,' Abigail said. 'I've never felt that at all.'

'Well, I get that feeling,' he said. 'Not getting it now, though. So things can't be all bad.'

And then he pushed her over, and she landed on solid ground.

'OK, so we have to –'

Abigail had no doubt that whatever Simon was about to say was integral to their plan, to the war effort, to the *world*, but there was absolutely nothing in her life more important than kicking Matt Temberley in the middle of his stupid face. She went from lying to standing in the time it took for him to step off the ledge, and only the look of sudden terror on his face stopped her hovering foot.

'Abigail,' Simon said very calmly, given the situation. 'If you kick him, he's going to fall off.'

She wouldn't even have to kick. Laid against his cheek as it now was, all her foot would have to do was tap –

'*Are you all right? Abigail? Simon?*'

It was Darcie's voice that stopped her. Matt nearly fell over himself when she drew her foot back and turned away. The rest of the climb was conducted in silence, Simon hiding them, Darcie guiding them and Abigail staying as far away from Matt as she could without compromising their veil of bent light.

The doors to Greaves's office were tall and wide and carved with the hand-and-hammers, and you could be forgiven for being captivated by them and not noticing the narrow set of stairs tucked behind a pillar beyond.

'*It's up there,*' Darcie murmured through the radio. '*But I've never actually . . . you'll have to describe it, and then we'll figure it out.*'

'Right,' Abigail said, and once again drew the stone blade she couldn't begin to think of as hers. The others drew theirs as well – Matt, who was *still* shirtless, and staring at her as if she might attack him, and Ed, who had managed to make his sword stay still for a moment, and Simon, who just shrugged, and let her lead the way.

It was a tall cylinder of a room, walled by diamonds of glass in sturdy iron frames. Abigail knew even before they stepped into the chamber that it wouldn't be an intricate device, some great astrolabe or lantern – this was the Order, and candlewards were just lights, and why be ostentatious when it was normality you were fighting this whole war for?

Rack upon rack of fat jars of oil, and in the centre a wide, stone bowl stacked with tinder higher than Abigail was tall.

The Tenebrous sitting on it smiled.

Hello, children, it said. **My name is Rout.**

30

WHO ELSE?

'No . . .'

The word came fast and high and hysterical.

'It can't be . . .'

Every particle within a few centimetres of Grey flashed to steam.

'You're *dead*.'

What is death, the Opening Boy whispered through its blank black face, **but one more misery I had to endure?**

If you wadded up the universe and slit it with the sharpest knife, drawing a hole in the shape of a child – *that* was the Opening Boy. A free-standing chasm, through which all the heat that had ever existed seemed to gleefully escape. Its outline bunched and wavered, as if fighting against the impossibility of its existence, and, within that deep and sucking void . . .

Stars, or faces, or turning cogs. Tiny lights amid the dark.

I did die, it whispered. **I think. I remember wanting to. The *pain* of it, that little shard of stone . . .**

Denizen remembered each and every plunge of that shard, long before it had been carved into a knife. He remembered the calm and mechanical way that Vivian had broken the Three apart, cracking clockwork to expose the stringy oil within.

But a piece of a thing is not the thing itself.

Mercy hissed as it balanced both feet on the neck of the King absently, just a boy at play treading over a branch.

We know that better than anyone, don't we, Mercy? The Man in the Waistcoat, the Woman in White –

It said the names with more venom than a Hardwick, and the air became so cold it drew a gasp from Denizen's throat.

– loved misery. He found her and she found him, and their appetites changed each other . . . but they never made me like it, no matter how they tried.

Grey's roar was barely human. The swordsman charged, blades a blur – and the Boy waved a hand. Grey's lunge turned to a tumble, as if every tendon were cut. He didn't even cry out.

Our misery never leaves us. Those doors never close. I've hidden in your shadow a long time, Grey . . . feeding on your misery, rebuilding myself, waiting for the moment I could avenge myself on those who had wronged me. Like Dragon was waiting. Like the Emissary was waiting.

The fallen monarch's golden fingers twitched, but the Boy's feet ground down and the King went still. Denizen had expected some sort of prison, some baroque enchantment or instrument of torture, not . . . *this*, something ancient and broken, abandoned in the middle of the ocean, trapped beneath the feet of a child.

I believe they were surprised to see me when I declared myself a Usurper, but they had their own vengeances to pursue, and killing the Order or killing a daughter is far less ambitious than mine. For a while, I even helped you. How shocked some Tenebrous were to Breach into the city of their hated enemy and find my freezing touch instead.

How pleased was Dragon when the sound of sobbing gave away his prey.

The sobbing that had made him go upstairs just before Dragon's attack. He'd thought it familiar, and he'd been right. He'd thought it human and been wrong.

Little touches. That's all it ever takes. A touch of guilt to make Grey join you . . .

Grey yawled against the frozen surface of the spire, drawn out and forlorn.

And anger and memory to cloud him, when he should have been doing his job.

Forced mirth in the Boy's voice then, thin as cracking ice.

Why didn't you call the Order, Grey? Wasn't that your mission? Your duty? The Order might have accepted you, but we know the truth, don't we . . .

Denizen hadn't thought it possible to feel any colder. *We could have called for reinforcements.* But Dragon, and Crosscaper, and losing Vivian, and sheer exhaustion and seeing those words carved into the ground . . .

Like the past had conspired to stop them. Like the weight of memory had slowed them down.

We are never free, Graham. Not of what has been done to us.

Unhand him. Mercy's voice was a whip crack. Hairs rose on the back of Denizen's neck at the building taste of lightning. *Get away from my father.*

Oh, but it's *fascinating*, don't you think? Our great and awful monarch, the Lord of all Tenebrous, He-Who-Is-*Endless*.

The words turned into a hiss so like the Man in the Waistcoat's that fire nearly punched its way through Denizen's ribcage, jerking him bodily forward, tightening sinews so that his hands came up curled into claws.

This was where the veil between realities was thinnest. This wind-scoured peak was where the line between here and *there* barely existed at all. The last time Denizen had been here the fire had hammered the underside of his skin like a swimmer trapped under ice, desperate to be free, to return to the Tenebrae from where it came.

The Boy did not possess eyes, but Denizen was sure it was looking at him.

All our little boasts. The *Endless* King, the *Forever* Court . . . all to hide what we really are. Impermanent. Temporary. We are ourselves as long as we can stand to be, and then we fall apart. Only misery is eternal. Only misery is unchanging.

'But you *helped* us.' Denizen had finally made his voice work. 'At Crosscaper. You helped me free Mercy.'

And I couldn't even die. Wind flurried at the Opening Boy's words, a blizzard of relentless hate. **I just wanted everything to *stop*.**

'Then *why*?' Denizen asked. 'Why are you doing this? If all you want is peace then why start a war?'

Because it will end me, the Boy said simply. **The Emissary, or *you*, or a challenger . . . or I will be King, and then I will have armies with which to scour this globe and every other until *something*, somewhere, kills me.**

And . . . Mercy's voice was soft with horror. **If nothing can?**

Then maybe when the entire omniverse is dead, when everything that exists is as polished and cold as beads of frozen rain on a string . . . then maybe I will know peace.

Grey fought to get his blades under him, to lever himself up on the points of his swords, but the Boy waved a hand and his struggles stilled.

Just let me, it said, not unkindly. **Just leave me with the King and his child.** The darkness of its fingers lengthened, splitting the universe until long blades of night and frost gently *tinked* against the ground. **I won't even make you watch.** It paused. **Why are you *still* fighting?**

Grey was just flopping now, struggling with every muscle his body possessed.

Stop it.

He did, and then he started again. It might have been comical had it not been so painful.

I said stop it. You can't change what will happen. No one can.

'You could.'

Denizen had tried this before, with the Redemptress of the Croits. Tenebrous were creatures of will. If you could change that, you could change them. If you changed that, you could change anyone. Even yourself.

Stop, it snarled. **I don't want to –**

'You don't want to *what*?' Denizen asked, though what the Boy wanted was rapidly becoming secondary to the inferno in his chest. As his determination to do something built, so too did the desire to *do something* that involved payback for everything they had gone through. Everything they had suffered.

Simon.

Abigail.

Vivian.

All because this creature wanted to die.

Give it what it wants.

Denizen struggled. He struggled for Mercy and he struggled for himself, because as much as the creature was crying out for death, as much as it had done . . . he didn't want to be the one who did it. He didn't want to murder this miserable thing because far too much of it reminded him of *himself*.

Tenebrous became like their obsessions, and Denizen had heard these arguments against hope before.

'Listen to me.' He tried to take a step forward, but his every molecule was bent towards holding back a cascade of flame. Every gulping breath of freezing air he took was held in the hopes it would somehow defuse the explosion building within. 'You don't have to do *any* of this. You can be whatever you want. You're just a *kid*.'

I'm not, the Boy said sadly. **I'm really, really not. The childhood was stripped from me a long time ago. I remember their laughter. Their screams. I remember –**

Oh no.

I remember Soren Hardwick begging for his life.

'Don't,' Denizen said, and light rode the word to sizzle frost from the air. 'Please don't.' The fortress of focus and control was disappearing like winter before summer, vanishing like the woman who had helped him create it.

I remember the Man in the Waistcoat practising the intonation so he could properly mimic it later, all the better to wring a tear from Vivian Hardwick's eye.

'Shut *up*,' Denizen snapped.

And we got them, you know? The Vivian you knew was the end result of a *long* process, and she fell through all manner of personalities before she landed on the engine of war you called *mother*. We beat her with your father's last moments, just as we planned to beat her with yours.

There was terrible laughter in the Boy's voice, not the mad cackling of a monster, but the quiet chuckle of a hopeless child.

Denizen had both hands pressed to his head, as if trying to hold those last walls up, and he honestly didn't know if the next words were for the Boy . . . or for himself.

'You. Have. A. Choice.'

Do you want to see? Do you want to see how little you matter?

Eyes frost-glued to the form of the Boy, Denizen had almost forgotten about Mercy until she surged forward, light spearing from her form. For a moment, she was the terrible avatar of storm and smoke that he had first met, all those months ago.

Don't!

The Opening Boy raised its claws, splaying them like clock hands, like the skinless wings of a bat.

This place, this Point . . . where the two worlds are one. Where you could step to the other as easily as taking a breath. Its fingers hooked into empty air, but Denizen *felt* the Tenebrae shiver, as if the Boy's claws had somehow sunk deeper. There was something familiar about the gesture. Denizen couldn't figure out what it was.

As easy as opening a seam.

It dug its fingers in deeper and *tore*, and Os Reges Point fell out of the universe, taking Denizen and the others with it.

Not a single mote of ice was disturbed, but Denizen's stomach abruptly climbed his throat like an aircraft taking a terminal dive. The stars above them wheeled and went out, replaced by . . .

DENIZEN! Mercy's voice was a snarl. ***CLOSE YOUR EYES!***

It was the one rule for travelling through the Tenebrae, whether you'd hooked your own fingers and torn a hole into another dimension, or whether a misery-driven monster did it for you. Because before bladecraft, before Cants, before even the Cost, Knights of the Borrowed

Dark saw in the dark, and that was exactly what Denizen was doing now.

He *saw.*

The Point remained, but the sea they looked on was different. Instead of grey and white, this ocean was *black* – seething, freezing black, the same black that Knights fell through every time they used the Art of Apertura. A black Denizen now saw through. His gaze fell through a million miles of arctic night to the secret geography beneath – a vast plain of crevices and cracks, like a crumpled sheet of steel sprawling from horizon to horizon, and all of it covered in teetering stacks of detritus and wreckage.

Denizen saw ships – oil tankers, galleons, even planes – sticking out from the drift like children's toys. There were structures that might have been ships, or statues, or skulls, but built to a scale and shape never intended for the human eye. There were *skeletons*, actual skeletons, so large they could have curled round the paltry planet Denizen called home, and mountains that weren't mountains but just piles of accreted junk.

They must have fallen out through Breaches, Denizen thought. *It's like the . . . back of the omniverse's settee. Like . . . like Everywhere's ocean floor.* You could have upended the entire planet Earth on to this wasteland and not filled a fraction of it. That meant . . . that meant . . .

DON'T!

Denizen looked up. It almost killed him.

Take a glass slide, and carefully cultivate upon it bacteria in as much complexity and colour as you possibly can.

Now let that sliver grow exponentially, stretching and stretching, and let every centimetre of it be covered in complicated *life*, viral, ever-multiplying, ever-evolving, and yet somehow *retain* that first detail, that microbe-level awareness of every moving part . . .

. . . and then place another behind with the same detail but different in *every possible* way and then another and another in a stupidly vast spinal column of jagged shapes grinding against each other like continents had gods . . .

Look at it, the Boy whispered, so close to Denizen's ear that had there not been the entire omniverse before his eyes he might have jumped. **What do you matter next to that?**

Mercy had told him there were other dimensions. She had thrown it out with a smile and a quip and he had laughed because the omniverse was real now, and weren't their lives ridiculous, and it was only now he understood that meant that his entire history and that of the Order and that of his planet and that of his galaxy were all just one place, and there was another step to the left.

This was what lay on the other side of the Glimpse. This was what Greaves made them see, before he asked children to take on a job with no victory in sight.

What's the *point*, compared to that? Just give up.

The voice was closer now, but Denizen was too busy simply staring. No wonder Tenebrous went mad. No wonder only the most determined of them could hold any kind of shape. Denizen was surprised that the sheer *everythingness* of it all hadn't pounded his flesh from his bones.

Just relax.

Denizen frowned.

'What?'

Had Denizen not jumped backwards, the Opening Boy would have cut him in half. As it was, the very tips of its claws tugged Denizen in a circle by the stomach, drawing bright drops of blood that froze as soon as they touched the air. They clattered on the ice like beads.

And Denizen remembered who he was, and where he was.

'I'm never relaxed!' he snarled, which was an absolutely dreadful battle-cry, as battle-cries went, but it had the desired effect.

The Opening Boy howled at him, as cold and sharp as winter, and Denizen wanted to howl back because there was a time for being a person. There was a time for trying your best. And there were excuses for being your worst, and standing on a dying god's fingers and listening to someone mock your dead parents was the best excuse in the omniverse. He knew. He'd seen it.

But . . . that wasn't how his mother had raised him.

Walls rose in Denizen's head and, for once in their strange partnership, he felt entirely in control of the fire. Maybe it knew he couldn't be budged this time. Maybe it knew that one way or another it would get the release it wanted.

Maybe they were family too.

It came to Denizen's hand, crackling as pure and strong as a *proper* dragon's fire, and with the flick of a wrist a summit's worth of snow was gone. The Boy skittered backwards, scraped a double handful of sparks from the ground with its claws, and came at Denizen with a shrieking laugh.

Helios Lance.

An arrow of light that the Boy dashed to pieces before –

Scintilla Scythe.

– twisting in mid-air to catch the blade of fire lashing from Denizen's fingers. The impact drove it to the ground, wriggling in a way a real child's joints wouldn't allow, and then it was on him again, fingers extended like the points of spears. Denizen rolled, instantly soaked, instantly dry, before lifting it from its feet with a snarl of Sunrise.

Keep your eyes on it.

Above them, the crazed shatterscape of the omniverse warred with the night sky of Os Reges Point as Mercy darted to her father and Grey clutched his skull and Denizen let Cant follow Cant follow Cant. Anathema Bends as sharp as knives, the bang of a Eulice's Ram, a Qayyim Myriad turning the air to stars and still the Boy came at him, again and again, like a predatory black hole.

JUST LET ME DO THIS.

The Boy was growing, the universe paring back along its lines to admit more night, more cold. It had once been a crowded galaxy inside the Boy, but now it was a window to deepest space, where nothing lived and nothing ever could.

And Denizen began to realize, somewhere in the plummeting kaleidoscope of fire and impact and darkness, that he was going to lose. He was black to his elbows.

There were buds opening in his knees and back, motes of iron that the fire had to flow *around* rather than *through*. He was going to lose because he had only so much darkness to give and the Boy had already given up.

Yield not.

Ebony claws raining down.

Yield not.

No breath in his chest. No Cants, no hope, just an entire galaxy pressing down on him until he shattered beneath it. The Boy's featureless head opened in a snarl –

And Grey split it in half.

The spoken steel disappeared into that sucking void, but Grey had already let it go, flinging the Boy backwards with a boot to the chest. The Knight was aflame, so bright Denizen could barely look at him – a star in the shape of a man.

The Boy had grown – *when had he grown that much?* – to tower over them both, a distended shadow still retaining the awkward physiology of a child, hauling claws the length of swords behind it. Grey never hesitated – weaving and slashing and cutting darkness away with every stroke.

It was the most superlative display of swordsmanship Denizen had ever witnessed, and he knew that the old Grey might have made a quip, or given a rueful smile, or kept something of himself back from that blur of blazing steel. This one just fought to avenge.

The Opening Boy didn't have time to stagger, slapped back and forth by the sizzling sword. It raised a claw and lost it, grew another and lost that too, and a backhand brought it to one knee. It wailed, as high and afraid as a child, and Grey's light flickered as, just for a second, he stayed his blade –

– and the Opening Boy's claw burst from his back.

Blood came as a waterfall of sparks, hissing as they hit the ground, and Denizen's breath turned solid and painful in his chest. Pinned like a coat on a hook, Grey didn't even fall, feet curling up underneath him, his sword clattering steaming to the ground.

Even the Boy seemed horrified, insofar as any expression could be made out on that blurring, jarring head. The stars in its depths slowed in their spin.

A moment of silence, from one edge of creation to another.

I just . . .

The Boy's voice was small. It began to slide those long claws free.

I didn't . . .

And Grey wrapped his hands round its wrists.

What are you –

There was a tight, crazed grin on Graham McCarron's face. An exultant grin. A triumphant grin.

He took a step forward. The Boy took a step back.

It struggled, and twisted, and tried to change shape, but the Tenebrous was rigid in its misery, and the Knight gripped it in a dead man's grip. Step followed step, and the beast howled pleadingly, but Grey didn't stop and the Boy could not, until they teetered on the edge, hundreds of metres above the sea.

Not you, the beast croaked. **Not . . . not you.**

'If not me . . .' Grey whispered, 'who else?'

They fell without a sound. Silence descended. The sky zipped back up along whatever seam the Opening Boy had slit, but Denizen's vision still wasn't right, and it took a long time before he realized he was crying.

Get up. He didn't know how long he had been kneeling. The wind had died, and, despite the November chill, the unnatural cold the Opening Boy had brought with him was dissipating. *Get up.*

It had to be over now, Denizen thought, as he pushed himself to his feet. Didn't it have to be over? He had reunited Mercy with the King. That was the mission, wasn't it? That was the thing he had to do. He didn't . . . he didn't have anything else to *lose.*

Mercy was kneeling over the King, cradling his head in her one good hand. The other lay across her chest like a promise. Like a plea.

Denizen's eyes met hers, and then she broke her father's neck.

31

ROUT

Humans were predators.

It was a fact Abigail was aware of, but had never quite believed. When you thought *predator*, you imagined nature red in tooth and claw. You didn't think soft brown skin, or neatly trimmed nails; you didn't think conversation and board games and movie nights. Even Abigail, who had more natural defences than most, didn't think of herself as something designed to hunt and kill.

But Rout had taken everything that was possible to sharpen about the human form and sharpened it – its shoulders backswept barbs, hip bones like fish hooks, stomach muscles a clenched fist straining against skin. It smiled with a mouth like an autopsy scar, and *predator* was the only word that came to mind.

Tell me, it murmured. **Do you know what the word *rout* means?**

Abigail did, as it happened, but more than that she *knew* this beast. During the summer, when all they'd had to face was the frivolous worry of a potential apocalyptic war, they'd learned that Tenebrous were changed by what they envied, and every King should have a Court.

The executioner of the Endless King – though it was possible, Abigail thought numbly, that it was now looking for other employment – stepped daintily from the pile of tinder and brought its umbra down on them like an axe-blade.

Simon fell over. Matt and Ed dropped their blades with a clatter of steel. Abigail had felt something like this before, when the Clockwork Three had flung misery at them in Crosscaper's courtyard a year ago, but not this powerful, not this . . . this sharp.

I want to hear you say it, Rout crooned. **Say what my name means.**

'An overwhelming defeat.'

The voice was crisp. Eyelids tore as the Tenebrous blinked.

'Or the dispersal of a defeated force in complete disorder.'

It wasn't Ed. Or Matt, or Simon. Abigail didn't know that from looking around; she couldn't tear her gaze from the half-moon curve of monster looming over her. She just knew that calm and collected tone.

The Tenebrous was peering at her. Maybe it didn't know what a radio was. Maybe it thought she was speaking. Either way, it let out a delighted purr.

Very good, girl. Very *neat*. Now –

'A bit like your first recorded Breach.'

Just for a second, the despair paralysing Abigail faltered and then, as the beast refocused, it returned tenfold. She saw her court martial. She saw two Hardwicks buried at once, and then her parents, because old age was a fight that nobody won –

'*1410 – the Hundred Years War. You sought to destabilize the Second Peace by masquerading as the border lord Henri Desson. This was before your ascension to the Forever Court, of course –*'

What are you –

'*And then you were hacked to pieces by a cadre of Knights led by Oliver Princeless. While fleeing, I believe.*'

Skin fissured as the Tenebrous bared its teeth, and, though Abigail still reeled beneath a slew of futures she had yet to let down, every time Rout focused on Darcie there was a little bit more space to think.

You –

'*Resurfaced again in 1545 in the form of a pair of skeletal children, their hands bound in ribbon –*'

Stop –

Falter turned as slowly as a sundial in Abigail's hands. Rout didn't see it. Faces were struggling under its skin. For an instant, there were two – hatefully young, hatefully thin – and then Rout's botched-surgery features were back, but Darcie kept speaking and it could not turn away.

'*Before your schemes were both figuratively and literally torched by Malleus Caterina Segurana. You resurfaced again,* much *diminished –*'

Stop –

'*We did our research, Rout,*' the radio said softly. '*We found you every time you raised your head, and every time you did we cut it off.*'

The blade was almost turned now, ready for a single upright stab. Rout stared down at her, as fascinated as a cat staring into the mirror.

'*What does that say about you, Rout? What does that say?*'

That . . . that . . .

Rout's eyes narrowed. **That your *pathetic* Order will never stop me.**

'*Oh*,' said Darcie. '*Well, I suppose* –'

Abigail stabbed upwards just as Rout pulled away. Instead of skewering the creature's throat, Falter slid between the bone of the jaw and the slick skin stretching across it. Flesh separated, an eye popping free like a pea from a pod, and half the Tenebrous's face came away in gobbets of wax.

Rout screamed.

The blade clattered away, and Abigail dived after it. It spun under a rack of jars, but before her fingers could close on it a claw punched through the wood and pottery above her head, her hair suddenly matted with shards and oil.

She fought it every step of the way, but it dragged her across the floor as if she were nothing, and though the flames of her heritage bayed to be used, there was oil squidging between her fingertips and dying in a fire was no victory at all.

It raised its other claw –

And Matt went high, Ed low and Simon just flung himself at the monster's stomach like a rugby player. A *terrible* rugby player. The three Neophytes swung like streamers from Rout's form, and either they were screaming or it was, but with a spasm it flung them all free . . . all except Ed, whom it gripped by the throat.

Where's the knife?

Rout's muscles rippled like water breaking over a shark's back. Skin split as bones grew faster than muscles could surround them. It stepped up on to the pyre, crouching like it was about to take flight, face still steaming from the touch of Denizen's blade.

Where is it?

Roooouuuuuuttttt, it growled, its voice reverberating in its new-made barrel of a chest. ***Roooooouuuuuuuttttt.***

Ed brought up a Costless hand to protect himself, but Rout nudged it aside with a talon, and drew another delicately from forehead to chin. Ed's scream shook the windows, and Rout leaned into it as if searching for music in the pain.

Matt was staggering to his feet. She had no idea where Simon was. And –

Where is Falter, oh God, where is it?

You've lost, child. The Order. Humanity. We will break everything you have built . . . and it starts with here.

Ed stopped screaming. Abigail would never have described anything about the Neophyte as dangerous, but there was a sudden note in his voice all the same.

'What?'

Not one stone of Daybreak will remain. We will dismantle it. We will unmake it.

The Tenebrous was enjoying itself now. The Neophyte had gone very still in its grasp.

We will annihilate the very –

Ed drove Falter into the side of Rout's head.

The Tenebrous squealed, flinging its head back. Ed spun away like a sycamore seed, Falter coming with him, and, pawing at its face, Rout fell to one knee . . . right on top of the pyre.

The first jug shattered against its skull in a burst of golden oil, gumming its sickly white skin with folds of honey-thick liquid. It bellowed wetly, not understanding: . . . but Abigail did, and after Matt and Simon heaved the third amphora over its malformed skull it took barely a whisper to light it up.

The metaphysics of the Order were Darcie's department. All Abigail had ever wanted to be was on the front lines. She knew *what* candlewards were, she knew the job they did, how they pinned the sagging wallpaper of reality back to itself so that the damp couldn't seep through . . . but the *how* was beyond her.

She'd only had one day of school, after all.

But you didn't need to be a *Lux* to feel the holy heat of that sudden fire, breathe the smell of honey and wood washing over her, feel *wrong* become *right*, and if Rout tried to howl or plead she couldn't hear it over the crackle of flame.

Rout collapsed like a smoked-out wasps' nest, and above them chimneys captured and tidied away the smoke. Abigail wouldn't have minded it sticking around because the glow from the massive candleward had nearly blinded her.

'Come on!'

It was Simon. Abigail stumbled after him down the stairs to find Matt sitting with Ed outside Greaves's office, holding a cloth to Ed's face that was doing absolutely nothing to stem the bleeding.

'Do you . . .' Ed was murmuring. 'Do you think it'll scar?'

Matt grinned. 'Oh, you've no idea! And I cannot *wait* to tell everyone how you got it. You hero. You absolute hero.'

Abigail left him half hugging, half holding on to the other Neophyte and turned to Simon.

'I'm sorry,' the tall boy said. 'I couldn't think what to –'

'No, no, you were brilliant,' Abigail said. 'I just can't believe –'

Her hand went to her hip. The radio clip was still affixed to her belt, but the radio had snapped clean off.

'If Tenebrous are will-based, then reminding them of past defeats might eat into the self-belief that allows them to hold together in the hostile environment of our realm.'

Abigail stared at him.

'Is probably what Darcie would say,' Simon finished. 'I don't know. Can we go and sit down?'

They'd already broken so many rules that Abigail couldn't even muster the slightest regret at sitting in the Palatine's chair. It hadn't even been looted by Tenebrous and for a moment she just *sat*, breathing in clean and uncorrupted air.

It was very nearly dawn. Ed had bound half his face with cloth so that he looked somewhere between Red

Riding Hood and a very small pirate. Matt had pressed his head to one of the windows. Abigail could see the first blush of rising sun on the horizon, though the windows outside seemed clogged with swirling, matted smoke. It almost looked like . . .

'Huh,' she said.

'What?' Simon asked, laying himself out flat on Greaves's desk with a groan.

'I was just wondering what happens when you light a candleward that big this close to Tenebrous who are only in this world because they found a hole to crawl through?'

Simon sat up, staring at the dust. 'Do you think . . .'

Abigail craned her neck, suddenly assailed by a reverse of Rout's coils of despair – *hope*, the foolish-and-yet-not-entirely-unbelievable notion that maybe they had somehow defeated the invading Tenebrous with a single act, that Greaves had been wrong and wars could be ended with decisive strokes.

And then the last of the windows collapsed under something that was not a roar, not a bellow, but too loud to be either. For a single, swaying second, Abigail thought it was Daybreak finally collapsing, or the city itself punishing her for letting it down. And then realization crashed down on her, and she knew it was far worse.

They hadn't lit a candleward. They'd lit a beacon. A challenge.

Do you feel you're good enough, Abigail Falx?

32
THE ENDLESS KING

When Denizen was six years old, he had seen a shooting star.

He'd been sitting at the lookout point on the cliffs at Benmore above Crosscaper. Simon was . . . somewhere else. The other children were somewhere else too. Denizen didn't remember. He remembered very little of that day but the prickle of grass underfoot, the little stroke of light making its way across the heavens and the terror.

Denizen had been a dinosaur kid. Most of the children in Crosscaper were. It was what had led him on to fantasy – these great and terrible creatures, separated by mist and time. So that evening, watching that star, Denizen hadn't felt excitement or joy or a sense that the universe was full of amazing and wonderful things . . . He'd thought it was a meteorite, and that they were all going to die.

And the thing was, for once in his life, Denizen hadn't catastrophized. He hadn't run to Simon, or cried for parents he didn't have. He'd just sat there, watching the star inch towards the horizon, and waited for the end of the world.

'Mercy,' Denizen said slowly. 'Did you come to me for help or . . . or did you use me to get rid of all your potential rivals?'

The Tenebrous had gone still. Not human-still, where there were always movements if you knew where to look, but still as a photograph, her aura of lightning now a thousand static thorns.

Her voice was smooth. **Can't it be both?**

The Endless King's face was turned towards him now, mask slightly ajar. Grey's sword lay on the ground halfway between them, and Denizen looked at it and Mercy did too.

You don't need that, Denizen.

'You just . . . You just . . .' *Can't it be both?* He'd said those words long ago, when Vivian had caught him and Mercy about to kiss.

She's not a girl. She's a monster.

Can't she be both?

Yes.

Mercy was very good at explaining things. She would justify herself any minute now. There was an explanation for what he had just seen, what he had just heard, and she just needed to say it.

Denizen could see through his iron eye the darkness of her true form, soft and spinning droplets, planets in the galaxy of her. Was that sadness in the sharp, spare face of the King? Or accusation?

'Answer me,' he said. 'Did you come to me for . . . for *me*, or did you just use me, use *all of us*, to take out your enemies?'

She stared at him for a long time.

'Answer me!'

The Emissary would have come for the Order, she said, one hand, her *injured* hand, gracefully tracing the fall of ice dust through the air. **He despises you, almost as much as he despised his King. You witnessed his humiliation, after all. Dragon was bound to this fate from its creation. And . . .**

'What are you *talking* about? Stop talking about fate and *tell me the truth.*'

I AM TELLING YOU THE TRUTH.

Denizen didn't feel his feet leave the ground, but his shoulder-blades were kind enough to inform him when he landed. Breath steamed a contrail in the air. He staggered to his feet, every instinct, his training, his mother's voice all screaming at him to *attack* –

But Mercy hadn't moved. That terrible solar bellow echoed out over the ocean, but the girl who had made it was just a bundle of delicate lines on the air.

This is what it is to be a King, she said quietly. **Everyone an enemy, everyone a piece to be moved. A King must be ruthless. Must think on a dozen planes at once, always working, always scheming just to stay in place. Ever since Crosscaper . . .**

'Ever since *Crosscaper*?' Denizen couldn't believe what he was hearing. 'You're saying that this was a *plan*?'

Plan? Mercy's cackle was bitter, but it was still the most human noise he'd ever heard her make. **Does this look like it might have been someone's *plan*? You think I planned**

for the Clockwork Three? To be taken, to be captured, for my very existence to be used against the creature that had given me life?

'But you just killed him!'

No, Mercy said. **I replaced him.** Her face was still expressionless, her best approximation of the mask at her feet. **What do . . . what do you think I *am*?**

For a moment, Denizen was back in the basement of Crosscaper, with a mother shot and an apocalypse impending, and Mercy asking him questions that sounded academic but were in fact the most important thing in the world.

'I . . . I thought you were the daughter of the Endless King.'

Tenebrous don't have daughters, Denizen. We are mutable. Always mutable, held together only by will. It is our weakness and our strength. A Tenebrous stole fire from a faraway place and used the power of it, the *symbol* of it, to show a world that he should be King.

She shook her head.

And then the fire was taken, and, instead of adapting, evolving, he *hardened*, stung by pride and what he had lost. He had risen so far, and could not accept the thought of loosening his grip.

'But he gave us the Cants –'

You had the fire. What good were the Cants to him? Just another mark of shame for what he had lost. He turned away from you. *Let them have their fire. Let them have their world.* And when a voice told him that this

was not enough, told him that he should help, told him he was wrong to let you live and die in unceasing war . . . he cut it out.

'Some say he is *the Tenebrae, and all the Tenebrous his stray and hungry thoughts, bleeding over into our terrified world.'*

My father has kept me a secret for a very long time.

He called me Mercy, the Tenebrous whispered. **He should have called me Hope.**

Denizen couldn't. He just couldn't. He couldn't wrap his head round it. Everything they had shared, everything that he had believed was a lie. Fiction. But that was what Tenebrous were, weren't they? False shapes and wrongness.

You have to understand –

'*Do* I?' Denizen yelled at her. 'Because I *don't*! You're . . . you're telling me that you're some sort of . . . some sort of *trick*? You're all his nice feelings scooped up and torn out and walking around and that's why . . . that's why . . .'

You have to understand there wasn't a plan. There never was. There are no prophecies, no guarantees . . . only what you can *take*. And every change brings opportunity.

'Explain.' The word came out cold and flat. 'Explain exactly what you mean by that.'

The Emissary and Dragon would have come for the Order, no matter whether I lived or died. Dragon was made of the King's worst impulses, the Emissary a would-be King from an earlier, more brutal age. They would have always come. I gave you *warning*.

'So we'd kill them.' The coldness was spreading through his voice, through his mind, through his heart. He welcomed it. It was the only way he could find his voice. 'So we'd remove your rivals.'

Would you prefer them as King? Can you *imagine* them as King? Either of them?

Denizen scowled, but she was already continuing.

The Concilium served a similar purpose – throwing the Court off balance while opening talks with the Order, establishing myself as someone they could trust . . . at the same time offering any in the Court with divided loyalties a chance to make their move and expose themselves.

'Did you . . . Did you *know* about the Croits? The Redemptress?'

Do you remember what I told you in the garden? About my mother?

My mother was only ever a story to me.

If any event gave me life . . . it was her betrayal. But I did not know the scale of what she and the first Croit had built. Believe that.

Believe that. Denizen could have laughed, if he thought himself ever capable of laughing again.

'Anything else? Any other secret reasons?'

Mercy's eyes glittered. **I wanted to see you.**

'How can . . .' The sky above had settled back to his world's dome of stars, but Denizen reeled as if their fall had never stopped. Everything that had happened between them, everything that had happened since leaving *Crosscaper* . . . and she had used it.

Used everyone. Used him.

Running through Dublin's streets, her laughter music, ice-pure and warm at the same time.

Teaching her Frowns No. 1–27, her fingers on his face to feel his skin.

'I've heard about kissing.'

The things they had done together. The things he had done for her.

'What am I to you?'

The drifting specks of ice seemed to slow at the words. Just five simple words, but they were the most important words he had ever said. More important than Cants. More important than *peace*. The only words he had left.

You are all this moment has.

'*Stop saying that!*' It took him a moment to realize he was stalking towards her. No more walls, no more control – just a raging, howling inferno battering at his soul. Cants circled the blaze, and Denizen felt the shapes they could make if he let them, and he advanced on her as if he were going to attack, as if he were going to . . .

And, in fairness to her, she did not back away or avert her gaze.

'Am I just part of your plan? Is that all I've ever been? Just a tool, something for you to *use*?'

Yes, Mercy whispered. **I am using you. I am using you and I am using the Order and I'm using my people and I'm using myself. That is what a ruler has to do. And is it not *necessary*?**

Her voice shook, not with the eldritch tremolo of the Tenebrae, but with rage and pain and . . . triumph, a terrible kind of pride.

Dragon was a monster. The Emissary is insane. The Opening Boy would have destroyed the entire universe just to silence the misery in its heart. I'm not doing this for power, Denizen. I'm doing it because, if I don't, billions will die. My people. Your people. How is that wrong?

'Because . . .' The Cants crowded Denizen's head, making his thoughts disconnected, nonsensical. That was why he couldn't think of a response. *Right?* 'Because . . .'

You have no idea what it's like, Denizen. Not knowing if you're real or just someone's stray thought that started thinking for itself. Well, I *am*, Denizen Hardwick. I will save my world from itself, and no one will doubt the will that holds me together.

And, as she spoke, she *shone*, a glow fierce enough to combat the one blurring the horizon's edge, and in the face of that rising light all Denizen's could do was die away.

He said it. Why not? Even if he only said it once, at least it would be said.

'I thought you liked me.'

She rippled like a pond disturbed by stones.

Denizen . . . I do. Now it was she who drifted forward, her eyes wide and bright and as round as moons. **I was trapped in a realm not my own, trapped with the worst of my kind and a warrior of the Order that hates and fears us . . . and you . . .**

A smile, meteor-quick.

You were just stomping around and complaining and completely out of your depth and you *offered to help*. A human helping a monster. Do you have any idea how *rare* that is? And the more I got to know you, the more I realized how special that gesture was.

Denizen looked away, but suddenly she was *there*, right in front of him, her hair drifting around them in smoke and strikes of lightning.

You've spent your whole life trying to close yourself off from emotions, trying to distance yourself, steeling yourself for disappointment and pain . . . and yet when someone needs you you're *there*, blood and bone.

'That's not . . .' It was *very* hard to think when she was standing that close, and not for the first time Denizen wished there were some way you could feel just one thing at a time. 'I just did what I had to do. That's all.'

No, Mercy said. **That's *everything*. That's why we're here. There are no great schemes, just opportunities and those with the will to take them. I didn't plan any of this, but when I saw a chance to help people, to make things right, I *took* it.**

There's no such thing as neatness, Denizen. It's only afterwards that people tuck in the loose ends. It's only afterwards that they make us into stories.

That smile returned, and Denizen could see now that it was just a curve of the lips, lonely and sad.

And what a story we'll be . . . the renegade King, and the Knight who loved –

'Don't,' Denizen said, but there was no anger in the word. 'You don't get to say that. Not when . . .'

I understand. Her eyes narrowed. **And I'm sorry. But this story isn't over.**

The air bent and deformed over the body of the King as a hole tore itself in reality, a graveyard of stars in the shape of a child.

It is if he wants it to be.

The Opening Boy.

Why do only the people I love stay dead? The sun in Denizen's chest might have had confused feelings about Mercy, but about the Boy there was no confusion at all. His body shaking with exhaustion already, he marshalled himself, Cants already fighting to be heard –

The Boy held up clawless hands and made no move to attack. Instead, it angled its head to return Mercy's cold gaze, the air around her hands sizzling as if expecting her blades.

No fighting. Not any more. I just want to hear you say it. I want to hear you tell him the truth.

Denizen honestly didn't know if he could handle any more truth. Instead of speaking, Mercy simply raised a hand, and once more the sky began to shift and change, less violent than under the Boy's slashing claws, but still with that lurching vertigo.

He knew enough this time to gird himself for the awesome totality of the Tenebrae, and *pointedly* kept his gaze on the two Tenebrous in front of him and not the cosmos above, but nothing could distract from the sucking infinity on either side. Once, he had thought standing on the top of Os Reges Point to be a dizzying experience, but to teeter on a peak above an entire dimension . . .

'What . . . why are we here?'

The words came out hushed, shrunken and scattered by the view. Denizen didn't move. How he had fought and ducked and dived against the Boy just a few moments ago was utterly beyond him now. He didn't dare lift his feet for an instant in case he was simply swept away by the sheer vastness, the gravity of what he beheld.

Because we have a chance to change things. To fix things. For good. I gave you those Cants for a reason, Denizen. No . . . not a reason. At the time, I didn't know. I couldn't have known that we would escape, that we would become friends, that someday we could be standing here with a chance to end a war. Not a reason. A hope.

'Please,' Denizen said. 'Just tell me. I can't . . . I can't deal with any more of this.'

And he couldn't. He was fourteen years old. He should have been worrying about getting his first job or exams or real human girls who didn't have any interdimensional wars to start or finish at all.

He was so *tired*, and all he wanted to do was be alone so he could start to mourn his mother, and his mentor, and everyone else who had died because of the ambitions of things bigger than them.

The Cants, Denizen. They are a language of control, of shaping. A language my father developed, but could not learn to use himself. But humans can.

The sun always rises, Denizen. I said that to you when I first gave you the Cants, do you remember?

'Yes,' Denizen said. And then he understood. Knights learned so few of the Cants because to them the fire was a weapon, because they did not know it had once been something else. And Tenebrous were ever-changing, and what else could they have become in the dark but monsters?

'You . . .' The audacity of it staggered him. 'You want me to return them. You want to light the Tenebrae again.'

And give my people another chance to change.

Inside Denizen's head, the Cants strained and battered each other in a frenzy of need. He had spent an entire year trying to keep them separate, under control, and always he had known that there was a *shape* to them, an order, an urge to let them build and build on each other . . . And now he knew why.

'Would it work?'

I don't know. You would speak them, and I would shape them.

'That's why you're made of light,' Denizen whispered, and she nodded.

It might work. It might not. I've practised weaving light my entire life, but fire . . . fire is not kind to such as me. And if you speak all the Cants, all at once . . .

'Oh,' he said. '*Oh.*'

The Cost. He could feel it inside him – the soft popping in one knee as iron slid over flesh, the itch of metal in his eye. To speak all seventy-eight Cants . . .

What will be left of you, Denizen? When this is over?

Denizen turned. The Boy stood there, outline tattered from its wounds. One arm ended in a stump – *Grey* – its former size now a distant memory, and Denizen was abruptly struck by how it could have easily been his shadow, worn and tired and trembling.

Bloody cuts across his chest. Arms iron to the elbow and more besides. A family lost to a war they never asked for, and a girl who had done nothing but lie to him now asking him to give his life for monsters that had only ever tried to do him harm.

And even if he did survive – what then? Lug a body of cold iron home to a world that might be dying, an Order decimated and friends that could be dead? What was he fighting for if his reward was simply to go home and mourn for what he had lost?

Haven't you done enough, Denizen? You have a choice. Giving up is a choice. The reward for fighting is just more fighting, the reward for surviving just *more* surviving . . .

Mercy didn't argue. She couldn't. The Boy was right. Denizen had made a choice in a garden long ago to stand between a child and a monster, but bravery hadn't got easier; it had got harder. He came out of each fight more ragged and in pain than before, and, even if somehow Mercy's plan did work, there was every chance Denizen wouldn't be around to see it.

Why then? Why keep fighting? Why keep going?

I can take it away, Denizen. Claws were budding from the ends of the Boy's fingers. **I can make all your pain stop.**

They stared at him, a creature of darkness and a creature of light, one who had lied to him and one who spoke only truth. Denizen could give up. None of his friends, his Order, none of them were around to see it.

He sighed.

'I know you can.' He looked up, and, though the crushing immensity of the omniverse drew tears from his eyes and a shudder from his spine, it gave him strength too.

'But this isn't about me.'

He turned to Mercy. 'What do you need me to do?'

The Boy let out a world-splitting howl and lunged, claws birthing in sprays of black, but the Cants were quicker, diving as the fire rose, and for the first time since that night in Crosscaper Denizen didn't stand between them. Instead, he faced Mercy, her eyes bright with silver tears, and, as the Boy screamed in fury, his head dipped to hers.

I'm sorry.

It's OK.

Their lips met, and the suns rose.

Fire roared through Denizen, and he let it, flinging open every door in his extremely compartmentalized head. He fed it his fear, and his doubt, and he fed it the notion that he was owed *anything* because there were actual heroes out there and right now he was all they had.

His heart screamed. His veins sizzled. His skin creaked with the effort of holding more flame than he'd ever held before and just when he thought he'd burst from joy the Cants swooped down and drank them in.

They'd always been hungry to show him what they were, and now Denizen just let them, arcing from the soles of his feet to where his lips brushed lightning. Given free rein at last, the Cants *aligned* – and Denizen realized that they weren't words but a *sentence*, a command, a calling.

The Endless King had bound all his hope and desire to change in a daughter, and this was the other half of that equation – the tools to command that fire and bring it forth, ready for her to use –

Though probably not in this exact way.

It was lucky that his head was a shifting, streaking matrix of constellations because, if not, he'd probably overthink what he was doing and ruin everything. His hands had somehow found hers, and Denizen had no idea what had happened to the Boy because he had assumed having your eyes open while kissing was *very* weird, but he could feel light pushing like fingertips down on his eyelids, and maybe that meant it was working.

And then . . . as night follows day, as death follows life, Denizen felt it.

The Cost.

The fire was drawn out of him, more than he had ever channelled before, and with perfect clarity Denizen felt the sting of his leg bones becoming heavier, his sinews pinching tight, his stomach become a leaden labyrinth of black. Breath became harder, even as Mercy's mouth tightened on his, and Denizen could *feel* the inside of his lungs frost over, *feel* his heart force another beat, and another, like an old man climbing the stairs.

Pull back. Fight. It's a lie, a Tenebrous trick. She was using you and now she's using you up –

No. It isn't. I trust her. And I want this war to end.

And as her lips left his – or maybe that was just the feeling retreating, deserting lips iron and dead – Denizen's heart beat one more time . . . and stopped.

33
CAPABLE

The Neophytes' descent from Daybreak's summit was in every way a reversal of their ascent. Pounding down stairs instead of doggedly climbing, the air now clean instead of fermented and rank. Where once they had crept scared, now they scrambled – footsteps echoing wildly as if an entire army marched at their heels. It should have made it easier.

The barrage of the Emissary's return challenge had not diminished. Why would it? There was no human throat to tire, no human lungs to empty – just a ceaseless, blaring war-cry, a drawn-out detonation of sound. At least this time they didn't have to circumnavigate the hole Dragon had carved, which was good, because with the way the castle shook they would have definitely fallen in.

Aside from that first awful unveiling, the Emissary had hidden from the Order. Abigail had asked Darcie and she'd listened in on communications – they hadn't seen hide or hair of the beast, but now it unashamedly announced its presence with a bellow that rattled Abigail's brain in her skull.

Maybe it was a call to arms to the rest of the Tenebrous, to stiffen their waning morale and bring them back to a fight they could still very easily win. Maybe it wanted the Order to know its location at last, so they could feel every second of its terrible advance. Or maybe it simply no longer cared.

Every muscle fibre of Abigail's body ached. No one spoke. They hadn't the breath. The only consolation was that each heaving gasp she dragged from the air was pure and untainted, but she *knew* that if they got too far away from the candleward above, the rot would descend once again.

Wasn't that what darkness did? Retreated to the edge of the light and no further? Darkness was the natural state of the universe. Eventually all light ran out.

Denizen's knife was tight in her fist.

Terrified energy could only push them so far, and Ed was still losing blood. Their run became a stagger, and eventually all they could do was walk until a staircase finally deposited them at the entrance hall, the door that led out to Adumbral long gone.

'The courtyard's empty,' Matt panted, over the still-echoing roar. 'We should make a run for it. Lose ourselves in the city –'

'I don't think that's an option!' Simon shouted. 'Look.'

And across the trampled muck of what had once been the courtyard there were *shapes* – a riot of spines and frills and fangs and smiles. The world still felt clean and steady and safe, but now Abigail knew where the edge of the darkness was, and what could resist its scouring touch.

She shouldn't have been surprised. The Clockwork Three had smashed the lesser candlewards of Seraphim Row as if they were nothing but sticks of wax, and these were creatures made in that image – solidified madness, calcified hate. Anything less would have been dashed apart.

'They're waiting,' Ed finished, still holding his face together. 'Waiting for us to make a run for it. Like hunters waiting for a hound to drive us from cover.'

The slyness of it made Abigail want to retch. This wasn't *loyalty*. This was no honour guard waiting for their would-be King. If the Emissary became their ruler, it wasn't because they loved it, or even because they feared it. They were following it the way jackals circled lions . . . waiting for the scraps from the kill.

They were just letting it go first.

'What do we do?'

With a start, Abigail realized they were all looking at her. 'I . . . I . . .'

'I could hide us!' Simon said. 'We could go to a tunnel, or . . .'

'Once we leave the candleward's aura, they'll have us,' Abigail replied. 'In any direction. There's nothing we can –'

She stopped mid-sentence, because the roar had stopped too, and in its wake came a silence that was somehow more expectant, more awful than any fanfare for a conquering king.

And one of the buildings on the far side of the courtyard stood up.

The Emissary of the Endless King had grown since their last meeting. It unfolded – ten metres, twelve metres, more – an industrial sprawl of metal and stone and pumping, breathing black, like a Victorian factory come to life, a place where children were brought to die.

It was *huge*, filling Abigail's senses until she could see nothing else, so massive it possessed its own gravitational pull, and she was nothing but an orbiting fleck of dirt.

Like a nightmare. Just like her nightmare.

The Emissary of the Endless King roared. The Tenebrous that lolled in the shadows roared with it – a hideous, bawling chorus that left Abigail's throat stinging with bile. The *smugness* of it. As if they'd already won. As if the Order had already lost.

One of the Neophytes let out a soft whimper. It might have been Matt. It might have been her.

The Emissary's voice was deep and cold, a rip-tide you knew you did not have the strength to beat.

Well *done*, children.

I wish they'd stop calling us that.

A fire lit against the dark. That is what the Order has always been, has it not?

Even its voice had changed. Fattened by its achievements, it had discarded the stilted, monstrous way in which it used to speak. Now its tones were swollen with indulgence and amusement. A ruler scoffing at a rebellion that had never got off the ground.

Each of its steps took an age, a tectonic procession of foot and knee and hip that shook the ground beneath

Abigail's feet. How could it be so *big*? Even the blurred glimpse she'd had of Dragon could not compare, for Dragon had been a long and spindly thing, all tendon and wing, and the Emissary was squat and wide, built for brawling, for demolishing, for swinging that monstrosity of a blade.

But at the end of the day, Abigail Falx . . .

She might never be able to listen to the sound of her own name again, not after it dripped so callously from the gap beneath that helm. The Emissary angled its huge head upwards to stare at Daybreak's summit, at the candleward, or the Glimpse buried deep in Daybreak's guts.

. . . candles go out. You know that as well as I.

Abigail shifted her grip on Denizen's stone blade and looked back at the motley cadre behind her.

Matt, standing with feet splayed and blade raised, ready for the blaze of glory he'd talked about so much. Ed, eyes *still* closed, his lips moving in a mantra or the names of his family or both. And Simon, who gave Abigail a lopsided smile as she held out the stone blade.

'He'd want you to have it,' she said.

'No,' Simon said. 'He really wouldn't.' Tears ran freely down his face as he closed her hands over the knife. 'But thank you. I –'

They held on to it together for a moment.

'I wish he was here.'

'Me too,' Abigail said, and it was that thought – the thought of her friend, and her Malleus, and poor D'Aubigny, and . . . and Grey that made her step out into the doorway and the pre-dawn chill.

Candles go *out*, Abigail Falx, it repeated, and she knew it didn't care what or if she answered. It was speaking for its own benefit. For its own ego, and the cheap pleasure of the crowd.

She answered anyway. For herself alone.

'Then we go out fighting.'

And a crossbow bolt shattered against the Emissary's helm.

It didn't so much as leave a mark, but the Emissary shook its head like a wet dog and dragged its massive frame to face the courtyard's south side. She saw the mob of Tenebrous turn too, heads and sort-of-heads looking about in confusion, and it might have been her imagination but the night seemed to suddenly become a little less dark.

It's morning, she thought, but then a single voice rang out, pure and clear and human, and a hundred sibilant hisses marked a hundred more arrows and Abigail realized it wasn't the dawn at all.

It was the cavalry.

'*Knights of the Order!*'

Greaves's voice was half joy and half rage.

'*Charge!*'

It was the first order Abigail had followed all day.

34

THE BORROWED DARK

Darkness.

Utter darkness, perfect and total and complete in a way that human words couldn't describe . . . because it was something a human world couldn't achieve. Oh, the *word* was thrown about a lot, but there were a million shades between the dingy black of coal dust, the glossy pitch of a raven's feather and the sloe-shine of its onyx eye.

And all imitations, pretenders, borrowed from a greater dark.

Don't be dead.

Even in the deepest dark, you could still find yourself. That was how the human body worked. Every sensation, every nerve signal, formed an expectation, a map, so even in nothingness you knew where you were.

Please don't be dead.

The words drifted down and, like navigating a pitch-black room, structure and shape followed.

The voice sounded panicked. Why were they panicking? Why were they panicking?

I hope they're not panicking about me.

That was a new thought, and the darkness trembled with the weight of it. If there were a *me* then there was someone thinking, and, once that thought was established, thousands more burst free from it, striking like lightning, like the synapse flickers of a birthing brain.

And Denizen could ignore them. The only dark that mattered was the giving-up dark. Everything else was solvable. Everything else was light.

Please don't be dead.

Each falling word a lifeline; each spark of thought a plea.

Wake up!

Denizen woke, and for once didn't immediately regret it. Usually, when he awoke after doing something ill-advised and/or heroic – they were usually one and the same – the relief at being alive was engulfed by all the pain patiently waiting for him.

But his eyes had been open for three whole seconds now, and nothing had groaned or ached or gone *sproing* in his innards, and that made no sense at all because he'd been a ball of bruises *before* he'd arrived at Os Reges Point and the Opening Boy had pounded him to marmalade for a good five minutes and that was before –

Denizen sat up.

My heart stopped.

He had felt it, that gasping, ponderous *push* of blood through ossified, creaking veins . . . and then his heart had stopped.

His hand went to his throat, fumbling for a pulse, and fingers met skin with the softest of *clangs*, two bells gently meeting.

Denizen.

You became very aware of yourself in service to the Order. Training made you intimately familiar with what your body could and could not do, including climbing the stairs and lying down without screaming. Battle made every vein in your body light up like Christmas lights and the aftermath made them as dead and dull as December trees.

You learned. You learned to tell Cost from flesh.

His arms were harder than he'd ever been able to make them through a year of training, his shoulders tight and brambled with black. Slowly, Denizen got to his feet, overbalancing slightly at the new weight. *Breathe.* He drew in breath as slow and purposeful as an archer nocking a bow, feeling the new heaviness to his chest.

It wasn't *unpleasant*. The Cost had never been unpleasant. It was just . . . there. A slow and rooted darkness that moved when he moved.

'But how . . .' he said. Even his voice was different, a deepness that sounded like he'd missed the floor for puberty and ended up in the basement. 'The Cants. I felt my heart stop. I felt the Cost swallow me. How did . . .'

It worked!

Denizen turned, and again felt that altered gravity as the Endless King smiled a smile of golden flame and held out her iron hand.

The girl of light and frost and storm was gone. Features that had changed constantly were now stiffly defined, her cheekbones jagged cliffs. Her hair was a briar-tangle of rigid black that left white scrape marks on her bare shoulders. Once she had shifted through all the colours of the rainbow in the time it took Denizen to draw breath and now she was a rough-carved statue, her lines choppy and sharp.

And her eyes . . . her eyes were fire, incandescent, and when her mouth creaked open it spilled forth laughter and light.

It worked!

If Denizen's voice was a cavern, hers was an iron mine lit by crackling flame, a wholly different kind of beautiful than it had been before. She stretched with a rasp of metal on metal and, before he could ask a single one of a hundred *million* questions, she raised a rugged iron hand and pointed up.

There was sunlight on his face, but they were in the Tenebrae. They were still on that soaring peak, and unreality and strangeness still shivered the air, but they were in the *Tenebrae* and there was an orb of light hiding that insanity-inducing view, the way the sun hid the stars.

Now the sky was blue, and, as he watched, the white-gold sphere was joined by another, this one a streak of shimmering light that raced back and forth across the sky.

The Helios Lance.

Denizen knew it. Of course he did – it had spent over a year in his head, after all, and there were others: a curving scythe, a snare of snaking gold, an entire army of suns orbiting and dancing and tangling with each other as if delighted to be free.

No. Not an army. He'd served as their unwilling host. Denizen knew exactly how many of them there were: seventy-seven suns, or Cants, or something in between that Denizen wasn't even going to try to explain. It wasn't his universe, after all.

He turned back to her, but she was staring down at the dizzying view and he couldn't help but do the same. The swirling, darting suns had turned that immeasurable junkyard into a marbled, mutable landscape of light and dark. A dappled world, constantly in movement.

I think it will suit them, the Endless King said. **And without looking into a billion other realms . . .**

'They won't constantly change,' Denizen said. 'All that . . . pressure is gone.'

They can still be visited, I imagine. Even seen. My people can still change . . . if they wish it.

Her smile was blinding.

The same as everybody else.

'OK,' Denizen said, a little breathlessly. There was definitely a frown coming, but he'd lost his grip on exactly which one. 'Was *this* your plan?'

I had thousands of plans, Mercy said. **And a lot of hope. This one worked out . . . passably, I think. Don't you?**

'If I do a mental checklist up here, I'll black out,' Denizen said. 'Honestly, I will.' He looked down at his iron hands and froze. There was a lot of time and a lot of iron between him *now* and him *then*, but he remembered the first blot of Cost on his palm – just a dark little penny pushed into his skin.

And it was gone. The rest of the iron was still there, but there was a tiny spot of pink skin, as if it had been gently lifted away.

'I don't understand. How –'

You spoke seventy-eight Cants in an order they have never been spoken. The effort should have killed you, fluency or no. The Cost is your world's response to the power of the fire, yes?

'Yes,' Denizen said. 'But . . .'

She shrugged, backlit by seventy-seven unearthly suns and a scrapheap so large you could have dropped Denizen's solar system into it.

We're not in your world, Denizen. And while the Cost did come for you – you are a product of your own world, after all – I was able to . . . get a finger underneath it, like a child lifting a scab. And we are shapers and changers and builders . . .

She lifted the jagged claws of her hands.

Even if this is not the medium I would choose to use.

'You took the Cost from me,' Denizen said softly.

As much as I could. Enough to keep you alive, at least.

She frowned, with some difficulty.

I didn't do the organs. Nobody does the organs. You're more iron than you were. I did what I could, I was . . . I was worried I'd kill you.

Bodies were a difficult thing to think about in percentages, as there were floppy bits and lighter bits, and

Denizen's hair stuck out a lot of the time, but, at a *guess* and without a mirror, he'd say that he was over sixty per cent iron. More than most of the Knights he had ever met. More than Vivian, and she had fought her entire life.

Denizen and his mother had spent so long building a fortress inside him that now that there was one there for real he had thought that her death would hurt less. But strength and sadness weren't opposites, he supposed . . . and ignoring it would mean ignoring her.

I'd rather hurt, he thought, and gave a rattling sigh. Mercy was staring at him. He forced a smile.

'Thank you, Mercy,' he said. 'I mean it. You told me you hated the idea of just being one thing and now you're . . .'

She closed her eyes, claws clenching into fists, and her profile suddenly *shivered*, as if vibrating from within. With a crack that reminded Denizen of ice floes and blacksmiths' hammers, a thin veil of dust seemed to fall from her skin.

When it had been carried away by the breeze, her features appeared a fraction closer to human. *A second draft*. The effort seemed to drain her, and she staggered. Denizen went to catch her and they both nearly went down. She was very, very heavy.

Iron is difficult, Knight's iron most of all . . .

Denizen thought of Dragon, and then suppressed the thought. This was nothing like that. A sacrifice, not a mockery.

But I have always been good at learning new things.

'Yes . . .' Denizen said. 'About that. There are seventy-seven Cants in the sky.'

Yes.

This close to her, Denizen could feel the heat radiate from her, the sunrise just the other side of her skin.

'You kept one. Didn't you? In the only body that could contain it.'

We do not have such a thing as succession, Denizen. To rule I must be a ruler. I must be audacious. Bold. I must show them that there is nobody as powerful, as daring, as the King who put the suns back in the sky and who kept a Sunrise for herself.

Denizen knew he was being pedantic, but it had been a long night of confusing things being explained to him, and a petty, stupid part of him needed to gain some ground.

'Em . . . Queen, actually, I guess.'

Mercy didn't have eyebrows, but he imagined she would have raised them if she had.

Human words. Irrelevant.

'Fair enough,' he said and then another thought occurred.

'Wait . . . did you take on the Cost to save me or so you could show off to your people?'

Can't it be –

'*I swear to God, Mercy.*'

They stared at each other for a long moment and then both burst out laughing – heavy, iron-creased chuckles. Mercy, She-Who-Was-Determined-To-Be-Endless, and Denizen Hardwick, fourteen, sceptical of almost everything, laughing as they watched the suns they had loosed upon a sky. It was, he had to admit, not the worst thing that had ever happened.

You know I have to go after this.

The laughter died in Denizen's throat.

If I am to be King, I must go and be King. I must assert my will, watch over my people, show them a new way to exist. To give peace to your people and mine, I have to go.

There were a lot of things Denizen could have said. He could have said it was unfair. He could have said that it wasn't right, that she could ask so much and give nothing in return.

He could have asked why everyone kept leaving him.

But he didn't. There wasn't a reward for being *good*. That was for stories. The reward for being good was the same as the reward for surviving – more surviving. He just nodded, and looked away.

Mercy's fingers traded one universe for the other. The sky rippled back to blackness and densely packed stars, and Denizen felt a rush of heady anti-nausea as for the first time in what felt like forever he was actually in his own world instead of pinballing around another.

Os Reges Point was much as they had left it – water puddled everywhere, occasionally pocking and papping with rain. And a hole in the air, slumped and small, a prone form in its one remaining arm . . .

'Grey!'

Denizen went to run, but Mercy's hand hooked him backwards hard. She clomped forward – another difference. Gone was the form that could drift and vanish from one spot to the next like a trick of the eye; now she was inarguably, unstoppably *there* – and she stared down at her wayward subject, and the man splayed beneath it.

I had to cut myself free of him.

A flower of frost had bloomed where the Opening Boy knelt. It was even now melting away.

His stomach had turned to iron. To . . . trap me, I think. It was valiant. It was so valiant.

The Knight was very pale. His eyes were closed, hair a smudge of darkness against his brow. There was no blood, or maybe it was too dark. Grey had lit candles when they had trained together. *He said he'd miss colours.*

Now he was a portrait in black and ashen white.

I just wanted it to end. That's all.

Mercy's voice was a purl of steam. **I know you did.**

Denizen was barely listening. He was tearing Grey's shirt open. The Cost – if he was right, if they were lucky, if he was allowed to ask for *one more* ridiculous thing to happen today –

It was a fight to be gentle, to push fingers against the vein in Grey's throat hard enough to feel a pulse through iron, and in the end all he could do was bend the bare skin of his forehead against his mentor's neck and hope.

And then –

'He's alive!'

Ice painted the air as the Boy let out a long and painful sigh.

Good. Good.

Denizen didn't take his head from Grey's, but he heard the Endless King kneel before the hurt child that had nearly brought an omniverse to ruin. He heard the Boy tilt the featureless scrape of its head and make a simple request, and he heard the Endless King as she placed hands of fire on a heart of fractured cold . . .

And showed mercy.

It took her a long time to get to her feet, and tears of flame had cracked the unmoving mask of her face. Denizen was already reaching into the back of his head for the Bellows Subventum. It took him a minute to find it, like searching for a book on a shelf, and it struck him that normally he'd be fighting them off.

Even the fire was slower, as if exhausted. As if sated.

He could already feel the Cost waiting to be paid, but that was OK. It was a . . . a good cause.

Grey made a soft little noise.

'Just a little further,' Denizen whispered. 'Just a little further.'

35
READY

The Knights' first salvo of Cants was a hammer blow, a fist of a hundred falling flames, and, when the first line of Tenebrous wavered and fell, Abigail ran through their collapsing bodies to fling herself at the second.

The courtyard fell away. Daybreak fell away. There was nothing but the wretched, warping forms of monsters and how right Denizen's blade felt in her hand.

She slashed. She cut and she stabbed and sang Cants with every breath she could spare. A thing with a mouth of knives screamed at her, and she screamed back. An apish, fumbling hand grabbed her throat and she gouged her own skin cutting it free.

The world was a chaotic swirl – like a Tenebrous, and she in its body, trying to kill it like a cancerous cell. Sometimes there were Knights around her and sometimes there weren't, and had you asked her name she wouldn't have been able to tell you because nothing mattered but this.

'Abigail!'

A face hung in her vision, red and blurring, and she brought the sticky, matted length of her blade up to slice it in half, but it grabbed her wrists, gabbling in some nonsense tongue. *Hands pinned. Other options.* She dragged in breath, a Cant spiralling down to drink flame from her soul and leap from her mouth and then –

'*Abigail!*'

Matt. It was Matt. Blood-drenched, fitfully glowing and talking at her. The battle had rolled them like a grape on a tongue and somehow spat them out on to a patch of clear flagstones. Just a few metres away, iron and steel warred with madness and black and yet they were ignored.

Awareness crashed back into Abigail, who she was and what she was doing, and sudden nausea splashed up her throat and on to the flagstones at her feet.

'Abigail! We need –'

He tried to clutch her arm, but she tore free of his grasp. It was so *difficult* to realign herself, to snap back to human speech. For the last . . . however long . . . her only language had been –

'We need to –'

And then the battle came back in like the tide, and a coil of combatants took them once again. Suddenly Abigail was face to face with a yammering *thing* – something like a vulture, something like a wolf – and stabbing her knife into the fetid gap of its armpit again and again and again –

And then Matt was there, like a magic trick, and his eyes were wide and panicked and he was saying something over and over again, but the battle was so *loud* – a ceaseless, clanging clamour, with individual cries kicking to the surface like swimmers trying not to drown.

'Please get up. Please, please get up!'

DIE!

'We need to run.' Matt. Matt was here. And he was saying, 'We need to get *away*.'

'Get away?' Abigail started to laugh, a high, mad laugh born of adrenalin and bloodlust. 'This is where we're supposed to be!'

Something staggered into their path and they stabbed it repeatedly until it went down. It didn't seem to even know they were there.

'You are,' he said, wheezy with panic. 'You're supposed to be here. I'm not. I . . . I'm not a Knight. I'm a *nobody*.'

'What are you *on about*?'

They were shouting at each other now, but it was the only way to be heard.

'Look at you!' he snapped. 'Your family go back ages. All your families do. They all go back a million years and I'm the . . . I'm the . . . I'm the *first*.'

The bravado. His obsession with lineages, and sounding cool, and *stories*, and the way he knew her family before she'd even told him her name, and Abigail wasn't sure if it was the apocalyptic battle around them that had made her not understand it, or how *bloody stupid he was being*.

'Is that *it*?'

He spat fire across her shoulder into a spindly creature with the mad, unblinking eyes of a prawn, and she pulled him close so she could pop Falter into something else's bulging throat.

'What do you mean, *is that it*?' he snarled when there was breath enough in his lungs. 'You all have ancestors going back centuries and –'

'So do you, *you idiot*!' Spin, and kick, and jam the blade into a jaw, and *pull* so hard that Falter rattled out all of its teeth. 'They're just not *Knights*!'

Matt looked as if he'd been poleaxed. 'Well, that's not . . . that's not . . .'

'*Look*,' she said, grabbing him by the back of the head and pulling him close. For a moment, just a moment, the battle seemed to lose its hold on them, Knights and monsters sliding around them like pebbles on a riverbed. 'You're the first. I get it. It's a lot of pressure. So be *worthy* of it. You want a lineage people are going to be talking about in a hundred years?'

His eyes were very wide.

'Then *start now*.'

His grin was sudden, and hesitant, and then he bent his head –

'*What are you doing?*'

He jerked back, his face bright red under dirt and blood. 'I thought –'

And then he was gone, and she was off her feet too, slamming into torn-up cobbles before she could even cry out. She tried to make sense of what had happened, but all she could see was that vast semicircle of ground that had somehow just been cleared away.

Very slowly, Abigail looked up. The Emissary was shaking blood from its blade, and preparing for another strike.

Matt.

Abigail's howl was swallowed by Sunrise, her very first Higher Cant. It loosened teeth and scorched her tongue on the way out, but before it had even hit the Tenebrous she screamed another and another.

The Emissary rocked on its heels, actually taking a step back. The battle around them seemed to open like a flower in shock. The Emissary stared at her. She stared at it.

And then it came for her.

She managed to dodge the first swing by flinging herself to the ground, but the wind of its wake sent her into a bruising, bouncing roll. Tenebrous and Knight alike died on that blade and the Emissary, uncaring as to how many of its own it killed, heaved the blade round and then brought it down again.

Terror. Terror lent her agility and speed, and a distant part of her was explaining that the weight and length of the sword made it unwieldy so *really* it was just a matter of maths, and every other part of her was screaming that the sword hadn't even stopped as it had torn Matt in half, and it would do the same to her, and then the world –

It stomped towards her again, Tenebraic distortion twisting the air in a multitude of colours and her vision into stars and agony.

Move.

She couldn't even get to her feet because its footsteps shook the ground. How had she ever thought she could fight this? How could one person even hope to amount to more than a smear on its boot?

Absurd. Idiotic.

She crawled on her hands and knees as fast as she could, knowing she would never be fast enough to outrun that long black blade. She could *feel* the eagerness of it, dragging at the Emissary's fist, urging it on to carnage.

Cants cracked against the Emissary's shoulders, and she saw a Malleus hammer take a whole armour plate away before black threads darted out and simply pulled it back into place. Abigail watched her life tick down in moments, measured in the arc of that rising blade.

And then it paused. There was no expression and no face to make it with, but she felt it was no longer looking at her, and a mad, prideful bit of her was insulted. It was taking a *break*?

She flung a Helios Lance, but it paid no attention, so she threw another, and another, and then a Sunrise to crisp carvings from its flanks. This annoyed it enough to look down, and it caught her next Helios Lance on the blade of its sword, the Cant for a moment turning it to a dazzling mirror.

Abigail's eyes widened.

The blade was notched. It had been perfect the first time she saw it. She remembered every centimetre – the horrible, living majesty of it – and, though the edge had shifted and warped with every breath, it had been whole. But now there were chips and nocks and nicks in it.

From the blows it had struck. From the lives it had taken.

They had *notched it.*

The Emissary stepped over her, still staring upwards, and a moment ago that would have been more proof that she was useless. A moment ago, she might have noticed the indefinable change in the feel of the battle – Tenebrous turned from their reaving, raising heads to the sky like animals sensing a storm. But she didn't. She was *busy.*

Abigail was busy realizing that she'd been broken by the idea that one person couldn't make a difference. Everything Grey had said, the hopelessness of their crusade, the scale of the beast blotting out the sky . . . they made her small. They made her not matter.

And she didn't. There were things in this world that were too big to stop single-handedly. There were things too big to face alone.

Abigail's hand tightened on Falter. *But I'm not alone.*

Every Knight that had fallen beneath the Emissary's blade had cost it. Just a little. Some core or chunk of iron, some little impact – each one leaving a notch or a chip or a crack. Alone, that was all they'd accomplished. Alone, one person could barely accomplish anything at all, and maybe that was why the Emissary had hidden from them until enough candlewards had been destroyed, so that it wouldn't be alone either.

Because if enough people chose to do something, if enough people *chose* to fight . . .

'Hey!'

She picked up a chunk of rubble and bounced it off the side of the Emissary's helm. It didn't even notice.

'Hey!'

This one actually went into the helm, rattling around like a stone in a tin, but the gigantic Tenebrous just flexed its gauntlets as if preparing itself for a new battle.

'I'm down here!'

And it turned. Faster than Abigail would have believed possible, with a booming snarl that was definitely more annoyance than anything else. The blade hummed towards her, a thundering terminator line, and Abigail had just enough time to pick her spot.

The blade she held had once been a hammer, pinning the Emissary to the palm of its enemy in a desolate prison. Now it was just a sliver of stone, a sliver small enough to fit into a notch the way a key fitted a lock.

Abigail took two steps forward, and maybe the nick she chose was the one Matt had left behind. She'd have liked to think that. She would.

Her blade parried the Emissary's, and the Emissary's broke.

The snap of the sword was deafening, echoed almost delicately by the bones of her left arm. The impact threw her three metres, luckily, because that meant she was nowhere near the night-black shards whickering into Tenebrous left and right, or the Emissary as he overbalanced, crashing to a knee with a sound like an entire forest downed at once.

The blade curled in on itself like a beheaded snake, and its wielder let out a mournful wail of grief, a grief that was picked up by every Tenebrous in the courtyard. Some bolted. Some were cut down where they stood. Some simply disassembled, shedding their forms in showers of black.

And there was light. More light than a flurry of Cants, more light than the sun itself could provide. The air was suddenly warm and shining gold, and the Emissary keened in fear.

No. No no no no no no no . . .

Rents were opening in the air, and *Knights* were jumping forth, wrapped in steel and wreathed in flame. She saw Ed holding Simon up, Tenebrous fleeing . . . but Abigail Falx had been raised to be thorough, and she knew as soon as she flipped the stone blade with her one good hand that it was not meant for throwing, but it was a very large target she was aiming at, and Abigail had been practising since she was very, very young.

It didn't make a lot of difference.

But it made enough.

The blade spun tip over hilt before disappearing into the hole in the Emissary's chest. The beast shrieked and pawed at itself, black oil popping and steaming like tar, and abruptly it shrank, armour moulting from it like scabs. Its helm jerked from side to side, shedding barnacles and rust.

Help . . . Help *meeeeeeeee* . . .

Black was slopping out from its joints now, drying up in the light. Abigail raised her good hand, wearily ready to defend her kill . . . but none of the remaining Tenebrous seemed very interested in their would-be King. Most had fled. Others were hacked to pieces, the courtyard a wasteland of scavenged debris. The few that remained were looking at . . .

Slowly, Abigail turned round.

The hole Dragon had torn in Daybreak was still there, a darker gash in sooty stone, but now light spilled out from it, as bright as the candleward but contained in the shape of a girl.

Mercy.

It was Mercy but . . . not. No longer blue and white and ever-changing, but instead a statue of black and red – as if someone had taken a suit of Hephaestus Warplate and crafted it to be beautiful instead of brutish, an artist's deftness in every line and curve.

The armour of a King.

Mercy stepped from the crater's lip and fell like a stone, crushing cobbles beneath her feet. A moment, on one knee, as if waiting to be knighted, and then she rose with a growl of iron. Every eye was on her – the Order's forces frozen as if unwilling to break the eerie peace, the Tenebrous in crouches of wary respect.

Like they had been with the Emissary.

Something was at stake here. Everything was at stake here. Silence, as Mercy stalked across the courtyard to the Emissary's hunched corpse. Carefully, she lifted the helm from in between the sagging shoulders. It was still massive, but she hefted it easily above her head.

And then she crushed it between her fingers.

Dust came raining down and, as if at a secret, unspoken signal, the gathered Tenebrous began to come apart. Some loped towards Daybreak and the Breach there, shedding matter as they went, and others simply vanished, bodies collapsing as the nightstuff within slithered away.

Soon all that was left were piles of refuse, a hundred scattered grave markers of rubbish and filth, and the bodies of the Knights strewn between. Mercy waited until all of them were gone, and then turned without speaking to the doors of Daybreak, and the boy who had stepped out into the light.

Now Abigail's legs gave out, and she found herself sitting on the cobbles without somehow crossing the intervening space.

It was Denizen.

They stared at each other a moment longer . . .

And then Mercy was gone as well.

EPILOGUE

SUNRISE

Denizen,

This is something I have to do. We love you. We will always love you.

Vivian Hardwick

Denizen stared at the note in his hands. Spring sunlight dappled the windows of Seraphim Row, getting tangled in the spiderwebs and painting the sheets of Grey's bed in charcoal and amber.

The Order had some extremely expensive private clinics – public hospitals having a tendency to ask problematic questions like, *Why is this your third disembowelling this year?* or, *Why are you turning to iron?* – and Greaves had strongly protested about moving him, but as soon as Grey was well enough to travel he insisted, and it was a lot easier to argue with Greaves since the full body cast.

Eventually, there would be questions. Interrogations. Possibly a court martial. But these things took time, what with a lot of the people that *normally* conducted these things having taken quite the battering, and so this was the quiet space beforehand.

'When did . . . when did she give you this?'

He asked the question, knowing the answer, and the Knight, drawn and haggard in the most ridiculous pair of pyjamas Denizen and Simon had been able to buy, shrugged in reply.

'Just before she . . . well. She'd obviously had it a while. Maybe she just carried it around anyway, or maybe she always knew she'd need to give it to you. I don't know.'

There was one street in Adumbral that was not undergoing reconstruction. It had at first seemed odd to Denizen that they would restore an empty city at all, but Adumbral was a symbol, and symbols were important, and that was why one street would always be marked with the piecemeal corpse of a dragon and the woman of black iron standing on its chest, her snarl just as fierce as her kill's.

Apparently, they couldn't find any way of getting the hammer out of her hands. Denizen wasn't the least bit surprised.

There was a number at the bottom of the page:

136

'This was her page in our Book of Rust. The obituary she filled out when she thought she was going to her death against the Three. The one she ripped out.'

Grey nodded. 'How have you been?'

Denizen swallowed. 'It's hard. Really hard. I keep . . . I keep thinking of things to say to her? Just little things. But I'm glad I got the chance to know her. Even if it wasn't for long. And I'm . . . I'm glad I know what happened and who she was. Because she was brilliant.'

Grey smiled. 'She was, wasn't she?'

'Why did you keep it until now?' Denizen frowned. 'Wait. Let me guess. She said not to give it to me until it was all over, because it would be a distraction.'

Grey nodded. 'It's very her.'

'Yes,' Denizen said. 'It was.'

The first year after the Siege of Daybreak there were only thirty Breaches worldwide, an unprecedented low. The next year there were twelve. The Order – very unused to peace or inaction – rebuilt, retrained and recruited to cover the losses they had suffered.

Years passed with fewer and fewer Breaches, and some Knights began to tentatively seek part-time work. Not all of them, obviously. It was amazing how unqualified magic made you for jobs. And some Tenebrous had fled to this world for sanctuary, and *that* needed fixing, although despite Palatine Greaves's best efforts the Order never found out what they were looking for sanctuary from.

Denizen fought too, for a while. Things cropped up here and there. Maybe he was looking for something. Maybe he felt it his duty. He was a Hardwick, after all.

Abigail went into private security.

Ed studied architecture, and Daybreak now rises higher than ever before.

Simon and Uriel eventually stopped emailing and began hanging out, and that hanging out turned into something else, and Denizen was delighted.

(Even if it did mean Simon got dragged into the return of Ambrel Croit and the Wire Daughter's War, but everyone escaped with only minor trauma and with this profession you took your happiness where you could.)

Grey and Jack spoke long into the night the day he arrived back in Seraphim Row. What was said stayed between them.

Darcie was too valuable to let go, but with more time on her hands the subjects she studied became ever more complex. They would sit up late, and Denizen would try to describe everything he had seen, and she would take notes. He had no idea what she was doing with them, but it was *Darcie*, and so he wasn't worried at all.

And Denizen began to teach. He studied and then he graduated – Ed and Simon made him throw his hat and they had to go looking for it – and through some kind of decision or no kind of decision at all he ended up at the doors of Crosscaper just as Mr Colford was entering retirement.

There was a new batch of children in Crosscaper now, ones who weren't afraid of the dark, who weren't afraid of anything, and Ackerby was delighted to have a . . . veteran in the school, and had to be stopped from budgeting for swords.

It was in his second year of teaching, eleven years after the Siege of Daybreak, that Mr Hardwick waved his students to their next class, staring, as he always did, out of the window to the sea. He'd thought once or twice about hiring a boat . . . or even speaking a certain set of phrases just to see what was on the other side.

No. Palatine Greaves had expressly forbidden the Art of Apertura in case it disturbed anything, and Denizen didn't want that on his head. *Besides*, he thought with amusement, *I'd only be the one who has to fix it.*

Someone knocked on his door.

Very slowly, Denizen's hand dipped to the stone blade taped beneath his desk. It wasn't the noise that had startled him. The three things students learned about Mr Hardwick in their first few classes were that: 1) he always wore scarves, and gloves, no matter how warm it was; 2) he had an unexpectedly heavy tread for such a thin, small person; and 3) he was not an easily startled man.

But something trilled through the air in the wake of the echoes, brushing his synapses so they crackled and fizzed.

'Hi,' said the woman in the doorway. Her skin was the colour of honey under street lights, her hair long and curly and black. She wore black lipstick, and black nail polish, and black rings sat shinelessly on her fingers.

Only eyes as sharp as Denizen's – one grey, one black – would have noticed that though a breeze breathed in through the windows, stiff with Atlantic belligerence, her hair didn't move. Not a millimetre. Not an eyelash.

'Hello,' he said, and took his hand away from the knife. 'It's been . . .'

'A while.'

'Yes.'

'I had a lot of work to do,' she said. It was a statement, not an apology. 'Had to be everywhere at once for a while. Now I have people in place. Makes it easier.'

'Do you trust them?' he asked.

She smiled. 'I trust them to keep a certain shape.'

'Ah.'

Her smile vanished. 'I'm sorry for disappearing.'

'No,' Denizen said. 'Don't apologize. I've had a lot of time to think about it. And it's OK. It . . . it worked out OK.'

She nodded. 'I'm glad.'

'You've got very good at the iron.'

'Thank you. Took a while.'

The light overhead flickered, just a little. Ackerby was probably evacuating the school.

'Why are you here?'

She sighed. 'As I said, the right people in the right places. I can leave. For just a little while. So . . .'

He looked at her, his eyes the colour and sharpness of a nail. 'So?'

She held out her hand.

How about that omniverse?

There's always another sunrise.

A FINAL SECRET ABOUT WRITERS . . .

. . . is that nothing is ever really final, and the ending of one story is always the beginning of another. I wrote my first-ever story as fan-fiction for the good folks at ImperialLiterature.net, and someone was kind enough to comment:

'This is pretty good. What happens next?'

So this is all their fault.

The Endless King is the end of a story, one that's been set in stone ever since the first chapter of *Knights* was written in a windbitten hotel in the West of Ireland on 1 November 2012. It's also got its own set of beginnings and endings, some more final than others, and even features an ending that hasn't begun yet.

(The Croits have their own fate, and their own ruin. We may see it yet.)

And so, in much the same way as *The Endless King*, some of these thank-yous are very much for this book, and others go all the way back to the start.

Firstly, to the Ruddens, close *and* extended – thank you

for being tirelessly supportive, impressively resourceful (I still can't believe we got those books to Thurles) and often embarrassingly vocal about the trilogy. There's a reason why the core of these books is family.

To the rock-star wizard ninja supernova diamond queens of Darley Anderson Children's Agency – Clare, Sheila, Mary, Emma, Rosanna and the entire team – thank you for your patience and diligence and ferocity and wisdom. I couldn't wish for a better cadre to be at my side.

My editors Ben, Caroline, Wendy and Jane for being guiding lights through Adumbral, and Eloquence, and Seraphim Row – thank you for all the weird and glorious structures we've built together. Thank you as well to the incredible team at PRH UK and Penguin Ireland for all their incredibly hard work bringing the trilogy into the world. (And for occasionally reminding me to eat.)

Deirdre Sullivan gave me Denizen Hardwick as a name; Sarah Maria Griffin made me give Denizen an omniverse for an ending ('Hasn't he suffered enough! Give him a break!'); and Graham Tugwell gave me words to live by. Doomsburies, now and forever.

Huge thanks to Alexandra and Beth at Inclusive Minds (a brilliant team of consultants working to support diversity and inclusion in books) and particularly thanks to two of their Young Ambassadors for Inclusion: Habeeba and Luca. I can't recommend them enough. Thanks also to CBI, Authors Aloud, Jackie Lynam, and the literal hundreds of teachers, librarians and organizers who've allowed me to be a ridiculous avalanche of a man in front of readers. It is genuinely my favourite part of this job.

Finally (but not really finally, never finally, I hope) thank *you* for reading. Meeting you, hearing from you, seeing your art, your fan-fic – it's so surreal and lovely to meet people who know and love characters that I made up in my head.

I hope you enjoyed the journey and its end as much as I do.

There's only really one question left.

'What happens next?'

LEXICON

A GLOSSARY OF NAMES

DRAMATIS PERSONAE

Denizen Hardwick: To be a 'denizen' of somewhere is to live there; it often has a wild or negative connation. The motto of the actual Hardwick family is *safety through caution*. Deirdre Sullivan handed me the name, like a gift, like a prophecy, on 1 Nov 2012.

Simon Hayes: 'Simon' means 'good listener,' while 'Hayes' comes from the Irish *Ó hAodha*, meaning 'descendant of Aodh (fire)'.

Abigail Falx: Falx is a word originally meaning 'sickle' or 'scythe'.

Darcie Wright: *Lux Precognitae* translates to 'forewarning light'. In an order of warriors and destroyers, Darcie is a 'wright', someone who creates or mends.

Grey: A man suspended between light and dark.

Fuller Jack: A fuller is a groove in the flat side of a blade.

Corinne D'Aubigny: Named after Julie D'Aubigny, a seventeenth-century opera singer and duellist who makes all the adventurers in this book look like amateurs.

Edifice Greaves: An edifice is an imposing building or set of beliefs.

Mottos: Both the motto of the Order (*Linguae centum sunt oraque centum ferrea vox*) and the Knightly Hardwicks (*Tu ne cede malis, sed contra audentior ito*) come from Keat's translation of the Aeneid, a story where a hero, aided by a mystical woman, descends into darkness.

Adumbral: From the Latin *umbra*, meaning 'shadowy'.

The Family Croits: From the French verb 'croire' – 'to believe'. The Croits are all named after medieval saints, while Uriel is an archangel.

Seraphim Row: *Seraphim* is the highest rank of angel in the Christian hierarchy.

Vivian Hardwick: From the Latin word *vivus*, meaning 'alive'.

BESTIARY

Tenebrous: From the Latin word *tenebrae*, meaning 'dark'.

The Man in the Waistcoat & the Woman in White: Creatures so immediately, awfully recognizable they don't need identifying names, only descriptions. The Man in the Waistcoat uses 'Ellicott' as an alias, a reference to a famous family of clockmakers.

Os Reges Point: From the Latin *Ossa Regis*, meaning 'bones of the king'.

The Redemptress/Coronus: Designed after the Wire Mother experiments and named after Coronis, the lover of the Greek sun god Apollo. Coronis was guarded by a white raven who failed to stop her abandoning Apollo for another. When the raven delivered the bad news, Apollo was so furious he burned the raven's feathers black.

Malebranche (Covet, Mabinogion, What-Men-Called-Muinnin): Named after a gang of demons who torment the corrupt, a collection of old Celtic stories, and for the Norse raven of memory.

Rout: A crushing defeat.

Mocked-By-A-Husband (the *Fatale Monstrum*, the Smile Kuchisake): Named after a line in Shakespeare's *Measure for Measure*, 'I hope you will not mock me with a husband', and after a Japanese urban legend of a malicious female spirit with a torn-open smile.

Pick-Up-The-Pieces (pursuivant of the Endless King): A pursuivant is a name for an officer ranking below a herald. Pursuivants are often countered by the Knights Peregrine, wandering cadres of Knights who wear sword pins as ties.

The Endless King: A promise. A threat.